Tight Quarters
By Samantha Hunter

Two hearts converge...until fear runs love off the rails.

In the years since a horrific car accident left her with a long list of phobias, Brenna Burke has overcome them all except one. Crippling claustrophobia—not a good trait for an aspiring travel writer.

With an interview for her dream job looming, Brenna forces herself to board a train for a weekend tour through New York State...only to find her berth has been double booked.

Retired NYPD detective Reid Cooper isn't happy about the mix-up, or his attraction to his petite, sexy roommate. But as their up-close-and-personal weekend progresses, something remarkable happens. Being with Reid makes Brenna feel normal, unafraid of anything.

After one passionate night, both are thinking beyond a mere weekend fling. But when Brenna's last phobia pounces at the worst possible time, she could miss the final boarding call for happily ever after.

Warning: This book contains a hot-to-the-touch hero and sizzling sex at high speeds.

Ticket Home
By Serena Bell

Is that a cell phone in his pocket...or is he just happy to see her?

When Amy Moreland left Seattle, she never expected to see her workaholic ex-boyfriend again. Encountering him on her Connecticut-to-New-York-City commute is the surprise of her life. He seems hell-bent on winning her back, but every time his cell phone rings, it's a painful reminder of how he failed to put her first.

Jeff Havers can't help that his phone keeps interrupting his carefully composed apology speech, but having Amy sic the Metro North security team on him is a bit much. Once he talks his way out of handcuffs, he focuses on coaxing Amy to talk about the fears that drove her away.

As the train ride takes them through the landscape of their lost life together, sparks fly and remembered heat reignites. But if they're not brave enough to overcome the still-fresh pain of old wounds, it could be too late to pursue what really matters—their ticket home.

Warning: This book contains steamy train-car action, sex on the stairs, and a hero determined to give his velvet-and-heels-clad woman exactly what she's looking for.

Thank You for Riding
By Meg Maguire

The last train of the night might just be the start of something good.

Stung ego or not, Caitlin's relieved her fizzling relationship is over, even if she's just been unceremoniously dumped between the copier and a dead ficus tree. At least she has an excuse to ditch the lousy office Christmas party in time to catch the last subway home...to her cat, and early-onset spinsterhood.

Instead of a lonely, chilly ride, she gets an unexpected holiday treat in the form of a nearly familiar face—a handsome stranger she encountered last week at the blood drive.

At the end of the line, neither can seem to let their chance meeting end—until their extended flirtation finds them facing the prospect of spending a frigid winter night locked in an unheated subway station. And they wonder if keeping each other warm is merely a delightful form of rebound therapy...or a memorable first of many more dates to come.

Warning: Contains dorky, harmless flirtation that heats up into some spicy, third-base action.

Back on Track
By Donna Cummings

What's a little lie between strangers?

Allie Whittaker is in a dating slump, too busy getting her fledgling marketing company off the ground to have a personal life. All that could change, though, if she can get baseball superstar Matt Kearns on the cover of a charity calendar. Except Matt won't even talk to her.

Matt is in a slump, worried his career might be over. A Napa Valley wine tour isn't enough to take his mind off his troubles—until sexy, funny Allie plops into the adjacent seat and tells him three things about herself. One of them, she says, is a lie.

Matt can't resist playing along, and soon the afternoon getaway becomes an interlude with lies, truths, and desire flowing as fast as the wine. Then Allie lets slip one truth too many...and they both realize they're playing for keeps.

Warning: A handsome hunk, a determined lady and a few glasses of wine. Throw in a little on-the-run action, and what more do you need to while away an afternoon?

Big Boy
By Ruthie Knox

He'll be any man she wants—except himself.

Meet me at the train museum after dark. Dress for 1957.

When Mandy joins an online dating service, she keeps her expectations low. All she wants is a distraction from the drudgery of single parenthood and full-time work. But the invitation she receives from a handsome man who won't share his real name promises an adventure—and a chance to pretend she's someone else for a few hours.

She doesn't want romance to complicate her life, but Mandy's monthly role-playing dates with her stranger on a train—each to a different time period—become the erotic escape she desperately needs. And a soul connection she never expected.

Yet when she tries to draw her lover out of the shadows, Mandy has a fight on her hands...to convince him there's a place for their fantasy love in the light of day.

Warning: Contains sexy role-playing, theatrical application of coal dust, and a hero who can rock a pair of brown polyester pants.

Strangers on a
Train

Samhain Publishing, Ltd.
11821 Mason Montgomery Road, 4B
Cincinnati, OH 45249
www.samhainpublishing.com

Editing by Anne Scott
Cover by Angela Waters

Tight Quarters, ISBN 978-1-61921-377-7
First Samhain Publishing, Ltd. electronic publication: April 2013
Ticket Home, ISBN 978-1-61921-434-7
First Samhain Publishing, Ltd. electronic publication: April 2013
Thank You for Riding, ISBN 978-1-61921-337-1
First Samhain Publishing, Ltd. electronic publication: April 2013
Back on Track, ISBN 978-1-61921-376-0
First Samhain Publishing, Ltd. electronic publication: April 2013
Big Boy, ISBN 978-1-61921-530-6
First Samhain Publishing, Ltd. electronic publication: April 2013
First Samhain Publishing, Ltd. print publication: February 2014

Contents

Tight Quarters

Samantha Hunter

Dedication

Thanks so much to my Strangers on a Train partners Ruthie, Sarah, Donna and Cara who made the adventure of writing this series so much fun, and for all of their support and advice along the way. This was about as perfect as any group writing experience could be, from start to finish.

And thanks to whoever it was on Tumblr who took all of those pictures of guys on trains, inspiring our idea in the first place. ;)

Chapter One

Brenna Burke forced herself to relax, her bags bumping against her hip with each step even though the middle aisle of the train was more than wide enough for two people to walk abreast.

She was feeling good and rocking this trip so far. It was the fifth time she'd boarded this train in the past year, but this time would be the *one*.

Everyone was on her side. The porters had cheered her on when she'd arrived, and the conductor had even given her a thumbs-up.

"You can do it, Brenna. You'll clinch it this time," she heard someone say, and she looked up to see Sean, the bright-eyed, young car attendant who had showed her the suite a few weeks before. He was helping a disabled woman to her seat.

"Thanks, Sean," she said with a smile that was sunny and positive.

Because that's who she was, she reminded herself. In all areas of her life, Brenna took the bull by the horns and lived. She loved her friends, her home and her work as a travel editor. If she could tame this last demon that had kept her down for the past twelve years, she would be good to go.

The first time she'd tried taking the weekend train from Lake Champlain to Niagara Falls, she'd choked up inside the door and had to get out, nearly plowing over several passengers in her hurry to escape. Each of the subsequent times, something had gone wrong at different points before departure, and she'd had to leave.

This was her chance, and life wasn't waiting for her. On the cusp of turning twenty-nine, she dreamed of the world *out there*. She thought about turning thirty in Paris. Or on some amazing beach in the Caribbean. This was the next step to making that happen.

If Brenna could do this—spend four days on a train—she could do anything.

Something jolted her. She paused in the middle of the aisle, caught in thought. People were lined up behind her; the aisle was full. Too full, making her feel closed in.

Breathe.

She inhaled something spicy...cloves? No, sandalwood. It was nice. Calming. Then she realized it was coming from whoever was standing right behind her, breathing down her neck, their body inches from hers, crowding...

No. The poor guy was stuck there, waiting for *her* to move. Turning slightly, she smiled at him.

"Sorry," she offered, proud of how steady her voice was, considering that his chest completely blocked her view. He was big. Not rotund, but large. Muscular. Broad. Solid.

Shit. She was staring. He was staring back, though it was more like he was trying to exert some superpower through the force of his brown-eyed gaze—namely, the ability to make her move forward. Then he smiled, and that didn't help her stop staring.

"No problem," he said. "Take your time."

Innocent enough—polite even—though his voice was the closest thing to sex she'd had in a while. Unfortunately, her problem with close spaces had taken its toll on intimacy as well. Trying to make love while asking the man she was with not to crowd her didn't usually work out very well.

Brenna somehow made one foot move in front of the other, continuing down the length of the long car. Taking her mind off of where she was and what it all meant, she focused on the beautiful train she was boarding for the weekend. The 1930s Zephyr had been retooled to include all of the amenities that contemporary luxury travel had to offer—including spacious sleeper cars that replaced the original *roomettes*, which had barely had enough space for the pullout bed.

Though its "Silver Streak" namesake was one of the fastest trains of its time, this one would roll along at a gentle pace, allowing everyone to enjoy the view while making frequent stops for shopping and sightseeing. For Brenna, those detours were also an escape hatch, if need be.

A glance behind told her that *he* was still there, keeping step, right behind her. That, in and of itself, wasn't a huge deal, except that as they passed room after room, other passengers found theirs, and eventually it was only the two of them making their way to the end of the car. Brenna had asked for the end room—a suite—specifically, since it had more windows. Four windows in ninety-five square feet with one double bed and one pullout half-twin.

The berth was advertised as big enough for three people, with its own small bathroom, but it was just barely big enough for her to be comfortable inside with the door shut. Though it had cost her enough, she knew it would be worth it. She'd tried to get comfortable in the smaller rooms, but she wasn't able to.

Maybe he had simply missed his room number, she thought absently, still aware of him.

As they reached the end of the car, however, her pulse picked up. Something was askew. Suddenly she felt very alone in the hallway. She reassured herself that if she screamed, people would certainly hear her.

Brenna turned without warning and planted a hand on the man's chest, stopping him in his tracks. His expression more surprised than menacing.

"Why are you following me?" she asked, looking him in the eye. His were deep, dark brown, like the best chocolate and coffee. His hair was curly—not shaggy, but not styled either. A little wild, actually. Slightly darker than his eyes.

"I'm not following you. Not in the way that you mean. I'm going to my room." His eyes dropped to her hand.

She removed it, her lips twisting in doubt.

"The only room left in this car is mine. Yours must be behind you."

"No, mine is right down there." He gestured to the end of the car.

She detected a hint of Brooklyn in his tone, or maybe it was New Jersey or Philadelphia. She could never quite sort them out.

"That's not possible. I specifically reserved that berth," she said pertly as she turned and walked away.

When she slipped the key card into the slot on the door, it flashed green. She smiled, stepping inside and looking at him victoriously.

"See? Yours is back there somewhere. Have a nice day." She closed the door in his face.

Turning her back to him and the door, she looked at the room.

Just as she remembered. Except for the bouquet of flowers on the table by the window. Curious, she walked toward them, picking up the card. They were from her friend Mel, wishing her luck.

The windows were small, with shades, but they let in enough light. The bathroom was also narrow, fitted with the bare necessities, but if she left the door open, she would be fine.

Brenna felt good. A thrill ran through her. She could do it this time.

The door behind her *clicked*, *buzzed*, then *clunked*. The same noise it had made when she was opening it with her key card. Shock had her fingers fisting around the handles of her bags as she turned to find *him* standing there in the entry.

He smiled, waving his key card at her.

"Well, look at that," he said and winked at her with wicked satisfaction, stepping inside and closing the door behind him with a click of finality that echoed in her brain.

Numbness set in. This couldn't be happening. Brenna's mind blanked as she confronted the one thing she couldn't ever have prepared for.

Reid Cooper watched the woman standing in the middle of the suite turn her back to him, facing the window as she started mumbling something to herself. She was breathing too quickly, her entire sweet body tense as a wire.

He frowned, regretting the smart-assed move. This was clearly some sort of mix-up, but he hadn't meant to scare her.

"Just because I'm afraid doesn't mean there's danger," she whispered over and over.

"Listen, I'm sorry. I didn't mean to freak you out, but I'm not going to hurt you. Promise. I was just makin' the point that this is my room. Or that one of us got the wrong assignment," he said, trying to sound reasonable. "We should, uh, go straighten it out, don't you think?"

She kept chanting. Great. He was stuck with a crazy person. Exactly what he was trying to get away from. It was why he'd quit his job in the NYPD in the first place.

He'd dealt with every kind of crazy in his job—funny-crazy to psychotic, dangerous crazy. The last one had nearly killed him. The memory made him cautious as he walked up to her and put his hand on her shoulder.

"Hey, listen, I said—"

She bolted so suddenly that he reached for his weapon reflexively before he realized he didn't have it anymore. As she plastered herself against the wall, it became clear she posed no danger to him. In fact, she was white as a sheet and about to pass out if she didn't get some air.

"Listen, I'm *not* going to hurt you, okay? My name is Reid Cooper, and I'm a cop. NYPD. You're safe, I promise. There's just been a room mix-up. You need to calm down. Breathe more slowly, in, then out."

Old habits coming back as he took a deep breath, trying to get her to do the same.

"Get out. You're...t-too big!" She gulped breaths in between words, watching him closely and taking smoother breaths as the seconds passed.

After a minute or so, she seemed much calmer, though she still clung to the wall as if she could crawl up it to escape him if she had to.

"Wait, did you say I'm too *big*?"

Her comment landed in his mind a few seconds after the crisis had passed. He stayed in good shape. Ran, swam a few times a week, and he had even started taking a martial arts class.

And pottery. He'd always wondered about using one of those wheel things. It was kind of girly, and Reid was the only guy in the class, but he liked it. He was expanding his horizons, something he'd thought a lot about over his six months of recuperation from three gunshot wounds. Two hit the vest, one didn't. It made a guy reconsider his priorities.

But he was back in form, a trim six-three, two-oh-five. Not too big.

She pointed to the door.

"*Out.*"

His eyebrows rose, arms crossed.

"No way. We leave together, sweetheart, or I stay here and we can call the passenger director to come here and help."

"Brenna," she said shakily.

"What?"

"Brenna. Not sweetheart."

She was clearly annoyed, but also less panicked. Reid took that as a win.

"Brenna," he repeated, trying it out. "Nice. So what will it be? You let go of the wall and come with me, or we wait here for someone to come help?"

Her mouth flattened, and she took one arm away from the wall, then the other.

She was a sexy little thing, with her colorful dress swishing around a very nice pair of legs, her labored breathing drawing attention to a great rack. Short, shiny, dark hair. He liked that too.

But it was her face that got him.

There was something odd about her features, a tilt of her nose, which was slightly crooked, and a slant to her lips that seemed perpetually disapproving. It made him feel like doing something to earn her censure. As if reading his mind, the slant deepened as she watched him.

He put his hands up. "Listen, honestly, I'm harmless. I really just want to get the room situation figured out, that's all."

There was a cute mole at the base of her throat. She was different pretty. Sexy pretty, though not in the way that would ever be seen on the covers of fashion magazines.

She was *real* pretty.

Reid took a breath, refocusing. It had been a while for him, clearly. Recovery and retirement had put a big dent in his love life, and it seemed his timing was still way off.

"Okay, I'll go," she muttered. The *rather than be stuck in here with you* was silent.

It took her another few minutes to actually move from her spot. Reid went first out the door but stood holding it until she joined him. Brenna insisted he go ahead of her, and she kept several feet behind.

"Harmless, right," he thought he heard her say under her breath.

Crazy. Or afraid, he realized, all too familiar with the things that could make a woman that worried about a man, although she hadn't seemed afraid of him in particular.

Finally, they reached the office to find several other irate people in line. The train was getting ready to leave, and the poor woman fielding the complaints looked like she wished she could jump from it.

Brenna eyed him warily, still standing a good distance away from the group.

"Hi," he said pleasantly to the passenger director, hoping to provide some contrast to the angry folks she had been dealing with. "We have a problem."

The woman looked directly to Brenna. "Brenna, are you okay? Do you need to exit the train? Because we're about to get underway."

Reid blinked. The passenger director apparently knew Brenna personally, and looked past him like he wasn't even there.

"No, I'm fine, but we have a problem, Trina," Brenna said.

As Brenna explained about the double-booking, Reid waited patiently.

"You know I reserved that room and why I need it," Brenna said meaningfully, and the two women shared a look.

Reid wondered what *that* was about. Was Brenna up to something? Meeting someone else?

"Well, it also appears that I reserved the room," Reid

interjected, trying to sound as pleasant and unthreatening as possible.

"Let me check," Trina said.

A few minutes later, she looked up from the computer. "Oh, this is a mess. There have been several double bookings. I have no idea how this happened, but there are limited options, I'm afraid. I'm so sorry. The train is full, so the best option is that one of you should reschedule. Mr. Cooper did reserve the room first, online, but for some reason, it didn't show up when we booked you in person, Brenna. If one of you wants to reschedule for another time, we'll do so at half price. We'll be leaving the station in fifteen minutes, though, so you have to decide now."

Reid looked at Brenna. She looked at him.

"I'm not leaving," he told her flatly.

"Me, either." There was a spark in her eye now that she had stopped hyperventilating. "Why should I go?"

"Because you're the one with the issue. I'm too big, remember?" He couldn't repress his grin as color heated her face. "And I booked first. Trina said so."

"If he won't leave, I'm afraid you'll have to reschedule, Brenna. I'm so sorry, but he reserved the room first."

"If you were a gentleman, you'd let me have the room," Brenna hissed.

He tilted his head in acknowledgement. "That may be, but the best I can do is offer to share. I'm willing to do that if we get fifty percent off of our tickets."

"I can do that." Trina clearly wanted to solve the problem, and quickly.

Some barely repressed, frustrated noise escaped Brenna's lips, which made him fight hard to stifle a grin.

"It's It's not safe for a woman to be in a room with a strange man," she sputtered.

"I can understand that. Maybe Trina could find us same-gendered passengers we could pair up with?" he suggested.

"I can check, but—"

"I can't share that berth with *anyone*," Brenna cut Trina off, sounding slightly hysterical.

"So it's not just me? I'm flattered." Reid pinched the bridge of his nose for a second. "Listen, I can understand your reservations, but I promise, I'm a safe bet. I was a cop, you can check with my captain, the NYPD, my father, whoever—I'll give you a list of references. We might not even see each other that much. I don't plan to spend a lot of time in the room."

The whistle blew, signaling their imminent departure.

"Fine," Brenna bit out. "We can share, and maybe we can work out a schedule or something. Rules."

"Sure." He tried again to repress a smile. "We'll get right on that."

She turned red again and spun in the other direction to walk quickly back to their room.

Reid decided to let her be for a while and located an empty seat in the dining car to relax as the train pulled away from the station. He'd get some breakfast, enjoy the view and deal with his new roommate later.

Chapter Two

Brenna had it all figured out.

It had taken her a few hours, but she'd come up with the perfect system for sharing the space. She'd made notes they could stick to the outside of the door to make sure no one walked in and interrupted any personal time. It had helped her refocus as the train pulled away from the platform and she knew there was no going back.

If she and Reid Cooper didn't find a way to get along, the trip would be a waste of time for both of them, and she had other things to focus on besides him. Not that he wasn't very nice to focus on. After she'd calmed down, she could admit he was a hottie, and he seemed nice, more or less. There were probably worse men to be stuck with, if she had to be stuck with a man. At least he was a cop, and he hadn't made her feel wary at all. Not personally, anyway.

He had a nice smile, even when he was chuckling at her in that annoying way. And kind eyes. And really, really cool hair. She wondered what those waves and curls would feel like tangled in her fingers, and then caught her train of thought.

Ha, *train of thought*. She smiled at her pun, feeling more relaxed.

Making her way through the cars, Brenna scanned the space and found Reid reclining with a book and a beer. The beer she would have expected, but the book surprised her, especially since she knew it.

"Oh, I loved that book," she commented, helping herself to the seat across from his. The book would make it easier to break the ice.

"You read it?"

"Yes. I read any travel writing I can get my hands on. It's my favorite genre."

"You travel a lot?"

"No, not much." *Not at all. Not until now.* "I guess that's why I like to read about other people doing it."

"I picked it up more for the story of how they got this farm going. Total wreck when they bought it."

"But such an adventure. And they knew their dream when they saw it."

"Not much of a dream at the start. Broken-down place, no water, and she doesn't even speak the language."

"That's the adventure part," Brenna said with a laugh. "And they were in love, so that helped. They shared that dream."

"If you say so. I'm looking forward to reading about how they renovate the place."

She smiled back, her fingers touching the schedule she wanted to show him. But maybe she needed to get to know him better first.

"I guess." She wondered how renovation could be more exciting than reading about the romance and beauty of southern France. But to each their own. "So, you're a police officer?"

"Yes. Well, I was. It's still habit to say it even though I retired six months ago."

"Retired? But you're so young!" she blurted.

"Thanks, but I learned the hard way that life's too short. Take it from me."

"Why should I? Take it from you, that is?"

She'd meant to fish for more details about him, but the innuendo landed between them, making her cheeks flood with warmth again.

"I mean, what happened?" She pretended she didn't see the twinkle in his eye.

"I was shot one night when I was out on the street. Almost died, and took a hell of a long time to bounce back. When I did, I decided to get out, move on. It was a wake-up call, I guess," he said, so casually he might have been telling her what the weather outlook was.

"You were shot? You almost died? Someone *shot* you? With a gun?"

He grinned. "Yeah, with a gun. That's the usual way. I was lucky. Two hit the vest before one missed. A lot of guys have had it happen more than once. I decided I wasn't willing to risk a repeat performance, much to the embarrassment of my old man."

"Your family doesn't approve?"

"Long line of NYPD. They would have stuck it out." He broke eye contact for the first time in the conversation, though his tone remained casual.

"What are you doing now?"

"I'm taking a train ride," he responded lightly.

"Seriously."

"I am serious." His gaze met hers again. "At the moment, I'm just enjoying some free time and scoping out the possibilities."

"In other words, you don't have a plan."

"Do I need one?" He seemed so thoroughly amused that she found herself tightening her fist around the papers that she'd written the schedule on.

"What have you got there?"

She let out a heavy breath. "I worked up a schedule for the room. When we could both have, um, private time there."

"You wrote it up?"

She nodded.

"Let me see."

She unfisted her hand, unfolding the paper and pressing it flat the best she could, handing it to him. "We can make changes based on your input, of course."

He nodded, scrunched up the paper and tossed it on the table.

"Why did you do that?" she asked. "It took me all afternoon."

"That was time you could have been out here, enjoying the start of the trip, Brenna. Think about it. We can just talk to each other. You need some time alone, you tell me and vice versa. It's that simple. We don't need a constitution."

She frowned, feeling foolish. "You make it sound so simple."

"It is. Just tell me what you want, okay? I'll do the same. Like I mentioned, I don't plan on spending much time in the room other than for sleeping, so it will be easy, I promise."

She bit her lip and nodded, feeling like an idiot.

"I made notes too," she said, then regretted saying it out loud.

"Notes?"

"On Post-its. You know, to hang on the door. Things like *Don't Enter until Note Is Removed* so we didn't have mishaps. Like walking in on one another while we're dressing."

He pursed his lips. "I see. And would that be so bad?" he asked, the mischief rising to the surface. "I think we should just take our chances."

She fought a smile in response. He leaned over the table, holding his hand out.

"Give me the notes, Brenna."

She resisted, but then pulled them out of her bag, putting them in his hand. She watched him dispose of them like he had the schedule.

"Are you up for an adventure of your own, Brenna?" He picked up the book, looking at it. "Because that's what we have here, right? A chance to live our own adventure."

"I—I don't know."

Though she did know. She wanted that adventure very much, but she wasn't sure she could have it.

"What holds you back?"

"I'm claustrophobic."

"Most people are, at least a little."

"Did what happened when we were in the room seem like a little to you?" she bit back.

"No. But all the more reason to take it by the balls and squeeze, Brenna. You're here. Make it count."

She shook her head. "I'm more successful, more comfortable, if I can control my environment." Her eyes slid over to where the schedule lay in waste.

He stared at her and then took a breath, sliding out of the booth to land on her side, beside her.

"What are you doing?"

"Showing you that you can't control your environment all the time. There are too many variables. Me, for instance. Things you can't control by drawing boxes around them. Like how this train will follow the track and tilt to the inside as we go around that upcoming curve. It will make my body shift a bit closer to yours. But it's okay to be uncomfortable. To know you can't control everything. Maybe you can even learn to enjoy it."

Her mind scrambled as she looked out the window at the curve in the tracks he was indicating. It was a wide, long curve circling around the base of a tall, stony hill. In just moments, the train would be only yards from the rock face, and she was bare inches from Reid, trapped between the two. Her throat tightened, strangling her voice as she put both hands on his shoulder, intending to push, needing to escape. He didn't move.

Big. Solid. Close.

Her heart slammed, her breath shortened, warmth infusing her entire body, but she knew it wasn't because she was afraid. The entire time they rode around the curve, she was focused on Reid. What she had perceived as the threat somehow suddenly became safety, and she felt herself holding more tightly to his arm.

As he predicted, his weight shifted slightly toward her, pressing against her hip. He did nothing to brace himself or keep the motion from bringing them closer. His dark gaze burned into her, and she returned it as they swept around the other side of the hill. He leaned in, much more than was necessary from the slight tilt of the tracks, and smiled.

Brenna wasn't at all sure she was even breathing when he put his face against her hair, whispering into her ear.

"See? You'll be just fine, Brenna."

Then he got up, took his book and left. Brenna wrapped her arms around herself, feeling chilled in the absence of his heat and wondering what the hell had just happened. Eyeing the papers on the table, she grabbed them, balling them up and dumping them in a receptacle as she made her way to the dining car. All the while, she could hear Reid's whisper in her ear, the challenge in his voice. She couldn't forget the heat in his eyes, and in her heart the sparks of a possible adventure flickered.

Chapter Three

Reid wondered who the hell Mel was. He'd noted the flowers when he was in the room earlier but hadn't thought much about it as he calmed Brenna down. The name on the card that came with them was androgynous enough to make him curious. Not that it was any of his business.

He'd just been flirting with her, loosening her up. The woman was wound so tightly that she might spring a gasket any second. Still...he'd enjoyed getting up close and wouldn't argue if they could get closer over the trip.

Melvin or Melanie? Melissa?

It had to be Melanie—no one named their kid Melvin anymore.

That settled, he poked around some more. Old habits were hard to break. He couldn't help but investigate the scene. She'd neatly stacked all of her things on the side of the room with the actual bed, leaving him to use the pullout.

He could deal with that. Especially if there was any chance he might end up over on the other side.

More interesting was the waste bin half-full of wadded-up paper. He checked out a few—drafts of the schedule she'd showed him and some rather funny discards of the "signs" she had drawn up.

No Farting Allowed in the Berth.

All Underwear Must Be Picked Up and Put Away.

He laughed out loud. Brenna had a sense of humor—except that she was probably dead serious. He thought about hanging up the farting sign, just to see her turn red again.

As for underwear, Reid wondered what she wore. Something secretly sexy, or neat white cotton? He'd enjoy sliding either one off of those rounded hips. It wasn't likely to happen, given her clear dislike of him and whatever issues she had, but it was nice to think about.

His duffle was thrown, unpacked, on his small bed. He hadn't brought much. It was only a four-day trip, and if he needed anything, he'd buy it when they stopped. *Live in the moment.* That was his current motto.

He *had* brought condoms. Live in the moment, but hope springs eternal. Sharing a room might not be conducive to having any of that kind of fun on the trip, unless he found himself spending the night in someone else's berth, which might be the best thing for everyone.

Grabbing the tablet he'd brought with him, Reid was relieved to see that the free wireless offered on the trip was working well. After checking email, Twitter, and a few other routine items, he found himself typing Brenna's name into the search box.

Editing and magazine credits...no Twitter or Facebook, interestingly. Some comments on blogs and articles for people with phobias and about their therapy. Compared to many, Brenna didn't have an extensive online presence, and he found himself a bit disappointed. And intrigued. Not many resisted the trap of social media these days.

Then his eye caught an old newspaper article on the third page in—a car accident.

The picture of the mangled, twisted metal was barely recognizable as a vehicle, and the caption said it all: "Rescue workers take three hours to free teen from crushed vehicle."

Reid swore, not needing to read the article. He knew who the teen had to be. Brenna had been caught in that for three hours?

Suddenly, being shot didn't seem like such a big deal. How had she survived? It appeared the other two people, the driver and passenger, hadn't.

He swore again, turning off the screen as Brenna walked in. She paused, stiffening as she saw him. For a moment, he thought she knew what he was looking at, but there was no way she could. Then her shoulders softened, and she closed the door, standing there like she didn't know what to do next.

No visible scars, no disfigurements or even so much as a limp from the accident. Apparently, the scars had all been left inside.

"What?" she asked, her eyes narrowing.

"Huh?"

"You're staring holes through me." She wrapped her arms around her front.

"Sorry, I wasn't staring at you so much as just...staring."

Liar.

But he wasn't going to tell Brenna he'd been snooping. He wanted to tell her he was sorry for being so cavalier about her phobia. Anyone who had lived through that hell would end up with some kind of damage, and she was fighting it. Trying to subdue it.

Admiration and desire tripped over each other, but this wasn't a woman to be played with. She had some serious shit going on.

She was uncomfortable, shifting her gaze away. She walked nervously to her bed and sat, grabbing a large bag and pilfering through it as if she needed to find something to do.

"Um, listen, I need to stretch my legs," Reid said, feeling uncomfortable as well. "I'm going to walk for a bit, find some dinner. I heard there was a movie being shown tonight. You want to come with?"

She shook her head, not even looking up.

Great. He couldn't blame her, after his come-on earlier. Probably the best thing he could do would be to make himself scarce as much as possible and let her have some peace.

"Thanks for asking. But I'm tired and I think I'll turn in early."

"Okay. Well, then. Night."

Outside the room, Reid closed his eyes and paused for a moment before walking away. Maybe he'd meet someone else at dinner or at the movie, but for some reason, he found himself wanting to go back to the room and talk to Brenna. To smooth things out and let her know he wasn't a jerk.

No doubt, those condoms would stay packed away this trip. It was as much as he deserved.

Brenna spent the rest of the night in the berth, telling herself she was getting used to the space.

Right.

She was an idiot. She'd frozen like a frightened deer when she'd stepped inside the room, and clearly, it had put Reid off. She knew that happened, because she'd been through it before. She couldn't entirely help her reactions to things, but sometimes it was difficult for other people to deal with, as well. Over the years, her erratic behaviors had lost her friends, lovers. Even her family had seemed relieved when she'd gone to college.

In truth, this time it had nothing to do with her phobia. The intensity of his stare and the way he was looking at her had stunned her. No man had looked at her like that, ever. Like she was a ripe, succulent grape that he wanted to peel and swallow whole.

It had paralyzed her. She felt like the idiot that he now surely believed she was. Why couldn't she just be *normal* for a change?

Any normal woman would have started taking her clothes off at the door and not stopped until she had his off too.

How's this for an adventure, Reid? she could have said in one of those smooth, sultry tones. *What do you say we start off this trip with a bang?*

Right.

Instead, Brenna had scooted to her bed, digging through a bag for nothing in particular so he wouldn't be able to read her face like a book. On top of that, she'd stupidly turned down his invitation for company.

It wasn't her claustrophobia that was keeping her from getting laid. Blatant stupidity clearly had something to do with it.

What was Reid doing now?

Why should she care? She'd known him less than a day.

It was late, but he hadn't returned. She'd rehearsed in her head what she would do, what she'd say, if he did.

But he didn't. Maybe he'd found someone else to watch the movie with. Spend the night with.

Well, good for him.

After changing into her nightgown in the tiny bathroom, she went to bed, putting herself to sleep with a mental litany of promises about how tomorrow would be better and enumerating all of the ways she would not act like an idiot around Reid. There were three days left. She could redeem herself.

Brenna couldn't say what woke her, but the first thing that hit her was the total dark.

Not dark, but encompassing blackness. Nothing felt right or familiar, and it took her a few seconds of gasping, lurching wakefulness to realize where she was and what had happened.

When she sat up, she saw the teeny orange running lights along the bottom of the wall, the streak of moonlight through window as her eyes adjusted. Her breath started to even out, her grip around the blankets loosening as she focused on the points of light.

Reid must have come back and turned the lights off.

Brenna rarely slept with less than a nightlight—the dark being much the same as any closed-in space—but she couldn't exactly tell Reid that.

Well, she had, but he'd thrown the note out about leaving at least one light on at night.

As the roar of panic settled, she laid back down, breathing evenly. Suddenly, she became aware of his breathing too. Another unfamiliar sound. How long since she'd heard another person sleeping in the same room at night?

Reid was less than ten feet away, crunched into the small pullout bed on the other side of the berth. He'd obviously come in after she was asleep, and the thought made her feel curiously vulnerable.

Still, it was a comfort, strangely, knowing that he was there. The easy rhythm of his breath soothed her, and she relaxed. She was starting to ease back into sleep when her peace was splintered again.

"I'm hit, I'm down," Reid called out loudly, and Brenna heard the even pace of his breathing speed up. He groaned, mumbled something else. Sounds of thrashing, then a slam as his knee or elbow hit the wall.

She'd felt guilty taking the larger space, but the small one had felt too close. Still, he was going to hurt himself if he kept thrashing, obviously having a nightmare.

"*I'm hit,*" he said again, more loudly.

A nightmare about being shot.

Brenna slid from the bed. She didn't know what to do exactly, but she'd lived through years of her own nightmares. She couldn't let him just suffer through it alone. Approaching him tentatively, she saw he wasn't thrashing now but curled up as if in pain, breathing hard.

It broke her heart, and she forgot her own misgivings, reaching down to touch his shoulder.

"Reid? Reid, wake up," she said gently. She didn't want to startle him, but she hoped to get through whatever held him in its grasp.

"No!" he shouted. His hand moved with lightning speed and closed down tightly on her forearm. She cried his name, panicked for a moment.

He froze, everything around them suddenly quiet except for the rhythmic engine pulsing through the body of the train, harsh breathing like static in the air between them.

Brenna didn't dare move with his hand still clamped around her arm. He might not be awake, or clear on what was happening.

"Brenna?" he asked, sounding confused.

"Yes. You were having a nightmare, and I was trying to wake you, and—"

"Fuck, I'm so sorry." He released her as if she were radioactive and swung his legs over the side of the small cot to stand.

Light suddenly illuminated the berth.

Reid looked like he'd been through hell—his hair tousled, his face still reflecting the pain he'd suffered in the dream. He rubbed his hands over his face as if trying to scour it away.

"I thought this was over with," he muttered, more to himself than to her.

Sympathy welled and then turned warmth to heat as Brenna

took in every inch of taut, hard muscle exposed and covered in a light sheen of perspiration. He wore only a pair of shorts to sleep in.

"Are you okay?" she asked from where she stood by his bed.

His eyes pinned her as he moved in.

"I'm fine. Let me see your arm."

His face carved into a deep frown, his eyes still wild as he got up close and took her arm in his hands to inspect it. He winced as he saw the light marks from his fingers on her skin. Sitting down on the side of the cot, he pulled her down with him. Not that she had any choice—her knees didn't exist. His hands were hot, and Brenna swallowed hard.

"I'm so sorry," he said again, shaking his head. "I'm not used to anyone being around when that happens."

Something hopeful in her heart jumped for joy upon hearing that.

"It's okay. Believe me, I know what it's like. As long as you're okay." She tried to ignore the way his thigh muscles stretched and bunched as he moved.

She wanted to slide her hand over them so much that she twitched slightly, holding herself back.

He misread it as a flinch.

"I know I was out of line earlier, but I'd never hurt you, or any woman, knowingly. I can get out at the stop tomorrow, and you can have the room. I should have done that in the first place, but I...well, never mind. I'll pack it up tomorrow and reschedule the trip."

Panic fluttered in her chest that had nothing to do with fear. She reached out, covering his hand with her own.

"I wish you wouldn't. I'm fine, really. I promise."

Reid studied her hand on his for a long moment, and the air shifted, thickening around them. When he looked at her, embers of heat were banked behind the caution she saw in his gaze. His body had stilled but hardened. He kept himself separate, the only place they touched where her hand covered his. His eyes fell to where the thin material of her gown covered the slope of her breasts, and she saw him swallow, control making his jaw tight.

He was being careful with her, and that tipped her over the edge. Made her brave.

In this moment, Brenna was the one who could comfort Reid, make him feel better. He was the one who had turned the lights on, escaping the horrors that followed him back from his sleep. She suddenly wanted to try to make all of it go away.

The train rocked slightly, and she let the motion ease her closer to him, her breath catching as her side, her breast, pressed against his torso.

"If you leave, what kind of adventure would this be?" she asked, and then answered the shocked surprise in his eyes by pressing a soft kiss to his mouth.

Brenna sighed into the kiss and closed her eyes, shameless as she threw her leg over his thighs, straddling him so that she could make the kiss deeper and feel more of him against her.

Reid groaned into her mouth, his tongue rubbing against hers like she was the tastiest thing he'd known in some time, but he held back, not holding or touching her in any way.

Didn't he want to?

No, he was being cautious with her, still shaken.

"You can touch me, if you want," she said against his mouth. It sounded gauche and stupid, and doubt started to tamp out her desire as long seconds stretched between them.

But then he was there, big hands underneath her gown, kneading her back, her butt, then rising to bury his fingers in her hair as the kisses turned feral and hungry, more desperate than she would have imagined she could ever be. She met him where he was hard and needful.

He was big. Not too big, but definitely big.

Hunger shredded the rest of her inhibitions as she pressed down against him, soaked through the light material of her panties, seeking what she needed.

"Sweetheart, we have to slow this down, or we're not stopping at all."

He broke the kiss on a harsh breath, but she sought him

again, not wanting to think or reconsider or question.

He captured her face between his hands, and she focused on him, finding it utterly amazing that *she* had put that desire in his eyes. His heart pounded so hard, she could feel it where she pressed against his chest.

"What?" she asked, dazed and wanting.

"I don't want to take advantage—"

Brenna chuckled. She didn't feel at all like herself, and that was...fantastic.

Right now, she wasn't herself. Not entirely. She was someone else, hurtling through the dark on a train in the middle of the night with a strange man whose eyes were devouring her as they watched each other.

The sparks of adventure turned into a blaze. Whatever this freedom was that took her over, she wanted more of it.

"Do you want me, Reid?" she asked as she pushed his hair back from his face, loving how silky it felt.

"Yes, but—"

"No buts." She kissed him again, pressing her breasts against his massive chest. "I want you too."

Reid's eyes widened at her statement, as if he couldn't believe what he'd just heard. Brenna couldn't quite believe it, either, but it made her happy somewhere deep down inside.

Reid bit out another curse, his nostrils flaring as he banded his arms around her, apparently convinced. Falling backward, he brought her down on top of him, and as they kissed and touched, he paused to reach up above him for something.

His bag. When he dragged it down, everything fell out of it, dumping everywhere around them, not that either of them cared. She focused on the planes of his chest, the scar at his waist. Where he was shot. She ran her fingers over it, studying the angry mark, fascinated.

"Does it still hurt?" she whispered.

"Sometimes, but not too bad. I still take pain pills, though, if I need them, though I need them less and less." Brenna heard the sound of paper ripping, then foil, and her heart slammed hard into her chest.

God, this was real.

She didn't think, didn't look at anything except for Reid as he shucked the shorts and covered his erection while she stood and shimmied out of her underwear before crawling back over him.

"What do you want, Brenna? What do you need?" he asked, taking command even though she was the one on top.

"Just this," she said as she planted her hands on his chest, finding a good angle. She enjoyed, for the sweetest second, the feeling of him poised at the center of her body, and she wanted to remember this particular moment forever. She rubbed back and forth against the broad tip of his cock, making both of them groan.

"Honey, if we don't do it now, I hate to admit it, but it's going to be all over for me," he said with a harsh chuckle, arching against her. "It's been more than a while."

He couldn't have said anything more perfect, and Brenna watched him, their eyes on each other as she took him slowly in until he was completely buried. The fullness inside her was incredibly erotic, more so than she had ever experienced before. Such sweet pressure. She rocked slightly, her own muscles tightening in response.

"Oh, Reid. God," she moaned.

His fingers snuck down between her legs, played with her clit for a few seconds before she was rocking harder and digging her nails into his chest, flying apart in a blinding, soul-rendering orgasm. She wasn't even aware of his fingers digging in on her hips, holding on hard as he surged up under her. Then his neck arched back as he let out a moan rent with male satisfaction, collapsing back to the cot, his gorgeous chest heaving.

Minutes later, the two of them were still fused together, breathing hard, bodies hot. Brenna didn't feel like herself at all, but whoever she was right now, she liked her a whole hell of a lot better.

Chapter Four

Reid looked at his watch as he stood outside on the train platform, waiting for Brenna to emerge. In spite of their intimacy the night before, she'd insisted on leaving while he used the shower, and then he had done the same for her, since she needed to leave the door open. It was strange, considering that they'd seen each other naked from a variety of angles, but come morning Brenna had tightened up, closed off. She clearly needed her space.

He'd gone along. It seemed like a small sacrifice to make her comfortable. Rome wasn't built in a day and so forth. Not that they were "building" anything, but the thought still applied.

But he'd been waiting an hour. The train had almost emptied out as passengers left to enjoy a full day in Saratoga Springs.

He'd started to climb back on board when he saw her walking toward him. Any impatience evaporated immediately. She was beautiful, and there was an extra glow in her cheeks this morning. Hopefully he was the reason for that.

"Hey. Ready to go? There's a wine tasting in a half hour downtown."

When he leaned in to kiss her and she backed away ever so slightly, he knew something was wrong. Her body was tense, and she didn't have a sweater or bag.

"I think I'm going to stay in for the day. You should go have a good time, though. I'm sorry," she said in a rush, turning away as if they would leave it at that.

Reid stepped forward, stopping her progress by closing his hand over one shoulder.

"Whoa. What's this about? You were the one who was all excited about the town, seeing the historic buildings and the racetrack? And suddenly you don't want to go?"

She didn't meet his eyes, wringing her hands. Reid dropped his from her shoulder.

She didn't reply.

"Um, okay. If this is about last night, we can talk about that. It was a moment, Brenna. Neither one of us planned it, and if you're feeling any pressure, don't. We could spend some time together today, or not. We don't have to be joined at the hip just because last night we...were," he said, hoping to lighten the moment in spite of his own disappointment. "You can do your own thing, or go with someone else, if you want. No harm, no foul. You don't need to hole up on the train just because of me." He meant it. Mostly.

He'd looked forward to spending some time with Brenna out of bed, but she obviously wasn't feeling the same way. Okay, fine. They'd had a great night, and he could leave it at that. At least, he wanted her to believe that was true.

"It's not you. Really, it's not."

"Brenna, are you really going to say 'It's not you, it's me'?" He chuckled and tipped her chin up so they were eye-to-eye. "Listen, seriously, it's fine. Last night was great, but you don't owe me anything. We can go our separate ways, no pressure, okay?"

She bit her lip in a way that made him want to lick it—especially now that he knew how she tasted—but he pushed the impulse away. Normally, Reid wasn't so needy with women. He enjoyed them, and had even had a few almost-serious relationships, but overall, a one-night vacation fling would be fine with him, as well. Getting laid was getting laid, right?

Except that deep down he wasn't buying his own line. He'd been looking forward to spending some time with Brenna. He was disappointed. It had to be the influence of the pottery classes; maybe he should stop those.

Brenna nodded, and he nodded back.

"Okay. You have a great day, and...thanks. Last night was amazing, and so are you," he said with a smile and leaned down to kiss her cheek before he turned back to the doors.

"I'm afraid I won't get back on," she said as she rushed up behind him.

He turned to find her looking panicked, her fingers digging into his upper arm.

She'd grabbed on to him like that when he sat with her the day before, when he'd flirted with her, and last night, when she was flying apart around him. Like he was her anchor. Something solid.

He liked it, but right now, it confused the hell out of him.

"What?"

"I *want* to spend the day with you, Reid, I really do. I'm not trying to give you the brush-off, please don't think that. I don't usually do...*that*...you know, like last night, with someone I don't even know..." She trailed off, clearly stressed. "But as I was getting ready this morning and thinking about being off the train, I really started worrying that I might not get back on. That's not just some lame excuse, and if I don't get back on I'm really screwed. I'd have no way home."

He stared for a moment and wiped a hand over his face.

"I'm sorry, Brenna. I thought you were just handing me a line. You're really worried about that, huh?"

She nodded. Relief almost made him laugh, and then he realized she'd think he was laughing at her and choked it back. But this he could deal with.

"What if I give you no choice?" he proposed.

She blinked. "What do you mean?"

"You come spend the day with me, and I'll make sure you get back on the train, even if I have to carry you back on," he said on a low tone, pushing a stray lock of hair back behind her ear. "If you want me to."

"You'd do that?" He liked how her voice became breathless.

"Whatever you need me to do, I can do. You set the limits, but I can do whatever's necessary to make sure you get back on board."

The spark of excitement in her eyes set off responding ones inside of him.

"You might have to restrain me, or keep me from screaming for help," she said tentatively.

By the way her lips parted, the color infusing her cheeks, Reid knew they were playing the same game now.

"I can do that." He stepped even closer. "Go get your stuff. I promise, no matter what it takes, you *will* be back on this train tonight. If nothing else works, I still own handcuffs, and I brought them with me."

"Why would you do that? Bring them with you, that is."

"Because you just never know when you might need them," he said with a grin.

Her eyes widened, and she popped up to plant a quick kiss on him before she turned and hurried back to the berth to get her things.

Reid smiled. As much as he wanted to see Brenna successfully get over her phobia—and he did—a part of him truly hoped she wouldn't be able to get on the train that evening. He would spend all day long thinking about what fun he could have keeping his promise to make sure she did.

Brenna was having the best day she could remember in a long time. Quite the opposite of what she'd thought would happen as she had agonized alone in the room that morning, afraid to leave in case she couldn't get back on board.

The problem had never occurred to her before, as she hadn't made it past departure any of the other times, and worrying about it had made her miserable until Reid had promised to help. She'd worried he would think she was a total whack-job, but he'd been there for her.

How she'd come to trust him so quickly was a mystery, but one she was totally enjoying as her eyes met his over the glass of Shiraz they were currently tasting.

"This one is sexy," he murmured over the top of the glass, with a wink in her direction.

She nodded, taking another sip. "But subtle. Mellow at first, but then it surprises you with some spice as it goes down."

His eyes darkened, and she fought a smile as she finished her glass, feeling a pleasant buzz set in. This was fun, and she was so glad he'd talked her into getting off the train.

Clearly Reid had no long-term plans for what was happening between them. He'd made that clear back on the train, when he told her they didn't have to spend any time together just because they'd had sex. But Brenna *wanted* to spend time with him.

Maybe it was foolish, but she did. Partly because she wanted to have sex with him again. She hadn't had much sex over the years, and she'd never had any that good. It seemed very likely at the moment that she'd get her wish.

But she also wanted to be with Reid because when she was with him, she felt safe. She felt normal. When he'd promised her he would make sure she'd get back on the train, she'd believed him. He'd taken something she was self-conscious about and made it into a sexy game, taken it out of her hands and into his. It was good to be able to put those concerns aside and let someone else worry about them for a while.

Today, she felt free. It was a heady thing.

Her mind drifted to his comment about handcuffs.

So many possibilities.

"What next?" he asked. He stepped closer, his mouth near her ear.

"There's a buffet lunch downstairs," she suggested, watching several other train passengers head that way. Spending time with the group didn't seem as appealing as being alone with Reid.

"I spotted a nice place down the street with an outdoor café in back that looks over a garden."

"Sounds nice."

"Glad you think so, since I already reserved a table," he said with a grin.

"That sure of yourself?" she teased.

"I was hoping, that's all."

Pleasure blossomed from her toes upward, and she let him steer her out of the tasting room toward the doors.

"We have to do something first," he said, and before Brenna could even ask what, he'd pulled her with him into a small alcove, his arms around her and his lips on hers, hot and demanding, wiping out any question she might have had.

"The Shiraz is even better this way," he whispered, licking at her bottom lip before invading her mouth again in a way that had her knees shaking.

Brenna held on tight, returning the kiss without reserve, and she caught her breath as his hand found its way inside her top.

"Reid." She looked past his shoulder, concerned if anyone else was around.

"No one can see." He made sure of that, turning her inward toward the wall.

When her back hit the hard surface and he pressed into her, Brenna froze. Then his thumb moved over her nipple, and her mind blanked, but not from fear.

"You okay?"

"I'm fine. Just don't stop doing that," she said as she pulled him down for another kiss.

It was amazing. The kiss, the touch, and how much she wanted to just let him take her right here—not possible in this semipublic space, but so tempting.

Reid apparently had other ideas as he pressed a thigh between hers. She gasped, and he swallowed her moan as he found the right spot, his hand traveling down to her backside, helping her move against him as they kissed.

The small, dark space of the alcove, the possibility of being seen—all fell away as she gripped him tighter and gave in to the need, her hands clawing into his back as she let a swell of release shudder through her.

He kept kissing her even as the sensations ebbed, his hands soothing her back, lips gentle. But when he backed away, his eyes were hot.

"I love making you do that," he said, tilting his forehead against hers. "You're so soft, so responsive."

"I'm a fan too," she said shakily, and felt his chest rumble. "I've always fantasized about that, being up against a wall, but I couldn't... Now, here...with you. It's amazing."

"Anything I can do to help," he said with a wicked smile as they walked out of the alcove. "Sex therapy for phobias? Maybe we've stumbled onto some new cure."

"But we can't be sure yet, so we should keep doing it."

"No argument from me."

Brenna laughed, feeling light. As they walked out into the sun, people they passed seemed to pause and take them in. Brenna felt like she was shining from the inside out.

It was Reid. If not for him, she'd still be sitting in her berth back on the train, curled up into her own fears. Instead, she was out here, living her life.

As they made their way into the restaurant, she took his hand in hers. She liked that he squeezed her fingers back as they walked to their table.

"So, you're retired. Are you just living the easy life, or are you starting a new career as a sex therapist?" she asked when they'd settled in.

"I think you might be my only client for that," he said with a wide smile. "But I have a few other ideas. I grew up in the city, but my parents used to take us up to Vermont and Maine, all through New England, for vacations. I thought maybe buying a hotel or an inn might be interesting. That's where I've been living, for now. In Burlington."

"I live right next door in Plattsburgh. I thought ex-cops all became detectives, private security or at least opened up bars," she teased, somewhat surprised at his new interests.

"Many do. But there's no reason I couldn't do both—you know, run a small inn and solve a murder now and then. Just like in the detective novels. It would probably make my family happier."

"They don't approve?" she asked more seriously, remembering he had said something about that the night before.

"They don't understand why I would quit. I think it disappointed them, on some level."

"That's too bad. Will they come around?"

Their lunches arrived, and their conversation paused as Reid looked out over the gardens before picking up his burger and taking a large bite.

"It'll be okay. We're not estranged or anything, but it's that elephant in the room, their disapproval of me quitting the force, as if I'm letting the family down or something. My father thought I was in the closet when I told him I might move up here and open an inn." He gave a rueful shake of his head.

Brenna rolled her eyes. "Well, it's an older generation. My parents try to be supportive, but sometimes I wonder if I'm claustrophobic because of the car accident I had as a teen or because they kept me so close to home after it."

"Yeah, I, um, I looked that up online. It looked pretty horrific."

"You looked me up online?"

He shrugged. "Sorry, sort of the downfall of being a former detective. I was curious who I was sharing a space with. I wasn't sure I was safe with you." He gave her a dangerous smile, making her chuckle.

He made her laugh more than she could remember doing for a long time.

Brenna thought about that for a moment, then returned to her lunch. "I suppose it makes sense. For all you know, I could be a fleeing felon."

"Good thing I brought the cuffs then."

"Sure is."

"So the accident was the trigger for your phobia?"

"It was the trigger for about a dozen of them. Claustrophobia is the only one I still need to work with. I cycled through all kinds of fears and anxiety attacks, drugs, therapy for post trauma in the years after the accident."

He ate, watching her thoughtfully. "You've been through a lot. The only survivor too?"

That still put a knot in her chest, and Brenna knew it always would. But she mentally untied the tightness and took a breath.

"Yes. My best friend and her brother were killed. He was older, back from college, and we were so young. We had no idea he had been drinking before he got in the car. I still can't remember a lot of it, just being stuck in there, unable to breathe. It was hot." Her

45

voice choked a bit, her chest tightening up.

Reid reached over and covered her hand with his.

"You don't have to talk about this."

"It's okay. It's good for me." She gripped his hand and took a few breaths. "It was a long time ago, but I suppose in some way, it will always be with me. But not this phobia. I got rid of the other ones, and I'll beat this one too. I have to."

"You're pretty amazing," he said, and her anxiety melted away, turning to something warmer and much more pleasant under his admiring gaze.

"Thanks, but I don't feel all that amazing most days."

"Most people don't, and they haven't had to overcome what you have."

"You have," she said. "Do you have nightmares often?"

She wasn't sure he was going to answer. He focused on his lunch for a few minutes, then shrugged, setting down what was left of his burger.

"I did, for a while. Though the dreams always seem to mix up different events. Not just the shooting—that's consistent—but they bring back other times, other moments, that got stuck in my head too. But they'd gone away considerably after I moved up here. I'd apologize for last night, except I'm really glad you were there when I woke up." His sidewise grin twisted her heart.

Brenna had to remember that this was just a weekend fling and not to fall hard for this man. He didn't know what his next move was, and she wanted a job that would take her away from home often. Not a great time to start a relationship—not that one was being offered.

Still, Reid was the first man in years to make her think in those terms, and it was very hard to keep hope from sprouting tender roots in her heart.

"There's no need to apologize. I was glad too..." she said quietly, their hands still linked. "It was nice to be able to help back. To comfort someone else for a change."

They didn't say anything else for several long moments, unlinking their fingers and finishing their meals as they admired the gardens and each other.

"What do you want to do next?"

"I might go to the Yaddo Gardens—it's an artists' retreat, but you can walk through the gardens. I think they might have a show there this weekend, displaying some of the work of the artists in residence. It would make a nice write-up for me when I get back. A small article to show at my job interview. But I understand if you would rather do something else."

"What interview?"

"I've been working freelance out of my home office, but now there's a spot open for a travel writer. It's domestic travel only, but I'd really like to try for it. Unfortunately, I haven't done much travel, so I'm trying to prove to my boss that I could do it."

"Ah, so that's why this trip in particular is so important."

"It is. She knows about my problems, and she's sympathetic, but you can't hire a travel writer who can't travel."

Reid nodded. "You're doing great so far."

"Thank you. I have you to thank for a lot of that. It's hard to believe I only met you yesterday. It feels like...more." She felt her face heat and hoped he wouldn't take that the wrong way. "I mean, not to suggest that—"

"I know what you mean, Brenna. I feel it too. It's nice. Let's just enjoy it." He stood and pulled her chair out, dropping a kiss on the back of her neck as she rose. "Yaddo sounds like a great idea."

He was right. She needed to stop analyzing every moment, every thought, and go with the flow. It wasn't something she'd ever been good at, but maybe it was about time.

"Okay, off to Yaddo?"

"Lead the way." His hand settled at the small of her back as they left.

Brenna could get very, very used to having Reid around, and that worried her. She was supposed to be taking this trip on her own—to prove to herself she could do it. Was she using him as a buffer or a crutch? What would happen when she had to do it alone?

Shit, she was doing it again. Overanalyzing every single stupid thing.

When she was with Reid—in the berth last night, in the alcove that afternoon, with his hands on her, among other things—she didn't think at all. She felt, lived and enjoyed. And her phobia disappeared.

As Reid's thumb slipped just under the waistband of her jeans and caressed the skin there as they walked, she made herself think about nothing but this moment and this man.

For now, it was enough.

Chapter Five

Reid noticed a change in Brenna after lunch. Her walk was lighter, her smile easier. She'd even pulled him behind a shadowed hedgerow in the garden for a hot kiss and had nearly driven him out of his mind.

He couldn't wait to get back to the train. All he wanted was Brenna alone in their berth for the night so they could continue what they had been teasing about all afternoon. He couldn't remember ever being this hot for a woman. The shooting and his recovery really seemed to be behind him now; life had returned, and he was living it again. Brenna freed up something inside of him—made him feel lighter too—and that was as addictive as anything.

They made their way back to the train, hand in hand, after stopping for some dinner. Brenna had shopped while he talked to a local innkeeper, and his plan to open his own place had solidified. Cops didn't make much, but Reid had lived simply, working most of the time, and he'd invested what he could. Even with the market troubles, he'd rebounded and had done pretty well.

That, with his severance, gave him the chance to do whatever he wanted, and he wasn't going to waste the chance. Almost dying had driven that point home. He wanted to squeeze every moment dry, including his time with Brenna.

They approached the train platform to hear music playing, and Reid remembered there was a dance planned in the dining car, which had been cleared out for the event.

"You doing okay? Need me to cuff you or throw you over my shoulder caveman style and carry you in there?" Reid said as they reached the entry.

Brenna grinned. "No, I think I'm okay, amazingly. I'm not going to overthink it, I'm just going to walk on inside. I have to be able to do this on my own, or it won't mean much, will it? Though maybe once we're in there, you might still have some use for those cuffs, who knows?"

He groaned with mock distress, hand to his heart, making her laugh.

"Honey, you're gonna kill me talkin' like that, but if you think it wouldn't trigger your phobia, I'm all for it." His breath caught as every muscle in his body tightened at the thought.

"I'm willing to try," she said, smiling again as she pulled a hand down his chest. "And I love when you go all Brooklyn on me, did I mention that?"

"Any time," he said with a grin, and he took her hand, leading her to the doors and up inside the train without a problem.

Reid found himself impressed and completely proud of her, and as much as he wanted to get her back to the berth and take her up on her offer of using the cuffs, he paused inside the door.

"We should celebrate this—your success. Being able to kiss me in small spaces and getting back on the train with no problem. Let's go dance for a while, you think?"

"I haven't danced in years, but that would be fun," she agreed. "I'll go drop off these packages and change. Meet you back here?"

"I'll be waiting at the bar," Reid said, and watched her walk away, very much enjoying how her jeans fit. She had a cute walk, Brenna did.

Heading to the bar, he found an empty spot and slid up on the seat, ordering a beer as he studied the cool Art-Deco work on the bar. It wasn't part of the original train, but it had been built to match the time period, and they'd done quite a nice job. Reid loved vintage design, and the more he thought about it, the more the idea of fixing up old B&Bs or homes appealed. Maybe instead of buying one to run himself, he could buy ones that needed fixing, live in them for the duration, and then turn them over for a profit.

"Hey, you look lonely." A woman's voice interrupted his musing, and he turned as a slim blonde slid onto the seat next to his.

"Nope, not at all." He knew the look in her eyes all too well.

He'd seen her around, flirting with other guys, clearly on the trip to have some fun and get lucky. Nothing wrong with that, but he'd already won the jackpot.

In fact, he wondered what was taking Brenna so long to get back.

"I'm Susan. Buy me a drink?" the blonde asked with a pleasant smile.

"Sure, to be friendly. I'm actually waiting for the woman I'm with to join me," he said, letting her know in no uncertain terms that he wasn't a prospect for anything other than a drink.

He and Brenna might only be enjoying a weekend fling, but Reid didn't multitask in that particular arena. He'd never really dated much, in the strict sense of the term, preferring a sort of loose serial monogamy or no involvement at all. At least for the next day or two, he was with Brenna.

"Oh, you mean that girl with the mental issues? We thought you were just being nice," Susan said with a sour frown. "Or are you just into that kind of kink?"

Reid nearly choked on his drink. "Kink? She's claustrophobic, not crazy. How do you know that, anyway?"

"Everyone knows. Some of the train staff were talking, and word gets around."

"Well, I wouldn't listen to everything you hear, Susan. Now if you'll excuse me." Reid rose, intending to go find Brenna.

Susan shrugged and muttered something about it being his loss. She moved at the same time he did, their feet tangling them up. Her hand was on his shoulder, and she laughed brightly, tilting her forehead against his chest for a second. Reid put his hands on her shoulders, steadying her while he extricated himself.

As he turned, he saw Brenna in the doorway, watching him. He paused and took note of the feline smile on Susan's face out of the corner of his eye. Damn it.

Brenna looked amazing. She'd changed into a short blue dress that showed off every curve, and he couldn't take his eyes off of her. Then he remembered Susan was still there. Something cold landed in his stomach—fear that Brenna would think he'd been flirting with someone else the minute her back was turned. But she smiled at him and walked in, linking her arm through his.

"Time to dance?" She looked up at him as if Susan wasn't standing right there. Reid decided that was the best plan of all.

"Absolutely."

He took her hand and led her off to the dance floor, where he ignored the fast-paced pop tune that was playing and pulled her in close, hugging her tight to him before loosening up his hold and leading her in a slow dance.

"So who was your friend?" Brenna asked.

"Not a friend. Just a girl at the bar," Reid said dismissively.

"So she wasn't trying to pick you up?"

"I wasn't interested."

Brenna smiled. "That's nice, though you don't have any obligation to me. You can spend your time with other people if you want."

"I don't want. Not that. Just you."

Her eyes reflected her pleasure at his declaration.

"Well, she's probably thinking you're one of those guys who's into crazy," Brenna joked, and his amazement at the accuracy of the statement made him blink down at her, wordless.

She laughed, shaking her head.

"I've been this way for over a decade, Reid—all through high school, when everyone knew about the accident. Some people even blamed me for it."

"How could they?"

"They'd lost their friends, and I'd survived. It didn't make sense, but it just was what it was. I got through it. Then in college, it didn't take long for word to get around about my issues. Some people are kind, supportive, nonjudgmental, and some aren't. I learned a long time ago to ignore it."

Reid was surprised at her acceptance and her good humor about the situation.

"You're really something, you know that?" He smiled, nuzzling her nose.

"What I know is that when I'm with you, I don't seem to notice anything else, like how crowded this dance floor is." She nuzzled him back.

Her words warmed him, and that quickly turned to heat as they shared secret, intimate touches—the press of her breasts into his chest, the graze of his fingers over her hip, the way she nestled his increasingly hard-to-hide erection in the cradle of her thighs.

Reid thought he might explode and embarrass himself in public if he didn't get her back to the berth. Apparently, Brenna agreed, taking him by the hand and leading the way.

They stopped to kiss and work each other up even more along the way, eventually falling down into a large, luxurious train seat in the empty lounge. Most people were at the dance or had retired for the evening. The train chugged along to its next stop in the Finger Lakes, and Reid pressed Brenna down into the deep recesses of the seat, exploring her mouth as deeply.

God, she was sweet, and it touched him that she trusted him enough to let him cover her like this without panic. She was gorgeous, strong, and sexy, and he wanted to touch and taste every inch of her to let her know it.

Not here, though—they couldn't risk that. Train staff made the rounds through the cars every so often. But right now, they were alone.

Running his hand down her hip, he sprawled his fingers over her knee and then moved them lightly up underneath the skirt of her sexy dress. She gasped, breaking their kiss as his fingers slid higher, and Reid's heart nearly stopped when he realized she wasn't wearing anything underneath.

"Reid, stop. Someone might come along. That was a surprise for back at the room," she whispered. She looked left and right, though in her position she couldn't see much.

He checked, leaving his hand where it was, and smiled down at her.

"No one's here but us." He slipped his finger in between soft folds of flesh, groaning as he felt how wet she was already.

Her gasp turned into a moan, and she writhed under his touch, her eyes closing. Reid took that as a green light. Her thighs fell apart, encouraging him. Lifting the skirt, he took in the view of this beautiful woman splayed out before him, letting him touch and watch her in such an intimate way.

He was turned on as all hell, but he also felt warm and protective. Possessive. As if she was *his*. That was new. It made his heart slam hard against his chest as he slid down to the floor on his knees and bent to kiss her thigh, and higher. He listened to every sigh and moan, knowing what touch pleased her and what made her tremble.

He wanted to know it all.

Taking another quick glance down the center aisle of the train car, he bent to touch his tongue lightly against her clit, enjoying how her nails dug into his shoulder. She cried out his name as his fingers discovered how hot she was inside.

Tight. Seeking, clenching. For him.

In seconds, she broke apart, flooding him, spent and breathless. He watched her, her eyes heavy-lidded, cheeks flushed, lips parted. This single moment, this vision, would stay with him until his last day.

Reid took her hand, not trusting his voice, and hurried her back to the berth, where he didn't take the time to completely undress. He freed and covered his throbbing cock quickly, anxious to do what he'd been fantasizing about all day.

When he turned around, she had completely lost the dress, and she stood waiting for him like some sex goddess come to life. All ripe, wanting woman. He stalked forward and pressed her back against the door of the berth, then lifted her and slid inside, deep and sure, as a shudder of pure male lust rippled through him.

"Fuck, you feel good, Brenna. I've needed this all day. I can't believe how much I need this." His tone reflected wonderment, every word of it true.

"Oh, yes. More, please," Brenna begged, her legs wrapping around his hips, her hands on his shoulders as he bent to suck a hard nipple in between his lips. Her ass was like velvet in his hands, and he held her firm as he started thrusting hard, pushing her up against the metal door in a frenzy of need. If she needed him to be careful, he was too far-gone to know it.

But she didn't stop him—quite the opposite. Her cries of pleasure heightened until she crashed around him, holding on, her inner muscles tightening and surrounding him, drawing pleasure from his body into hers, making his knees shake with the force of it.

He lowered her from where he'd pinned her against the door, pushing her hair back from her face, still catching his breath as he pulled her against him. Had he ever known a woman as passionate and giving as this? So willing to tackle her fears and to live life head-on?

Her arms locked around him too. They walked back to the bed, and he pulled her down against him.

"You are rocking my world, Brenna Burke," he said with a chuckle.

He could feel her smile against his chest.

"Mine, too. I can't believe how...free I feel."

"Want to really put it to the test?"

Propping up on one hand, she looked down at him with definite curiosity and smiled slightly.

"The cuffs?"

"Maybe later. I was thinking I could really use a shower, but maybe you'd like to join me?"

Unmistakable apprehension filled her expression.

"It's so small in there. I had to do breathing exercises the entire time I was in there alone to get through my own shower. Though I could use one."

"It's okay, baby." He pulled her in close and kissing her neck. "No problem at all. Maybe another time. We can work on it, one day at a time." The words were out before he realized how they sounded.

She pulled back. "That's a nice thought, but we only have two more days of the trip left. Unless you were thinking, you know...um, that maybe we'd see each other after."

He hadn't been thinking that, not consciously, but he knew the minute she said the words that it was something he wanted.

"I'm sorry," she said, the words rushed as she stiffened. "I didn't mean to suggest—"

"That would be nice," he interrupted. "If you'd want to see me. Maybe go on a date or something." He smiled and kissed her. "We don't live too far from each other."

"Unless I get the new job. Then I might be on the road a lot, or I might move to be closer to the home office," she reminded him, sighing as he kissed his way down to her pretty breasts, full and warm in his hands. He fondled her nipples until they were hard and dark and then pushed them together to take both between his lips.

For several long, luscious seconds, he sucked, and she moaned, lifting her hips against him for more of what he wanted too.

When he broke away, he looked down into her face, knowing that even though it had been a mere twenty-four hours, he wanted to see more of Brenna. As often as possible.

"We'll figure it out. I can't possibly get enough of you in these few days." He reached for another condom, thinking he'd have to be sure to pick up more at their next stop.

She parted for him lazily, and he accepted the invitation, pushing inside her warm body, settling down between her legs, lying over her, not in any rush.

"This is nice," she said, her hand on his face, her eyes aroused but also serious. "Nicer than you could know."

He moved just so, tightening their connection. He loved how her lips would part when he did that.

"Oh, I think I have some idea." He sought another kiss.

She shifted under him. "I mean, I've never done...this. Not easily. Not like this."

He pulled up again. "Done what?" Reid was sure she hadn't been a virgin

"Lay underneath a man like this. It's always been impossible for me. I don't like feeling trapped. But I don't feel that way now. Not at all." She dragged her fingernails up and down his chest in the most hypnotic, incredible way. "I want more. Deeper."

"If something gets to be too much, you say so, and I'll stop."

He buried his face in her neck, unable to resist the need to move.

"I will, but if you'll just keep doing more of that, I think we're good." She chuckled, then sighed as she linked her ankles up around his thighs.

"I aim to please," he said lightly.

"Aim a tad to the left, then, if you can," she said, making him laugh even as his body tightened and surged inside of hers. They both forgot their conversation, words abandoned as Reid made pleasure the goal of his entire night.

Chapter Six

Reid woke up alone, twisted in the sheets of the bed. He lay quiet, sated, and listened for sounds of Brenna moving around, but the room was silent.

Maybe she had gone to get breakfast? Rolling over and looking at the clock, he groaned. It was almost noon. The train was also still—they'd already arrived at their next destination, Skaneateles, New York.

Pulling himself out of bed, he stretched sore muscles. Brenna inspired him to have the endurance of his twenty-year-old self, but his thirty-six-year-old self sent up a few protests as he headed to the shower, wincing as his side reminded him he'd overexerted.

Totally worth it.

Brenna probably hadn't wanted to wake him. He'd been sleeping like the dead.

A few minutes later, he was dressed and out to search for her, his stomach grumbling. The train perched on a hill at a train station that looked down over a sparkling lake, and the small town at the top was visible from the other side of the car.

Very pretty, he thought absently as he looked for her.

Finally he saw her. She sat alone on a wooden bench on the platform outside the exit, looking over the lake. Reid stepped forward, putting his hand on her shoulder as he took the seat next to her.

"Hey, good morning, gorgeous."

He leaned in to kiss her cheek. She didn't turn to meet his lips. She looked miserable and didn't say a word, which didn't bode well. "I thought maybe you'd decided to leave without me, since I was in danger of sleeping all day. You wore me out," he joked lightly, rubbing a strand of silky hair between his fingertips.

"I went for a walk." Her voice was faint as she looked at the doors.

He paused and pulled back a bit. "By yourself?"

She shrugged one shoulder. "It seemed like a good idea. I felt great yesterday, so right. Like I was...past all of it. My phobias. So this morning, when I came down for some coffee, I bumped into a few other passengers who asked me if I wanted to take a morning walk before breakfast. I thought it would be fun, and I said yes. You were sleeping, and there was no need to wake you."

"You could have."

"I didn't want to."

"So what happened?"

"I went, and it was very nice. Until I tried to get back on the train." She swallowed hard. "And I couldn't do it. Every time I tried, I just felt like my breathing was going to stop, and I had to back up. Some of the other guests tried to help me, taking my hand to try to tug me up inside—they didn't know—and I kind of freaked out. They really do think I'm crazy now," she said miserably. "So I've been sitting here, trying to get up the nerve to try again, but I couldn't."

"Aw, Brenna. You should have had someone come get me. I would have helped—"

She stood, walking away, pacing nervously and shaking her head.

"No. Don't you get it? I need to do this on my own. You're just a crutch, and depending on you won't help me get over this problem. It's holding me back. I never should have let this happen. I came on this trip for a specific reason, and I lost focus. I shouldn't have done this," she repeated, clearly agitated. "What's the point of this whole trip if I can't do this on my own? You won't be there come Tuesday, and then what? Then what do I do? Clearly, nothing has changed."

"Brenna, there's no shame in letting me help you—" he started, trying to ignore the sting of her words. She was just upset.

"Don't try to save me, Reid. You're not a cop anymore, and I'm not some damsel in distress," she bit out. Then she laughed, though it wasn't a happy sound. "But I guess I am, aren't I? God, how pathetic. Why did I even think I could get that job?"

Reid wasn't sure what to say. It killed him to see the tears staining her cheeks, the tension in her form, but she didn't want to be reassured, didn't want to be helped. She didn't want him, apparently. For all he knew, she had just had her fill of him and was giving him the brush-off. Maybe this was all some kind of act, some kind of game she played. Or maybe she really was crazy.

"I don't know what to do for you, Brenna," he said helplessly.

"I don't want you to do anything. I—I want you to leave me alone. I have to get back on that train myself, or nothing else matters."

Reid frowned. He might be hurt, and pissed, but he wasn't about to leave her out here by herself in this condition.

"Brenna, your stuff is all on the train. You can't just stay here. What will you do? Just let me help you back on." He stepped toward her and reached out.

She backed away, wrapping her arms around herself, her mouth pressed tight as she shook her head.

"I mean it. Leave me alone. I can take care of myself. One way or another, I have to." With that, she turned and walked off.

Reid wanted to follow—and not. What had he gotten himself into with Brenna? He'd known her for three days, and it had just been sex. A fling.

So why was he so angry and hurt at her rejection?

That she wouldn't let him help.

That she could walk away so easily.

Cursing, he shook his head and closed his eyes.

"For fuck's sake, Cooper, you're starting to act like a girl," he growled to himself and forced his eyes to look away from Brenna's retreating form.

If she wanted to go, fine. They'd had some fun; that was it. He was going to get his stuff and enjoy the day. Maybe she was right. Reid had come on this trip for a reason too—to celebrate his new life, to think about what he wanted to do next and maybe even to scout out some places to move or live.

He'd lost his focus on that, as well. He'd gotten a bit carried away the night before, thinking about pursuing something with Brenna after the trip. He was starting a new life and hardly knew what he wanted next. He didn't need to tie himself down to a woman, especially one with problems like Brenna's.

It was what he told himself as he made his way into town to find some breakfast; maybe if he repeated it enough times, he'd start to believe it.

Brenna was miserable.

She'd asked one of the train staff to please get her things for her before Reid got back, and her bags had been delivered to the station holding area.

She hadn't gone anywhere else the rest of the afternoon, but instead had paced the platform over and over again, not knowing why she couldn't get back on the train. She'd gotten on it so many times before. What was the problem now?

She'd wanted to get back on so much—she'd actually stopped on the walk that morning and bought some beautiful pastries at a bakery in town, hoping to go back and surprise Reid with them, but then...she *couldn't*. The worst part was that she didn't even know why. She just hadn't been able to do it.

The train was gone. It had left a few hours ago, moved on to the next stop, with Reid on it. Glad to be rid of her, she imagined. She'd booked a room in town and would stay there until she could get home. She could rent a car, probably, and drive the distance in small sections of highway. It was only a few hours.

That idea freaked her out too. What if she couldn't get back into the car halfway home, in the middle of the New York State Thruway? Right now, she couldn't trust herself.

Tears stung. She was stranded, and she felt unbearably stupid. She should have given in and let Reid help her onto the train, but she'd been so embarrassed for being dependent on him. It wasn't how she wanted to be.

She'd been furious and upset with herself, and she'd taken it out on him, Brenna knew. She hadn't meant to hurt him, but she hadn't been able to stop the things she was saying.

As she sat on a pretty bench by a white gazebo that looked out over the lake, watching townspeople and tourists walk around her, she'd never felt more alone in her life.

She tortured herself, wondering if Reid would take the sexy blonde from the bar up on her offer. Or maybe someone else. Some lucky woman who didn't freak out at the idea of taking a shower with a man because of the small space or who could get in a car or a train.

Clearly, the new job opportunity was out.

There had been moments—only a few in her life, but this was one—when she wished she hadn't made it out of that accident, either. Everything was just so damned hard.

The breeze was cool, and she thought she should get up and go to her room. Still, she continued to sit, looking at the water as if she didn't have a care in the world, when in truth she was loaded down with them so heavily, she didn't feel like she could stand up.

Knowing she needed a lifeline, she grabbed her phone and dialed desperately. Melissa Garvis had been her therapist for years, though their relationship was mostly one of friendship now. Brenna had quit regular therapy years before.

Mel answered. "Brenna? I didn't expect to hear from you this weekend—did you get my flowers?"

"I did, thanks. They were gorgeous." She tried to sound normal and failed miserably.

"Hey are you okay? Where are you?"

"In Skaneateles, a small town in Central New York. By the lake. It's a beautiful place," Brenna said with a sniffle.

"What's going on?"

"I met a guy. We sort of... Well, we ”

"Oh my God, that's fantastic! Is he hot? What's his name?"

"Reid. But, well, things didn't quite work out. I'm kind of in a jam. I left the train this afternoon, and I'm not entirely sure how to get home."

"Oh, no." Mel's tone softened. "What happened? Did he hurt

you? Did you have to get away from him? Was he crazy or something?"

Brenna couldn't help but smile. "No, I think that would be me, actually."

"Tell me about it."

Skipping the sexier parts, Brenna related what had happened. Mel did what she always did, listening intently as Brenna poured her heart out.

"He sounds wonderful, Brenna. What do you think made you run?"

Brenna blinked. "Run? I didn't run. I just couldn't get back on the train. Without his help anyway."

"So why not let him help you?"

Brenna sputtered. Mel didn't sound as sympathetic as she usually did. "Well, because I need to do this on my own. I need to prove I can do this so I can apply for that job."

"Really? Are you sure that's it?"

"Of course. What else would it be? It's this stupid claustrophobia, and I couldn't do anything without him there to help. I thought I was getting over it, but I wasn't. Not really."

"Hmm."

Brenna straightened her spine, irritated. "Don't *hmm* me. You aren't my therapist anymore. You're my friend."

"And as your friend—who used to be your therapist—I'm wondering what you're really afraid of here."

"You're not making sense, Mel," Brenna said stubbornly, letting her head fall into her hand as she rested her arm on the side of the bench. She was too tired for guessing games.

"Bren, think about it. You hadn't had a single problem getting on or off that train in all the times you had visited, preparing for this trip, and even leaving. Suddenly, after you get close to this man—and I assume you got very close—you feel the need to bolt in the other direction? I don't think you need a therapist to figure that out. You just need to be honest with yourself about what you're afraid of."

"I want to be happy. I've worked hard to be happy."

"But you keep clinging to this final problem, don't you? And when you met someone who made you feel like the problem went away, you pushed them away—doesn't make sense if you ask me. Why would you do that?"

Brenna just stared at the lake, unable to answer, though she knew, deep in her heart.

"He wanted more. To see each other after the trip."

"And?"

"I don't know. It's like everything changed with him, and fast. I went from being myself—my messed-up self—to being...normal. I didn't know if any of it was real, I guess. And it wasn't—I couldn't get back on the train by myself."

Mel was silent, and Brenna hung her head in self-disgust. "I guess because I was afraid what I had with him wasn't real, either. Or that when he got to know me, the real me, he wouldn't be able to run fast enough."

"Sounds to me like he did see the real you, and he could handle it."

"I guess."

"Listen, it's up to you. If you wanted out and if you aren't ready for that yet, then that's cool. But you do have to be honest with yourself about it. Don't hide behind the phobias. What you're going through is what every other red-blooded woman on the planet has experienced when they fear something with a great guy won't last. Welcome to real life, Bren," Mel said gently, with a smile in her voice. "But if you want him, you're going to have to decide that too."

"I couldn't just depend on him to help me feel like I didn't have this problem. I had to be able to do it on my own."

"Why?"

"Why what?"

"Why do you have to do it on your own? Everyone needs help. You came to me for help, years ago. You're calling me for help right now. We all need help. Why was his so threatening?"

"You really think I'm just making excuses so I don't have to risk failing?"

"I think your phobias are real, and you'll deal with them to some degree for the rest of your life. But sometimes limits can get comfortable, and getting outside of them, well, isn't."

"I don't know, Mel. I just don't. I felt like I had lost so much ground, back to square one."

"Oh, honey, you are nowhere near square one. You were a total mess at square one."

Brenna laughed, and it felt good.

"Reid made me feel normal. Maybe being normal is scarier than I thought. It doesn't leave me with any excuses anymore, does it?"

"I think you may be on to something there."

"Okay...well, thanks."

"Let me know what's going on, and if necessary, we'll work out a way to get you back here, okay?" Suddenly, Mel sounded slightly distracted, and Brenna heard her whisper something to someone in the room with her. "I have to go, Bren."

"Okay, thank you. Bye, Mel."

They hung up, and Brenna groaned the second she did. She'd been so involved in her own drama that she had forgotten to ask Mel how her own weekend was going—especially meeting her new fiancé's parents.

Was it always like that? Brenna considered Mel a friend now, not her therapist, but maybe the one-sidedness of their relationship had carried over from their professional interactions. Could it be that Brenna's phobias had been such a huge part of her life for so long, defining her, that she had become more comfortable with them than she realized? Reid had freed her of almost all of her limitations, and maybe it had been too much, too fast.

But it had also been wonderful.

Maybe having that closeness with Reid hadn't been scary, but the possibility of losing it was. If she was so dependent on him, what would happen if they didn't work out?

But how could she know unless she tried? If she could be "normal" with him, that meant she could be normal without him too, right? It really was all up to her. Confused, she got up from the bench and walked until she was exhausted, trying to figure it all out.

Chapter Seven

Back in her room, Brenna stared at the television without watching it, looked at a book without reading it, and finally gazed at the game of Solitaire that waited patiently for her next move, but nothing stopped Mel's words from echoing in her mind the entire time.

Was she really afraid to be happy?

Reid had brought up being together after the trip. He wasn't at all upset that she couldn't handle the shower because the room had been too small, and he had immediately offered to help her get back on the train without treating her like she was deficient in any way. All of the worries she had were purely her own—he hadn't been anything but wonderful. Even when she had treated him so badly that previous afternoon, he hadn't wanted to leave her. He'd only wanted to help.

He actually made her feel the opposite of helpless, in every way.

Capable, sexy, comfortable.

And she'd pushed that away and then run in the opposite direction.

Coward.

Getting out of bed, she cursed at her own stupidity. It was probably too late to do anything about it now—Reid was likely glad to be rid of her once he thought about it—but maybe not.

Brenna had to try, at least.

Everything she wanted was there, right within reach, if she let herself reach for it. Energy that had been spent on self-pity and feeding her own rationalizations for why she couldn't do the things she wanted to do thrummed through her.

She could do it. She *would* do it.

Taking a quick shower, she ignored the squeeze in her chest when she closed the door and imagined Reid in there with her. She wanted that.

After a few minutes, her breathing came easier—maybe a little too quickly when she found herself fantasizing about all of the things they could do in a shower. Getting out and dressing as quickly as she could, she noted the time on the bedstand clock. She could catch the train as it pulled into the station at Niagara if she left now—and drove straight through.

Brenna clasped the keys to the rental car she'd procured after the train had left, and her fate was set. They dug into her skin, but she didn't really feel it. Everything was dark and quiet outside the inn, the streets abandoned. She stood by the driver's-side door and reached deep for the resolve she needed, getting inside.

If Reid didn't want her when she got there, well, she'd deal with that then.

The Toyota wasn't big inside, but it was all the rental place had offered. The dark made it worse, but Brenna focused on Reid, thinking of how much fun they had had and how much fun they could have as she pulled out onto the thruway.

About twenty miles down, fear caught up with her, and she found a parking area, getting out of the car and pacing the parking lot, taking in as much fresh air as she could.

Eyeing the car again, she wondered if she could get back in and make it the rest of the way.

She had to push past it. He was worth it. She wasn't afraid of the car, she told herself. She was afraid of failing with Reid, and that wasn't acceptable. It wasn't how she wanted to live her life.

Taking a deep breath, Brenna got back in and got back on the highway, keeping to the slow lane, eyes on the prize.

Except for one stop for gas and coffee, she made it the rest of the way by blasting the satellite radio eighties classics station and singing at the top of her lungs to relieve any tightness in her chest.

It worked.

She was exhausted and running on adrenaline, but as she found her way to the train station, she was relieved to see she'd arrived early. Dawn was just breaking over the parking lot, and she locked the doors and dozed for a while until the familiar sound of the train's powerful engines woke her up.

In rolled the gorgeous silver train, and Brenna watched, taking a deep breath.

Whatever happened now, things would be okay.

She'd never driven that far before, and she had no doubt she could get herself home if she needed to. If Reid wasn't interested in her apologies, so be it, but she had conquered the fear that had held her back for so long.

Still, the idea of Reid's possible rejection put a dent in her bright moment as she walked to the train. It was so early, he was probably still sleeping. Maybe she could let herself in and surprise him—or maybe that wouldn't be a good idea.

She struggled with the issue all the way to the platform, where she saw Sean stepping down from the train, prepping for guests to exit as they awakened.

"Brenna! How did you get here? Trina said you left the train in Skaneateles."

"I did, but...well, I didn't want to give up. I drove here overnight."

"You drove all that way?" Sean asked, his eyes widening. "Good for you! I bet I know why. He's been miserable without you, you know."

Brenna felt her skin blush to her roots, but she couldn't resist asking, "Really?"

"Kept to himself, didn't eat much, retired early with a couple of beers from the bar. I think he'll be glad to see you again."

"I hope you're right." Brenna faced the entrance to the train as if confronting an opponent.

"Are you going to make the return trip with us?"

"I don't know. I guess it depends."

"Well, we'll head back around four this afternoon, dinner on board, and back to Lake Champlain by morning. Just so you know," he said. "You can, uh, go on board, if you want. Maybe get some coffee."

Her energy was fading, as was her optimism. Catching sight of her reflection in the train window, she looked like she had been up driving all night.

Great.

But none of that mattered.

Taking a deep breath, she did what she hadn't had the courage to do the afternoon before and stepped up on to the train.

She smiled as she heard Sean's quiet cheer behind her.

It was that easy. She was fine.

The hard part would be facing Reid.

After walking down to her—their—*his* cabin, she stood outside for long minutes, her fingers turning the key card in her pocket around and around.

Should she just let herself in, or knock?

Or wait in the breakfast car for him to come out?

Call and leave him a message on his phone?

People were starting to stir, a few doors opening as guests headed out for food. Her stomach grumbled. She hadn't eaten since lunch the day before.

Brenna lifted her hand to knock and jumped as the door opened and she found herself face-to-face with Reid.

"Oh," she said, words suddenly deserting her.

He looked awful—and wonderful. Tired, unshaven, and not very happy to see her.

"What are you doing here?" he asked, sounding groggy and sleepy.

Peering past him, Brenna saw he had taken more than a couple of beers back to the room, and most of them looked empty.

"I— I came back to apologize."

He continued to frown, but his gaze seemed to clear over several long, silent seconds.

"Wait. How'd you get here?"

"I drove. I got a car, and I drove all night."

That seemed to wake him up even more. "You did? Why?"

"Because I was an ass yesterday, and I know it. I shouldn't

have said the things I did. I was using my phobia as an excuse not to take a risk—if I held on to that, I could avoid the job, avoid taking a chance...with you."

He didn't say anything. He stood there, looking at her like she was nuts. Maybe she was.

"I'm so sorry, Reid. You were so good to me, and I was terrible to you. If nothing else, I wanted to be able to say that to you, and let you know I...enjoyed our time together. But I don't blame you for being pissed at me, so I'll just go, and—"

She turned away, eyes stinging. She didn't know what else to say, but she wouldn't cry. She'd made it here, and she'd said what she needed to say. He wasn't thrilled to see her, that much was clear. Now she had to get over it.

"Brenna," Reid said roughly, stopping her with a hand on her arm. "Come back. Come in."

Inside the cabin, Reid sat down on the bed—the one he'd avoided all night because it was a lot lonelier without Brenna. He thought he might be having some kind of alcohol-and-insomnia-induced delusion when she appeared at his door. Now, as she entered, though she seemed apprehensive, he knew she was really there.

The relief was humbling.

"I missed you. Isn't that weird? I've only known you for two days, and I missed you like hell." He couldn't hide the raw emotion in his voice.

She crossed the room to sit by him and nodded. "It's crazy. But I missed you too."

"And you drove here, by yourself? And got back on the train, with no problem?"

"It was touch and go, but I figured it out. I wanted to. Getting back to you was more important than giving in to my fears."

"Oh, honey, that's fantastic," he said as his arms wrapped around her and pulled her in close. He was so damned happy she was here and that she'd managed this huge accomplishment, he couldn't find any adequate words.

Then the shame set in. That he had left her behind, and that she had driven all night, alone, because of him.

"I'm so sorry, Reid. I was afraid, but I wasn't even sure what I was afraid of until Mel gave me some tough love," she mumbled against his shoulder.

He pulled back, the frown back in place. "Mel? Who sent the flowers?" He wasn't sure if he liked where this was going.

"Yeah. She's my best friend—used to be my therapist—and she let me know I had my head up my ass, basically."

"Sounds like a fantastic friend," he said with a smile. He pushed her hair back from her face, relieved.

"She is. I think I'll always have to deal with these fears on some level, but I was holding on to them because they were familiar and safe. When I realized that...and I realized how much I wanted to be here with you, it was easy to let them go. But I was so afraid I had really messed things up," she said, her voice catching.

"Aw, hell, sweetheart, don't cry. I've been kicking myself for getting back on the train and leaving you behind. I felt like all kinds of a dick not staying and making sure you were okay."

She shook her head. "That's not your job. I mean, I appreciate your help—it's made all the difference in the world—but the fact that you didn't stay helped me realize what I had to do. It was good that you walked away; I deserved it. You weren't a crutch. You were a...miracle. You made me realize what I *could* do."

He was so moved by her words that he had none of his own. He pulled her in close again, running his hands over her back to keep touching her and making sure she was really there.

"Well, you're here now. That's what matters."

He loved the feel of her hands on him too. When she pressed a kiss into the side of his neck, his blood turned hot, need overcoming his exhaustion.

"We were both up all night," he whispered against her cheek, the edge of his lips touching hers.

"Yeah." She sighed, turning her mouth toward him, her hand sneaking up under his shirt.

"We could probably use some sleep before the trip back," he

added. "Might not make it out of the room for the rest of the morning, at least."

"I agree. Though I thought maybe we could take my car back, if you want to. We could...take our time. See some of the sights. Stop at some of the inns, maybe get a room with a nice big shower?"

He smiled. "That sounds perfect." He captured her mouth in a hot, hungry kiss, which she returned just as greedily.

Clothes were removed without haste as they explored each other and got reacquainted on this new, exciting level. One with promise and a future. Reid pulled Brenna down with him, suddenly not feeling tired at all.

"You sure you want to be stuck in a car with me for a few hundred miles?" he asked, rolling over her and covering her. "It could be even closer quarters than these."

"I guess you'll have to find ways to distract me if I tense up. Maybe in the back seat?"

She smiled up at him, linking her feet over the backs of his calves as she pressed up against him, already wet, more than ready.

"I promise I'll do whatever it takes," Reid agreed as he set to driving both of them to distraction as thoroughly as he could.

About the Author

Samantha Hunter lives in Syracuse, New York where she has written for Harlequin Blaze since 2004. *Tight Quarters* is her first release with Samhain Publishing. When she's not plotting her next book, Sam likes to work in her garden, quilt, cook, read and spend time with her husband and their dogs. She's also an unapologetic TV addict. If you would like to learn more about her books, current releases and news, please check out her website at samanthahunter.com.

You can also email her at samhunter@samanthahunter.com and look for her on Twitter and Facebook.

Ticket Home

Serena Bell

Dedication

To Mr. Bell, for whom I would cross a continent.

I am grateful to Donna Cummings, Samantha Hunter, Ruthie Knox and Meg Maguire for being my partners and cheerleaders. I'm thrilled to debut among such talented writers. Ruthie and Sam also deserve extra hugs for being there on a daily basis to keep me—wait for it—on track.

Thank you to Anne Scott, a terrific editor, and to Nalini Akolekar who advised and supported me.

The denizens of Twitter, especially the early-morning crew, have been invaluable. Thank you, Edie Harris, for your astute comments on the manuscript, and the Wonkocrew and the New England Chapter of RWA, for your support.

To Ellen Price, who believed first, and to Brad Parks, who gave me my mantras—you are among the prime movers. And my mother is the original prime mover—I know that some days if you could send back the genetic gift/curse, you would, but thank you—THANK YOU—for the words.

And last, but by a very large margin not least, thank you to my family, Mr. Serena Bell, Miss A, and Mr. C, who have borne the trips to Fictionland, the unwashed dishes, and the ups and downs, and are still enthusiastically contributing titles and book ideas. I love you guys and couldn't have done it without you.

Chapter One

"Is this seat taken?"

Amy had been dozing, her head lolling on the vinyl train seat, a victim of Metro-North's gently rocking progress over the aging tracks on the way to Manhattan. The sweet shug of well-fitted metal on metal and the slight hitch in the train's forward motion had soothed her to sleep like a fully grown baby in an industrial-strength swing. But at the sound of that male voice, her eyes flew open, and she looked up into a pair of eyes that were more familiar than her own.

"Jeff!"

His name burst out before she could bite back the joy in her voice. If he hadn't surprised her, she would have said it coolly, would have pretended away the shock and, yes, elation. She would have held him at bay. But it was too late now. All her excitement, all her hope, was right there in her voice.

His smile told her he'd heard it.

He'd come for her. Six months too late, but he'd crossed the three thousand miles she'd put between them and come for her. *He loves me,* she thought, drinking in his long-lashed brown eyes, strong jaw, and dark brown hair that had gotten longer since she'd seen him last, long enough to fall over one eye.

"Hey," he said. "I can't tell you how good it is to see you."

"Yeah. It's...good to see you too." That was the understatement of the century. "But—what—? You're on my *train*. What are you doing on my train?"

"I flew in last night. I didn't want to wait until tonight to see you."

She felt a rush of pleasure at that, melting warmth she'd forgotten he could call up at his whim.

"Your cousin told me where to find you. I got on at White Plains. I couldn't— I wanted to talk, Ames."

Ames. No one had called her that in six months. She could feel herself softening like caramel on a sunny day, as she had so many times back in Seattle. But she made herself be patient. He had apologizing and explaining to do. Recanting and reforming. She was supposed to be angry at him.

Where have you been all these months?

Why didn't you try to stop me when I left?

Why wouldn't you at least entertain the idea of my taking this job?

Because that was what had precipitated all this: their breakup, her flight across the country, these months of separation. She had gotten a job offer in New York, a chance to move from financial aid officer to director of financial aid, to work for her alma mater, and when she'd told him—

She could still see his face when he said it. *There's no way that could work.* Pure dismissal.

He couldn't have made it any clearer.

It wasn't just that she was *supposed to* be angry at him. She *was* angry, the memory of it returning with a fast, brutal strength. Hardening her against him.

She was grateful for it. She needed that hardness, because without it, he broke her heart, over and over.

Yet it was surprisingly difficult to sustain her anger. To be as cold and clear and unmoved as she knew she needed to be. For one thing, even without looking at him full-on, she was aware of the muscles moving in his upper arm and shoulder beneath his suit coat as he clung to the metal bar above his head. She wanted to ogle him, to remember the exact nature of that shift and bunch, muscle and sinew,

"Amy—" He swayed as he loomed over her, suspended from the metal rail above. His eyes were luminous and dark under those gorgeous lashes, filled with something big he wanted to say to her. Hope expanded like a brilliant bubble in her chest. "I'm so sorry, Ames. If I could go back and do it differently, if I could go back and hear you out, and not be such a stubborn son of a bitch, I'd do it. I don't know why I reacted the way I did. I don't know why—"

A head poked out from the seat in front of hers, and a thick Brooklyn accent said, "D'ya mind? You're not the only ones on this train."

Jeff made a sound that might have been a laugh. He leaned closer, close enough that she could see the day's beard growth clinging to his jaw, and asked, "Can I sit with you?"

She hesitated. She was afraid, afraid of her own susceptibility to his physical presence. Afraid if she let him slide into the seat, if he sat that close and smelled like Jeff, she would fall back into her old ways, forgetting that she had ripped herself away from him, Band-Aid from skin, and crossed an entire country to escape exactly this weakness in herself.

People had stacked up behind him, waiting to get by, and she still hadn't moved from the edge of the seat, so he sat diagonally in front of her. When the other passengers passed, he turned around in his seat and tried to catch her eye. "I was so surprised." His voice was low but clearly audible over the train's clack. "You never said anything about wanting a different job, let alone one in New York. And you never mentioned you were applying for anything."

Guilty as charged. She had clobbered him over the head with the news that she'd gotten the job, but everything had happened so fast—she hadn't had any choice. And that didn't excuse—

"It's not an excuse. I know you hate that."

Ha, he remembered. She did. She hated an apology followed by an excuse.

He frowned. "I was harsh. I was dictatorial."

"You were medieval." Her voice surprised her. Louder than she'd meant it to be.

"Guys," said the heavyset dark-haired guy in front of her. "I can watch all the reality TV I want at home. Can you save it?"

There were chuckles from some of the other passengers. Amy blushed.

Jeff leaned across the aisle toward the commentator. "Tell her she should let me sit with her. If I sit with her, you won't have to listen to our conversation."

"Don't push your luck, dude," the guy told him. "On the other hand—" He twisted around to address her. "Lady, can he sit with you? Please? For the good of the rest of us?"

She willed Brooklyn guy to vanish. Jeff too. Hell, she wanted the whole goddamned train full of laughing observers to disappear. "I'd rather he didn't."

But Jeff had risen from his seat and planted himself on the padded vinyl beside her, and she had to scoot away from his muscular thigh. She'd been chilly a moment earlier, and now she desperately wanted to sink into his heat. To press the side of her body to his, turn to him and draw every last ounce of his warmth into her skin. Her mouth.

Instead she slid herself as far into the corner as she could, against the cold molded plastic and metal trim. She brought her knees up to get more distance from him. Still, she could smell him over the ambient train smell of vinyl and disinfectant. He smelled like—like him. Like freshly dry-cleaned wool suit and dry-erase markers and Old Spice deodorant. Like power and success. *Not*, she told herself firmly, *like* home.

Not unless he'd changed.

"Amy."

She didn't turn toward him. She was terribly afraid that on top of all the heat and nearness, the sight of him so close would be too much for her.

"Fine. I'll talk. You listen. Or don't listen."

It was impossible not to listen, of course. His mouth was a foot from her ear. His voice was a low, dark baritone that had always weakened her knees. She could scramble the words in her head, but that voice would crawl inside her and twine itself around her vulnerabilities and wear her down.

"I was medieval," he said. "And it was inexcusable. But—"

She sighed, the whisper of it loud over the train's shushing.

"I'm sorry," he said again. "I want— I want us to talk about it. Now. What happened. About working things out between us."

There was a sound in his voice she'd never heard before. She thought it might be desperation, and she found the possibility tantalizing. He had always been the alpha partner. He was older, he was established. He earned more money. He had influence outside their immediate sphere—the Seattle Chamber of Commerce, the business community, the larger world of technology. He went to conferences, gave talks. Their apartment had been his. Most of their friends, the people they saw regularly, were his friends first. She liked the idea that she was now in control, that she now had the power.

"Your hair is different," she said, without looking at him, without thinking.

She liked how it hung in his face. How it had begun to wave. It was soft, and it softened him. Not that anything could blunt the edge of his jaw or strength of his chin.

"Yours is exactly the same."

She put a hand up to touch it. It was long and dark and straight, pulled into a ponytail. Exactly the same as it had always been. But *she* was different, inside. She had decided not to live with a man who wasn't there for her. She shook her head. "I don't think so. I think it's different."

She turned to the window, watched the edges of another town rise from hills to cubes and spikes and fade back to hills, like time-lapse photography.

"I was wrong. I was wrong to do that. I was wrong not to talk to you about it." His voice was lower now, in the register where it vibrated in her chest and her thighs. She put her hand on the cold exterior wall to steady herself against the sensation.

"Amy?"

He was waiting for a response from her. She felt the suspension in the air, a thick, potent thing.

"I accept your apology. And I owe you one. I didn't mean to blindside you. It happened so fast. Not an excuse," she added hastily.

"Still, once I got over the initial surprise, I shouldn't have been so—"

"Medieval," she repeated. She saw the quick flash of her own white teeth in the window and clamped her lips shut. *No smiling.* That way lay capitulation on a scale she didn't want to consider.

He took a deep breath. "So...?"

"So what?"

"Can we talk? Can we work this out?"

"Why are you here now, asking me this, after six months?" She stared out the window. The sky was nearly light, a gleaming pale-blue tribute to morning over the increasingly urban landscape.

He shifted, and the seat creaked. "Are you asking me why it took so long for me to come out here?"

She nodded.

"If I answer that, will you tell me why you left without trying to work things out?"

She pressed her nose to the window. "I didn't think there was anything to work out."

Not a lie, but not the whole truth either. She hadn't believed he could change. And she hadn't wanted to hear him claim he could. Hadn't wanted to listen to him lie about that.

"We had a good thing, Amy. A really good thing. God—"

The way his voice broke off then, the tension, made her think of the weight of his body and the short, harsh sound of his breathing when he was inside her.

No, it didn't. It couldn't.

"It doesn't always feel that good." His voice was hushed.

So he'd been thinking something similar. She closed her eyes and tried not to see his face, drawn and straining, his fair skin gleaming in the dark. His expression tender and solicitous, his attention fixed on her, a thread she could grab and follow wherever she needed to go.

"I should know. I've been in enough relationships to know."

She'd left a patch of foggy breath on the window, and she used her thumb to draw a zigzag line through it. She was losing her will to resist him. Maybe she should tell him the truth. That she couldn't be the second most important thing in his life.

She opened her mouth, but as she began to speak, his phone rang. That distinctive, slightly musical, real-phone sound he liked so much.

She saw the look that crossed his face—close to panic—and for a split second she thought maybe he wouldn't take the call. Then he pulled out his phone, and the bubble in her chest burst, leaving flat, dark emptiness in its wake.

"I gotta take this."

She shrugged like it meant nothing to her. Meant nothing that he always took the call, would always take the call.

She turned away as he answered the phone. "Yeah?" The single word clipped and impatient. Out the window she saw the Bronxville station fly by, one of the platforms the express didn't stop for. Behind her, he spoke a flurry of words, dictating to-do items to one of his many underlings. She could hear a nervous woman's voice on the other end, and she guessed it was probably his admin and knew the conversation could go on for a long time, each of them remembering things they'd forgotten.

Amy had eaten a lot of dinners like this, sitting across from him as he spoke urgently into his phone. She had learned to lose herself in her own thoughts so she wouldn't be impatient, waiting for him to come back to her. She did it again now, letting her mind fly out into the world beyond the confines of the train. Just to remind herself that there was a world out there. That she had a choice.

She didn't have to sit here. She didn't have to be with him. She didn't have to let him remind her, over and over, that she came second in his life.

Hoisting her bag, she slipped out past him, ignoring the brush of her leg against his. Ignoring the startled expression on his face.

He put out a hand to stop her, but she shook it off and jerked away from him, breaking into a near run once she was clear of him and in the aisle.

She looked back, but he hadn't followed, and for the first time since she'd looked up to see him, she filled her lungs with air.

She took a seat several cars up.

A few minutes later, she heard the hitch and slide of the door at the end of the car. She peeked back, and there he was, carrying his briefcase and suit jacket. The phone was nowhere in sight.

People didn't change. How many times had her mother said that very thing? *People don't change. Not really.*

"Ames," he pleaded.

She ignored him.

"Amy, *please.*"

"Jeff, no. Just *no.* Go home."

There was a rustle as the people in the seats around her began to display their displeasure with the noise. They'd left the Brooklyn guy behind, but it was only a matter of time before someone would berate them for bringing their fight on the train.

She heard him sit. He was diagonally behind her, and she sensed him leaning forward.

Her breath seized. She had to get away from him, far enough away that she couldn't feel his presence. Far enough that she couldn't smell him, because as candle-faint as his scent was, it had a grip on her like a determined hand. And for God's sake, far enough away that if his stupid phone rang, she wouldn't hear it.

"Excuse me?" she called to the conductor. He was standing a few seats forward of her, punching tickets, a white-haired man with a trim mustache and a cliché of a cap.

"Yes, miss?" He slid a ticket under a leather strap and approached her seat.

"The man sitting diagonally behind me?" She kept her voice low so Jeff wouldn't hear.

"Yes, miss?"

She clutched her computer bag to her chest. Her mouth was dry. She lowered her voice more. "I'm going to change cars. Would it be possible for you to ask him not to follow me?"

"Follow you?" The conductor frowned.

"Yes. I'd— I'd like to move to another car, and I don't want him to follow me."

His eyebrows formed a sharp upside-down triangle. "Has he been following you?"

She'd somehow, foolishly, thought this would be simpler. The conductor had reminded her of a British butler in a BBC drama, so she'd assumed he'd be all discretion and eagerness to please. This guy was more perplexity and alarm.

"Never mind." What did she think she was playing at? She was making things worse. "No. No, he hasn't."

The conductor peered at Jeff, his eyes hard. He set his chin. "Go ahead, miss. I'll do what I can to keep him from following. And we should talk to security when we get to New York."

God, no—what a disaster that would be. "Oh, no. No, no, no. He hasn't done anything wrong."

"But his behavior is suspicious?"

"No. No. His behavior isn't suspicious. I know him. He's fine. I just don't want him following me."

"Miss," he said gently. "I have to report this incident. *See something, say something.*"

"No. He hasn't done anything wrong. You can't report it."

She and the conductor both peeked at Jeff. His dark brown hair hung over one eye, and he swiped it back. Her breathing hitched.

The conductor must have heard the hitch and taken it for fear. He turned to her, his face determined. "Let's get you out of here. Come with me."

She hesitated, but her need to get away overrode everything else. She took her laptop case and followed the conductor, not looking back but feeling Jeff's gaze on her neck. Trailing down the length of her spine, following the flare of her hip, teasing its way down her thighs. *Yes.*

No.

Safely ensconced several cars down under the watchful eye of her new protector, Amy gazed out the window as her heartbeat steadied. The train ran express from here into the city, gathering speed and pouring itself along the rail until its rhythms synchronized with hers. She felt its hum in her bloodstream and in the soles of her shoes, and she watched the landscape change like video in fast forward, scraggly growth on the embankment giving way to an industrial landscape and then to the open plains that surrounded Co-op City, the buildings like quadrangular tumors.

The train began its elevated journey over the tops of the multifamily units in the Bronx, and she played the game she always played, trying to imagine the families that crammed into those boxy, exposed houses—the mothers who hung their underwear out for the commuters to see, the children who played on those balconies and back porches, some of which should have been condemned.

He had not followed her, and she breathed more easily.

They stopped at the 125th Street station. Here, the city finally began to edge in close to the tracks, and buildings crouched, blocking out the world. The train was packed now. A heavy woman with a frayed backpack sat down beside Amy. The woman and the backpack crowded her, but she didn't mind. If anything, she felt safer.

Then they were underground. Inside the tunnel, features flickered into and out of existence, advertisements and station signs rushing past as Metro-North's route merged with the New York City subway. She was almost there. He had not followed her. She prayed he'd given up.

Chapter Two

He was waiting for her on the platform at the end of the day, leaning on a pillar, a study in male nonchalance.

Her insides got tangled as her heart tried to leap at the same time her stomach tried to sink, and then she knew half of her had hoped he'd go back to Seattle while the other half had been hoping just as hard he'd be here, on the train.

Stupid workaholic Jeff with his stupid phone.

As she stepped through the sliding doors, he pushed himself up off the pillar, an uncoiling of muscle, and closed the distance between them. Aligning himself at her side, matching her stride.

She sped up, ran for the train, and he chased her, bounding on behind her and following her up the aisle.

There was, of course, no place to go. No way to get away from him. Unless—

There was a conductor at the end of the car, and she started toward him, but Jeff caught her wrist again and spun her around to face him. He was very close, so close she could see the circles under his eyes and the brown stubble on his jaw. So close she could remember the exact feel of that well-formed lower lip.

"No more games."

It was a command. It was a growl. She felt it, everywhere.

"Do you know what I spent my morning doing?"

She shook her head. From behind her, someone said, "Excuse me," and Jeff sat abruptly in an empty seat and tugged her down to sit beside him. A group of passengers went by and distributed themselves into the seats beyond.

She tried to get up, but he held her firm.

"You're hurting me."

He released her instantly, and she rubbed the place where his fingers had dug into her.

"Your little stunt this morning with the conductor got me detained by the transit police for questioning. Apparently they take 'See something, say something' very seriously in the year of the tenth anniversary of September Eleventh."

"Oh *God.*"

"It's okay. It turns out I don't have a police record or obvious links with terrorist organizations, and I haven't traveled out of the country in the last couple of years."

"Jeff, I'm so sorry."

"Yeah, well. You can make it up to me by not running away. Okay? Just talk to me."

She shouldn't have sicced the MTA police on him, but that didn't mean she wanted to be trapped here with him. It didn't mean she wanted to rehash bits of their relationship better left behind. And it definitely didn't mean she wanted his body a few inches from hers, tension rolling off him like fog off the early-morning Pacific Ocean. If she let her eyes flicker sideways, she could see that his thigh was tensed, the muscle straining the wool of his dress slacks.

"I'm not playing games," she said. "I don't want to talk. I don't want to fix things up. I want you to get off the train and leave me alone. It's over."

"And I want you to come home with me."

He said it so simply, it stopped her dead. She eyed his soft, wavy hair, the lean strength in his neck, the rough line of his shoulder under his dress shirt, and she couldn't move.

The train began to pull out of the station, gathering speed in the dark tunnel. Her own mind started moving with it.

It was too late to put him off the train. He was going to ride with her now, and no matter where she ran, she wouldn't be able to get away from him.

I want you to come home with me. Of course he did. He'd said as much this morning. But there was something about having it spelled out for her that made it more real.

"I'm not coming home. There is no *home.* There was, but there isn't anymore."

He turned his body more fully toward hers, his knees almost touching her thigh. His expression was earnest. "I had a lot of time to think today. And I decided something."

For a brief, giddy moment, she imagined he was going to say what she'd always dreamed he would. *I want to spend more time with you. I've been spending too much time on work stuff. I'm turning over a new leaf.*

"I'm not going home without you."

It took her a few seconds to recover from her shock. "What, are you going to just ride the train back and forth with me until you wear me down?" As she said it, she felt a flash of panic. If that's what he decided, there'd be virtually nothing she could do to escape him.

"I don't want to wear you down. I want to talk to you. About what happened."

If he had any idea how easy it would be to overcome her resolve, she'd never get him off the train. "No, Jeff. No. It's not an option."

She had not expected this of him. Not the grand gesture of showing up on the train in the first place, not the willingness to stick it out after she'd sicced security on him. And definitely not the stubborn look he gave her now. This Jeff—this grand and stubborn Jeff—was a complete stranger to her, despite months of living with him in Seattle.

Yet now that she thought about it, she had known at some level that he had a stubborn streak. It was stubbornness, in fact, that defined his relationship with work. He insisted to himself that things couldn't function without him, that the company that had so desperately required his nurture in its early days still needed him like a newborn needs its mother.

Ego, that's what it was.

"I won't change my mind," she said again.

"I'll change your mind."

Ego.

"How will you do that?"

"I don't know yet. But I'm going to ride this train until I do."

They were coming to the end of the tunnel, daylight visible ahead.

"What will you do about Streamline?"

Streamline was his company, his baby. The other woman at the distant end of the phone.

"I can work remotely. I'll phone in." He patted his pocket, where she could see the outline of his iPhone like a futuristic implant under the tight pull of his pants. And then, as if reflexively, he pulled the phone out of his pocket, swiped a finger across the screen, and glanced down.

"You don't have the slightest idea, do you?" she asked.

It took a long time, the slow motion of a train-wreck disaster sequence, before he dragged his eyes off the screen and back to her face. There was a slight daze of concentration on his features as he asked, with absolutely no irony, "The slightest idea of what?"

Wednesday morning Jeff woke in his hotel room in New York City before his alarm went off, so eager to see her, a mess of nerves. He rode the train outbound, got off, crossed the tracks, and rode inbound to her stop, watching out the window as she boarded, tall and remote and beautiful. She chose a forward-facing seat, a two-seater. Today she wore a ruffled cranberry-colored blouse with a deep V-neck and cloth-covered buttons. Her hair was pulled back, the whole dark mass of it anchored in a low ponytail under crisscrossing black elastics. He wanted to tug it loose and bury his face in it.

"Mind if I join you?" he asked instead.

"You? Or you and your phone?"

After he'd taken out his phone yesterday, she'd refused to talk to him. He'd been unable to draw her out, unable to get her to so much as shrug her acknowledgement.

"Me."

"Sure. Right."

She was very angry. He deserved her anger, but he hated

being the object of it. The way she had softened toward him yesterday—he had felt hopeful. A lightening of a darkness he hadn't realized he'd been carrying with him. For the first time since he'd boarded the plane to New York, he'd believed his grand gesture might work after all. Then he'd checked his phone. And the shutters had closed, the gates banged down.

"I'm not going to talk on the phone."

"Are you going to check your voice mail? Your email? Your texts? *Twitter?*"

He shook his head.

"What if it's an 'emergency'?" Her voice was laced with sarcasm.

"Even then."

"I think this is the part where I'm supposed to feel grateful."

He kept being surprised by these gusts of anger. He'd been such an idiot to think that flying across the country would be enough to win her back. After what he'd done. After what he *hadn't* done.

"Sit."

Startled, he looked down at her. The hard lines around her mouth had softened just a little. He had always loved to kiss those lines. He had loved being able to distract her from the thing that made her angry.

Now he was that thing.

"Just sit," she repeated. "You can't hang out in the aisle forever."

He noticed she didn't shrink into the corner as she had yesterday morning. You could consider that progress, even if she was staring straight ahead, refusing to meet his eyes.

"How's the job?" he asked her. "Still enjoying stealing from the rich and giving to the poor?"

She looked startled, like she hadn't expected him to remember. "It's good. I love being a director. I feel like Tom Cruise in *Minority Report* with the fancy computer, fingers on everything, moving all the pieces around, seeing things come together."

The job was the reason he was here, stalking her commute.

She'd been doing financial aid at the University of Washington, going along perfectly happily, until someone at NYU had gotten the bright idea to recruit her. Then he'd pulled his medieval act, and here they were.

"The food is great. A catering company does lunch every day."

"Intensifying the impression that you're the Prince of Thieves?"

She didn't quite smile, but the corner of her mouth quirked. "Yesterday it was sloppy joes. On the softest egg rolls I've ever eaten." She bounced a little on her seat, something she did when she was excited about a song on the radio or chewy chocolate chip cookies. A habit of hers he had always loved, because it was like watching her enthusiasm burst out at the seams. That big Amy life force, the vibrant, buoyant essence of her. Of course she would love what she was doing. It was who she was. You could plant her anywhere and she would thrive, leaf and flower and, before long, grow roots.

Roots that would keep her from coming back to him. The thought made him queasy.

"How's..." She appeared to be struggling for a topic to keep the conversation going, "...your sister?"

"Good," he said. "Jake's nine months. So cute. Not walking yet. Going back to work was stressful for her, but I think she's pretty happy with her balance now."

They were talking. It was so much better than the fighting had been.

"How are Sasha and Porter?"

Porter was his partner in Streamline, and Sasha his girlfriend. The couple were their closest friends. Before Amy had left, they'd had sushi with them almost every single Friday.

He hesitated. This was trickier territory. Porter had bought an engagement ring and started talking about popping the question.

"That bad?"

Because she was staring straight ahead as she spoke to him, he had an opportunity to drink in her beauty. The sleekness of her hair, her noble forehead and regal nose, and the surprising sensuality of her mouth, which seemed out of place with the aristocratic rest of her. Watching her made him antsy and aroused, his lips and tongue craving the softness of hers, his fingers recalling the silkiness of her hair and the satin feel of her skin under his hands. "No. No. Things are good. They might get married."

A little hitch, as if in the regular forward motion of time, and then she laughed bitterly. "Good for them."

They sat without speaking, the disturbance of Sasha and Porter's success in the face of their own failure heavy in the air. The two couples had gotten together around the same time, and Sasha and Amy had commiserated about their boyfriends' preoccupation with Streamline's needs.

The train chimed and slowed to a stop in Hawthorne. Amy tapped the window. "There's a good diner here. Sometimes when I'm too hungry to make it all the way home, I stop."

"I haven't eaten anything except breakfast cereal, eggs and takeout since you left."

"So you do miss me."

Time stopped.

Her face got pink, streaks of color on her cheekbones. She hadn't meant to say it, he could see. "Only at breakfast," he said lightly. "Otherwise, nah. The apartment's a lot cleaner without you in it. Well—a lot less cluttered, anyway."

She smiled. That pleased her.

What he hadn't said was that the apartment was also a lot more bare. She had taken away the scarves and posters and cushions, the vases and tchotchkes whose names he didn't know. Once, he had made fun of her for those things, even as he'd secretly admired the way she could take those disparate objects, those unrelated bits of girlish fluff, and turn a series of blank white boxes into rooms with personalities. Now—

He missed it, the way the rooms breathed paisley or floral or slightly fringed, this one almost a Renaissance feel, this one firmly Pottery Barn circa 2002. All Amy.

He sought, again, the lighthearted tone he'd been trying for. "I open the mail every day instead of once every three weeks."

"I opened it more than once every three weeks!"

"Are you sure about that?" he teased. "I remember some pretty big stacks. I distinctly remember not being able to find at least one of the kitchen counters. For quite some time. It's a good thing neither of us actually cooked."

She grinned, guilty as charged. "Yeah. And also that no one ever needed to get in touch with us."

"But think of all the Publishers Clearing House lotteries we won and missed out on."

"We could have been rich," she said, in a mock-dreamy voice.

"Yeah. I've been getting rich since you left. But on the downside, it's possible the toilets haven't been cleaned in six months."

"Eew!"

"And I'm pretty sure you could do an archeological dig through the dust."

They were both laughing, leaning toward each other, all the anger gone.

"Amy."

"What." A statement, not a question.

"I miss you. Nothing's the same without you. The apartment feels big. I don't feel like going to any of our old haunts. Nothing's right."

He heard her exhale, a cross between a sigh and a sob. "Don't do this."

"Amy, please. Listen. I was an idiot. I was wrong. I need you to forgive me."

She shook her head. "I can't. I can't."

"You keep saying that. Is it because of your dad?"

She glared. "What the hell's that supposed to mean?"

"You never talk about him."

"Because he's not worth wasting the breath on."

"So is that why you ran away?"

"I ran away," she said through gritted teeth, "because you were an asshole."

He held up a hand. "Okay. I'm sorry. Yes. I was an asshole. We both agree on that. But—your dad, he was an asshole too, right? The original asshole?"

She smiled a little. "Yes. The original asshole."

"The asshole against whom all other assholes are measured?"

Now she was definitely smiling. "You gave him a good run for his money."

"I did. But—" He took a deep breath. "I'm really sorry." And then he blurted out, "Why did you leave?"

She turned and stared at him. "Are you serious?"

"No, I mean, I know what I did was obnoxious. But why didn't you just yell at me? Why did you leave and go all the way across the country?"

"You were a fascist, Jeff. You acted like it was a crime against nature for me to suggest that my career might compete with yours in importance."

She was angry again, that tight, hard sound in her voice. The anger poured off her in waves, as if her muscles were tensed so tight they were giving off a particular UV heat spectrum.

They'd been doing so well. He should have kept going with the niceties. But God help him, he wanted to have a real conversation with her. He wanted to know what she was thinking and what she was feeling. He wanted to crack her open and suck out all the sweetness. Or all the venom, if that's what it would take. He could do that.

"So you should have said, 'You're a fascist, Jeff.' You should have yelled at me. Not packed up and moved out and gotten on a plane." And there it was, plain as day—his anger. Anger he'd suspected was buried in there somewhere, but that caught him off guard anyway, the heat and depth of it.

It had apparently caught her off guard too. Her eyes were big, almost scared. Now would probably be a good time for him to shut up. But apparently, once the anger was out, it was like the proverbial genie. "So why don't you tell me what you're so mad about, really? What you were so angry about that you had to fly all the way across the country instead of having a conversation with me?"

There was a long silence, silence that seemed to have spread over the whole train car, which probably meant a good number of their fellow passengers were avidly listening. Great.

"I think you know."

"No. I don't."

She sighed.

Something about the fatigue in her sigh calmed him enough so he could say, "Whatever it was, I know it was a big deal to you. And I know the thing with the job was the final straw."

She fidgeted with the fabric of her pants. "There wasn't. There wasn't anything else. Not anything you could do anything about."

He wanted to pound the seat in front of him. What she had said was in the same category of awful relationship utterances as "It's not you, it's me" and "I think we'd be better off as friends". There was a flaw in him that made it impossible for her to love him the way that he loved her. And that—that sucked so much. "Oh," he said.

If that was the case, the smartest thing he could do would be to get off the train at the next stop, take a cab to the airport and fly home.

Except the way she was looking at him now didn't seem to match what she'd said. She eyed him gravely. Her eyes full of heat and interest.

His heart started to thud. She was staring at his mouth, he was sure of it.

She looked away, and it was as if none of that had happened.

What the fuck?

The race of heat under his skin told him he hadn't imagined it. But there was no hint of it now.

"It's the work."

"What?"

"The work. I got so sick of it, never seeing you. All the phone calls at the worst possible moments, not ever being able to go away on vacation."

Dread crawled under his skin like a thing under the bed at

night. Not the work. Streamline needed him, now more than ever as the company gathered momentum. Porter wanted to hire in a new management team, had even talked about cashing out now while the valuation was so good, but Jeff had said no. Streamline needed them both, needed their vision and energy and commitment. There were going to be years, still, when going away on vacations would be touch and go, and if Amy couldn't handle that—

"You never said anything before—"

"That's not true. I said it a million times. A million and one. I got sick of hearing my own voice. Nothing ever changed."

"I—" He took a deep breath. Tried to uncoil the fear. There was a way to fix this. He could work less. Differently. Be more attentive to her. Of course he could.

"You should go home. Before either of us gets hurt any more than we already have been. You work there. I work here. Neither of us is interested in negotiating, apparently."

"I am. I will. Tell me what I can do."

"Okay, let me put it differently. I'm not interested in negotiating." She turned abruptly and looked out the window.

But earlier, she had looked at him with hunger. She had laughed with him the old way. Maybe before this morning he could have given up and gone back to Seattle. But today had sharpened his longing for her. It had reset his determination.

Chapter Three

"Come home with me," he said.

It was Wednesday evening now. She was being slowly worn down like a stone in the middle of a river. "No," she said.

"Please."

There was something intoxicating about a powerful, well-dressed man pleading. It should be a controlled substance. And this wasn't just any powerful, well-dressed man. This was a man who had always had the ability to reduce her to naked neediness—and that was before that bit of wavy hair had started hanging over his eyes.

Also, she hadn't remembered his mouth clearly. How did it manage to look so soft and so masculine at the same time?

"No."

"What do you have against second chances?"

"The fact that nothing changes."

"That might have been true with your father. It isn't true with me. I will change. Whatever you need. I won't talk on the phone during dinner. No phone calls when we're in bed."

The phone calls in bed. She'd blocked those out. He'd never actually answered a call while they were making love, but one time, she was pretty sure he'd driven them speedily to the logical conclusion in order to check his voice mail. She'd been mad as hell, had walked around for days thinking of it, but she'd never brought it up because it would be too easy to deny. If he'd told her he hadn't done anything deliberate to hasten the happy ending, what evidence would she have to the contrary?

"Long vacations in exotic locations. No broken dates. I'll be on time."

What other concessions could she demand from him, and

would it make a difference if she did? There would be no guarantee he would keep his promises. No guarantee that he *could* keep his promises. Once she'd given in and come home, she wouldn't have any leverage.

"No."

He banged the back of his skull on the soft seat behind him. "Amy."

Why was that sexy? What was wrong with her? It was too many hours spent too close to him. Months of living with him and having constant access to sex had conditioned her to associate the sight, smell and sound of him with mind-blowing orgasms. And then she'd deprived herself of all sexual contact for six months, and this was the inevitable outcome. He banged his head on the seat, and she wanted to climb on and straddle him.

"I want you to tell me about your father," he said.

"This has nothing to do with my father."

"This has everything to do with your father."

He looked fierce. So much for the softer Jeff. He was all boss today. And, well, she liked him that way.

She took a deep breath. "I told you my parents split when I was ten."

"Yeah."

"What did I tell you about it?"

He tilted his chin up. "Not much. You told me he was a colossal jerk."

"Yeah, that's about the shape of it. Only I probably told you the abbreviated version."

He nodded.

"The first time he left, I was ten. I don't know absolutely every detail, but she caught him cheating and kicked him out."

Amy remembered the day he'd left. He'd found her playing paper dolls on the floor of her room. He'd loomed over her, a tall, beefy man in a red plaid flannel shirt and baggy jeans. A fixture of her life, not threatening. Not someone whose presence she'd ever questioned until that moment.

I've gotta go, he'd said. Only that. Nothing about how long or how final, just *I've gotta go.* A kick in her gut, and that was before she'd felt the full weight of fury at her mother. The real anger hadn't started until ten-year-old Amy had realized that if her mother had been more forgiving, Amy would still have a dad living in her house with her, making Saturday-morning pancakes.

Breakfast had always been her favorite meal. The only essential meal in a day. Jeff had known it so well that he'd developed a policy: He never went to bed until he checked to make sure the apartment was locked, the dishwasher loaded and primed to run, and a healthy supply of Wheat Chex and two-percent milk—her favorites—on hand. More than once, he'd made a late-night cereal run over her protests, so she wouldn't have to wake up without. *For me, it's coffee,* he'd said. *Everyone's got a morning addiction.*

He'd made it a casual thing, but every time he did it, she got a little teary. A cigar wasn't always just a cigar, and breakfast wasn't just breakfast to Amy.

"He was gone about six months—he was living with the woman he'd been cheating with. Then he came back and wanted another chance. He begged. I overheard. I had just read *Harriet the Spy*, and I had a spy notebook, and I hadn't figured out yet that eavesdroppers never hear anything good. He said he wasn't in love with this other woman, that he was in love with my mother, and that he couldn't bear to live without the two of us. He was very persuasive. I think he's probably technically a sociopath, you know, charming and totally devoid of conscience? Anyway, she agreed to give him a second chance."

Amy had forgiven her mother and welcomed back her father. Saturday mornings were Saturday mornings once again, the Bisquick box and Aunt Jemima and the feeling that everything was right in the universe. A parent on each side.

"We were all together another eighteen months, and then he left again. All told? I think he came and went five or six times. Finally, he emptied our bank accounts and took off for good."

His knuckles were white, his mouth a tight line. "Why didn't you tell me that?"

"Other guys I dated had this way of using that story against me. 'Oh, you have daddy issues. Trust issues.' Whatever. Maybe I do, but I got tired of hearing about them."

He frowned. "I wouldn't have—"

She went on, her words overlapping his. "My mother said it was her fault for not trusting her instincts. She said she shouldn't have even let him talk to her. She used to say once she'd let him onto the porch, it was inevitable that he'd manage to sneak into the house, and once he was in, it was only a short distance to the bedroom."

"Oh."

"Yeah." She finally turned and looked at him full-on. "So now you see."

As she'd gotten older, she'd stopped blaming her mother for sending her dad away and started blaming her for being weak enough to readmit him, not once but many times.

"Well, here I am. I'm in the house. Metaphorically speaking. And I'm not your father."

It would almost be better if he were. If he were as much of an asshole as she'd convinced herself he was. Because then she wouldn't be sitting here, her face close enough to his that if he only leaned a little closer—

She turned suddenly and looked out the window.

Behind her, she could hear his breathing, ragged, uneven.

"I'm not your father," he repeated. What a gut-wrenchingly bad story she'd told. The original asshole had been a true original.

"You took an awfully long time to come looking for your second chance." Her words were almost lost in the soft *shhh* of the train.

Everything made sense now. Why she'd been so quick to anger, yes, but more to the point, why she'd fled instead of giving him a chance to explain.

"I was angry too. That you'd walked away so easily."

"It wasn't easy."

He leaned closer, catching the lemon scent of her hair. His fingers and lips tingled with longing to reach out and touch. Comfort, apologize, forgive. "It happened so suddenly. And being angry was easier than feeling hurt."

She nodded.

"I let my anger make me stubborn about coming to find you, even though I knew I'd behaved badly. I tried to get in touch, and—"

"And I blew you off."

"But I understand why. I do." He spoke almost into her neck now, and if he leaned a little closer, his lips would touch her. Could she feel his breath, moving across her skin?

She made a small, incoherent sound. A whimper.

"Amy." Her name was barely more than a puff. He reached for her, put a hand on her shoulder. She didn't shake it off, and he felt her warmth through the thin blouse. Felt the sharpness of her bones and a slight tremor. That, more than anything, set him off. He leaned closer, anticipation gripping him around his chest and in his groin. His balls tightened, and his cock hardened. He pressed his lips to the juncture of her neck and shoulder and to the smooth, hot skin there, the feel of her electrifying.

They'd been together almost a year, and in that year they'd made love hundreds of times, but this was like brand new—this was like before they'd ever touched, that crazy-prickly, whole-body wild desire that made you do things you shouldn't.

Another tiny sound slipped from her lips. A groan that caught him off guard and was like a touch, almost pushing him outside the bounds of control. He groaned too, and several things happened at once, then. She laughed, turned toward him and shushed him loudly.

"We're on a train," she said.

"I don't care." He leaned in. It was awkward, but he managed to find the V of her blouse with his mouth. She groaned again, a little louder than last time, and without lifting his head, he said, "Doesn't sound like you care, either."

"There are a million people on this train."

"There's no one sitting across from us."

"Yet."

"Then let's not waste any time." And he kissed her for real this time. A puzzle piece fit into place, like a tiny internal click deep inside him. It took only a second for her to open to him, for her tongue to find his, for her to begin to make those familiar little whimpering noises that had driven him completely wild in bed from the very first time they'd made love.

He wasn't sure he'd ever told her this, but it was those noises that made him come, every time. Sure, there was all that heat and friction and wetness, all the grappling and groping, her fingers reaching into the space between where their bodies met to move slickly over his balls, his thumb finding her clit, and all the kissing, endless hot, wet and hungry—but every time, those little whimpers were the final straw, picking him up and hurtling him into mindlessness. He guessed it was how helpless they made her sound, like she was awash in what was happening to them.

He had to wrench himself away, or he was going to make a spectacle of himself, of them. When he broke apart from her, she was panting, and so was he.

"Don't stop," she said.

"We're on a train."

"I don't care."

He sank into kissing her. He skimmed the lace of her bra under her blouse, and beneath it, the hard, tight knot of her nipple. They were superconnected, and touching her set off a chain reaction in him, like he wasn't in control of anything he was doing or feeling, caught in the spiral of their need. She arched up into his hand and made another sound, a different, rawer sound, as he brushed his thumb back and forth.

He slid his other hand to the seam of her slacks, where heat radiated. He rested the palm of his hand there, not willing to push her too far, but she slid forward to meet him and ground herself against him, hard. "Christ," he breathed, and she whispered, "Please don't stop," and you couldn't have paid him to, nothing could have made him stop touching her or kissing her. He felt the tension in her body growing to match the tension in his. He moved his hand against her needy grinding, closing his index finger and thumb over her nipple, and felt, rather than heard, her yell her release silently into his mouth as the train clattered to halt in a station somewhere in Westchester County.

The doors opened. A new batch of people climbed on, and a middle-aged couple sat down across from them.

Chapter Four

Amy turned her whole body toward the window to hide the physical signs of what had swept through her. Also, there were tears of release—and relief—in her eyes. Behind her, Jeff said, "Impeccable timing."

"For me," she murmured. "Can't imagine it's going to be a very comfortable rest-of-the-train-ride for you."

"No. God, no. Ouch."

"Wish I could help you with that."

"No, you don't. This is your revenge."

"Well, there is that."

Gradually her breathing returned to normal. Gradually the heat in her face retreated. But her nipples were still hard little peaks, and she was swollen and damp where he'd rubbed her with the big, strong palm of his hand. God, she was shameless. They were on a *train*. This was her *commute home*. Which brought her abruptly back to reality. This was crazy. They lived on opposite sides of the country. He was a workaholic, and all the promises he'd made wouldn't change that. The fact that he was the indisputable master of her body, that he could bring her to climax faster than she could bring herself—and that was saying something—shouldn't enter into things a bit.

And yet entering into things—his entering into things—his entering into her—was precisely what she could not stop thinking about. Sex had a way of screwing everything up. All one's best laid plans. All one's best intentions.

"You know," he murmured behind her. "I can't think about anything right now except being inside you."

Her body should've been taking a break, but she felt a sharp jolt of renewed enthusiasm. Which scared her. She could keep going. They could keep doing this. It could spill off the train and into real life, and then what?

"We can't do this," she said.

"Why not? I think we're pretty amazing. I've always thought we were pretty amazing."

For a moment, she let herself think about it, really think about it, and then she realized exactly how much of a complete and total mess she'd made of everything. "How would that work? I live in New York—well, Connecticut—and you live in Seattle."

"Come home. Come home with me."

She got itchy with anger then, all of a sudden.

No, it wasn't all of a sudden. She'd been angry the whole time, and what he'd done to her body had been a fabulous distraction, but here it came, roaring back, anger and hurt. "I won't. I can't. Not until you realize how ridiculous it is for you to say that. Why is Seattle home, just because you work there?"

"It was home first. It was our home." Now he sounded angry too. "I took that for granted. Maybe that was crazy of me, but we were living there together, and it didn't occur to me that you would just upend that."

"I didn't just upend it. I tried to have a conversation with you, and you wouldn't have it."

"It wasn't a conversation! It was an ultimatum!"

They were both silent for a moment. Around them, unfazed by their anger, unfazed by their distance, their attraction, their needs, their desperation, the passengers on the train continued with their low chatter, the clattering of keyboards, the buzzing of cell phones.

"I don't know what you mean by that," she said finally.

He sighed. "I shouldn't have said that."

"You should have, if you meant it." There was a part of her that wanted to reach out. That wanted to stroke his cheek, to feel the rough texture of his skin, slightly blotchy from arousal. But she kept her hands to herself.

"I thought at the time— It seemed like maybe you were...trying to push me into proposing."

She couldn't help herself; she laughed out loud. "Really?"

"Weren't you?" It was framed as a question, but his body language, his crossed arms, his stern face were all accusation.

Had she been? Not consciously. But she was well aware that very little was done consciously. She turned to the window.

"Whatever I was doing," she said, finally, "I seem to have put us in an impossible situation."

"Not impossible. Challenging."

She experienced a brief, almost blinding surge of hope.

His phone rang again.

He looked at her. She gazed steadily back. Her eyes stayed on his through eight rings. Then silence.

She liked that, but she didn't entirely believe it.

He was still staring at her. "Can I—?"

His expression was pained. Whatever he'd been about to ask, it wasn't coming easy. Served him right.

He sucked in a deep breath. "Can I get off the train with you?"

She knew what he was asking, both the little question and the big one. He wanted to go home with her, make love to her in her bed. He wanted to step outside this perfect, protected realm and bring cold, hard reality into their peaceful interlude. He was asking her to be with him in the bigger, realer world.

Could she?

She had loved Jeff in the bigger, realer world. She had loved the little private things, the hummed lullabies and the ever-ready breakfast cereal. But she had also loved the way he was with other people, relaxed, at ease. The power he had to convey his own confidence, to make other people open up and spill themselves into the room. At parties, he could get anyone past small talk in under five minutes, a steady unreeling of questions that drew out a person's essence while she stood nearby and listened. While she watched him, the strength in his face, the regularity of his features, and that gift he had for making people enjoy themselves from the inside out.

He had done it to her too, once when they'd first gotten together, and again on this train ride—drawn her out of herself and into him.

In her mother's endless retelling of how her father had showed up in the living room and claimed his ill-fated second chances, she had often said that there were "real" and "fake" second chances. That some petitions for second chances were genuine and others a ploy. But how could you know which was which? What if she let him get off the train with her? What if she let him make love to her? What if she let herself fall in love with him? And what if when it was all over, he still wasn't interested in compromise?

She should make him commit first. Negotiate first. She should get him to agree that any outcome where he kept his job and she lost hers wasn't fair. Because after he made love to her—

Well, she was in a position of power now. He wanted her. She could see it in his eyes, dark and hungry. She felt a flare of answering heat at the apex of her thighs.

After she made love to him, she would be the needy one. Making love to him had always had the power to reduce her to a pathetic state.

She opened her mouth to tell him she couldn't, not unless he could promise her more.

And then closed her mouth, because she had realized something important.

She wanted to make love to him even if he couldn't promise her more. She wanted him inside her to a degree that stripped her of reason. And she didn't want to issue an ultimatum she'd hate to have to enforce.

"You're thinking of your father," he said flatly.

Ha! "No. Well, I was. But no. I was thinking about—" She grinned, lowered her voice, and lied. "That thing you do with your tongue. The flick." Her nipples tightened abruptly, the way they did when he took one firmly but gently between his teeth and flicked his tongue relentlessly back and forth over the tip. *Gaah.*

"Is that a yes?"

Was she really ready to do this to herself? To give up leverage and sanity and three thousand miles of hard-earned perspective?

He leaned close, his lips touching her ear, his breath sweeping hot across the sensitive folds. "Do you like it better when I do it to your nipples or your clit?"

She grabbed his arm hard, steadying herself, although she wasn't sure if she was bracing herself against the movement of the train or the precipitous sense she had of falling into a void. "Yes," she whispered.

"Yes, what? Nipples?"

She shook her head.

He lowered his eyebrows. "Clit?"

She shook it again, and he wrinkled his forehead in confusion.

She put one hand to her cheek. Her hand was icy cold, her cheek burning hot. She closed her eyes briefly and gathered her nerve. "Yes, it's a yes."

Chapter Five

The world outside the train and his head was a blur as they jogged up the stairs to cross the platform, then down the side toward the parking lot where she'd left her car. She opened the trunk, and he slung his bag in. He had so much to say that it crowded his chest, but he knew if he opened his mouth, nothing would come out. He wondered if she felt the same way.

They both slid into the car. Even though they'd been physically closer on the train, this felt dark and intimate in a completely different way, and he could sense her presence, magnetic, beside him. He turned to look at her. She was looking back.

They fell into the kiss, or that was what it felt like, anyway, like being drawn into some deep, dark void, into a velvet-hot center. Her lips were cool, but her mouth was scalding, and then her hands were on his shoulders. She slipped the fingers of one hand into his hair, and the familiarity of the gesture seared him. He grabbed her ponytail so she couldn't pull away and set about exploring every tiny crevice of her. Until it got to be too much for him, the smell of her skin and the taste of her mouth, and he plunged his tongue in deep to show her what he wanted to do to her.

She groaned and tried to pull him closer over the ridge of the parking brake, and they broke apart, laughing. "Trains, planes and automobiles," she said. "Let's get to a non-moving location."

"Drive fast."

She started the engine, then hesitated with both hands on the wheel. "I still have the IUD."

He nodded.

"And—I haven't been with anyone else."

Relief flooded him. "Me neither."

She didn't look at him, but he saw her shoulders relax an inch and realized she'd been worried too. He wished he'd said it sooner.

For a while, they were quiet in the dark. He absorbed the feel of the car, its enclosed, quiet smoothness after the jostle and life of the train.

"The train is strange, don't you think?" she asked.

Of course. He had missed the way their minds worked in parallel, the way she'd sometimes voice his thoughts before they'd fully taken form.

"We're all going to the same place. Point to point. We're all in it together. But then—we're not, either. We have our different destinations in our heads the whole time. So it's like, the train is bursting with all the missions of the people it contains."

She did that, kept quiet and then opened up with a little piece of philosophy, words that were almost poetry. He could only nod. If he said anything, his emotions would spill out over both of them.

Maybe she knew, because she cast a quick glance in his direction. She reached out and touched his thigh. The muscle clenched involuntarily, and he made a choked sound.

That brought out a definite, real grin. "Yeah. Me too." She left her hand there, her fingers playing very slightly over the lightweight wool, a terrible, wonderful ticklishness. He kept an iron grip on the door handle, as if that would somehow translate to an iron grip on his self-control.

The long, winding road they were on gave way to smaller neighborhood streets, any suburb in any town in North America.

She pulled into the driveway of a small split-level, lit in front with a single bulb in a cast-iron lamppost.

"Is your cousin home?" It was the first time logistics had occurred to him.

"She's out tonight."

He followed her up the stone walk. She unlocked the front door, and he went in behind her. She flipped a light switch, and they stood together in the tiny entryway, a wall-mounted rack of coats and sweatshirts looming behind them. Her face was flushed, her eyes bright. The life force in her moving at the surface of her skin. He took a step toward her.

She drew back. "Do you want some food?"

"No. Later. After."

Her eyes got bigger and darker, and her lips parted a tiny bit. The subtle show sent a swift rush of blood to his already hardening cock. He'd always loved that about her, how evident her desire made itself.

He kissed her, hard, pressing his knee between her legs, easing her against the wall at the foot of the stairs. Under his hands, her body was warm, strong and supple. She arched her back, exposing her throat to him, and he nipped it, loving how concentrated the scent of her was there, reveling in the slight saltiness of her skin. She made a little noise, somewhere between a hum and a whimper, and the sound burrowed into him and took up residence as an ache. "We should go to the bedroom." It would be a better venue for the kind of life-changing, mind-altering—fuck that, ragingly possessive—sex he wanted to have with her. He wanted her to know everything. His desperation, his fear, his determination. What she did to him, how she made him feel. "I didn't get off the train with you so we could do this somewhere else half-assed—"

But he couldn't finish, because she reached up and locked her hands behind his neck, drew him down and ate his mouth like a starving woman. Nibbled, bit, licked, devoured him, sucking the breath out of his lungs. And he kissed back, wanting to pour himself into her. To make her believe what he believed. That this could work. Was working.

She broke the kiss off. "I used to fantasize all the time about you doing me on the stairs in the townhouse."

Fuuuck. "You did? You never told me that." It was a rush—his Amy, that revelation—like discovering that an object you'd always loved for its sentimental value was also eighteen-karat gold

"There was never time. You worked and worked, and then we went to bed, and we did it, and it was good, don't get me wrong, and you always made sure I got mine, you were a total gentleman, but there wasn't time to...figure things out."

Although he wanted to believe she was wrong, or that it was

only her version of things, her wounded version of things, he thought she was probably right. There hadn't been any time, and that was because he'd been so busy. So oblivious.

He wanted to go back and undo it, but that wasn't open to him, so instead he took her face in his hands and held her steady in front of him. "I was an *idiot*. I will make time. From now on. I promise. I swear it." He leaned close and kissed her. Hard. Harder than he meant to, but she kissed back just as hard, sliding herself against him, rubbing herself on his thigh.

He broke the kiss and asked her, "What happens? On the stairs?"

"I'm wearing a skirt," she whispered.

Oh, that worked. That definitely worked. He had a whole set of fantasies involving Amy in skirts of varying lengths, with little to nothing underneath. How much fun could they have had on the train if she'd been wearing a skirt? Hmm, maybe it was a good thing she hadn't. But here, now? "Go change."

He saw the heat flash in her eyes and felt his cock jump in response. In Seattle, they'd had great sex, but it had been vanilla— in the bed, him on top or her on top, usually. Once or twice when he'd asked, she'd let him take her from behind, but she hadn't seemed terribly into it, which had diminished his enthusiasm. But now? "You like that, huh? When I boss you around."

She nodded, mouth pressed together in a tight line, like she was pleased and a little ashamed.

It was a wedge, prying his heart wide open, and part of him wanted to grab her and hold her, squeeze her so hard it would probably break every bone in her body, but this new Amy was a temptation, and he didn't want to lose the moment. "Go change."

She went up the stairs, her hips swaying a little before she disappeared down the hall. He heard drawers and doors opening and slamming, heard her mutter and swear, heard the sound of what sounded like two books hitting the floor—shoes, maybe?

She reappeared at the top of the steps, and his body revved. God, she was so beautiful. She'd taken her hair down. It spilled over her shoulders, masses of dark silk he desperately wanted to have slip between his fingers and brush his face. She was still wearing the cranberry-colored blouse, but she'd put on a black velvet skirt that skimmed an inch or two above her knees, stockings, and black high-heeled sandals. His mouth got dry, and all the blood in his body drained into his cock.

She came down the stairs until those sweet curves of hers were in his face. He reached out, grabbed her around the waist, and buried his face in her cleavage, breathing her in, kissing her, biting her. She yelped but pulled him closer. Roughly, he brushed the blouse and one lacy cup aside and did what he'd been dying to do this morning—took a mouthful of her. Felt the tightly beaded nipple on his tongue. His cock strained against his shorts and jeans, craving more contact.

She took another step down, which made them almost exactly the same height, and he took advantage of the access to rub himself on her hip, on the soft-over-hard inviting juncture of her thighs. She moaned his name. Everything felt both familiar and foreign. She was so completely Amy—smelled like her, tasted—he had to stop and reassure himself of that, his tongue sliding along hers—yes, tasted like her, felt like her in his arms. But she was a different Amy, a bolder, brasher, naughtier, sexier Amy, so hot she burned.

She turned away from him and rubbed her black velvet ass over the bulge in his jeans, and he bit the inside of his cheek to keep from coming. He had to make this good for her. He had to convince her, because nothing else he'd tried had gotten through to her yet. He had to make her see, feel, *get* that what was between them was not something you could set aside or replace. He wanted to overwhelm her, own her, ruin her for every other man.

She knelt on the steps and put her elbows on another step, and there she was, waggling her black velvet self at him and—

He closed his eyes, because taking a break from the visual marvel of her was the only way to stay in control.

He ran a hand up from her knee and encountered a lovely surprise at mid-thigh. Her stockings ended there in an expanse of warm, satin skin, and he knelt behind her and put his mouth on her thigh, kissing her, licking her, sliding upwards until he felt the edge of a skimpy pair of lace panties. He slid them down, and she wriggled out of them until she could kick them off, and he put his mouth to the place where thigh became ass and found her pussy from behind with his tongue. Found and teased and played until she was mewling, bucking back against him, and all he could think was, *Yes.*

She was sweet and butter soft and wet, and he was going to make her come in about half a second and follow her over the edge, so he said "turn around" in the same commanding voice he'd used earlier, because now that he knew she liked it, it had a corresponding effect on him, like a hand grabbing the base of his cock and squeezing. Steadying and provoking.

She turned and looked up at him from under her eyelashes. It maybe should have been too porn-girl cute, but it did him in, because it was *her*, and behind the play and the silliness he could see wonder and joy, her surprise at what this was turning into, how much fun and how oddly *sweet*. He kissed her nose so she'd know he knew, then he took her hands and put them on his belt buckle, and she unbuckled and unbuttoned and unzipped him, which made him feel unhinged, like someone about to catapult over an unexpected emotional cliff. Her hands slipped under the elastic of his shorts and around him and *Christ*—

"Amy, wait, stop—"

She laughed, a buoyant, delighted laugh that reminded him of how Amy she was, and he took her in his arms and kissed her all over her face and neck and ears and breasts. "Turn around again."

She did, presenting him with the sweet curves of her backside, and he knelt and kissed her inner thigh. He drew back and she gasped.

"Don't tease." Her voice was muffled, her face pressed into her forearm.

He hadn't meant to tease. He didn't want to tease. He wanted to give her exactly what she wanted. This. Everything. Whatever it would take to bring her home.

He took his cock in his hand and brought the tip of it to her silky-wet opening and drew circles until she was begging. He eased his cock between her lips and let her rub along the length of him, backing herself up and moving forward, until she shuddered and cried out. On the surge of her orgasm, he buried himself in her to the hilt—it was like being thrown up on the shore by a particularly cruel tide, waves that wanted to wring the last bit of resistance out of him, and that was exactly what happened, his own orgasm wrenched from him on a yell, and he felt like he was turning inside out inside her, so that he was surprised when he regained the world and was still half-standing, half-kneeling behind her, more or less intact. He slowly lowered himself, covering her warm, slightly sweaty back like a blanket.

She said something nearly indistinct into the hard wood of the stairs, but his brain picked the words out, like tracks in snow. She'd said *I love you*, and his chest tightened with joy. He'd been scared he'd never hear those words from her again.

"I love you too. Give me a few minutes, and I'm going to vividly demo to you how much. In bed this time."

His phone began to ring.

Chapter Six

She listened to the phone ring. Her body was still spasming around his. Her heart was thudding. His too, strong and fierce against her back.

The phone finished ringing, paused long enough for her to start to catch her breath, and began to ring again.

She already wished she hadn't said what she'd said. That he hadn't said it back. That—that she'd stuck to her guns. *Let him onto the front porch, and he'll find a way to talk himself in the front door,* her mother had said about her father. *Let him in the front door, and he'll find a way to talk himself into the living room. Let him into the living room, and he'll find a way to talk himself into the bedroom.*

Behind her, he withdrew, and all of a sudden, she hurt. All over. Her neck and shoulders from the way she'd braced herself on the stairs. Her knees. Her back, which she'd arched as she pressed against him.

"You can get the phone." It had stopped for the second time.

"I don't want to get it."

She stayed where she was, partly so she didn't have to look at him and see the struggle in his face.

"You can take it. Really."

"I'm sure it's nothing."

She stood up, straightened her clothes. When she turned around, she saw that his dress slacks and shorts were still around his ankles. Otherwise, they were both fully dressed. That had seemed insanely sexy a few minutes ago. Now it seemed sordid. "Someone doesn't call twice in a row like that for nothing."

"Probably wasn't even the same person." The phone began its refrain again.

"Just take it."

He looked for a moment as if he were going to fight her, then sighed and turned to dig his phone out of his computer bag. He produced it, frowning at it. "Oh, crap."

She wasn't angry. Or disappointed. Except in herself, for letting him on the train. Or not working harder to get him kicked off. She should have told the MTA police he'd harassed her. She should have told them he was a known terrorist with ties to Al Qaeda. She should have told them he'd asked her to plant a bomb in Grand Central Station.

"I gotta get this." As if she might care. "I'm pretty sure it's about the new client. I asked the office to handle it and only call me if things got out of control, so the fact that they're calling me means it's probably pretty serious."

She shook her head. A secret thread of heat began to trickle down her thigh, the wasted, pointless not-gift of him.

The phone began to ring yet again, and she turned away. Climbed the stairs and went into the kitchen, leaving him at the bottom of the stairs, phone in hand, pants around his ankles. Ridiculous.

"I'm so sorry, Amy," he called. The agony in his voice was real. She heard it, and she understood it, but it wasn't good enough.

Then he said, in a completely different voice, "Hello?"

He was silent for a long time. "I can't, Rob. Not right now. Maybe in a couple of days."

More silence.

"It always has to be me. Make them understand I'm not always there at a moment's notice. I have a life—" A pause. "No. I'm sick of this. Everything's an emergency with them."

For a moment, she held her breath, almost hopeful. She let it out with a rush as he said, in a voice closer to the one in which he'd spoken to her—one filled with confusion and indecision— "Yeah, I know. Okay. Thanks for booking me. I'll be on that flight."

He pulled his pants up, buckled his belt and climbed the stairs to the kitchen. She was busy making toast and wouldn't look at him.

"I've gotten them into the habit of believing I'll come when they call. It's not an easy habit to break. But I will break them of it."

She peered into the toaster. Her face was still flushed from their lovemaking, her lips a dark red that made him want to grab her, spin her around and kiss her until she was forced to acknowledge him, if not at the level of conversation, in a deeper, more primal place.

"We've made so much progress, Amy. Don't clam up on me now."

She wouldn't talk to him. She grabbed the toast when it popped up and put it on a plate, buttered it carefully, spreading the butter evenly and into every corner and crevice. She ate the toast, bite by bite, studiously not looking at him.

"I wouldn't go if I thought there was anyone else who could handle the situation."

She surprised him by raising her head and meeting his eyes. "I know." For a brief moment, he thought things were going to be okay. Then she asked, "What time's your flight?"

"Five thirty a.m." He peeked at the kitchen clock. It was a little after eight. There was enough time for them to eat and go to bed together. He'd have to be up by two, but there was time. He let himself fantasize about taking it slow the next time, making love to her languidly, like people moving through warm water. Watching the slight impact of each stroke shimmy through her and show on her face. If she wasn't too mad. "Amy. You could come with me."

She held his gaze, studying him. She held out her hand. "Give me your phone."

Unsure, he handed it to her.

She swiped it open, searched briefly, tapped something and handed it to him, already ringing. He looked down at the screen. GO Airport Shuttle.

"It's over," she told him.

He took the ringing phone, too shocked to refuse. He put his ear to it, and when the cigarette-smoke-clogged voice at the other end of the phone said, "GO Shuttle reservations, how can I help

119

you?" he booked the shuttle.

She kept up her manic puttering. By the time he hung up, she was scrambling eggs. He watched her, neither of them speaking. She was graceful and efficient, as if she cooked all the time, instead of approximately never. A thin corkscrew of pain had begun at his temple, making it impossible to think.

She set the plate of eggs and Canadian bacon in front of him, placed two slices of toast beside his plate. Drew his chair out and gestured for him to sit.

"Amy."

"It's *over*."

When the eggs were done and he set the plate in the sink, he tried one more time to reason with her. "I'll be back. I could be back by Friday. Monday at the latest."

"Don't come back."

"Amy, be reasonable. Sometimes the job is going to need me."

She turned away from him. She walked out of the kitchen and down the hall and shut the door to the bedroom. He followed her and knocked, but she didn't answer. He tried the knob and found it locked.

Then he got angry. Because it wasn't fair, it wasn't right, for her to ask him to choose between her and his job. He couldn't be who she wanted him to be. She'd known all along how important Streamline was to him, how invested he was in its success. There were going to be times work needed him. If she couldn't live with that—

"What do you want me to do, Amy?"

It came out almost a shout, and he took a deep breath and tried again. "Amy, what do you want me to do? I own the company."

Silence from behind the door. Not even the sounds of Amy changing clothes or quietly weeping. Nothing. As if she were holding perfectly still and waiting for him to leave.

"It's *my* company," he said to the door.

He gathered his things and went to sit on the front steps.

A light went off inside the house, and he sat alone in the dark.

When the car showed up, he was glad. Grateful. He wanted to get away. Away from her and her unreasonable demands.

The car took him away from Amy, relentlessly inserting miles between them. The car smelled of some terrible kind of air freshener mingled with the driver's potent body odor, and Jeff had to breathe through his mouth to keep from feeling sick. The peculiar quiet jarred his mood too. He had hardly registered the train's sounds until they were gone—the *shugga-shugga* of train on track, the wobble and shift of things moving in the older cars, doors swinging open and shut, people shuffling and speaking. The car whispered over the surface of the road, and the driver didn't try to drown the silence with the low drone of talk radio. So there was just the silence. Dark and absolute.

They were almost to the airport before he remembered that he'd left another suit hanging in the hotel room closet. A pair of jeans, a T-shirt and his briefs sitting in the anonymous hotel dresser.

Fuck it. He'd call the hotel and have them send his stuff along to him. It was time for him to get the hell out of here. There was only so long you could ride a train to nowhere.

Chapter Seven

"Hey."

It was Porter's voice at the other end of the line, solid and comforting.

"I'm at the airport," Jeff said. "On my way home." He was the only one at his gate, slumped down in a black vinyl club chair with all his electronics arrayed on the arms and the floor in front of him, charging merrily away. He'd sleep here, with his head resting on the back of the seat, until the gate woke up tomorrow morning.

"Is Amy with you?"

Jeff had told Porter and Sasha about his mission. They'd been fully in support. They missed Amy almost as much as he did. Well, no, nowhere near as much as he did, unless there was something he didn't know about their nighttime fantasies and dirty dreams, but when they'd heard his plan, they'd said, effectively, *Thank God you've come to your senses! Bring our girl home!*

"No."

There was a dark silence on the other end of the line.

"Look. I don't want to get into it."

"Don't think you're going to get away with that, man," said Porter. "No way. What happened? You said things were going well. You—I've got the text here. You said, direct quote, 'I love this girl. And I'm pretty sure she feels the same way.' That was fifteen hours ago. Are you trying to tell me you managed to go from that to 'I don't want to get into it' in fifteen hours? Jeff, man—"

"Don't." There was an ache in his gut, like heartburn, only worse, that had lodged there around the time Amy handed him his ringing phone. It wasn't food poisoning. It was the feel of life without Amy. He knew, because as soon as it had settled in there, he'd remembered it. He'd spent the previous six months with it there, and it had only abated the last few days. Only when he'd ridden the train with Amy, her slim body a solid warmth beside him. Even when she'd been angry at him, she'd been with him. Right there.

God, he missed her. As angry as he was with her for her unreasonable expectations and demands, he missed her.

"What happened?" Jeff could hear the stubbornness in Porter's voice. He wasn't going to give up until Jeff answered him. That was the goddamned thing about having a best friend. They knew.

He stood up, pacing to the end of his expensive white electronic tether. "She kicked me out."

Porter was silent. Jeff checked the charge level on his phone. Getting there. The silence went on for so long that Jeff started to think maybe Porter was going to leave it at that. Spare Jeff the gory details. But then his friend asked, his voice only slightly accusatory, "What changed?"

Fuck it. He'd rather tell Porter the whole thing now than have the details drip out under interrogation later. "I told her I had to go back to Seattle to deal with the Global Four fuckup, and she flipped."

Jeff watched as a man about ten years older than him wheeled a black carry-on into the gate area and began to engage in the same technological charging ritual as Jeff had twenty minutes earlier. Cell phone. Laptop. And what was that? Kindle, Jeff guessed.

"Wait a minute," said Porter. "You're on your way back here to deal with Global Four?"

"Yeah. Rob said—"

"Rob's full of shit, Jeff, you know that."

"I know, but—"

"But what, Jeff?" Porter sounded pissed.

"I knew you and Sasha were in Madison, and someone—"

This time the silence was bigger and deeper, and Jeff wasn't sure Porter was still on the line.

"—someone had to step in," he finished. His voice echoed in the nearly empty gate area.

He could hear Sasha's voice in the background. "Who is it, Porter?"

"It's Jeff," Porter said, and Jeff could see them clearly in his mind's eye—the two of them probably in their PJs, curled up together in a hotel room in Madison, his phone call an intrusion into a world they'd created. A world where whatever Rob Akres thought was so urgent was as inconsequential as a flea on a buffalo's back.

And he realized Porter hadn't asked him what Rob Akres was on about. What was going on with Global Four. Ten years ago, five years ago—hell, a year ago—that would have been the first question out of Porter's mouth. *Christ, man, what is it?* And the two of them would have powwowed all night, if that's what it took, bending their minds around solutions to whatever business problem they'd gotten themselves into.

When had Porter moved on? When had he stopped caring about the minutiae of Streamline's progress?

Once upon a time, their hard work, the fruits of their late twenties and early thirties, their late nights really had been the only thing standing between Streamline and failure. Their labor, their devotion, had been the thing that could make their dreams real.

But that had been a long time ago. Before Sasha.

Before Amy.

It didn't have to be that way anymore. Porter was proof of it. Porter and Sasha. At some point, without Jeff's noticing, Porter had left behind the old days. He hadn't stopped caring about Streamline, he'd only decided that Streamline didn't need his undivided attention.

He'd understood that the company would march along without his undying and constant vigilance.

"How's it going?" Sasha asked in the background, and Jeff imagined Porter rolling his eyes or signaling her to hang on or pipe down just a sec so he could finish up with Jeff the crazy loser who couldn't manage to convince the woman he loved to be with him. *Because he had the staying power of a goddamned chipmunk.*

With a falling sensation as distinct as lead plummeting in his gut, he remembered that *just yesterday*, he'd promised Amy he'd ride that train with her until he convinced her to come home. Only he hadn't, had he?

God, no wonder she was pissed. Not demanding. Not irrational. She was right. Exactly fucking right.

He was a workaholic cretin who didn't deserve her. Didn't remotely deserve wonderful, sexy, creative, expansive, *sweet* Amy.

His Amy. His second chance at *really living*. Not this crazy late-night-airport-inhabiting run-when-they-call crap he'd come to take for granted as life, but the long, slow, leisurely comings and goings he'd briefly experienced on the train with her. A promise of what life could be if you *hung up the fucking phone*.

But it had been hard enough to convince her to give him a second chance. How would he ever talk her into letting him near her, let alone giving him a third chance?

What if she couldn't forgive him?

His heart contracted agonizingly, the fear of losing her as big and dark as the windows that looked out on the nearly deserted runways. He looked over and saw the other lone businessman rest his head on the back of another, identical black vinyl seat. This life stretched out forever in front of him—this set of dead-end choices.

The phone had drifted away from his ear, and he clutched it back to his head. "Porter?"

"Uh-huh?"

Jeff didn't want to think about what Sasha was doing over there to give his best friend and business partner that abstracted sound to his voice. "Can you do me a big favor?"

"Yeah?"

"Can you call Rob in the morning and tell him he's in charge of working this one out for himself?"

Suddenly, he could tell, he had Porter's undivided attention. "Hell, yeah," his friend said. "Nothing would give me more pleasure." He could hear the smile in Porter's voice.

"And Porter?"

"Yeah?"

"Thought maybe I'd take some of the vacation I have coming."

"Good man."

"You can manage without me?"

"Hell, we'll have divided up your computer equipment by the time you get back."

Jeff laughed, sharp relief. Took a deep breath for what felt like the first time in years. "And can we set up a meeting when I get back? To talk about bringing in that management team?"

"You serious?"

"Never been more serious in my life."

A deep intake of breath on the other end of the phone that Jeff sincerely hoped was a result of Porter's joy at the thought of bringing in reinforcements, and not whatever Sasha was so quietly up to over there.

And then Porter said, "Holy fuckin' hell, yeah!" and Jeff figured he'd better hang up on that note while there was still enough ambiguity to go around. He had work to do. An early-morning train to catch. Miles to go, and promises to keep.

Amy's head was full of television static, white and gray snow. Her eyes burned, and her lids were heavy. She hadn't slept at all, because the noise in her head had kept her awake. It wasn't voices or recriminations. It was the sound of the train on the rails and the sound of Jeff's phone ringing.

Now she was on the commuter rail, and she could hear the shush of the train, which made sense, and the phantom trill of Jeff's phone ringing, which didn't. She wondered how many nights you had to go without sleeping before you started hallucinating.

"Where's your friend?"

The guy with the heavy Brooklyn accent who'd harassed her and Jeff knelt up suddenly in the seat in front of her. Great. Just what she needed. A total stranger interrogating her about her relationship with Jeff when all she wanted to do was hide in a corner and cry over what she'd lost and regained and lost again.

"He went home."

Brooklyn raised both thick black eyebrows. "Did you forgive

him?"

Was he for real? "Why are we having this conversation?"

"You owe me," said Brooklyn guy. "You bring your reality show on the train, you can't just take it off the air whenever you want. I need to know what happens."

He was older than she'd guessed, maybe fifty, with a heavy, jowly face that looked Italian in origin, with its first-thing-in-the-morning shadow. He had kind eyes. There was a gentle curiosity on his face, and she felt a pressure in her chest that she understood was her need to talk to someone, anyone, about how much Jeff had hurt her.

"What happens," she said slowly, "is that the guy is a workaholic, and when some crisis happens at work, he runs off to fix it and the girl remembers why she couldn't live with him to begin with."

"Huh. So, like, he just *left*?"

"You know I don't *really* owe you anything, right?" she asked, more for her own benefit than his. "I don't *have* to tell you."

He nodded. "You don't have to tell me."

"I know." Yet it was comforting, this total stranger who somehow, mysteriously, had become their—she'd been about to think *godfather*, but she decided that was vaguely discriminatory and settled on *guardian angel* instead.

"So he just left," Brooklyn repeated.

She nodded.

"And you—just let him go?"

"Well, what the hell else was I supposed to do? This is what he does. He makes promises he can't keep. He spends most of his time working. He thinks the job is *that important.*"

"You could tell him he's wrong."

"I *have* told him—"

She stopped. She thought back to the ringing of the phone, their intimacy cooling rapidly as the familiar sound floated in the air. To the train ride two days ago when she'd first fled from his endless conversation with his admin. To a hundred, maybe a thousand other phone calls. All the times she'd let him put her aside. Let him put work first.

She was well trained. The phone rang, and she melted obligingly into the shadows. *You want to abandon me? Again? Sure! Let me just get myself out of the way here.*

She had told him yesterday that she'd asked him a million and one times to work less, that she'd gotten sick of the sound of her own voice, but now that she thought about it, she knew the truth. That voice had been in her head. Rattling around, a shout, a scream. When it had come down to it, she had squelched her complaints and let things go rather than rock the boat.

She hadn't seen the connection because she hadn't associated each minor instance of Jeff's departure, his mini acts of abandonment, with her father's many goings. But that's what it was, right? As hard as she had tried not to be her mother, she'd missed the big picture. Every time he left and she gave him permission, every time he tuned her out and she complied, she made it a little easier for him to think he could keep going like this forever.

What would have happened if she'd stopped acquiescing? What would have happened if she'd stopped playing nice? If just once, instead of disappearing into her own head and letting him have the conversation, she'd wrenched the phone out of his hand and hung up the call?

She'd never know now, would she?

Unless—

Unless it was not, in fact, too late.

She looked at her watch as if it would shed some light on the larger issue of whether this revelation had come in time.

She could get off at the next stop, call in sick to work, get a GO Shuttle, and head to the airport. Find him. Tell him. Maybe it wouldn't change anything, but at least she would know.

The train was approaching White Plains. She stood up, lurching forward into the seat, nearly smacking Brooklyn in the face with her shoulder.

"Where are you going?" he demanded. "Don't go. I'll shut up. I promise. I was just trying to help."

She smiled at him, her stranger on a train, her guardian angel. "You helped."

"So where are you going?"

She stepped into the aisle.

"Home."

Chapter Eight

She hung on to Brooklyn's seat as the train swayed and pulled into the station, and then she heard it again.

Jeff's phone. Behind her.

What?

"I like happily-ever-after endings, myself," said Brooklyn to no one in particular. "I like romantic comedies. Not those dark little dramas at the Sunshine Cinemas, where someone has to end up dead to teach everyone a lesson about pride going before a fall."

Riiiing.

"Do you hear that?" she whispered.

"What?"

"That sound. The phone ringing."

Brooklyn was grinning like mad at her. Maybe because she was mad as a hatter herself.

People were climbing onto the train and making their way into her car. She shrank back into her seat. Even over the sound of footsteps and people settling themselves in, the ringing was clear.

It was getting closer, unless she really was hallucinating. Unless she really had lost her mind. She turned slowly.

"Mind if I sit here?"

That was Jeff's voice, and it was attached to Jeff. Her noodle legs gave out, and she collapsed back into the seat.

Jeff looked exhausted. There were circles under his eyes and a generous scruff along his chin and jaw. And there was something in his face. Contrition and determination and, wow, she had never seen him look that nervous. Not when he'd first approached her in a Peet's Coffee, cockier than she usually went for. Not when he'd asked her to move in with him, a genuine question but one he hadn't ever doubted her answer to. Not even when he'd shown up on the train on Tuesday morning, half apology and half certified-Jeff surety.

Now he looked green with anxiety. He looked the way she felt.

He leaned down, and when he spoke in her ear, his voice was rough from whatever combination of fatigue and nerves he was packing. "Hi."

"Hi."

"Is this seat taken?"

She managed to get enough of her muscles and nerves to cooperate that she could slide over and make room for him. Brooklyn had disappeared. She couldn't see the top of his head. He might not be tactful, but apparently he was discreet.

Jeff sat, bringing his heat with him. Lack of sleep had chilled her to the bone, and she wanted to lay her head on his shoulder and beg him to hold her.

"I came back," he said.

Noise rushed in her ears, like wind on a ski slope or a train passing through a valley. She had to lean her hot cheek against her cool hand to collect herself. This was what she had wanted, but the reality of it was overwhelming. "Yeah." It was the best she could manage.

He ran both hands through his hair, standing it on end. "I've been a crazy idiot," he said, a pileup of words. "I've done everything wrong. I've put the job first and you last and— Look. I know I don't deserve a third chance. Hell, I probably didn't deserve a second chance."

Slowly, dumbly, she was making sense out of the shock of the last few minutes. He had come back. He was here.

"I came back because I need you to give me another chance. When I climbed on this train two days ago, I was going nowhere. In a big fat fucking hurry. And then I sat down next to you and—and all of a sudden, even though I was riding in circles, everything made so much sense."

He reached out and took her hand, his fingertips painting teasing lines on her palm. Waking her up out of her stupor. "These last few days, riding the train with you, I've been alive. I've been grateful. I've laughed more and cared more, and for the first time in as long as I can remember, I've felt like I was moving forward, instead of being carried backward, away from some goal I can't see. And I realized: *This* is my reason for being. This is what I want to do. I want to be with you. Really *be* with you."

The frozen parts of her were thawing, and the import of his words, not only their literal meaning, was starting to penetrate her core.

"I'm going to take some time off. When I get back, we're going to hire a management team at Streamline. The bulk of the work, the worst of the every day—it won't be my problem anymore. There will be slack. I'll be able to walk away. Ignore the phone."

She felt a flash of elation and then a suffocating wash of terror, like someone had dumped cold water over her. Would he be able to walk away? Could he ignore the phone? What if she wasn't enough for him and, having given part of Streamline away, he resented the hell out of her?

"I love you, Amy. I know it isn't easy for you, but I really, really need you to give me another chance. I don't know what number we're on now, maybe it's way more than three, but whatever it is, I need you to give me one."

There were tears in her eyes, emotion choking her, as she said, "I don't want you to give up Streamline. You love that company—"

"No. I love *you*. And I'm not giving it up. I'm pruning it back, bringing it in line. I'm making it what it should be—a job, not the center of my universe. And—" He took a deep breath and squeezed her hand. "I'm asking you to sacrifice too. Because believe me, I know what it's like to have a job that's really important to you. I know how much courage it must have taken you to come out here, and I want you to know, I'm not telling you, I'm asking you—like really *asking*—how you'd feel about—"

She'd never heard him that hesitant. A tiny smile bloomed in her chest, grew into a grin and a laugh of pleasure. "I'm coming home. I'd already made up my mind."

She saw from the widening of his eyes that he hadn't known, hadn't been at all sure of his reception. He looked past her for a moment, out the window, and she realized he was trying to steady himself, to collect himself. Her Jeff, her bossy medieval guy, hadn't been sure.

"We could get on one of those cross-country trains." Strength gathered in his voice. "We could do some leisurely exploring. I don't want this to end yet." He gestured around them, and she knew he meant more than just the train ride. He meant the small secret world of the two of them.

She couldn't talk. He seemed to understand, because he took her hands and held them tight in his. Then he let go with one and reached into his pocket, and she knew, absolutely knew what was going to be in his hand when he pulled it out—

Only instead of a ring box, it was his cell phone.

He held it out. Put it in her palm. "Would you do the honors?"

She looked from the phone to him, puzzled.

"Come with me," he said, rising. She tottered down the aisle after him. He pulled the door open, and they walked into the swaying vestibule between cars.

"You could get in trouble for this," she warned him.

"The MTA already thinks I'm a terrorist. This can hardly lower their opinion of me."

"You want me to throw your phone out there? I can't do that."

"Sure you can."

She took a deep breath. All this time, she'd been afraid that if she asked anything of him, demanded anything of him, she might turn out not to have been worth his sacrifice. That she'd wake to find he'd left and taken breakfast with him.

I want to be with you. Really be with you.

She clutched his arm with the hand that didn't hold the phone. Looked up into his smiling face, his eyes filled with love and conviction. There was no doubt, no hesitation there. Nor was there any in her voice or her heart when she spoke. "I love the idea of a cross-country train ride."

"I know you love your job."

She shrugged. "I like my job. I love *you*. And I want to be with you too. *Really* be with you. I should have been clearer about that. I never said it. I thought I said it, and maybe I did once or twice, but I never told you to hang up the phone or come home or pay more attention. I was afraid. That you'd—" Her voice broke. "I was afraid you'd say no."

"I wouldn't have." His voice was ragged.

"I know. I know now. I should have had the courage to tell you I needed you. More of you." She shook the phone for emphasis. "I need more of you." She made herself meet his gaze. "All of you."

His eyes shone. "You have me. All of me." He reached for her with both arms, but she held back a moment.

She reached out and touched his cheek, rough from a day and a half's neglect. She drew her thumb across his cheekbone, and he leaned his head into her touch. He closed his eyes, his lashes casting long shadows, darker than the shadows under his eyes. Then he opened them and looked at her, but he seemed to be looking through her, at something in his own head. "I don't know when I decided that I was the only thing standing between Streamline and disaster," he said quietly. "But when I told Porter I wanted to bring in a management team, it felt like the weight of the world got lifted off me. I didn't realize what I'd been carrying around."

She let her hand touch his shoulder before resting it on the hard muscle of his arm. "I did. I just didn't realize I could ask you to put it down."

He leaned forward and rested his forehead against hers. "Amy." That was it, just her name. And he rested there for a moment, his breath brushing her face, mint and Jeff. She wrapped her arms around him and dragged him closer, bringing the hard wall of his torso against hers with a jolt that she felt to her toes. They stood there for a long time, swaying with the motion of the train.

Then he straightened and pulled away. He drew the exterior door of the train open and they looked out together at the embankment, flying past, a blur of dirt and scrub and litter. He reached out his hand, and she laid the phone in his palm. With one smooth motion, an abbreviated baseball windup, he hurled it out the door. It bounced out of their vision immediately, gone, just like that.

"The leave of absence has officially begun," he said.

"All your data, though? What if someone finds it?"

"I can wipe it remotely," he confessed. "Does that ruin the gesture?"

She was laughing and crying. "No. Not in the slightest."

He pulled the door shut and took her in his arms and kissed her, hard and fierce. "You come first with me. Always. Okay?"

He led her back to their seats, the two of them wobbling all the way and dodging the odd passenger who had stood to claim an overhead item. She sat, but before he did, he reached into his other pocket, and there it was in his palm, a black velvet box, and he snapped it open and said, "Amy, will you be my seat mate for the rest of my life?"

The rest of my life. He was serious. He had thrown away his phone and was hiring new people to run his company, and he wanted her to spend the rest of her life with him.

"Oh, Jeff... Oh, Jeff!"

"Holy Mother of God," said a gruff, Brooklyn-accented voice from the seat in front of them. "If you don't say yes, I will personally reach over the seat and strangle you both. I can't *take* any more."

There was laughter from the seats around them, and Amy laughed too, through her tears, and nodded her head as hard as she could, while Jeff removed the ring from the box and slid it onto her finger. It was too big, but she wouldn't let him take it off, just clung to it, and then clung to him while he kissed her and kissed her and the train pulled into the station with a squeal that might've been her own squeal of delight.

Jeff took her hand.

They watched out the window together as passengers disembarked and new passengers climbed aboard, their ebb and flow part of the train's pulse. The train pulled out of the station, and she turned to him, smiling, and he smiled back, and squeezed her hand.

The train gathered speed, a purr of contentment, a race of excitement, the beginning of the rest of their travels together.

About the Author

Serena Bell writes stories about how sex messes with your head, why smart people do stupid things sometimes, and how love can make it all better.

Bell wrote her first steamy romance before she was old enough to understand what all the words meant and has been perfecting the art of hiding pages and screens from curious eyes ever since—a skill that's particularly useful now that she's the mother of two school-aged children.

For a while, Bell took a break from penning love stories to explore the world as a journalist, where she spent time shadowing and writing about a cast of fascinating real-life characters, including a midwife and home-birth advocate, one of President Obama's key advisers on health care reform, and a U.S. Senator with a pivotal role in the 2010 mid-term elections.

When she's not writing or getting her butt kicked at Scrabble by a six-year-old, she's practicing modern dance improv in the kitchen, swimming laps, talking a long walk, or reading on one of her large collection of electronic devices. You can find her at www.serenabell.com, by email at serena@serenabell.com or on Twitter @serenabellbooks.

Thank You for Riding

Meg Maguire

Dedication

For those intrepid riders of the MBTA. Godspeed, ye daredevils.

And with many thanks to my smart, funny, and otherwise excellent partners in this series, Serena Bell, Donna Cummings, Samantha Hunter and Ruthie Knox.

Chapter One

Caitlin squeezed the stress ball in her fist.

Actually it was half a stress ball, one lobe of a foam heart. Squeeze, release. Squeeze, release. Blood snaked from the crook of her elbow through a tube, up to the benevolent, boxy robot standing beside her recliner, a red ribbon passing through a dozen whirring, rotating doohickeys.

Maria, Caitlin's favorite tech from the donation center, pressed gently where the needle met her arm. "Feels okay?"

"Yup. Fine." Squeeze, release.

The machine bleeped, and Maria squinted at the monitor. "Your first return should be here any time."

Caitlin waited for it—the funny chill of her blood coming back into her body, sans platelet cells. *Zing.* "Ooh, there it is."

"Still feels good?"

Caitlin nodded. "Like a refreshing ocean breeze."

Maria laughed and taped the tube in place, covering the insertion point with a wad of gauze. "Let me know when you want a blanket."

"Will do."

Maria wandered off to check on the other donors, and Caitlin relaxed back in her seat.

The donation took just under two hours. Two hours when she couldn't use her right hand for anything but stress-ball pumping. Couldn't reach the phone she'd intentionally left in her coat pocket, couldn't check email, couldn't accomplish a damn thing. Bliss. People would ask if she was cold, thirsty, hungry, how she'd been since she'd last donated, ask how she'd like to be entertained and if they could fetch anything for her. Like being a toddler again.

She fumbled left-handed with her earbuds and queued up the

audio book she'd downloaded. Other donors watched movies on ceiling-mounted televisions, screens angled around the crescent of recliners, but Caitlin's eyes were tired from a near all-nighter at the office, the one that had earned her this rare afternoon off.

She hit PLAY, ready to be sucked into the drama of the latest bestselling espionage novel. She could use the escape after the last few seventy-hour weeks at work. Get her head out of the spreadsheets and charts and into some made-up person's grand adventure. Her job had her feeling so compressed, so stuffed into the bottom of a dusty box and weighed down by deadlines, this break was like surfacing after a long dive, the idleness deep gulps of cool air. Of course, it would have been less physically exhausting to relax at home, but at home she could give in to the compulsions and check her work email, sit down and fill out *just one* report...which always turned into three or eight or a dozen. But here she had her hands tied—not quite literally, but close—and it was heaven, this forced laziness.

A few years ago, she'd never have let herself enjoy a moment's laziness. Young people new to finance had to appear eager and industrious at all times, go-getters to the nth. But she was seven years out of school now, her identity no longer defined solely by her job title. She ought to have a life outside of her clients' balances and returns, but it was a hard habit to break. Squeezing the stress ball, she wondered what other hobbies she could take up that would keep her this thoroughly occupied. Rock climbing, maybe. SCUBA diving. Plate spinning.

Just as the hero heard the baddies' footfalls down the echoing marble corridor, a tech interrupted to switch on Caitlin's heating pad and offer her the snack basket. She picked hastily, mind off in a bank vault in Eastern Europe. The tech opened her animal cracker package and left her be.

An hour into the book and two packets of cookies and one candy bar later, the author went off on a dull tangent about encryption methodology, and Caitlin woke from the storytelling trance. She glanced around the space as a tech across the semicircle of chairs got things set up for a new donor. Nice to see the place so busy this close to Christmas.

The donor emerged from the men's room, and Caitlin noted with a dreamy, fluid-deprived curiosity that he was awfully cute. Though since things with Kevin had become so...*meh*, it seemed she'd been noticing cute guys all over Boston.

No, bad eyes.

After the holidays and the end-of-year work madness were over, she'd have time to see Kevin again. See him properly, make a real, girlfriendly effort once she had the hours and energy. She wouldn't force the relationship to work, but she wouldn't quit because things had temporarily flatlined. Kevin was her colleague, after all. A secret office romance had been risky, so surely there was something there worth gambling on. Right? It'd be a waste to not at least *try*. Plus, he was just as stressed as her. If he'd been short and snippy lately, she of all people could appreciate why.

But she stole another guilty glance at the guy across the linoleum, now busy having the crook of his arm swabbed with antiseptic.

He looked about Caitlin's age, early thirties, but from perhaps a different side of the tracks, professionally. His jeans bore multicolored paint spatters, and he wore a gray thermal shirt, the sleeve of one arm folded up to accommodate the blood-pressure cuff. Dark, tousled hair, handsome eyebrows, pale skin, straight, dignified nose. He said something that made the tech laugh, and he smiled in return, a wide, uncensored grin that lit up his face.

His eyes rose and caught Caitlin's for a second. His smile wavered, and she glanced away. Thankfully too much of her blood was centrifuging around in the robot's belly to allow a blush. But she kept her gaze darting so he'd think she was just taking in the room...not taking *him* in, specifically.

The cute guy got distracted as the tech prepped his needle, clamping his eyes shut and turning his face away for the insertion. *Aww.* Caitlin always watched when they slid her needle in. She thought it was fascinating. Adorable that a grown man who looked like he worked a physical job couldn't handle the sight. Though maybe this was his first time.

Soon enough, he was squeezing and releasing, and the tech helped him prop a hardcover book on the pillow in his lap. She could see the library stamp across the tops of the pages.

Wow. A cute, platelet-donating, library-card-carrying man. Her fist squeezed the foam heart, *buh-bum, buh-bum.*

The audio book's narrator kept shoveling plot into Caitlin's ears, but she only registered the odd detail—train derailment, suspicious man with a pipe, blizzard. Every other sentence, her attention flicked to the cute man, but his didn't flick back. His book must have been more interesting than hers.

She watched as he caught Maria's eye. He got her to go to where his coat was hung by the door and fetch something for him, then smiled and said thanks, unfolding a pair of reading glasses. Caitlin's woman-area nearly succumbed to a core meltdown. She watched his hand as he turned the page. No ring.

Bad. Bad eyes.

She shut the troublemakers, wondering how on earth her story was suddenly in London. Was this a flashback? She hated flashbacks. She let the author's voice drift to the edge of her consciousness and peeked again. What was he reading? He looked awfully absorbed.

Caitlin's machine bleeped. Once, twice, then a third, more musical time, signaling that her blood wasn't pumping as vigorously as it should be. A tech strolled over to tighten her cuff and check her needle, and the guy across the way caught her eye. He glanced to her machine, her face, and back again, then at his own machine. He shot her a playful, smarmy look that said, *Check me out, being better at platelet donation than you.* He strained his face, pretending to squeeze his stress ball with epic strength.

Caitlin rolled her eyes and faked annoyance, noting by mistake the attractive swell of his arm muscle under his shirt. He squeezed a couple more times and wiped imaginary sweat from his brow.

She bit back a smile, shaking her head. What a weird place to flirt. She probably only found him so charming because she was missing half a pint of vital fluids.

She turned to the little screen on her robot, to the countdown clock. Forty minutes to go. Forty minutes and she'd bundle up and walk to Downtown Crossing and try to tackle some holiday shopping, avoid the siren song of work for another hour or two.

Mr. No-Ring Library Reading Glasses caught her eye again. He'd made his face exceedingly stern, and he glanced at his own monitor, then pretended to race her, squeezing his stress ball with spastic fervor.

She laughed noiselessly, and for the first time in a couple weeks, it felt, she relaxed.

Giving up the charade, the man looked down at his book, back at Caitlin for a split second, then back to the book. She saw him swallow, and she shut her eyes lest they invite any more trouble.

Caitlin's own book finally recaptured her attention, and before long her stress ball and cuff were taken away and she was left flexing her hand, waiting for the last of her red cells to be returned. The procedure was tiring as always, but the clear bag hanging from her machine was heavy with platelet cells, thick and yellow as the fat from a can of condensed chicken noodle soup. She looked to the cute man's bag, only half full. She waited until he glanced her way, then ignored the wriggle in her belly and shot him a snotty look, one that said, *Behold my vastly superior wealth of golden platelets, peasant.*

He glanced at his own bag and frowned, miming a bruised ego.

Caitlin was pulled from the exchange as the tech removed her needle and got her bandaged up. Probably a good thing. The footrest was lowered, and she tested her legs, waited for a head rush that didn't arrive, and deemed herself ready to walk.

The cute guy caught her eye one last time and brushed his fingers over his chest demonstrably. Caitlin blinked, puzzled, then glanced down and found her sweater dusted with cookie crumbs. Classy. She wiped them away, zapping him a little glare to say, *You win this round.*

But the boldness—if it could be called that—left her as she gathered her purse and iPod and snagged a granola bar and a bottled water from the kitchenette. She walked right past Mr. Cute to fetch her coat, but she'd lost her nerve and kept her gaze locked on the exit. Had he looked at her? Had he smiled? She'd never know.

And just as well. *Bad girlfriend.*

The sun had set. It was supposed to drop into the low twenties that night. Harsh enough on its own, much worse with a pint of blood freshly filtered from her body. But as she stepped into the brisk winter air, her cheeks were warm. In several hours' time, this post-pheresis tipsiness would leave her, and she'd feel a touch guilty for flirting, no matter how silly and innocent it had been. But for now, it felt awfully nice. A sensation she hadn't enjoyed in ages.

She aimed herself downtown with a spring in her step, right where she'd expected the exhaustion to be. This morning, the Christmas lights had only highlighted a hundred looming pre-holidays to-dos, but now they dazzled in the freshly fallen darkness. The honk of cars and the rattle of buses sounded like the beating heart of the city, the frigid wind invigorating, not punishing. She remembered Mr. Cute's smirk one final time and felt her lips curl. She pursed them and picked up her pace. Into the bustle of Christmas shoppers and harried commuters, banishing the memory of the flirtation.

Very bad, to have her face flushed from the attention of some stranger she'd shared a clinical room and basket of snacks with for an hour. That was Kevin's job.

Very, very bad.

Yet very, very cute.

Chapter Two

"Highs today made it to the low forties," the clock radio on Caitlin's dresser announced. *"Lows dropping tonight into the midtwenties for Boston, colder north and west of the city."*

She glanced down at her bare legs and shivered.

Still, the dress was worth it. Worth scampering three blocks to the train with a stiff breeze assaulting her womanhood, worth looking like an idiot clattering around in these heels, because when else was she going to get an excuse to dress up? The fanciest she got at work was a tweed skirt and flats, and that effort was only for when she had to meet with a client. If she was stuck feeling like she lived in her office twelve hours a day the final six weeks of the year, she'd be comfortable, goddammit—slacks and sweaters, padding around in socks, shoes abandoned under her desk. Everyone else was a spreadsheet-blind zombie, anyhow. No one noticed. They all just staggered in bleary paths to and from the printer, the bathrooms, the coffeemaker, ants following their chemical trails toward caffeine and toner.

And sure, it was an office party. She'd still be in the office.

But that made it all the better. Let all her coworkers see her looking fantastic, like a post-makeover scene from a dumb romantic comedy. Let Kevin know he wasn't the only one witnessing her secret hotness, and feel a little of whatever hormone made men toss their girlfriends across tabletops and ravish them soundly.

If anyone could use a sound ravishing, it was Caitlin. Her lady-business hadn't been manhandled in ages, not even by herself. Usually she liked a good manhandling as a matter of maintenance, but nothing sounded so seductive lately as a nice, long sleep.

Pathetic.

So no more *comfortable* tonight. In fact, she'd be pretty *un*comfortable, drafty up her dress and rickety in these ambitiously tall shoes. Drafty and rickety...hmmm. She wasn't really going for the dilapidated-building look. But no, she looked *good*. She'd gotten a weeks-overdue trim that afternoon, and the woman at the salon had smoothed her hair with some magic potion, banishing all her flyaways and frizz, leaving it so shiny it looked like she'd had highlights done. She modeled the spangly garnet cocktail dress in the mirror, flashed her heels under the bedroom lights so the beaded details glimmered. Kevin was going to blink and stutter and maybe even get an inappropriate workplace hard-on when he saw her. Saw her as a woman for the first time in ages, not just a coworker and neglectful, neglected girlfriend.

At six thirty, she buttoned her coat and unlocked the front door. Then turned back and spent fifteen minutes changing and unchanging her mind about what purse to take before finally settling on a silver clutch. Why bring a practical bag? Why wreck how perfectly impractical the rest of the outfit was?

She turned to the cat. "Night, Sarge. Don't wait up." She grabbed the wrapped box that held Kevin's Christmas present, a monogrammed chrome cocktail shaker. She hoped it wasn't too much. They'd only been going out for three months, but it was their first holiday as a couple. She'd give him his gift early and set the tone for the entire break, tell him, *Yes, we're an item and I like you and here's some shiny, monogrammed, nonrefundable proof of what a great catch I am. Now sully me, you fool!*

Before she even had the building's front door open, winter had her in its bony grip.

Clop clop, clop-clop clop went her shoes on the sidewalk, but by the time she made it to the subway she'd found her rhythm and equilibrium on the three-inch spikes. *Clop clop* into the subway, *clop clop* onto the escalator, *clop clop* through the turnstile and down to the platform. The journey took perhaps ten minutes, but she was sure she gave the backs of her thighs a good fifty covert feels to make sure that yes, the dress really was there, hadn't ridden up under her long wool coat.

The temperature had dropped several degrees by the time she

emerged in Harvard Square, but her office was barely fifty *clop-clops* from the station. She took the elevator to the twelfth floor, shedding her coat on the ride up and smoothing her dress over her butt one last time, ready for her entrance.

The first person to spot her was Gina, the receptionist. The girl's heavily lined eyes widened in the direction of Caitlin's legs.

Good shock, she prayed.

"Wow, Caitlin. Like, wow."

"Good wow?"

"Oh my God, yeah. You look...wow."

Bless you, hip twenty-two-year-old receptionist!

Caitlin strode past the front desk to find a glass of something to soothe her prickling nerves. *One drink*, she promised herself. Best not to test her balance on these shoes.

She tossed her coat on a radiator in the front room, avoiding everyone's eyes at first, afraid her own would give away her nerves.

"Caitlin!" It was her manager's voice.

She turned and smiled at Tom. "Merry...nondenominational holidays!" she corrected, and he laughed. He was only a couple years older than she was, and they found the corporate policies equally tedious.

He wandered closer. "Merry holidays. Well, you win."

"Win what?"

"Best dressed. You look fantastic." He leaned in and gave her a chaste pair of kisses, one on each cheek. He'd never done that before. The dress was making him all suave. Excellent. Test run: successful.

He stepped back. "Looking like that, I can only assume you've got a better party to go to after this one." He led the way to the open bar set up in one of the conference rooms.

She snagged a glass of chardonnay and shrugged. "Just felt like making an effort. Remind everyone around here what gender I am. Unless HR has a problem with that?"

They headed back to the lobby right as Kevin appeared, strolling in from the hall that led to the offices. Caitlin's heart gave a jump, and she worked to keep her face blasé, like she didn't think there was anything noteworthy about her appearance. *This old thing?*

He'd made an effort too. His slacks were creased from the dry cleaners, not from half a day spent glued to a chair, and his sandy hair looked nice, the one side that he habitually finger-combed into an anxious crest lying flat for a change.

"Merry holidays," Caitlin said.

"Are we allowed to say holidays?" he asked with a smile. "It's got 'holy' in it, after all."

"Joyous festive secular gathering!" she offered.

Tom laughed. She waited for Kevin to stutter over how she looked, but he seemed to be saving his reaction for once they were alone together. Perhaps a reaction that involved no words at all, such as the forceful push of Caitlin up against the wall of the supply closet.

Yes, please.

The three chatted about how relieved they were for the year-end chaos to be done, and Tom was called over by Gina when one of the firm's biggest clients arrived.

Caitlin turned to Kevin with a small, sly smile that invited inappropriate workplace advances. "So."

His gaze drifted downward, then quickly back up to her eyes. "So. What did you get up to yesterday? Our first day off in what feels like a year?"

"Sleep. Lots and lots of sleep. And I got brunch at a café, since I haven't had time to buy groceries since October. You?" *Tell me how awesome I look. Say it all huskily, under your breath. All clandestine and horny.*

"Oh, went to the gym. Found out exactly how atrophied I've gotten. Went out for drinks last night with some friends who were probably worried I'd died."

And I look...? "Feels like we haven't seen each other in forever," she said quietly. "Which is weird, since we've basically been living in this building since the fall."

"I know what you mean." He said it quietly too, but with not quite as much fond conspiracy as she'd been angling for. To be fair,

Kevin was a thoughtful, cautious soul, not one for flair. Certainly not at work. Though maybe after a couple more drinks...

"Do you have much planned for your week off?" Not especially subtle, but come on, this was her boyfriend.

He sipped his beer. "No, mercifully. You?"

"Not a thing."

Kevin stared into his glass. "I've been wanting to talk to you."

Her heart fluttered, praying for something heartfelt. Her guts clenched, ever the pragmatists. "Oh, yeah?"

He nodded, coming a bit closer, speaking more quietly. "It's been ages since I've seen you, it feels like. Properly seen you, away from this place."

"I know." Her heart elbowed her guts aside, excited now for what this might be about—what they'd talked about back in October, getting away for a weekend to the Berkshires, to some cozy little rustic cabin or bed and breakfast, where they could be a couple without risking witnesses and winding up the talk of the office. And maybe while they were there they'd make a decision, figure out if this thing was the real deal and decide to go ahead and out themselves at work, come what may.

"So—" His next words were cut off as Gina came over, one of his clients at her side. He waved, muttering "bad timing" to Caitlin.

"I'll find you later."

"I want to talk to you before the party's over," he said, a stern promise in his voice. It made Caitlin swoon a bit, that determined look on his face. If they'd been openly together, he would have pressed a firm, possessive kiss to her lips—she could just feel it.

Her own clients began arriving, and Caitlin did her duties as hostess, showing them around, playing matchmaker and introducing them to likeminded others—the CEO of the moving company with the GPS distributor, the cold-press coffee entrepreneur with the owner of the chain of up-and-coming boutique green grocers. Soon enough, all her clients had found more stimulating company than Caitlin herself, and though Kevin was still talking in a small, mingled group, he caught her eye meaningfully. What was that look saying?

Pack your bags, baby! We're going away next weekend! Well, maybe. Perhaps not with quite so much ebullience from her subdued suitor.

I've been doing a lot of thinking, and I think it's time we went for it.

Went for it? Kevin, whatever do you mean? Oh, how her eyelashes would bat.

Let's go shopping while we're out there. Let's find you a ring. What do you say?

Gee, Kevin, I'd say I'm not quite with you there. Maybe let's talk about that a year from now.

Okay, baby, all in good time. Damn, you look hot tonight. Let's get out of here.

And go where, Kevin?

To my place. Let's split a bottle of wine and screw all night.

And she'd already be halfway out the door, tugging on her coat and thanking God she wasn't having her period.

But likely, Kevin wouldn't say any of those things. He'd never once called her baby, not even in bed. They'd never once screwed all night, either, but speaking for herself, she had a backlog of sex to tackle, following the recent drought. And neither of them had anyplace to be for...carry the two...over sixty hours! They'd have to switch to her place lest her cat go hungry, but the change of scenery would be fun, like, *Round Two! Sex-fest recommencing in—*

"Caitlin."

She nearly jumped out of her skin, but thankfully it was held in place by her unprofessionally tight dress. "Kevin, hey. All your clients getting along?"

"Yup. They're talking about social media and word-of-mouth promotion and going viral with the youth demographic. That should keep them swapping inane marketing tips for hours."

She smiled, giving him a look she hoped was languid and seductive.

"You look wiped."

Curses. "I'm fine." A waiter strolled past, and Caitlin snagged a festive paper cup of eggnog. She sipped it, frowning internally to find no warm embrace of rum behind the cream and spice.

"So," Kevin said with a mighty sigh.

"So. You wanted to talk to me?" She said it as coyly as she dared, not wanting to wander over the border into Vapidville.

He scanned the room. "Would you meet me by the laser printer, nearest our cubes? I'll go the long way, and maybe you can pretend to need the ladies' room?"

She nodded, pleased by the sneakiness.

"Cool. I'll see you in a minute."

Caitlin headed off toward—and then past—the restrooms, heart thumping with happy nerves. She leaned on the deep windowsill between the printer and a rather neglected potted ficus. It was a quiet corner en route only to the emergency exit and server room. They could easily steal a few minutes' kissing here once they hammered out the Berkshires trip.

But the minute Kevin had estimated became two...three...five.

About seven minutes later than promised, he finally arrived, Caitlin's eggnog and mood both thoroughly cooled. But she stood up straight, smiling with all the fondness she'd felt before the long wait.

"Sorry," he said as he reached her. "Got waylaid."

"That's fine. So."

He took a deep breath, and Caitlin wondered exactly what about asking her to go away with him had him so nervous. He looked as if he was getting up the courage to ask her to the junior prom.

He exhaled with a sigh. "I think we should stop seeing each other."

She blinked. Unbidden by her brain, her mouth said, "Do you?"

He nodded, and that boyish anxiety she'd misdiagnosed outed itself as guilt and dread.

"Oh."

"It's just not working, is it? We haven't seen each other in weeks."

"It's that time of year," she offered, trying to sound like she was forgiving him for being an absentee boyfriend, not begging him to reconsider. She wasn't even sure which sentiment was the genuine one.

"It's not just that. We'd have made time, if it was really a priority, don't you think?"

She opened her mouth, then closed it on a protest. "Yeah," she said instead, slumping in defeat and acceptance. "Yeah, we probably would have." Tears were percolating behind her nose, hot with embarrassment.

He took a step closer, speaking more softly. "It was nice, though. Really nice."

"It was."

He gave her a quick hug, one Caitlin was spared having to return, as her hands were full. They separated, and she tossed her cup in the wastebasket. She was tempted to pitch his gift in after it, but instead she held it between two clammy palms, her cold sweat likely warping the pretty wrapping paper.

"Well, I'm glad we're on the same page," he said.

"Yeah. Me, too." Glad in a humiliated, Christmas-vacation-ruining kind of way. Peachy.

He pointed at the gift. "What's that?"

"Oh, that's...for Gina." *I've just been wandering around with it all night for shits and giggles.*

"Well, we better go make sure our clients are still walking that fine line between bored sobriety and drunken rowdiness."

"Yup."

"I'll go back the way I came."

"Yup." *And I'll go back the way that takes me past the open bar.* And she did.

She pulled a five out of her purse and slipped it into the bartender's fishbowl. "White wine. To the brim, please."

Chapter Three

"The next train to—Braintree—is now approaching."

Fucking finally.

Caitlin rose from the cold bench she'd been camped out on for a seeming eternity, waiting for this final train of the night. She tucked her purse under her arm and picked up Kevin's wrapped present and the ribbon-bedecked paper gift bag Gina had given everyone as they exited the party. Scotch for the men, champagne for the women. Stupid distinction. Caitlin had never wanted a shot of whiskey more than she did now, even as that second glass of wine faded from buzz to headache between her ears.

Stupid party. Stupid holidays.

Stupid Kevin.

Dumped, a week before Christmas. Dumped beside a dying ficus with a paper cup of virgin eggnog in her hand. Not a word about how great she looked. She nearly wished he'd found her so irresistible he'd put off dumping her until the morning, after they'd had sex one last time. But that was just a tender ego talking.

He should've grabbed her adorable shoes and snapped the heels off them, insult to injury.

It's just not working, he'd said.

And she'd agreed because yeah, it hadn't been working. But she still felt dumb for having bought him such an overpriced gift. That good mood she'd floated on, chatting with her clients, thinking that by the end of the night she'd have plans in place for a romantic getaway... Bleh. Must be true what they said about cats making their owners nuts. She had to have been breathing some major feline crazy-fumes to have talked herself into that wishful delusion.

But behind all the annoyance was genuine relief.

She was working hard enough at her job. Having to also find time and energy to work on a relationship on top of it...? Perhaps passive giving of the platelet donation variety was all she had the energy for, that and keeping Sarge alive so that he might continue poisoning her brain with his stupid-making cat-fume powers.

Why do relationships have to be so much work, anyhow? she wondered as the train rolled up. Or maybe that question merely meant she'd been doing it wrong. Maybe if it felt like work, it wasn't meant to be. But old people always talked about the key to their fifty-year marriages, expounding the importance of constantly "working at it". Exhausted by the thought, Caitlin sighed and boarded the subway car, squeezing into a seat between a hefty man and a woman with about six shopping bags that spilled from her lap into Caitlin's. Her three months with Kevin had been challenging enough. Fifty fucking years?

Still, five stops on the Red Line, two on the Orange Line, and she'd practically be in bed. Just a quick, cold dash in her pointlessly adorable, unseasonable shoes and short hemline, and she'd be warm, inside, scrubbing her face, petting her cat and climbing into her bed with an *actual* weekend to look forward to, for the first time since late November. Forty-eight hours of sleeping in, watching dumb made-for-TV holiday movies...drinking an entire bottle of champagne by herself. Possibly in mimosa form, if it was before noon when she popped the cork. Felt likely. She'd better buy orange juice first thing in the morning. Yes, she'd wake up and celebrate being single, dammit.

"Hey," someone said to someone else, a sharp sound amid the train's greater rabble. Caitlin wished she had her iPod with her.

Again, "Hey."

Glancing up, she was surprised to find she was the one being addressed. A handsome man in a sporty black coat grinned at her from across the aisle. Who was that? The guy from 15C? An old classmate from BU? Shit, she'd better pretend to know who on earth he was. *Not a client, please not a client.*

"Hey," she offered, waving cheesily, overcompensating.

"Didn't recognize you at first without...you know." He made a gropey hand gesture that had heat flooding Caitlin's cheeks, thinking he must have her confused with some woman who'd fondled him.

Oh, wait. He was miming squeezing a stress ball. It was Mr. Cute from the Red Cross, last week.

"Oh, yeah." Her flustered laugh admitted that she'd been stymied. "You too."

The train squealed to a stop at Central Square, and the lady with the shopping bags exited. Mr. Cute crossed the aisle to sit beside Caitlin. His boldness was both intimidating and refreshing, his friendliness a nice but foreign-feeling change of pace from Kevin's stoicism.

"You're not one of the usual Thursday people," Mr. Cute said. He seemed far bigger this close up. In a nice way.

"I donate all different times, but usually weekends. Whenever I can manage, with my work schedule. You always do Thursdays?"

He nodded, and she catalogued the exact blue of his eyes. Prussian. "Same time, every two weeks for..." He did some calculating. "Nine years?"

"Oh, wow. I guess you do know your fellow regulars, then."

"It's the only weekday I get off."

She paused, mustering the energy to flirt. It'd be a waste not to, dressed as she was. "Nine years, and you still shut your eyes when they stick you?"

He smiled. "Oh God, yeah. I hate needles."

"Maybe you picked the wrong charity."

"Nah. My little sister had leukemia, so it sort of chose me."

"Oh. Did she..." Caitlin frowned in a way she hoped gently conveyed her condolences.

He nodded.

"That's sad. But good of you to donate."

"Why do you do it?"

She smirked, feeling lame in the face of his loss. "It makes me feel sort of full of myself, when I'm done."

He laughed. "Good a reason as any. Whatever gets bodies in the door."

"And it's like three blocks from my house, and it keeps me from obsessively checking my work email for a couple hours at a time. I signed up for a blood drive at my office once, maybe two years ago, and then I went back on my own and they somehow smooth-talked me into pheresis." She shrugged.

"They're good that way."

"Good at charming people out of their humors."

He looked her over, a cataloguing glance at her bare legs. "You aren't a flasher, are you?"

She laughed and lifted the hem of her long coat enough to prove she was indeed wearing a dress underneath, albeit a brief one.

"Lemme guess. Office Christmas party?"

She shook her head sternly. "Just hearing you utter the C-word could get me a talking-to from HR. *Holiday* party, please."

"Oh right, my mistake."

"Probably not even a party. A festive social gathering neither endorsing nor condemning any one religious dogma."

"So, a Christmas party?"

She smiled, nodding.

"What's in the bag?" He sat up straight to peer past the curls of silver ribbon.

"Champagne."

"Nice."

"The men got Scotch. How sexist is that?"

"Very?"

She shrugged again. "Jeez, I dunno. I'm probably just punchy from the late night." *And getting dumped.*

"My name's Mark, by the way."

"Caitlin." She balanced the gift and bag in her lap, and they shook. She wished he wasn't wearing gloves so she might feel how smooth or rough his palm was. "What about you? What's landed you on the last train of the evening on a Friday night?"

"I work for a youth center. Not far from the Red Cross, actually."

"Oh, that's nice." He donated his vital fluids *and* he worked with children? Dreamy.

"I coach intramural basketball, and our team was playing some kids in Porter Square. Then I stayed to have a beer with an old roommate who lives over there."

"Did you win?"

He smiled. "Fifty-six to thirty-nine, thanks for asking. Go Dingoes."

"Dingoes?"

He unzipped his jacket to reveal a dark-green hooded sweatshirt with a cartoon of a vicious-looking canine silkscreened in white.

"Very...ferocious."

"That's what happens when the kids get to name the team. I campaigned for the Back Bay Bruisers."

"That has a ring to it too."

"I like to think so, but a coworker pointed out that sensitive parents might worry it condoned unsportsmanlike violence." He zipped his coat back up.

Caitlin bit her lip, forcing her gaze to quit dropping to his mouth. Nice mouth. And she was suddenly free to kiss any mouth she liked. Though not on a subway train, four hours after getting dumped beside a laser printer. She telepathically willed Mark to ask for her number.

The train emerged from the earth to cross the Charles. As always, the view made Caitlin's heart rise. She'd lived here a decade, but that skyline beyond the glittering river still thrilled her now city-hardened heart just as it had when she'd been fresh off the plane from rural Washington.

"Best view in the whole town," Mark said.

"It is." Pretty in the summer sun with sailboats and scullers crisscrossing the river, gorgeous under the black winter sky, the lights of Boston sparkling in the water's reflection. A postcard.

She met Mark's eyes. His awfully blue eyes. "Did you grow up around here?"

"No, Connecticut. But I've been here since I was twenty-three."

"Connecticut—that must be pretty."

"You've clearly never been to Hartford."

She smiled. "No, I haven't."

"But no, you're right. It's got its nicer points. What about you? You come here for school?"

"Yup. Transferred to BU my junior year. Did you?"

He shook his head, and the train doors opened at the Charles stop, icy winter wind gusting inside to pepper Caitlin's bare legs with goose bumps.

"I was a camp counselor when I was teenager," Mark said. "Then I worked full time at the Y as a youth sports coordinator for a couple years in Hartford, then got a chance to transfer to Boston. All my closest friends had gone off to college, and I didn't want to wind up like my dad and my uncles, all still farting around in the same neighborhood where they grew up, so I jumped on it. I figured eventually I'd save up enough to do the school thing, but with my salary and Boston's cost of living..."

She nodded her commiseration.

"But it's all working out, I think. I'll probably get appointed as director when my boss retires next year, which is a nice promotion. Plus, it's a lot of fun, and really satisfying. When I don't want to strangle the kids, that is."

The train trundled back underground, and Caitlin was disappointed her stop was coming up.

As they squealed through Park Street Station, she asked, "Were you always sporty?"

Mark shook his head. "I was kind of a lump, actually. Hands glued to a video-game controller. Then when I started high school, my folks were on the verge of splitting up, and I joined the track team just to have an excuse to avoid being home during all their fighting." He paused, blinking. "Sorry. That was probably TMI, as my girls would say. It's late. My social filters have gone to bed for the night, I think."

"I just got dumped at an office holiday party by a guy I didn't even really like all that much. Is that TMI?"

He grinned. "Probably. Guess we're even. Shit, you got

dumped, dressed like that?" He gave her legs an appreciative glance. Not sleazy—not that Caitlin would have minded so much.

"He must have been drunk," Mark said. "Or blind."

"Neither, I'm afraid—"

The speaker chimed. *"Now approaching...Downtown Crossing. Change here for the Orange Line."*

She stood, checking that her coat was covering all the important, drafty places. "Well, this is me."

Mark stood. "Me too."

"Oh. Where do you live?"

"You know where the Chinese Evangelical Church is?"

She laughed—the name of that place always made her scratch her head. Huh. They'd be getting off at the same stop. *Getting off together,* her brain repeated with a juvenile snicker. "Yeah, I know the place."

"Not far from there. You?"

"Not far either, but down Tremont a block and through that little park."

The doors hissed open, and they headed for the Forest Hills platform together, Caitlin's *clop-clops* sounding too loud to her ears.

"You rent?" Mark asked.

"No, condo. Tiny little walk-in closet of a condo, but this time of year my job hardly ever lets me go home, anyhow. My cat must worry where his next meals are coming from." *Did I mention I live alone with a cat? Just got dumped, workaholic who occasionally eats half a bag of shredded mozzarella cheese for dinner? With chopsticks? Get on this hot mess with your man-broom before someone else sweeps me up!*

"What do you do?" he asked.

"There's no way to make it not sound boring, but I'm an account manager for a financial firm. Nothing too evil, I promise. I specialize in small-business loans and investments. Leave the corporate stuff to my more ambitious colleagues."

"Cool."

She laughed. "If you say so."

Caitlin slowed on the stairs, out of practice at walking in heels, and they stood among the other late-nighters, waiting for an Orange train.

"You must be freezing in that," Mark said.

"A little, but it's only five minutes' dash to my place. Plus, I dress up maybe twice a year, so I can channel my inner twenty-year-old idiot and suffer the elements in exchange for wearing cute shoes."

He glanced at her feet, and she modeled one for him. "Those *are* cute."

"I know. Cute as a basket of yawning puppies." She gave Mark a quick once-over. "When I saw you at the Red Cross, I thought you must be a construction guy. You had paint all over your pants." *And quite sexy arm muscles behind your shirt.*

He looked perplexed a second. "Oh, no. Sadly, that was only evidence of how overdue I was to do laundry. Those are my crappy jeans I wear when I have to help with a mural or paint banners for games or whatever. But if they trick women into thinking I'm some kind of capable roughneck, maybe I'll put them into regular circulation."

She laughed, just as headlights winked from the dark tunnel. Twenty minutes ago she couldn't wait to be in bed, now she was almost sad how soon she'd be home. *Ask me out,* she beamed to Mark.

Yeah right, dum-dum. You told him you just got dumped. If he's smart, he'll run screaming, and if he's a creep, he'll think you're all vulnerable and easy.

Who cares? He's hot. Maybe I am easy.

Well, not quite. Not in practice. She wished she was the kind of girl who'd just take him home tonight, let him peel off her fantastic dress and hey, why not keep the shoes on? But she most certainly wouldn't be wishing all that come morning, after he disappeared down the hall and out of her life.

"After you," Mark said, gesturing as the doors slid open.

The car was packed with animated young adults heading home to Roxbury and Jamaica Plain from the clubs, leaving no room to sit. They were only going two stops, anyhow. Caitlin tucked herself into a corner by the far door, and Mark joined her, seeming to position himself in such a way that she might avoid having her legs leered at by their fellow riders. *Chivalry or jealousy?* Didn't matter. Either reason made her bite her lip to keep from grinning.

Their fists were an inch apart on the metal pole, and if his drifted down to butt against hers, she wouldn't relocate her hand. Come to think of it, his face was awfully close to hers. And he was a lovely height, maybe six-one, tall enough to make a slightly-taller-than-average girl in three-inch heels still feel adequately loomed-over. Woman, that was. Not a girl. Though she certainly felt like a college kid again, and her glass of consolation chardonnay had worn off an hour ago and couldn't be blamed for this giddiness.

She studied Mark's five-o'clock shadow, thinking idly how nice he'd look with shaving cream all over his face—that open face with its easy smile, temporarily stern to keep from getting nicked. Chest bare, towel knotted at his waist, the squeak of his palm across the glass as he cleared the fog from the mirror . . .

Here, let me help you with that... How do you like your eggs? Call in sick to work and have sex with you all day? Oh, Mark, I really mustn't. But I will. Paint my front hall wearing nothing but your mangy work jeans, you say? Excuse me while I orgasm.

"Caitlin?"

She started, blinking to bring his face into focus.

"Sorry. You said your name's Caitlin, right?"

"Yeah. Oh, yes. Sorry, the time must be catching up with me." *Pardon me while I redress you in my mind. And...there we go. Now I can form words.*

"I asked if you got time off for the holidays," Mark prompted.

"Yeah, I do. My company's year-end craziness wrapped up this week. Me and most of the people in my department are taking the week after next off, through New Year's."

"Doing anything special?" he asked as the doors opened at Chinatown.

Are you thinking of asking me out? If so, will I look cooler if I say I'm busy or if I say I'm doing absolutely jack shit? Oh, well. Let's be honest. "I'm doing jack shit. I can't wait."

He laughed, and his smile made her lady-region twitchy and demanding.

"Sounds good."

"Next stop, Tufts Medical Center. Doors will open on the right."

No. Boo. Ask me out. Ask me out now. Prey upon my recently dumped, vulnerable ego.

"What about you?" she asked. "Get any time off?"

He shook his head. "Kids are all off for winter break, which means I'm even busier than usual."

"Bummer."

He shrugged. "I'm not real big on the holidays, so I don't mind. I mean, Christmas is only fun if there's kids around. Me and my older sister have been slacking in the baby-making department, so I'm not missing out, staying in Boston. I'd just as soon hang around work and watch the kids there get all wound up about it."

"They make you dress up like Santa or anything?"

He laughed. "Thank God, no. Our facilities manager is...how can I put this delicately?"

"Built for the role?" she ventured.

"Yes, very diplomatic."

"Tufts Medical Center. Doors on the right."

The train slowed as they rumbled into the long, tiled length of the station. Mark edged through the crowd, and Caitlin followed in his wake, wishing she weren't quite so close and could discover what sort of butt one got from running around with kids all day.

They exited the car. The station was chilly, which meant it had to be even icier outside. Caitlin hugged her gifts to her chest as they stood on the platform. "I usually go that way," she said, nodding toward the less popular Tremont Street exit.

"Me too."

Oh, goodie.

They meandered toward the far end of the station, and she was pleased to note he seemed to be dawdling as well. *Ask me out.*

Ask me ooouuut.

"So," he said as they boarded the escalator.

"The final outbound train of the night has now departed. Thank you for riding the T."

"So," Caitlin echoed.

"You've been single for like an hour."

"Four hours."

"Oh, okay. That's totally different. That's enough time to recover, right?"

"Recover for what purpose?" She stepped smoothly from the escalator, feeling confident in a way that usually only arrived shortly after her third glass of wine in a dimly lit bar.

"I know I'm just some guy from the Red Cross, but could I maybe have your number? Maybe call you some time, see if you want to meet for a drink? Maybe right after we both donate so you'll be a really cheap date."

"No alcohol for twenty-four hours," she said, quoting the techs' release spiel.

They passed through the ancient floor-to-ceiling turnstile one at a time, its revolving metal teeth ushering them into the drafty corridor that would take them up to the street.

"Okay, fine. A coffee then. Or a drink the next day, once we're both allowed to do heavy lifting and vigorous exercise again."

What kind of vigorous exercise? "Yeah. I'd like that." Caitlin's heels clicked to a halt on the bricks, and she smiled at him, hoping her hair still looked fantastic and no traitorous zits had decided to make surprise appearances. The cold licked at her legs, but she couldn't care less. She was flirting with Mark, and she'd happily suffer through worse for the chance.

He tugged off a glove, fumbled in his pocket and pulled out a phone, queuing up a new contact. "Okay, shoot."

"Six-one-seven…"

"Six-one-sev—" The phone beeped three times, and the screen illuminating his face went dark. "Oh, shit. Stupid battery." He woke the phone back up, but it died immediately. "Damn. You have a pen?"

She frowned her apology.

"Well, I'll just have to remember it, then."

She told him the number, and he nodded, repeating it several times. "That's my mom's street number, plus the Dingoes' center's jersey number, then three four, which is Paul Pierce's number... Okay. I got it." He squeezed his eyes shut and fisted his hands, an epic charade of memorization. "Mom, Justin, Paul Pierce. Mom, Justin, Paul Pierce."

"Shall I take yours, just to be safe?"

"Yeah, good idea."

Caitlin opened her tiny clutch purse and frowned. She checked her coat pockets, but she already knew it was a lost cause. "Crap. I switched bags at the last second before I left my place. I don't have my phone."

They went through another digit-memorizing rigmarole, and hopefully *one* of them would recall the other's number by the time they each got home in ten minutes and could write them down. If they didn't, it just wasn't meant to be. But she dearly hoped her phone would buzz with a text not long from now, a *Testing, testing* from Mark, something like that. Something to put a smile on her face just before she fell dead asleep.

"Maybe when we go out," he said, "I could wear a tux, and *you* can look like the slob."

"You don't look like a slob. You're not even wearing your painting pants."

"True."

"I'm the one who looks out of place. I look like I should be stumbling home after too many shots at Tequila Rain or somewhere... Is that still a place?"

He laughed, flashing her that amazing smile again.

Quit smiling like that, or I'll sexually assault you in this subway tunnel.

Just then, the overhead bulbs went dark, leaving them in the dim glow of the emergency lights.

"Last call," Mark said with a sigh.

"You don't have to go home, but you can't stay here." They

headed down the corridor toward a metal gate that opened into a recessed brick courtyard a little ways off the street. "Though I'm quite happy to go home, frankly. That was a long-ass day."

"Agreed. Well, ladies fir—" The gate rattled with Mark's tug but didn't open. He took the handle in both hands and leaned way back, but nothing. Pushed hard against it. Nothing.

Another spirited, fruitless shaking, then his blue eyes swiveled to Caitlin's face. "That's not good."

Chapter Four

"The other side must still have someone working," Caitlin said.

They'd taken the unpopular route, barely more than an emergency exit. The more civilized, main lobby boasted ticket kiosks and an actual human being on duty beside the plastic gates.

"Only one way to find out," Mark said, heading back toward the platform.

"Oh..." Caitlin halted as they neared the turnstile, heart sinking.

"Shit." Mark jogged ahead and pushed at the metal bars, but it was as useless as she'd feared. It was a one-way, revolving-door-style setup, only designed to let people out, lest someone sneak into the station without paying their fare.

"Okay," Caitlin said, mustering calm. "Okay. There's got to be an emergency something-or-other, somewhere."

She headed back toward the street and heard Mark following. The cruel, cold breeze swirled around her naked legs. A small plastic window winked in the streetlight leaking in from outside. "Here we go."

Mark stood beside her as she opened the tiny door and punched the button labeled EMERGENCY INTERCOM. They waited for the speaker panel to crackle or hum or for a human voice to answer her summons, but nothing. She pushed the button and held it down. "Hello? Help?" She let it go, but still nothing. Mark took a turn pushing and speaking and listening in various fruitless combinations. They shared a long, nervous look.

"Let's keep searching," he said. "There's got to be a fire alarm, right?"

"Right."

They squinted in the dark corridor, but an extinguisher mounted by the gate was all they found.

Mark sighed loudly, voicing Caitlin's exact frustration. "Fucking MBTA."

"Indeed."

He headed for the turnstile, gripping the bars and shouting. "Hey! Hello! Anybody down there? We're locked in!"

They waited, but no reply arrived. Mark jogged back to the other end, rattling the gate barricading them from the street. "Hey! Hello!"

It was no use. They were in the theater district, but the tourists would have cleared out an hour or more ago, and the bars were all closed or closing, and hardly anyone was likely to be walking past in the direction of not-very-much. Even if someone did, what would they make of people yelling from a dark corridor in the middle of the night? If it were Caitlin passing, she'd probably glance fearfully down into the shadowy brick courtyard and walk faster, maybe have the courtesy and concern to dial 9-1-1 as she beat it the fuck out of there.

Mark sighed again. "Shit."

"Yeah," she agreed softly. "Shit."

He woke his phone again, but it went dead immediately with a defeated *bloop*. "Shit shit shit."

"Don't panic. It's what? Maybe one-thirty?"

"I think so." He pocketed his cell and rubbed his face with his gloved hands.

Caitlin took stock, looking for a bright side. She was trapped in a subway corridor with the cutest, most charming man she'd had the pleasure of getting asked out by in months. Life could be worse. Unless she lost a toe to frostbite. That might not be the best way to kick off a would-be courtship.

"This thing starts running around five," she said. "Even if we can't reach anyone, neither of us will drop dead in three and a half hours, not of cold or hunger or thirst, right?"

"Nah, we won't." Mark shook his head a bit too energetically, faking calm.

"You're not claustrophobic, are you?"

"No, no. Just..." He made a dramatic shuddering noise. "Feels weird. Being locked in. I've gotten so used to being the lone adult in a room or a bus full of kids, the one who fixes stuff. Just frustrated."

"Understandable. This ever happen at the Y?"

"Nope. No practice in this particular crisis." He studied her in the scant light and smiled. "Better it's you and me here, and not me and fifteen under-rested, over-sugared adolescents, like the time I was on a bus that broke down in Western Mass."

Just him and her? Better indeed. "Sounds very *Lord of the Flies.*"

He laughed. "Nearly."

"What'd you do?"

"Games, fun. Distraction. Trick the kids into thinking it was a sleepover."

"I wish I'd brought pajamas," Caitlin said. And slippers, and a nice fluffy robe.

"If we're stuck here until the morning, we should set up camp closest to the platform. Maybe they keep the station heated through the night."

"We can only hope. Less breezy, anyhow."

They wandered back to the revolving gate, and Caitlin sat on the floor as demurely as could be expected in her tiny dress—not that Mark would be able to see much if she accidentally flashed him, not in this paltry light. She slipped off her shoes and set them beside her with a sigh, flexing her toes.

"Funny how getting dumped at a holiday party suddenly isn't the worst thing that's happened to me today," she teased herself.

"Careful. Crappy stuff's supposed to come in threes."

"Oh, right. I wonder what's next?"

"Guess we'll just have to wait and find out."

On the positive side, at least she didn't need to pee. And though she didn't know Mark well at all, she did have a crush on him, and if someone had forced her to choose a person to be trapped in this corridor with all night, his was the name she'd have blurted.

Mark stretched his legs out in front of him. "So. You like it so far? Our first date?"

She smiled, glad he was finding the humor in things again. "I would have preferred that coffee, I must admit."

"You okay? Cold?"

She nodded. "Yeah, pretty cold."

He unzipped his coat.

"No, don't do that."

He ignored her, slipping it from his shoulders. He draped it over her lap, and she tucked the edges under her legs and feet, happy for the soft fleece lining...though she wasn't exactly cozy. The brick floor was turning her butt to stone, and the breeze still reached them, sucked from the street down into the station, off through the tunnels bound for other stops.

"Still think you can make it three or four hours?"

She nodded. "Yeah, I can."

"Lemme know if your feet go numb or anything. You want my socks?" He reached for his shoes.

"No, no." She tucked his jacket more tightly under her heels. "I'll be okay."

"Gloves?" He was already pulling them off, so it wasn't a question.

She slipped them on, liking how they'd been prewarmed by him, and how small her hands felt inside them. Mark slid his own hands into the front pocket of his Dingoes sweatshirt after flipping up its hood and cinching it around his face. His very handsome face.

"Thank you," Caitlin said, her voice sounding strange and disembodied in the dark weirdness of the space.

"Least I can do, after talking your ear off and getting us stranded down here."

She shrugged. "I'd been willing you to ask me out with telepathy, so really it's my fault. You were just doing my bidding."

He laughed softly, and she wished she could see his grin better. That'd warm her up.

"Why didn't you just ask me out yourself?"

"Well, I might've, except I'd already admitted I got dumped in the last few hours. That might quite rightly give a guy pause."

"Ah. What does it say about me that I asked you out anyhow?" Mark asked, a smile lingering in his voice.

"That you like 'em desperate and vulnerable."

Another laugh, a proper one. "Wow. I'm a scoundrel."

"Nah. You're cute."

He turned to meet her eyes, raising a brow. "Oh?"

She nodded. "I thought you were cute at the Red Cross, with your scaredy needle-face and your library book and your reading glasses. And the fact that you were donating your platelets in the middle of a weekday." *And your shapely, shapely arm.*

"How did you know I wasn't unemployed, just there for the free snacks?"

"I knew. The way you squeezed that stress ball..." She sighed for wistful effect.

"Oh?"

"Oh, yes. Women can't resist a man with strong squeezing hands. Tells us you must be great at, oh, I don't know...making juice. Opening jars. Crushing beer cans."

"Women really go for that, huh?"

She shrugged. "Maybe that's my own perversion, after spending seventy hours a week surrounded by guys who speak in financial code."

"All that mouse clicking, though. Dexterous fingers. Left click! Right click!" he mimed furiously.

"You make us sound so exciting."

"Enter that quarterly earnings data!"

"Indeed. Not nearly as exciting as what you do, I'm sure."

He made a dismissive *pfffft* noise. "In any given eight-hour period, I get mocked fifty times for not knowing who some pop star or rapper playing on the radio is or what a slang word means. And get told stuff like, 'Coach Holly, you're actually pretty cool. What are you, like forty?'"

She laughed. "And what are you, really?"

"Thirty-two."

"Ooh, burn." A chill overtook her, and she tucked Mark's coat tighter under her butt. "Thank you again, for lending me this."

"You've got nice legs," he said casually. "Be a shame if they snapped off from the cold."

"I wish I had something to offer you, aside from a uselessly tiny purse... You need lipstick? Or my T-Pass?"

"Save the lipstick for when we get hungry."

"Oh." She sat up straight. "I do have champagne."

He glanced at her, and she realized neither of them was sure if she was serious. Mark shrugged.

"Have to pass the time somehow," Caitlin said.

"True. Okay, sure. Bust it out."

She reached for the bag and freed the bottle from its tissue-paper nest. The idea perked her up, making it feel more like an adventurous date, assuring her she hadn't gotten all hussied up for nothing. She'd toast to that. "Would you like to do the honors, with your manly squeezing hands?"

"Sure."

While Mark unwound the little wire cage, Caitlin tore the pretty paper from Kevin's would-be Christmas present and slid the shaker from the box.

The cork escaped with an echoing pop, and she caught some of the fizzy overflow with the shaker's silver cap.

"Cheers," she offered, and clacked the cap against the bottle.

"To, um..." Mark took a sip from the bottle, seeming to think.

"To my first subterranean date," she ventured.

"Mine too. What a coincidence. To many more." He tapped the cap again. "And to the next date going a bit more smoothly, if you ever let me take you on a second one after this debacle."

"It's not your fault we're locked in. If only I were litigious, I'd lose a toe on purpose and sue the pants off the T. Not that they have any money." She sipped her wine. In a weird way, she didn't think champagne had ever tasted so nice. Considering the surroundings, it was all the more luxurious.

"In any case, it can only get better from here," Mark said. "The bar's been set so low. I planned it all this way, paid off the T employees."

"I'm sure next time you'll take me somewhere *really* nice. Like the North Station parking garage."

"Nothing but the best. Keep those standards low, Miss..."

"Dwyre."

"Miss Dwyre."

"I shall. Mr. Holly, is it?"

"Yup."

"Mark Holly," she repeated, nodding. "I like that. Very seasonal."

"HR probably wouldn't approve."

"No, maybe not. You'd have to change your name to Mark Nondenominational Winter Greenery."

He laughed, a soft chuckle that made her feel clever and pretty, momentarily warm.

"So you aren't allowed to say Christmas, but your boss is allowed to give you alcohol? And a martini shaker?" He nodded at it.

"Yeah, I know. Though the shaker wasn't a gift. Not a gift to me, anyhow. It was supposed to be for the guy who dumped me."

"Ah. Ouch."

She picked it up to show him, and Mark squinted at the engraving in the dim glow of the emergency lights. "Can't return it, huh? Bummer."

"Yeah. Do you know any KPDs who enjoy cocktails? I'll sell it to you at a very reasonable discount."

"It's a memento, now. Maybe you can make up an acronym to commemorate our little underground adventure."

She pondered it, nothing witty arriving. But if she wasn't mistaken, the wine was already taking effect, its fizziness bubbling through her veins, making her feel all mischievous and slinky, even camped out in quite possibly the least romantic spot in all of

Greater Boston. Except perhaps for that territory between the half-dead ficus and the laser printer.

"We're going to hit it off," Mark announced after a minute's conversational lapse.

"Oh?"

"And we'll have a real date and fall in love and get married and have about ten kids."

"Ten sounds like a lot," she said, playing along to see where this was going.

"Fine. Nine kids. And fifty years from now, everyone will gather around the parlor for our silver or gold or whatever anniversary, and we'll take the old martini shaker off our stately mantle, and regale everyone with the tale of how it brought us together. And you can drink champagne out of the cap, just like you are now."

"Deal," she said, and they tapped vessels again.

After another swig, Mark cleared his throat. "Provided we do survive the night and I don't mess this up, I *would* like to see you again." He sounded a touch vulnerable—nervous and hopeful, all the things she felt. It warmed her in a way the champagne never could.

"I'd like that too."

"Do you like dim sum? Or is that too lazy, since we both live so close to Chinatown?"

"I like lazy. And I love dim sum. I like the way the wasabi makes me feel like it's boiling my eyeballs for ten seconds, then suddenly it's gone."

"Sounds like a plan."

"Then if we don't mess it up, we could wander around and go into all those interesting shops that sell pickled fish and coffee-flavored chewing gum," she added.

"And those tiny prepackaged Japanese Jell-O shot things with the cube of mummified pineapple in the middle?"

She laughed. "Definitely."

"If I'm feeling particularly smitten, I'll buy you a lucky waving cat."

"A big gold one?"

He nodded.

"I'll be extra smittening, in that case. It might freak out my actual cat, but he could use a little friendly competition." They were quiet a moment, and the chill took hold of her, making her legs tremble and her back muscles knit in the tensing cold.

"You're shaking."

"I'm fine."

He smiled and shook his head. "Here." He spread his legs wider and patted the floor between them. "You'll be warmer, and I promise I won't grope you or anything."

Yes, because getting groped by a handsome, charming man hours after getting dumped by a workaholic iceberg was such a repulsive notion.

Caitlin carefully crab-walked herself over his nearest leg and sat in front of him, tugging her dress and coat flat beneath her frozen butt and rewrapping her legs in his jacket.

"Okay?" he asked.

Draping her hair over her shoulder and out of his face, she leaned back. He felt solid behind her, his voice so close by her ear. If she'd had any blood left in her extremities, it would've rushed to heat more womanly climes. "Yes, fine. Thank you."

She reached for her champagne, wanting a fresh sip to keep its pleasant, distracting tingle inching through her veins. As she swallowed, Mark slid his arms around her middle, encircling her waist a couple chivalrous inches below her bust. Not that he'd be able to cop much of a feel through her wool coat.

"What base is this?" she teased, but her voice came out all breathy and overwrought. Behind her back, his chest felt as solid as the brick wall, but leagues more comforting.

Mark's silent laugh warmed her ear. "Not any base I've ever gotten to. I think we've wandered off in the outfield someplace."

She could begin to feel his heat through their layers and hoped maybe he could feel hers in return. Maybe they'd just melt together, two truffles joining so their mismatched gooey centers might mingle. She blinked at the metaphor, wondering if it was dirty, the idea of his nougat canoodling with her raspberry crème.

Freak.

"You feel nice," she murmured.

"You too. And you smell nice."

She smiled at a thought. "I wonder if I'll tell anyone about this on Monday, if they ask what I got up to on my long-awaited weekend off."

"I will definitely *not* be telling my coworkers. They can't be trusted with gossip."

"It's a good story, though," Caitlin said. "How would you word it? I think I'd say, 'I got to talking with this cute guy I knew from the Red Cross, and the next thing we knew, the subway shut down and we got locked inside all night.'" *Suck on that, stupid Kevin.*

"Will you mention all this?" Mark asked, giving her a gentle squeeze.

"I'll tell my girlfriends about it, yeah. Colleagues, not so much. But they'll think it's funny, I bet, boring old Caitlin getting trapped in the subway. That's by far the most interesting water-cooler material I've ever had to contribute."

"After we fall in love, but before the ten kids—"

"Nine, you promised."

"Before them, we can get married down here. I'll walk you down the corridor and carry you through the turnstile. Hopefully your dress won't get caught in the bars. A conductor can officiate."

"And we'll string cans to the back of an Orange Line train en route to our honeymoon in...well, Forest Hills or Oak Grove, I suppose, unless we switched to the Amtrak."

"Very romantic. Except the cans would probably wind up breaking the train and they'd have to shuttle-bus us."

She laughed. "That sounds about right."

He sighed—a tired, happy noise—and his arms held her tighter. Or perhaps that was her optimistic imagination. She felt him go rigid for a few moments, could practically hear him thinking. About what, she had to wonder. About taking back all this flirtation, clamming up and retracting his silly wedding talk, as many a man would wish to do. But instead she felt his lips or nose brush the side of her face, by her ear, and her shiver had nothing to do with his chilly skin or the breeze leaking in from outside.

"Was that a kiss?" she murmured.

"Not quite."

She listened to him swallow, waiting. Was he waiting too, for her permission to take more official liberties? Then there it was— cool lips, warm breath. Just a faint graze to start, then a firm press, a real kiss on her temple.

"You smell amazing," he whispered.

"So you said."

Another tease, a drag of his lips along her cheek. The tunnel disappeared as their little shared space seemed to heat, and she simultaneously tensed and relaxed against his firm chest, inside his strong arms. If her breath steamed in the air, it was because her insides had caught fire, not because it was cold. Because it wasn't. It was suddenly very, very warm.

A strange man you basically just met is kissing you in one of the shadier corners of the MBTA. You really ought not to get turned on right about now. He could be some kind of homeless vampire smack-fiend pervert.

Fuck you, intuition. You should have warned me about Kevin dumping me when I was ordering that stupid martini shaker or mentally booking a room in the Berkshires.

To spite her lousy instincts, she turned in Mark's arms, resting her bent legs over one of his thighs. Their eyes met for a moment before he accepted her invitation, pressing his mouth softly to hers.

Just the whisper of his cold lips against hers to start. Soft, dry skin, the sweet touch of their noses. She felt the warm huff of his breath, the scratch of his stubble. Subtle and cautious. A gentleman.

His mouth opened faintly, and she let hers do the same, their lips brushing and glancing, becoming familiar, finding a rhythm of sorts in this new acquaintance. She put her hand to his jaw, swore softly, then pulled off the glove, cold be damned. As she slipped her fingers inside his hood, the kiss deepened.

The caress of his mouth felt lush, the promise and mystery of what would come next drawing energy low in her belly, hot and chaotic. When his tongue slid against hers, she just about melted. In the back of her consciousness, she felt that his coat had ridden up to expose a sliver of her thigh. To hell with it. She was half-tempted to grab Mark's hand and lead it right there. That'd heat them up.

He cocked his jaw, and she did the same, letting him take things a bit further.

Ooh, he was good. He was the best kisser she'd had the pleasure of doing this with in far too long. It was as sweet and exciting as a prom-night kiss, but smooth and practiced as a seduction. Champagne had never tasted better than it did sampled off Mark Holly's lips.

She wriggled her hand free of the second glove, the chill wholly worth it to feel his neck against her bare palm. She loosened his hood and pushed it back, wanting the soft brush of his hair and the view of his handsome face, unobscured. His lips plucked her lower one. If they were seeking an invitation, she granted it, parting to welcome him deeper. His mouth taunted, giving just the tiniest slide of tongue. She angled her head and was rewarded with a brief, wet sweep, scalding in the midst of their fogging breath. Another sweep, the slick, thrilling tease of his tongue against hers. She returned the caress, feeling his body tense, alert. She felt everything fivefold, the corridor like one of those isolation pods, maybe. His heat scorched hotter, his mouth tasted more male and primal, his shallow breaths louder in the dark.

What if he never wants to see you again after you show him you're tacky enough to make out with him in a subway station?

Fuck you, rational brain. I thought we were feminists.

She couldn't worry about what this little tryst would do—propel a romance or scare it away. She was too freshly cut loose to be trusted with overthinking this situation. *Just enjoy it for what it is. If nothing else, it's a great story.*

A better story would be, "You'll never believe how Mark and I met." It'd make a hell of a best man's speech, as well. Oops, where'd that come from? Who cared—Mark wasn't above joking about a basketball team's worth of children.

His mouth showed hers what he liked, and after letting him lead for a minute or two, she took ownership of the kiss. His energy shifted, an unmistakable swerve in a more sexual direction. She imagined insanely inappropriate things—how maybe his breath would go shallow and excited this way when she shimmied toward the foot of one of their beds to show him what else her mouth could do.

You're jumping the gun again, brain.

Whatever. You love it.

The weight of Mark's hand found her waist, strong and sure, exactly how she hoped the heft of his body might feel one night in the not-so-distant future, the confident push of his thighs spreading hers.

She wondered a dozen things in a single breath. How he'd sound and what he might say, if he'd order or flatter or plead, or if he'd simply moan and pant, abandoned by words. If he'd be as giving and thorough as she suspected, and how desperate or greedy he might grow when his turn came. How his tongue would feel, taking her pulse at her jugular, teasing her ear, taunting at the crease of her innermost thigh. How he'd smell and taste, what his face would look like in sleep if she woke first to find him beside her in a bed, hers or his. Smooth cotton sheets? Worn flannel? Jersey? White or striped or some unexpected color? Coffeemaker or French press or a quick run to Starbucks or Dunkin'? So many questions she wanted answered about this handsome stranger. But none she could reasonably ask.

His mouth broke away. "You all right?"

"Oh my, yes."

"Okay, good. You went sort of...distracted there."

She bit her tender lip, brain not quick enough with a smooth reply. "Just thinking about stuff. Sorry. You're an amazing kisser, I promise."

He pressed his lips to her jaw. "Can't be *so* amazing, if your mind's already wandering."

She laughed softly, vulnerability taking hold. Might as well own it. "If you must know, I was thinking about how bummed out I'd be if you never wound up calling me after all this. Because making out in the bowels of the Orange Line may not be the classiest move a potential date could make."

"What does that say about me, then?" he asked with a smile. "Plus this isn't the *bowels* of the Orange Line. The nostril, maybe."

She grinned. "I guess that's a bit better."

"But if this is starting to be too weird for you, we can stop. It was a nice diversion while it lasted."

"I don't want to stop."

Mark squinted thoughtfully and recited her phone number. "Right?"

"That's it."

"Well, unless you kiss me into some kind of brain damage and I forget, I plan on using those digits very soon."

"I'd like that."

"Me too." He reached over and handed her the half-empty bottle of champagne. She tilted it to her lips, the fizz igniting her excitement all over again. Mark took a drink as well and set it aside. His lips were cold as they grazed hers, his tongue sweet with wine.

Between kisses he murmured, "Classy women are overrated, anyhow."

She swatted his arm, their mouths already reconnecting.

Goodness, she'd forgotten how lovely all this was. Not just a man's newness and that nervous spark of this-could-really-be-something, but simply being this way with anyone—familiar or completely unknown. Her libido hadn't disappeared during her and Kevin's neglectful spell. If anything, it'd been angrier than usual, starved and left to pace around her belly, hungry and irritable. But having those feelings stir and actually getting them stoked by someone were so different. She'd nearly forgotten. She memorized every caress of Mark's lips and tongue and cool fingers lest she ever make the mistake of underestimating the awesomeness of this nonsense again.

She snuggled closer, sliding a hand under the collar of his sweatshirt to knead the hard muscle of his shoulder. The image of his pumping hand and strong, flexing arm from their Red Cross encounter revisited her, unlikely an arousal trigger as it was. If only they were someplace warm, someplace private. Then she could get him down to a T-shirt or less, get down to good old-fashioned man-ogling. He was welcome to ogle her in return. That gig's erstwhile overseer had slacked something terrible of late.

"You feel nice," she murmured. Their gazes flicked in the shadows.

"So do you."

She kissed him, hard and deep, stealing the reins for a minute or two. His hands stroked the back of her neck and her shoulders through her damnable coat. Her body wanted to know his—what it looked like, how it felt and might fit with hers, what it was capable of and how to make it react.

No longer caring what some dating coach might make of her eagerness, she reached between them to undo the top button of her coat. Mark took the hint, fumbling with the remaining two. She felt the uncertainty in his touch as he slid his hand inside, and the cold air that leaked in was canceled out by the flush that visited her as he rested a palm on her waist. Her body tensed, but the tightening had nothing to do with the icy breeze.

Stroking his chest though his sweatshirt—his perfectly firm, warm chest—she freed her mouth and smiled at him. "If anybody catches us down here, this is just some survival technique. Body heat or whatever."

He laughed. "If anyone finds us down here, I'm going to lose a lot of appeal real fast. Compared to some guy who can get you out of here, I mean."

Her rubbing fingers found his collarbone through his sweatshirt, tracing it as she stared at his throat, wondering what his skin tasted like. "You clearly don't know how good a kisser you are."

He let slip a prideful grin, but just for a moment before he pursed his lips, turning it into a smirk. "You're not so bad yourself."

I'm going to kiss him again soon, she decided. Kiss him hello before dim sum on a weekend morning, kiss him thank-you afterward and taste salt and spices on his lips. Or if all things went well, kiss him good night. Or if they went *really* well, kiss him awake the next morning. Yes, perhaps that last one. Maybe kiss him hello on a Saturday morning, kiss him goodbye on Monday as they parted ways at the train station or wherever. Just kissing him, really. Whenever, wherever, just wonderful.

Her happily wandering mind was drawn back into the present as she felt something else wander—Mark's hand drifting up her ribs, his thumb glancing the side of her breast. He moved so slowly, she knew he was welcoming a protest or correction. He'd just have to keep waiting. He was the sexiest, nicest man she'd met in ages, and he could grab her boob if he wanted.

Have at it, handsome.

She let her own hands wander in return, showing him just how fine she was with them tiptoeing across second base. His arm was as hard and muscular beneath his sleeve as she'd suspected, and she gave it an appreciative squeeze. She'd like to squeeze his biceps while he was braced above her in bed. Another notion to add to her mental checklist of Ways to Molest Mark.

The stroke of his tongue drew a hot flush up her neck, into her cheeks, fogging her brain. There it condensed and streamed back through her body, warming her chest and belly, fingers and toes, and some awfully neglected regions south of the equator. She scooted closer, and though she felt her dress ride high up her thigh, she also felt when her hip abutted Mark's crotch, which was far more interesting.

His kiss changed, as though she'd clicked him into a different gear, an eager one. This was the kind of kiss that *led someplace*. Wasn't it? She was so sex-deprived, if Mark sneezed on her she'd probably have rounded it up to foreplay.

The hand heating her side finally shifted, and he cupped her breast. Pleasure bloomed and spread through her chest, rising to make her head foggy. Was he hard? She couldn't tell, not with the fold of her coat between him and her hip. Jesus, she'd kill to find out.

The hand on her breast kneaded softly, tossing her deeper into the wilds of happy distraction. She shifted closer, as close as she could get without straddling the man. Which wasn't an unappealing thought, even considering it'd shove her dress up past her undies. She rubbed the bare skin under his collar, then his chest through his sweatshirt. His middle felt lean and firm, and she imagined how he might look, wandering in from the bathroom in just his shorts, heading back to the bed for an encore performance, perhaps. What kind of shorts? Boxers, Caitlin bet, with some pattern or other. Fine by her. They wouldn't stick around long before she flung them aside.

Mark's mouth moved to her jaw, then her neck when she tilted her head. It was awkward, the way they were sitting, but that was an excuse—if a lame one—to get relocated, drag them out of the outfield and back to the vicinity of second or third base. She broke their mouths apart and shifted to her knees between his thighs.

"This is probably forward," she said, "but I don't really care." She moved one leg to the outside of Mark's, and he edged away from the wall so she could straddle him. Her hemline rose to her hips, and she was thankful for the relative darkness. What felt hot in the shadows might look sloppy in the light.

Settling against him, she could feel him through her panties and his jeans, stiff. It was as shocking and forbidden and thrilling as the first time she'd ever touched a guy and discovered that a hard dick was so much...*harder* than she'd ever guessed possible in all her adolescent theorizing.

His mouth left hers to kiss her cheek, her jaw, her neck. One warm palm on her back, under her coat, his other fingers tangling in her hair. She felt the softest scrape of teeth, a lap of his tongue. *Give me a hickey,* she thought. Let everyone at work see.

But for better or worse—probably better—no self-respecting man over the age of twenty necked with such bruising fervor, Mark included. Instead of a hickey, he gave her a head rush, a pleasant, dizzying sensation as her mind drained of all thought, consciousness relegated to the wants of her body.

She cupped his head, the softness of his hair already seeming familiar. Maybe she'd stroke his hair this way when they made lazy love on a Sunday morning, or when they fucked like animals on a Friday night. She'd stroke his hair like this as they fell asleep after said fucking and/or lovemaking, kiss his temple or forehead, mumble sleepy fondnesses she was currently too riled up to guess at. Perhaps he'd give her a nickname, someday, a boyfriendly one. And she'd find out what he called her in bed, *baby* or *sweetheart* or something else, or maybe he wouldn't speak at all. He might just moan, giving voice to the low, soundless rumbles she felt brewing in his chest.

Their bodies shifted together, and he seemed as antsy as she felt. And between her legs, against his erection, something surprising was happening.

Oh, fuck.

I could come.

Through two pairs of underwear and Mark's jeans—and here, of all unromantic places. Her body begged her to keep going, but her brain butted in. *You can't come on some guy, not if you want to get asked out on a real date.*

Are you sure? He might think that's hot. Might do something Pavlovian to his ego.

It's not very dignified.

Neither's getting dumped ten feet from my cubicle. Watch me go.

"Mark."

"Yeah?" It was a sexy *yeah,* breathy and dark.

"Would it be weird if I...uh..."

His lips kissed her throat, slow and patient. "If you what?"

"If we keep doing this, I might...you know."

"Oh." A pause, then a laugh. "*Oh.* Jeez, I though you were going to ask to do something freaky to me."

"This whole dry-humping-a-stranger-in-the-subway thing doesn't count?"

"Heh... But anyhow, no, I don't think that's weird, if you...you know. I think it's kind of awesome."

"Okay. Good." She was glad of the permission, though she wouldn't pursue an orgasm, not intentionally. That would feel weird. Utilitarian. But if one happened upon her—upon him—well, that would be delightful.

Mark seemed to agree. His kisses changed, as did his hands. His palms held her hips, over her dress at first, then slipping beneath the hem. They were inviting Caitlin to move, urging her in tiny tugs. She did as they asked, rubbing against him, faintly to start. Within a minute, the motions took on a life of their own, and Mark echoed them with a tensing of his thighs, adding to the friction and Caitlin's mounting excitement. Her pleasure was champagne bubbles, forming and collecting, rising and bursting, but all at once it was as if someone shook the bottle.

Craving turned to demand. She heard herself panting, felt the push and pull of Mark's hands speeding alongside the undulations of her hips. The kisses heating her neck lost focus, and small noises punctuated each of his breaths, tiny grunts and sighs. The bubbles rushed together inside her, fizzing and crazy. As the first happy spasm arrived, she registered her nails raking Mark's back, beneath his shirt. Then she knew nothing but the pleasure, wondrous seconds that made up for everything crappy that had happened in the past few hours.

She came down from the high, tugged in opposite directions by euphoria and embarrassment. But the way he kissed her throat, so fond and excited, she knew there was no cause for regret. She leaned back to smile her delirium at him.

"Wow," he said.

She laughed. "Tell me about it."

"Here." His hands directed her to sit again as he edged back against the wall. She settled on her hip between his legs, knees bent over his thigh, and he wrapped his coat around her legs once more, tucking it tight then smoothing her hair from her face. A good idea, as the cold was finding her fast in the wake of the orgasm. She was still turned on, but it had lost some of its power to veil the elements. She'd just need to find another diversion.

Mark accepted her kiss eagerly. She let him know the fun wasn't over, just because she'd popped her cork. Her stroking hands got reacquainted with his shoulders and chest, his belly, then met his belt for the first time. She gave him a minute's intense kissing to signal that she should stop, but he didn't take her up on the chance. Bless him. His cool palm covered her hand at last and moved it lower, cupping it over his erection.

Even through his jeans, he was hot. He drew her hand up and

down, up and down, yet it was Caitlin who took things further. Her fingers were stiff with cold, but she curved the end of his belt through its buckle, eased it from the post, slid it free. His hand was eager, undoing his fly and leading hers to cover his cock through a thin layer of smooth cotton. *Boxers*, she confirmed.

He guided her touch for a minute or two, the bossiness giving her a preview of how he might get when he was all worked up and within sight of a bed. Nice. Maybe that ravishing she'd thought she'd been robbed of was still on the horizon. He let her hand go to touch her breast, his palm dragging against her in shaky strokes, the caress of a man who'd progressed beyond the graceful confines of foreplay.

"This is kind of embarrassing," he panted, "but I'm getting close."

Embarrassing? That'd be a sick double standard. Try fantastic. "Do you want to stop?"

"Do you want to?"

"No...but it'd be messy." And though normally she wouldn't have balked at the thought of swallowing... Well, just not here. His cock hadn't been rolling around on the floor of the Orange Line any more than his mouth had, but something about the idea was undeniably squicky, in the context. "You could just use your sleeve, I suppose. The walk of shame's awfully short, right?"

Mark's fondling hand and twitching hips stilled, and he began laughing, the quiet, happy sound like bells ringing in the darkness. "Sorry. I've totally sucked all the sexiness out of this."

"We're in a subway station. How high do you think my standards are?"

He cracked up harder at that, and Caitlin decided she'd never date anyone again whom she couldn't make laugh this way. It was as good as turning a man on, she realized. And you could do it anywhere. Except maybe a funeral.

"I'd hate to meet your ex-girlfriends and find out you take every woman to the back end of the Tufts Station on a first date."

"No," he said, chest still hitching. "This is our special place." The final word was gobbled up in a wheeze, and the peripheral light shone on the tears wetting his eyes. He sighed and wiped them away just as Caitlin succumbed to her own fit of giggles. He cleared his throat. "Okay. Sleeve it is, if it comes to that."

Caitlin hoped it would indeed come to that. With a few slow strokes, any stiffness he'd lost was back, the length of him the most wonderful, cruel tease, a mystery begging to be uncovered.

As he moaned, Caitlin imagined them in a bed, in the light and warmth, all the normal things. But screw normal. Where was the fun in that? Normal was dressing up, taking your boyfriend home after an office party and having reconnection sex in a pathetic attempt to save what didn't want resuscitating. What she had down in this creepy-ass brick corridor with a near stranger was far better.

She stroked him rougher, loving how he squirmed. His labored breaths told her maybe he wasn't up to much more, not without the finale arriving. She stole a glance at his face, wowed by the fact that it wasn't familiar yet. He was still some sexy guy she'd run into on the subway, yet here he was, panting on the verge of climax from what her touch was doing to him. Weird. Weird and awesome. A better gift than a monogrammed cocktail shaker, certainly, and even more personal.

His cold fingers brushed hers, then the smooth heat of his bare cock as he pushed his waistband down. He was scalding against her chilled skin. She must have felt like ice in return, but that wasn't what his face told her. Any discomfort he was feeling looked purely pleasurable. Short, harsh breaths huffed little jets of steam between them.

"Fuck, I'm close."

"Good."

Good, and then what? Two strangers, trapped together for another three hours or more, sobering up from sex and champagne in a brick tunnel of pure awkwardness.

I don't care. I like him.

You'll both be embarrassed once you're back to reality. He won't call.

You don't know that.

Mark's strained whimper hauled her out of the argument. One

of his hands closed over her stroking one, squeezing it tighter, moving it quicker. "Oh..."

She held her breath, body all at once flushed to see him so worked up.

He pressed his forehead to hers, their hands thrashing together as he came undone. On impulse, she slid hers up to cup his crown, just in time to feel his release, warm in her palm. Through a groan she heard her name, two desperate syllables, the best sound ever. After a few hitches, his body stilled, head dropping back to lean against the wall.

He blinked. He panted. He smiled.

She couldn't help but grin herself. "I'm going to do something really un-classy," she warned. Mark nodded blearily, and she grabbed the nearby wad of wrapping paper and wiped her hand. He laughed, lost again in a brief fit of giggles. A sighed warmed her neck. "Beats my sleeve."

Slowly, the tunnel asserted itself once more—the cold, the dark, the strangeness.

"I better..." Caitlin pulled back an inch or two to button her coat, find the gloves he'd lent her and slip them back on.

"Right."

She waited until Mark had his jeans done up and his hood re-cinched, then got herself settled between his legs once more, head on his shoulder, back against his chest, his jacket wrapped tight around her legs. He smoothed her hair aside and pressed his lips to her cheek. After a moment's shifting, he handed her the champagne bottle.

"To...well, you know. All that," he said.

She took a sip. They passed the bottle back and forth a dozen times, until the wine was gone.

"That was delicious, if unexpected," Mark said, setting it aside. "Thanks for sharing."

"You're very welcome. Thanks for helping. I probably would've ended up drinking mimosas all morning, then let half of it go flat. This was a much better use."

"Glad now they gave you champagne instead of whiskey?"

"I suppose I am." She let her body relax, her full weight resting on him. He closed his arms around hers to pin her pleasantly in place against him. "You know what else I'm glad about? That we got locked in here," she announced.

"Oh, yeah?"

"Yeah. This story's much more valuable than a good night's sleep."

"Speak for yourself. I have to be at work for basketball practice at ten."

"Oh, dear."

He hugged her tight. "You're right, though. It was worth it. Best accidental first date I've ever had."

"Indeed." And he'd made her come without even glimpsing her underwear. Actually, that was kind of a shame, considering she'd gone to all the trouble of matching the items. But hopefully there'd be more chances to spoil him.

I hope, I hope, I hope.

Chapter Five

Caitlin slept in fits and starts, deep enough to invite snatches of near-rest before something roused her—the cold, or Mark shifting behind her back.

She woke from a strange dream, its details gone before she could even recall them. A glance toward the end of the tunnel told her nothing. Even if it was early enough for the trains to start running, dawn light wouldn't follow for an hour or more. How long since they'd stopped kissing and chatting? Three hours? Ten minutes? She was almost glad his phone was dead. Checking the time and knowing how long they still had to wait could be a curse—

A clank echoed from the direction of the exit, and she tensed, her jolt or the noise waking Mark. Was it the sound of their escape being granted?

They shared a look, and Mark's wide eyes said he was wondering the same thing.

"Do you think...?"

He nodded. "I do."

She got to her knees, unsteady from the cold, or maybe the champagne. Mark looked away politely as she tugged her dress down to a more modest arrangement. She offered her hand, and he made it to standing on legs surely as rickety as her own. Her shoes were stiff as she fumbled to get them on.

She gathered the shaker and stuffed its wrapping paper and gift box in her coat pocket. Mark reached for the empty champagne bottle.

"Don't," she said.

"Don't?"

"No. You know what? Let's just leave it. I can't believe

somebody wasn't lying down on the job for us to have wound up locked in a freezing cold tunnel all night. The least they can do is recycle a mysterious champagne bottle they find down here."

He grinned but picked it up. "I'm taking it. Better drop some hints about your favorite kind of flowers so I can buy the right ones to fill this thing with when I turn up for our first date."

She blushed, the warmth welcome and humbling. "I like tulips. And gerbera daisies."

"Color?" he asked, picking up the cork.

"Surprise me."

He handed her the cork. "Here. You should have a souvenir, too."

She accepted it with another blush, and they headed for the exit.

Please let it really be unlocked, maybe on a timer. She prayed they might escape before any bewildered T employees found them. She was dead tired and didn't relish filling out whatever heap of forms might be required of them after such an ordeal.

The sky beyond the iron gate was still dark. She held her breath as they reached the bars, afraid to hope, but the gate swung out with an angry squeak when Mark pushed. They stepped into the brisk winter wind, the streetlamps and Christmas lights seeming exotic. Magic.

"Cheers to that." Caitlin tapped the bottle with the martini shaker.

She stared up at him in the streetlight, his blue eyes tinted greenish by the yellow glow.

"Do you still remember my number?" she asked.

His face went rigid with concentration, but he nailed it on the first try.

"Very good."

"The effort probably pushed my locker combination out," he said with a smile. "But it's a worthy trade."

Caitlin tenderly drew her hopeful heart from its nest between her ribs and stitched it onto her sleeve. "I hope you'll call me."

"I hope you'll answer when I do."

"If it's in the next half hour, I'll be dying of happiness in a boiling-hot shower."

"I'll try not to take it too personally, then. You must be freezing," he said, rubbing her arms through her coat. "Do we need to find you a cab?"

"No, no, I'm really close."

"Can I walk you home, at least?"

"You may."

She'd have preferred a leisurely stroll to draw the final minutes of their strange date out as long as possible, but Mark set a brisk pace, clearly more concerned with getting her safely home and into the warmth with all her fingers and toes still attached.

As they passed through the little park, he put his hand to the small of her back, the contact feeling dangerously like that of a boyfriend. Well, dangerous only if they never saw each other again. If he came to his senses and decided he didn't want to go on a real date with a woman who'd been dumped less than twelve hours earlier, lived alone with a cat, and had a tendency to fuck around with strangers in subway tunnels. So, dangerous, yeah. But awfully exciting.

"This is me," she said as they reached her building. She slipped off Mark's gloves and handed them back. "Thanks for those."

"My pleasure. Really."

She pursed her lips, watching his breath fog in the winter air, memorizing his face, his handsome nose, dark stubble, that little divot beside his lips when he smiled at her, as he was now.

"You may kiss me good morning, Mark Holly."

"May I?"

She nodded, a dopey grin wrecking any cool, casual façade she might have mustered, had she gotten any real sleep. His lips felt soft and familiar, their kiss rippling through her body, tingling in her fingertips and toes and chest. If only he could kiss her while she donated platelets. He'd get her warmer than any heating pad, keep her pulse higher than the tightest blood pressure cuff. Maybe on the Thursday she had off for vacation, they'd find themselves at the donor center together once again. Maybe side by side, sharing a movie.

She cleared her throat as they separated, cold winding itself around her bare legs. "What book were you reading, that day at the Red Cross? A thick hardcover one?" The question was spurred by both curiosity and a desire to stall, spend a few more seconds in his proximity.

He thought a moment. "Oh. Some book about behavioral disorders. Child psychology stuff. I've been thinking maybe I'd study that someday, when I'm too old and creaky to keep up on the basketball court."

She smiled at that, picturing a forty-year-old Mark in a classroom full of undergrads. *Will I be there to wish him luck on his first day?*

"You better get inside," he said, taking charge and pushing in the foyer door.

She slipped past, fishing her keys from her useless little purse. With a peck on her cheek, he said, "Take care" and stepped outside, the glass door hissing shut on him. She waved, and he waved back, and she headed into the wonderful, miraculous heated hallway.

Inside her unit, Sarge greeted her with an aggressive push against her leg, one that seemed to say, *And where have you been all night, young lady?*

"You wouldn't believe me if I told you." She stowed her keys, kicked off her stiff heels and made a beeline for the bathroom. Soon the shower was steaming, and her skin itched, going from frigid to broiled in an instant. But she adjusted, melted exactly as she had in Mark's embrace.

How easily that thought had crept in. Easy as Mark's smile and laugh and company. Easy as a new romance was *supposed* to feel, no making-things-work, nothing that felt like a second job, an obligation. Natural. Simple. Mark felt like a new friend, one she would happily kiss until her lips fell off. Just Mark plus kissing. Plus some other good stuff that came after all the kissing. If that wasn't simple, she didn't know what was.

But don't go getting your hopes up, she warned herself. So she didn't. She thought about how lovely it would be to go to sleep with the sun just coming up and not have to wake again until Monday morning if she didn't want to.

Sarge brushed her calf again as she emerged from the steamy bathroom, leaving long gray hairs clinging to her damp skin. Ah yes, back to glamorous reality. A reality where she was freshly single, where girlfriends who asked what Kevin got her for Christmas would be set straight and moved to look at her with loving pity. Reality, where her well-meaning mom would tell her to buck up and then list all of Caitlin's cousins who were having such great luck meeting people online, misquoting the names of the websites. *You should join that WebHarmony, honey. That's how Tina met her fiancé, and look how happy they are!*

As she finished pulling on her pajamas, reality intruded further in the form of a muffled tinkling noise. Heart thumping with cautious hope, she padded to the living room and fished her neglected cell phone from her other purse. A text was waiting for her. *It could easily have come last night, some guilty let's-stay-friends message from Kevin.*

Or not. Twenty minutes ago, it was stamped, from a number she'd no longer have to worry about forgetting. She tried to bite back a grin as she opened it, failing grandly.

If this is Caitlin's (spelling?) number, I hope you're enjoying your shower. And I hope maybe you're free sometime for dim sum—extra wasabi, just how your eyeballs like it. I work Saturdays but my Sunday is wide open. Give me a call if you're up for it. Oh and if this isn't Caitlin's number, sorry. Though if you were showering, I still hope you enjoyed it. Go hygiene.

Mark

She smirked and saved his number to her contacts. She would call him—oh, yes, she would—right after she took a nice long nap and ate breakfast or lunch or whatever meal was appropriate by the time she roused. Rest and nourishment would make for a more coherent digital flirtation. She wasn't coy enough to make him wait a whole day, but a few hours, sure. She could play it that cool. Then he'd meet her at the restaurant or her door, and her big old dorky grin would give her away. And she'd be just fine with that.

She waved her phone at Sarge. "Guess who's got a date, fatty fatty fur-pants?"

His tail flicked with disinterest.

"Fine. Be a jerk. But *I* happen to have a date, and no, it's not with Kevin." She wandered to her little kitchen to open a can of cat food. She mashed it up in Sarge's bowl and set it in its place, where he attacked it with an ardor not warranted by Caitlin's romantic news.

"It's with Mark," she said, ignored. "Mark Holly. He donates his platelets and coaches youth sports, and he's a really good kisser. And if I manage to get him back here to watch a movie and mess around, you better not watch us, all creepy and judgy."

Sarge settled on his haunches, tail whipping around behind him.

"You better not pee on his jeans either, like you did to Kevin's that time. Though in retrospect, thank you for that. You've got better taste than I give you credit for. And better intuition than me."

She left Sarge to his gorging, stopping in the bathroom to dry her hair before climbing under the covers. After half a minute's deliberation, she abandoned her cozy cocoon to jog to the front door, to where her coat hung. She returned to bed with the champagne cork, setting it beside her cell on the bedside table.

Just once more, she told herself, grabbing the phone and rereading Mark's text.

One quick message, she decided, abandoning her plan to appear cool in favor of the contact. She hit REPLY and typed a single letter in succession.

Zzzzzzzzzzz...

The moment she hit SEND, Caitlin second-guessed her missive.

That was me zzzzzzzzzing from exhaustion. Not because your text was boring, she typed, and sent it. She read it again. *Not because your text was coping.* Oh, fuck. Stupid predictive spelling.

That should have been boring. Not that your text was boring. Never mind. Dmplesmdyl adm oggusm, she finished, in a flurry of nonsense-typing. SEND. Fine. Done. Dignity surrendered.

She was still lamenting her dopiness when her phone chimed. She opened Mark's message with a little knot in her middle.

Oggusm? it asked. *Didn't we already exchange a couple of those in the nostril of the Orange Line?*

She laughed aloud, middle untying itself. Cute. Awfully cute.

See you Sunday, she wrote. *If all goes well, more oggusms to follow, preferably someplace a bit more civilized.*

She waited for another chime, and Mark didn't disappoint.

See you then. Enjoy your zzzzzzs. Going to snag a few myself, before I have to head to work. xx

She switched off her phone with a smile and wrapped the covers around her tightly. Tight like Mark's coat around her legs, like his arms around her waist. Tight like her chest would feel when she spotted him next, her breath drawn short from hopeful anxiety.

Tight like maybe his hand would feel around hers as they walked back to one of their homes, out of the brisk winter breeze and into the warmth. Tight like he'd hold her in bed, maybe.

Maybe maybe maybe.

Definitely, she corrected, smiling as she drifted off to sleep.

About the Author

Before becoming a writer, Meg worked as a record store bitch, a lousy barista, a decent designer, and an over-enthusiastic penguin handler. She loves writing sexy, character-driven stories about strong-willed men and women who keep each other on their toes...and bring one another to their knees.

Meg now writes full-time and lives north of Boston with her extremely good-natured and permissive husband. When she's not trapped in her own head, she can usually be found in the kitchen, the coffee shop, or jogging around the nearest duck-filled pond.

Meg welcomes reader feedback. E-mail her at meg@megmaguire.com, follow her on Twitter @megguire, or visit her website at www.megmaguire.com.

Look for these titles by *Meg Maguire*

Now Available:

The Reluctant Nude
Trespass
Headstrong

Back on Track

Donna Cummings

Dedication

This book is the perfect example of why I'm in love with Twitter. Someone tweeted a picture of a hot guy on a train one day, generating a lot of interesting commentary from the romance authors in attendance. One wicked tweet led to another, followed by excited brainstorming, and then five of us created stories about strangers falling in love on a train.

Huge thanks to Samantha, Ruthie, Cara and Serena for including me in this project, and for keeping me on track throughout. It was so much fun, and I hope we can collaborate again, on planes and automobiles. (I call dibs on the G6 and Jaguar.)

Also, many thanks to Anne Scott for the wonderful editorial guidance. I'm thrilled to have my words in your hands (and my apologies for all those unnecessary ones you helped me excise).

Lastly, a shout-out to Melissa, beta reader extraordinaire, because I truly appreciate your enthusiasm for all my writing projects, as well as your gentle suggestions for improvement.

Chapter One

"How did you talk me into this again?" Allie Whittaker gave her best friend a mock glare over her wineglass and then took a sip of Riesling. It was fruity and smelled like honeysuckle, and it made her taste buds incredibly happy. "Oh, that's right. Wine."

"Lots of wine." Sandra lifted her half-empty glass in salute. "And don't forget the wonderful scenery."

Allie glanced out the window. They were sitting in the comfiest club chairs on the Napa Valley Wine Train, watching sun-drenched vineyards pass by in a leisurely green blur. "You're right." She sighed with contentment, gazing at the hills in the background, which sheltered the acres of vines in their long, tidy rows. "It really is beautiful."

Sandra laughed. "I was talking about all the gorgeous guys on this train."

"I'd nearly forgotten about that part."

"I sure didn't," Sandra said, patting her perfect blonde hair into place.

Allie spun around in her swivel chair to avoid Sandra's pointed look. Pretend as she might, she knew exactly why she'd been dragged away from working this weekend.

There were clusters of men chatting with women throughout the lounge car, some of them standing in the aisle, others seated at the upholstered booths scattered among the club chairs.

All of them were laughing and drinking wine and clearly having a wonderful time.

Her heart sank at how effortless it seemed for everyone. "I barely remember how to flirt, or mingle, or any of that stuff."

"You do it with your job on a daily basis. Getting people to do what you want is your specialty."

"That's different. Plus, I'm failing at that right now too." All she needed was one more sports figure to say yes, and the celebrity calendar project would be a go. After that, she hoped to use the victory as a springboard to lure more lucrative accounts to her fledgling marketing business.

But right now, it was the hardest "yes" she'd ever gone after.

"You just need to get your mojo back. And this is the perfect place for it. It's only three hours. It's not in our neighborhood." Sandra ticked each item off on her fingers. "If you like someone, great. If not, you never have to see them again."

"Tell me again why I can't sit here and drink wine all afternoon?"

"You're in a dating slump."

Allie sat up, stung by Sandra's brash statement. "It's not a slump. It's just been a little while since I've dated."

"Months." Sandra dragged out the word.

"I've been incredibly busy with work," Allie said defensively. "It's not easy starting up a business. It takes every minute of my time—"

"Slu-ump," she continued in a singsong voice.

"Stop that. This doesn't qualify as a slump. I'm not sure I like that word."

"You're in a slump. I know. I've been in one before." Sandra shuddered. "And slump is a better description than dry spell."

"Oh God, you're right."

Allie took another gulp of wine. She gazed wistfully at the other people laughing and having so much fun. It had been a long time—too long—since she'd felt that carefree. It had been even longer since she'd had fun with someone of the male persuasion.

She was so stingy with her non-work hours, she barely spent time with Sandra, her best friend, which is why she had finally agreed to go on this trip.

Allie settled back in her chair. She deserved an afternoon off. Maybe it would help her figure out how to get her calendar project back on track. And as nerve-wracking as it was, she liked the thought of possibly meeting someone who could take her mind off work, even for a few hours.

"Nobody knows you," Sandra said in a beguiling voice, "so you can be anybody you want. Celebrities do it all the time. Julie in Accounting saw that funny weather guy here once, and hardly anybody recognized him."

"You know, speaking of celebrities, the stadium isn't that far from the train station. Maybe we could swing by there on our way home—"

Sandra gasped. "I can't believe you sometimes."

"I'm not thinking about work. I'm not." God, she was hopeless. "Okay, I was, but I promise I won't think about it for the rest of the afternoon."

"Yeah, right."

"I mean it. Just tell me what I need to do."

"Easy. You walk up to someone who looks cute—"

That snapped her back to reality. "What am I supposed to say?" She leaned toward Sandra, giving her a leer. "Nice wine rack you've got there."

Sandra laughed, waving her away. "We'll come up with something." She thought for a moment. "I know. Say you'll tell them three things about you, and one of them is a lie. They have to figure out which one is which."

Allie frowned. "I'm not sure that will work here—"

"It's a mingles thing. On a train. With unlimited wine." Sandra practically snorted. "The hardest part is going to be staying upright."

Allie giggled, and Sandra joined in after giving her a mock glare. "I meant because of the train bouncing side to side."

"It all sounds so—"

"Meat market-ish?"

"Yeah, I guess that's it," Allie admitted. "A mobile meat market."

"But that's the beauty of it! Like I said, if you don't want to see these people again, that's it. It's not like you're going to bump into them, unless you want to."

"Why does it seem like when you say 'bump into', you mean

something else entirely?"

Sandra chuckled. "That's your mind rolling around in the gutter. This is meant to be fun, so try to view it like that. Don't worry." She gave Allie the patented Sandra warning look. "And do not think about work."

"It's hard not to. I should charge extra for all the worrying I do on my own time."

"Not today."

Allie took a deep breath, ready to take on this challenge. "We're here to have fun, and that's what we're going to do." She clinked her wineglass against Sandra's. "Who should I try first?"

"Ooh, that's the spirit." Sandra perused the potential men, shaking her head occasionally. She finished one sweep of the room and started a second. Just as Allie thought they'd have to survey the occupants of another car, Sandra's face brightened. "Why don't you go chat with him?"

"The one with the baseball cap pulled down low?" Allie sighed. "Why do guys always do that? It makes them all look the same. You never know what hair color they have. Or if they have hair."

Sandra shrugged. "Maybe he's shy."

"Could be." Allie watched him checking out the rest of the passengers, as if he was doing his best to keep his distance from everyone. In a way, she sympathized, since she'd spent most of her life doing the same thing—using work as a shield to keep from getting too involved with anyone. Maybe it would give them something in common, make it easier to talk to him.

And maybe it would be easier to drink her wine and plot how to get her calendar project moving along.

"There's no guarantee this will get me out of my so-called dating slump."

"I know," Sandra said cheerfully "That's why I've got us signed up for stripper-pole lessons next."

Allie bolted out of her chair. "Okay, I can do this."

After all, how hard could it be to tell a couple of lies?

Matt set his wineglass on the table next to him. He didn't want to be here, but his best friend had assured him this was a good distraction, something to keep his mind off the possibility of being sent down to Triple A for rehab.

This might not be the best place to mention that particular word. It meant something entirely different in his profession, though.

The prospect of it didn't make him happy. He'd spent his entire life throwing a baseball faster than anybody else, and he didn't want that taken away from him. What if he got sent down and never made it back to the top?

"I can't believe you talked me into this," Matt grumbled, rubbing his shoulder although it felt fine. "I hardly ever drink wine."

"It's because you need to get out more." Troy didn't look in Matt's direction as he answered. He was too busy checking out a leggy blonde across the aisle who was practically blowing kisses his direction.

"Every time I get out more, I'm bombarded with fans."

That made Troy spin around in his chair. "Oh, boohoo. It's so tough to be the world-famous—"

"Ssh!" Matt said, tugging on his cap. "I'm trying to be incognito today."

"Yeah, yeah. Sorry. I forgot."

Matt smacked his friend's arm. "Liar."

But he was also lying to himself, because as much as he didn't want to deal with overzealous fans every time he left the house, he worried just as much that people wouldn't remember him if he was away from the pitching mound too long. He hated when the season ended before he was ready. And he didn't want to think about it possibly becoming a permanent thing. That was more painful than hurting his arm in the first place.

"I don't know what to do when I'm not playing," Matt admitted.

"I know. It's your identity."

Matt frowned at Troy's cheerful pronouncement. "I know it shouldn't be, and sometimes I wish it wasn't. But right now, when it feels like it might all go away... I could get sent down for rehab and then disappear for good."

Troy snorted. "You're not going to the Bermuda Triangle."

"Hey, players get stuck in the minors all the time. It could happen to me too."

Troy gave Matt his full attention. "Look, we've been friends a long time. Ever since I beat you up in first grade."

"You threw a sucker punch. While I was dutifully eating my PB and J before recess."

"Whatever. What I'm trying to say is, I know you, and I know how important baseball is to you. It has been for a lot of years. It's not going away any time soon, even though it might feel like it right this minute." He stopped to make sure Matt was listening to him. "But no matter what happens, you still need to add something besides baseball to your life."

Matt shook his head, not wanting to hear the words.

"Don't shake me off! I'm not your catcher."

"Thank God," Matt mumbled into his wineglass.

"You know I'm right about this. So try to have some fun today. It's only a few hours. About nine innings' worth, actually. And no, we're not going to stop by the stadium later."

Matt didn't have a chance to retort, because Troy gave him a cheeky grin and shot out of his chair, intent on talking to the blonde he'd been eye-flirting with.

Matt watched him go, envious of Troy's easygoing approach to life's problems. It was one of the reasons they had been friends for so long. Troy's casual manner blended with Matt's more driven methods, making them a great team.

And Troy was probably right—Matt knew he needed a diversion, something to get his mind off his worries about the future. But he wasn't exactly the best companion today. He leaned back in his chair, slowly rotating his arm, trying to convince himself everything would be fine. It had to be.

In the next instant, a goddess sat down in the chair Troy had just vacated. Matt blinked, taking in the shiny black hair she brushed away impatiently and pretty blue eyes that nearly made him forget all his troubles. She wasn't trying to hide any of her curves in the outfit she wore—a bunch of layered T-shirts and snug jeans—and there was something sexy about the toes peeking out from her gold sandals.

Most of all, though, he was struck by her tentative air and the way she inhaled, as if gathering her courage. He couldn't imagine what she had to worry about...

Unless she was about to ask for his autograph.

He nearly groaned at the realization. So much for his attempt to disguise himself.

"Hi," she said brightly.

"Hi," he answered, crossing his arms and tightening his mouth into a forbidding line. If he was lucky, she'd get the hint and leave him to wallow in his misery.

Instead, she smiled and said in a nervous rush, "I'm going to tell you three lies about myself."

Chapter Two

Allie watched his eyes widen, as if she'd just confessed to murdering someone in the dining car and needed his help throwing the body off the train.

"Well, that's a good way to start out," he murmured, chuckling.

She flushed. God, she was worse at this than she thought. "I meant to say I'm going to tell you three things, and one of them will be a lie. You have to figure out which one of them it is."

She took a gulp of the wine she'd brought with her, wishing she could knock back the whole glass. Why had this seemed so easy when she and Sandra had plotted it?

"Okay. I'm game." He smiled, and it was such an unexpectedly warm expression that she instantly relaxed. She could do this. It was a three-hour train ride, and she was capable of loosening up and having some fun. If it gave her a chance to improve her outdated dating skills, all the better.

She wished she had picked someone a little friendlier, though. Despite the killer smile, everything about his body language said "go away".

She would have to pretend he was a potential client and win him over, like she did every day.

"Okay. Here goes." Allie should have asked Sandra to help her out with her spiel, but she'd been too distracted by the thought of avoiding the stripper-pole lessons. "I was born in California, in the back of a taxi."

His lips twitched, but before he could say anything, she plowed on. "I have a bachelor's degree in hotel management, but I've only lived in hotels, never worked in them."

She wracked her brain, trying to think of a lie. Lying didn't come naturally to her, so she was searching for something that could pass as the truth. She couldn't think of anything, and when his fingers started to tap against his chair, she blurted out the first thing that came to mind.

"My name is Allie. Which is short for Allie Kazaam."

She wanted to cringe, but he surprised her by laughing. "Well, it's obvious which one is the lie." He finally uncrossed his arms, adjusting his hat so she could see his eyes were twinkling. "Nobody in California uses taxis."

She joined in his laughter, relieved that he had a sense of humor. This might work out just fine.

"Your turn," Allie said. "Tell me three things. And I can guess which one is the lie."

"Sounds good," he said.

She sat forward, her chin on her fists, waiting for his answers. He picked up a glass filled with a pinot or merlot and spent a minute or two thinking, as if he was trying to decide where to start.

He glanced at her a couple of times, and then a huge smile brightened his face, and Allie could swear his eyes were twinkling again. Or maybe they were sparkling. It was hard to decide. She was definitely mesmerized, so much so that she almost missed what he said next.

"I'm Matt Kearns."

She gasped.

"Have you heard of him?" he asked casually, swirling the wine in his glass while he studied her face.

Heard of him? She'd been trying for months to convince Matt Kearns to pose for her client's celebrity calendar. Unfortunately, his manager made sure she never got to talk to the baseball superstar, even though she had called every couple of weeks to make her pitch. But Allie couldn't let this guy know about that.

Especially since she'd realized about five seconds ago he really was Matt Kearns.

Allie nearly shivered. She'd seen a couple pictures of him when her client had waved around a wish list for the calendar. At the time, she had thought his pics were gorgeous, but now, up close, he was incredible. Handsome in that rugged way that made modern women melt, even when they swore they were immune to such things. His eyes were an intense blue, and his skin was tan from being outside all the time, making his smile seem more brilliant in comparison.

She didn't have the strength to check out the rest of him. Well, except for his long legs encased in skin-tight jeans. And a button-down shirt that covered up what everyone knew was a killer body. Baseball uniforms didn't leave much to the imagination, after all.

Allie needed to fan her face, but she couldn't, because then he would know she was thinking about his physique. She supposed she could blame her red cheeks on the wine she'd consumed.

If only he had agreed to be part of the calendar. It was for a worthy cause—rescued greyhounds. But he'd refused repeatedly, his manager saying Matt wanted to be known for his baseball skills, not the results of his strenuous workouts.

Now here he was, sitting right next to her.

But she was confused. Did he want her to know who he was? Or had he told her his name in the hope she wouldn't have heard of Matt Kearns, and he could hide in plain sight?

She had thought coming up with one lie would be the tricky part of this whole scenario. Now she had to figure out whether to act like she believed him or thought he was lying.

The only thing she knew for sure was she couldn't blow this opportunity. The calendar was way more important than ending her dating slump.

She glanced again at his baseball cap. "Matt Kearns." She tapped a finger against her lips, then tilted her head to the side. "Isn't he the one who catches footballs or something?"

His eyebrows shot up with obvious surprise, and she thought he growled before saying, "He's a pitcher. With one of the best arms in the league. An ERA of 2.92, and three-time winner of the Cy Young award."

Allie covered up a smile. "Oh, him. Now I know who you're talking about. That's a good one. Funny you should mention him." She leaned forward and looked from side to side before whispering, "I dated him for a while."

He choked on his wine. "Seriously? You dated m— I mean, Matt Kearns?"

Allie nodded, watching the puzzlement float across his features.

This was way too much fun, this lying thing. Only now she had a good reason for it. He was trying to stay incognito, keeping a low profile, and who could blame him? It was a funny way of going about it, telling her who he was, but maybe the hiding-in-plain-sight thing worked for him sometimes. Who would expect a famous pitcher to be on the wine train? Allie certainly hadn't.

After his injury-ending season, everyone in the world wanted to know what Matt Kearns was going to do next. If she had anything to say about it, he'd be taking off his shirt to pose for her calendar.

"Wow." Matt blinked, several times. "You dated Matt Kearns."

He couldn't believe it. He'd actually encountered somebody who didn't know him. And to his huge surprise, he'd gotten defensive about it, reeling off his stats like a rookie, trying to impress her rather than worrying about her being a completely delusional fangirl.

He looked at her, enjoying the open, fresh-faced expression she wore. She wasn't anything like the groupies who normally followed him around, trying to get his attention—well, except for that aura of sexiness that surrounded her. Of course he was attracted to her, but that wasn't the interesting part. He couldn't remember the last time he'd been so intrigued.

They were two people enjoying a glass of wine on a leisurely train ride for a few short hours while they told each other lies. Or things that sounded like lies.

He sat back in his chair, relaxed for the first time in weeks. This was going to be a great afternoon.

"So," he said, "what was it like, dating a famous baseball guy?"

Her eyes were filled with mischief when she answered, "I don't kiss and tell."

Great. Now all he could think about was kissing her. He

actually envied the fictional version of himself, the one she'd dated, even though it had never happened.

"He's probably happy about your policy."

Matt leaned forward, tempted to steal a kiss. Her lips were pink and pouty and filled with all kinds of promise.

"So?" Allie prompted.

His heart lurched for a brief second, as if she'd read his mind and was urging him to move things along.

To his relief, she laughed, asking, "How'd you come up with that whopper? Since the Matt Kearns thing was obviously a lie. I'm surprised you started with that one."

He chuckled. "What makes you think it's a lie?"

Allie sat back and covered her mouth—which was a shame, since it was so sexy—and she shook with laughter.

"I dated him, remember?"

He shrugged, trying his best to look sheepish. "Can you blame a guy for trying?"

"Not at all. I loved it." She smiled. "It's going to make it tricky to top that one, though."

"I'll do my best," he answered, lacing his fingers behind his head. He could have outed her right then and there, exposing her falsehood and declaring her the grand champion of the lying game.

But this was fun. *She* was fun. All of a sudden, he was hoping the train ride wouldn't go so fast. It had been too long since he'd had an easy, relaxed time like this.

And he didn't have to hide his identity from her. Hell, he'd come right out and told her who he was. He'd done it as a test, to see how she'd react. He never expected her to say she had dated his imaginary self.

"You can't think of anything else?"

Matt couldn't think about anything but her and the couple of hours he had to enjoy her company, sipping wine and telling tall tales. Who knew those would be the ingredients for a perfect day?

He almost told her he'd lived in fourteen different states, or that he'd shaken the hands of three different US presidents. They were both true, but he decided on something else instead.

"I haven't dated for a while."

She gazed at him, her eyes slightly narrowed as she considered his last statement. It was the truth, but anyone who paid attention to the press surrounding Matt Kearns might consider it a lie. Women found him attractive, and he usually had a beauty accompanying him to his various public appearances. But he didn't have anyone in his life right now. It would be great to have someone like her, a woman who was sexy and funny and easy to be with.

Even if she was lying through her teeth.

"Okay, so you're Matt Kearns." Allie snickered, which seriously ruffled his feathers for some reason. "And you haven't dated for a while." She rolled her eyes. "You've got to come up with at least one non-lie. What else have you got?"

"I find you very intriguing."

That was definitely the truth, and he could see from the look in her eyes that she was both shocked and delighted by that statement. She blushed a little. Which made him want to know more about her.

"I'm not sure you're playing this game the way it was intended," she chided.

"Maybe not. But I'm having a helluva lot of fun with it."

Matt reached across and picked up her hand. She shivered but tried to hide it. He smoothed his thumb over the back of her hand. He was about to suggest they move to one of the tables across the way, needing to be closer than the club chairs permitted, wanting to talk with her more intimately—when his worst nightmare appeared.

A group of college-aged guys came barreling down the carpeted aisle, laughing and chattering. Not the typical wine-train crowd. One of the young men glanced his way and did a double take. Matt shook his head in a silent plea, but he was too late or the guy was too filled with wine to understand the request.

Matt stood up, Allie's hand gripped in his. "Let's go."

Fortunately, she didn't hesitate.

Chapter Three

Allie loved the feel of his hand in hers, and even though he was racing through the train, obviously to duck some overzealous fans, it gave her a chance to check out the rear view of his fantastic physique while he tried to find someplace for them to hide.

"This used to happen all the time when I dated Matt Kearns," she said.

He turned around and grinned. "So you should know all the tricks."

"And evasive maneuvers," she added. "Here."

She saw an alcove that looked like it held luggage, or possibly supplies. He gave her a look that made her think he had more than evasive maneuvers on his brain. She nearly melted on the spot. But to her surprise, he shook his head. Instead, they kept barreling forward, and all she could do was hold on tight and hope he knew where he was going. At some point, they would reach the end of the train, and the fans would catch up to them.

Allie wanted to stay away from them as much as he did. She didn't want them forcing him to confess he really was Matt Kearns. He was having way too much fun *pretending* he was the superstar. And if he confessed, she would have to as well—if she wanted him to be halfway amenable to her pitch about the calendar.

He obviously knew she hadn't dated him, but he seemed to enjoy the subterfuge. Probably because it let him stay incognito, getting to act like a regular guy with a girl who didn't know who the hell Matt Kearns was.

Allie nearly groaned. How had this gotten so complicated? From one simple lie meant to improve her dating prospects? No wonder she wasn't good at this dating stuff. There were way too many elements to keep track of.

Her mind was in such a whirl, she didn't have a chance to pay close attention to where they were going. They passed through the Silverado Car, a Western-themed area complete with steer horns on the red walls. Matt paused and shook his head before continuing forward at what was obviously an easy pace for him, thanks to those long legs of his.

Allie pulled more air into her lungs. It was hard keeping up with a world-class athlete. Clearly, she spent too much time behind her desk. She made a mental note to see about extending her gym membership.

They finally stopped at the Vista Dome Car, a two-level car with a bubble window overhead designed to showcase Napa's finest vineyards and the cloudless blue sky.

"This ought to work," Matt said, his voice filled with satisfaction. He stood in front of the carpeted stairs leading to the dining area, a metal chain draped across the entrance.

Allie tugged at his hand. "The sign says PRIVATE."

"Perfect," he said with a wicked grin. "I could use some private time with you."

Allie's giggle was a soft, sexy sound that had Matt thinking he wouldn't mind a ton of private time, not to mention something with a hell of a lot more privacy. For now, he'd make do with a corner booth in the dining car.

He moved the chain and, still holding Allie's hand, sprinted to the top of the stairs. His heart raced—not from the exertion, but from the thought of spending an uninterrupted hour with the beautiful and sexy liar known as Allie. His thoughts were so far into the future he almost plowed into an imposing maître d', who wore a dark blue suit and a scowl. Matt bit back a curse. He'd bumped chests with umps who were less forbidding.

"Do you have reservations?" the man asked. His tone of voice said he knew the answer was no, and he'd have no qualms about turning the both of them away.

"Uh, no." Matt took off his cap and ran his fingers through his hair. "Well, I usually do, but this time..." He glanced back at Allie, his eyebrows lifting quickly, asking her to play along.

She nodded, making him feel relieved...until she blurted out, "Why don't you tell him you're Matt Kearns?"

He shushed her in case she drew a crowd and pulled her closer to his side. His body had no complaints. Well, just one. There wasn't anything he could do except wish they had someplace else to go. The curves he'd only admired from a distance previously were now pressed against him, and it made him lightheaded, not to mention wracked with desire.

"He's Matt Kearns," Allie said in a stage whisper.

Matt laughed, a theatrical sound, and gave a broad wink to the maître d', who was now examining his face like he expected to have to describe it later to a police sketch artist. Matt leaned in and whispered, "Help a buddy out, can ya? I told her that, you know, as part of my game."

The maître d' looked a little more forbidding. Matt saw out of the corner of his eye that Allie was gesturing to the man. Whatever she did, it seemed to make the man thaw a tiny bit. In fact, Matt could swear his lips lifted in the briefest smile. "No problem. Right this way, sir."

Matt exhaled his relief and turned toward Allie. "What did you do to convince him?"

A slow, sexy smile appeared. "What makes you think I did anything?"

"I saw you doing something. I'm just not sure what it was."

"Then it doesn't matter. If you keep dawdling, we're going to lose our nonexistent reservation."

The food was incredible, the sort of gourmet experience Allie rarely indulged in, since she usually ate takeout in her office while working into the wee hours. And sitting across from the most handsome man she'd ever met, chatting about the luscious scenery while drinking glasses of Napa's finest—well, that was definitely another plus to the whole dating thing.

She'd never think of an amuse-bouche the same way again.

Matt set down his fork. "I want to hear more about you and Matt Kearns."

Allie nearly choked on the roast chicken she'd just put in her mouth.

"I'm starting to think you've got a crush on him," she said as innocently as she could. "Or you're a stalker."

It was his turn to choke. He dabbed at his mouth with the linen napkin. "I'm trying to figure out what was wrong with the man if he let you get away."

"You are too sweet," she answered, enjoying the compliment. And she had to admit, she liked the back-and-forth banter they had going between them. It made it easier to rid herself of the bad-dating mojo than she'd expected.

Of course, lying wasn't the usual cure for relationship woes.

"I mean it," Matt said. "He didn't deserve you."

"Everyone always thinks he's the one who ended things. But he's not. I did."

"I *knew* it. I'll bet he's a selfish blowhard, the kind that's always talking about himself."

"In the third person," she said primly, taking a bite of risotto.

He laughed. "I wouldn't have guessed that about him."

"Oh, there's plenty you wouldn't expect. Believe me."

He leaned forward, his eyes pinning her to the spot. "Too bad you won't kiss and tell. You've got to have some great stories."

"I do." She drew the words out, hoping it would seem as if she was reluctant to spill the beans. She didn't know anything about the man, obviously, so the best she could do was make up outrageous stuff that would keep him entertained. He knew he was hearing lies about himself, but he was such a good sport about it.

"He's probably got all kinds of weird superstitions too," Matt said with a great deal of glee in his voice. "Does he wear mismatched socks that haven't been washed in months? To keep a winning streak alive?"

She shook her head, biting back a smile.

"Really?"

"No. He wore smiley-face footie socks. With a tiny pompon in the back."

He choked but covered it up with a cough into his fist. "Why

217

would he do that?"

"He said it made him happy."

"Those crazy sports stars."

She sighed, theatrically. "I know. It was maddening at times."

"Is it why you broke up with him?"

"No. I didn't mind the socks. They came in handy, actually, when I couldn't find any of my own to wear."

"Ah," he said.

The waiter stopped by before she could add anything else. "Did you save room for dessert?"

"Yes, definitely." Matt pushed his empty plate away. The beef tenderloin had looked scrumptious, but Allie wondered if the tiny portion had come close to filling his stomach—even with the roasted potatoes and green beans added to the mix.

"We've got some wonderful dessert wines." The waiter described an ice wine that sounded luscious and sweet and completely indulgent. Allie opened her mouth to decline, but Matt had other ideas.

"We'll have a bottle of that as well," he said.

"I hope there's a sleeping car. I'll need it after this." Matt's eyes lit up, and Allie couldn't hope to stop the blush. "I mean because of all the good food and wine—"

"Me too," he said, but his eyes were putting the lie to that statement. He had something else in mind, and now she couldn't think of anything but that either. She fussed with the napkin on her lap for a few seconds while she tried to regain her composure.

"So, the reason you broke up with Matt," he prompted.

Allie grabbed the glass of sparkling water, needing a diversionary maneuver. She'd told so many outrageous tales already. Now she was starting to run out of stories to tell. She searched her brain, and it finally came to her.

The perfect opportunity.

"Well, Matt's a great guy. There's no doubt about that."

"That's what I hear."

"But—"

"What?" He seemed nervous, although he tried to hide it. It made her feel bad about deceiving him when he thought she was about to say something awful.

"Well, there was this charity that asked him to participate in their project. And he kept refusing to do it."

"He must have had his reasons." His demeanor got stiffer, but Allie pressed on. It would be easier to broach the subject of him posing for the cover of the calendar later if she could warm him up to the idea of helping out some anonymous charity now.

"I know," she said with a wistful sigh. "But it was for such a good cause."

"I bet he gets asked to do a ton of those things. He can't possibly do all of them. How many of them are even legit, you know?"

"That's exactly what Matt said!"

He smiled, but it was still a little tense. "Well, I can understand how he would feel. Nobody likes to be taken advantage of."

"True." She pushed away the guilt niggling at her. "I was hoping he would discuss it with me." She debated whether to tell him more about how the greyhounds were being rescued since they couldn't race anymore, but she decided she'd done enough for the moment. Plus, she didn't know for certain how much his manager had told him about the project. "Anyway, it caused a bit of friction between us, so I thought it best if we took a break."

He leaned forward, clasping both her hands in his. "So you didn't break up with him? You're just taking a break?"

Now she was getting confused. Especially with his intense blue eyes gazing at her like that. It wasn't easy to tell stories to someone while imbibing alcohol. It was much harder to do when she was telling the stories *about* that someone.

It almost seemed as if he wanted her to have broken up with Matt Kearns so *he* could have a chance with her.

Even though he was Matt Kearns.

She had made herself dizzy. And she might have sprained a brain cell or two.

He was so easygoing, and fun, and completely different than she had expected a baseball superstar would be. Of course, he could be all of those things because he thought she had no idea he was a famous sports star. Although she hated the deception, it was the only way they could truly enjoy each other's company.

Not that he would be thrilled if he ever discovered she'd known all along who he was. She winced at the thought.

"Are you okay?" he asked. "I didn't mean to upset you."

"You didn't. I think I drank a little too much wine."

He smiled. "That's the tricky part of being on a wine train. There's a lot of wine around."

"I'll say."

He slipped out of his side of the booth and came over to sit next to her. Before she could think to protest, he was pressed to her side, his arm wrapped around her protectively.

How could she try to resist that? Why would she want to?

Chapter Four

She had to be the craziest woman he'd ever met, and Matt couldn't get enough of her.

Here she was telling lies about dating Matt Kearns, a man she'd obviously not met, and he'd never been so entertained in his life. The worst part was wanting to convince her that Matt was no good for her so that she'd make their "break" a permanent one, giving him—the real Matt Kearns—a chance to date her.

He had lost his mind. All because of her.

She was doing a great job of making him forget about going down to Triple A to rehab his arm. For the past hour, he hadn't worried at all about his less-than-stellar future. Hell, she was even getting him to rethink his resistance to that charity that wanted him to pose half-naked for its calendar.

Thank goodness she wasn't the one asking him to be in it. There wasn't any way he could tell her no. Not after today.

Allie made him think the future was going to be just fine. No lie. The best part? It felt like they had something special going on between them.

All he had to do was make her forget about that Matt Kearns guy.

"So were you really born in the back of a taxi?"

He felt her stiffen and almost wished he hadn't asked, but there was so much he wanted to know about this woman who had dated the faux Matt Kearns. He still had his arm around her, and he smoothed his fingers down her arm, intending to give comfort. It apparently worked, because she turned toward him and smiled.

"That's something I've never told anyone. It's kind of embarrassing."

"Why?" he said with a laugh. "It's not like it was your fault."

She chuckled, her eyes lighting up with mischief. It made his heart give a thud for some reason. "I was too impatient to get my life moving, I guess."

"It sounds like you did a lot of that. Living in hotels, starting out life in a taxi."

She blushed, but then her chin came up, defiantly. He tucked a strand of her hair behind her ear before pressing his lips to the same spot. A hint of something exotic tickled his nose. She wasn't the type to wear a delicate floral scent. She was bolder, and more than a little outrageous. She was just his type.

He never would have guessed it before today.

She turned her head slightly. "If you keep doing that, I might need you to repeat your question."

He kissed the shell of her ear, treasuring each of the heavy breaths that resulted. "It wasn't really a question. More of a comment."

"Well, that's a relief."

"But I do have another question." He nuzzled her neck, enjoying the way she ducked her head and the goose bumps that instantly appeared on her skin.

"Then stop tickling me. If you expect me to answer."

"This?" He nipped at her earlobe. "This is making you ticklish?"

She shook her head. "No. Not that."

He ran a trail of kisses down the side of her neck. Which was easy to do, since she had tilted her head to the side for that exact purpose. "This makes you ticklish?"

"Yesssss."

Her soft moan of pleasure was almost too much for him to bear. The train wasn't designed for quickie trysts, but he couldn't think about much else. The way she kept responding to his touch—

"You're trying to keep from answering my questions, aren't you?"

"I'm happy to answer your questions. If that's how you want to spend our time together."

"It's not easy to do much more than ask and answer questions."

Her breath caught. "True. So it's my turn."

"Now we're talking," he said.

She laughed. "I meant my turn to ask you some questions."

He grabbed his wineglass, but it was empty. "Damn. There goes that option."

She wrapped her arms around his and squeezed, laughing. "Don't be afraid. I promise I'll be gentle with you."

"So we're telling the truth now, right?"

"Of course!"

He practically snorted at her way-too-innocent expression, her widened eyes intensifying the blue color. In that moment, he didn't care what was true and what wasn't. He was drowning in sensation, having her pressed close against him. She felt real, more real than any woman he'd had near him in ages. He knew they had another hour or two together, and that was it. But he didn't want it to be done.

Which surprised the hell out of him.

He laced his fingers through hers, smoothing his thumb across her skin. "So what did you want to ask me?"

She nibbled on her lip, her eyes narrowing as though she was going through a number of potential questions. His heart bounced around while he wondered what she most wanted to know about him. It made him nervous thinking about being so exposed. Which was ridiculous, because he'd told her all along who he was.

Maybe it was because he wanted her to know *him*. The real Matt, not the superstar one. Or possibly the former superstar Matt. Depending on how things went with his arm.

"Why haven't you dated for a while?"

He nearly did a double take. That wasn't the question he was expecting. And he'd have to take a couple of minutes to come up with an answer.

All of a sudden, it was important that he give her the right information. Not only so they could enjoy the rest of their time together on the train, but so they might have a chance for more

223

time with each other once this excursion was over.

His expression must have been too serious, because she wagged her index finger near his nose. "Don't try to give me any nonsense about the tough life of a baseball superstar, buddy. I know what that's all about."

"True. And whenever I try to forget, you love to remind me about you and Matt Kearns." He scooted closer, placing his arm around her shoulders again. "Although why you would want to think about him when you have me here—I can't figure that one out."

She chuckled, leaning her head against his chest, and he nearly sighed with contentment. "It's as much of a mystery as why you keep bringing him back into our conversation."

He gave her a squeeze, loving the way she squealed in protest. "You're the one who brought him up this time."

"So," she prompted. "Nice way to duck the question, by the way. Now I'm imagining all kinds of horrible possibilities."

"About?" He'd already forgotten the question. Holding her close like this made it hard to think straight.

"About why you haven't dated for a while. Like maybe you live in the basement, with your mother and your maiden aunt."

"I don't have a maiden aunt."

"That's a relief."

"And I've discovered the attic is actually a lot more comfortable."

She giggled. "But it must cramp your style. Dating-wise."

He expelled a huge sigh. "True. Mother hates when I bring women home, and women hate when I bring Mother along on our dates."

She shuddered. "No wonder you pretend to be Matt Kearns when you finally leave the house. I would too."

He buried a laugh in her hair. When was the last time he'd had this much fun?

He finally leaned his head back so he could see her face. He opened his mouth to answer but found himself nervous about abandoning their bantering. It was a nice refuge, their little game of lies. But he also wanted her to know how he truly felt about her, as crazy as it was.

"I haven't dated for a long time because—"

She lifted her eyebrows, waiting for his answer.

"Because it always felt like work. Or an audition or job interview. It wasn't enjoyable." He smoothed his hand down her arm. "I know it sounds crazy, but I haven't had this much fun in about a million years. I—"

Before he could finish, the waiter stopped by their table, bringing their dessert. He was a real pro, not even hesitating when he saw both of them on the same side of the table. He merely set their plates down and silently poured some of the ice wine into a glass for Matt to taste.

Matt removed his arm from around Allie and slid the glass toward her. "I think you know more about this than I do."

She swirled the glass before taking a delicate swallow. A slow smile appeared. "Perfect," she said. The waiter glanced at Matt, and they were both thinking the same thing. Perfect was the best description. Of Allie.

"Enjoy," the waiter said.

"I definitely will," Matt answered.

"I'll make sure you're not disturbed," the waiter added in a voice only Matt could hear, earning himself a *huge* tip.

After the waiter left, Matt watched Allie take a bite of the dessert she'd chosen—something with chocolate, and filled with chocolate, and covered all over the top with chocolate. The pure bliss on her face nearly made him spill his wine. He shifted in his seat, trying to find a comfortable spot, which was next to impossible at that moment. Hell, it was going to be impossible the whole rest of the train ride.

He practically stabbed the dessert in front of him.

"Ooh, that looks good," Allie said. "Can I have some?"

She's talking about the food, he told his body. But it wasn't convinced. Her voice was soft and sensual and filled with desire. He couldn't resist anything she wanted.

With his fork filled to overflowing with the lemon raspberry thing he'd ordered, he lifted it, holding it out toward her.

Her eyes sparked with something fiery and exciting. It made his hand wobble, and it was a wonder he didn't drop the damn thing in his lap. Before he could guess what she might do, Allie leaned forward the tiniest bit, her mouth open.

He inched the cake closer and bit back a groan when her lips sealed themselves around the dessert, her eyes locked on his the entire time. When he slid the fork away, her pink tongue darted out, moistening her lips to catch a stray crumb.

He wanted so much to taste her.

He leaned forward. Allie tilted her head at just the right angle. His breath came faster, waiting for their lips to touch. He couldn't seem to get enough of her. No matter what lying words tumbled out of her mouth, her body's reactions were truthful. He was sure of that.

The train hit a bend in the track, bouncing the car, jolting them off balance. Matt wrapped his arms around Allie to keep her safe, and she fell against him. He heard her sigh right before she looped her hands around his neck and pulled his head toward hers.

He'd been resisting all afternoon and didn't have any more left in him. Her lips were soft and inviting. Normally he would be suspicious of a woman who made the first move, but there was no artifice in Allie. At least, not in the way she kissed him. She seemed tentative, as if she wasn't entirely sure of his response. He tightened his arms, holding the nape of her neck, leaving her with no uncertainty about his feelings.

She moaned, and his body hardened, instantly. He nibbled on her lip, hoping to hear her moan again, even knowing that what he wanted to do right then wasn't possible. He nearly groaned his frustration. "Where can we go?" she asked.

He rested his forehead against hers. His mind was so far gone, he thought she'd taken the words right out of his mouth. As close as they were, it could have been possible, but in the next heartbeat he realized she wanted the same thing he did.

He closed his eyes and placed a kiss at her temple. "There's nowhere to go," he said. "Not unless we jump off the train."

She glanced over his shoulder, looking out the window. "It might work."

He laughed, giving her a squeeze. "It's been a few years since I've had to do the stop, drop and roll routine."

"I'm sure we've had enough wine that we're all loose and easy. That should keep the injuries to a minimum."

He pulled her closer. "Yeah, but as much as I'd like to get us into a room with a bed, I don't want it to be a hospital room."

She kissed him again. "You do have a point." She rubbed against him. "An excellent point actually."

He was tempted to ask how he compared to the infamous Matt Kearns...but then he saw a small crowd hovering nearby, ignoring their waiter's pleas to stay away. One of them had their camera phone trained on him and Allie.

"Oh, hell."

Chapter Five

While Matt practically ran through the train, trying to stay ahead of the devoted fans, Allie couldn't think of anything but him and his chest—his naked chest—with her hands all over it.

It was no longer a matter of seeing him on the cover of a calendar, with her client praising her for accomplishing the impossible. Now it was all about taking care of *her* needs and what she wanted. She could tell herself this was about ditching that dating slump, but it wasn't even close to the truth.

He held her hand as they navigated the narrow aisles. When they reached the connector area between the two cars, she tugged, halting him so she could catch her breath. He turned around, his face creased with concern. She smiled to let him know she was okay, but clearly there was something else giving away her thoughts, because his lips tilted up in a knowing manner. Obviously this happened to him a lot. He was a sports star.

Allie nearly stumbled on that thought. Oh God. Did he think she was another groupie trying to add a celebrity notch to her belt?

No, he couldn't. She'd convinced him she didn't know who he was. She'd told him she dated a version of him that didn't exist.

Now she was making her head spin again.

She probably shouldn't have kissed him. He was a celebrity, and it didn't make sense to kiss him. But kissing rarely involved good sense. That's what made it so delicious.

And his kisses were off-the-charts delicious. The swaying motion of the train bumped her against him once more, and his arms folded around her as if they'd been designed for that reason. She braced her palms against his rock-hard chest, and then, since they were alone, her hands smoothed up his chest to his neck, wrapping around it and pulling him down for another kiss.

He didn't hesitate. The expression on his face was the clue

she'd been looking for: he wanted this as much as she did. His arms pulled her tighter against him, rocking his body against hers in the most wonderful way. Why didn't all first kisses happen on a train? It was the most intriguing sensation. She stepped closer, and his head tilted so he could deepen the kiss.

She kept telling herself this was madness. How could she kiss someone without letting him know she knew who he was? But her brain was overruled.

Thankfully.

Because it was the most intense kiss she'd ever experienced.

Heat radiated off him, intensifying the woodsy, clean scent he wore. Allie could taste a hint of the sweet wine they'd shared earlier. She pulled back to see his expression, and then she leaned in again. His lips tilted into a grin of extreme satisfaction before he claimed her mouth once more.

That gave her the shot of courage she needed. No more second thoughts. How could she get herself back on track if she hesitated at every second? It wasn't her style at work, so she had to adopt that mindset for her personal life too.

Allie smiled up at him and winked. His fingers tightened on hers, a silent signal that he would follow wherever she was going.

She pushed on the door to enter the rail car. It was almost impossible to open, but it finally did, once Matt gave it an extra push with his superstar arms. Allie nearly shivered at the thought of what she was doing. It was crazy. And she so wanted to be crazy right now.

She saw the *Restroom* sign and ducked into the miniscule room with Matt following right behind her. There wasn't time to think twice about her decision. She turned, and his arms were around her. He pulled her into his body, leaning against the door at the same time, and she felt his arousal and his racing heartbeat and knew there was nothing better than this moment.

"Perfect," she murmured, right before she captured his mouth with her own. His lips were soft yet insistent, as if he'd been wanting this as long as she had. She wrapped her arms around his neck, stroking the tendrils of hair that escaped his hat, wishing he wasn't wearing the thing. He must have read her mind, because he snatched it off and tucked it into his back pocket without moving his mouth from hers.

"What a pro," she murmured.

"An all-star," he said with a grin against her lips.

Her heart lurched for a moment. Had he figured out she knew who he was? She didn't think so. How could he?

And why was she worried about that right now? His body was solid everywhere, and it was pressed so tightly against hers, it was leaving a lasting impression.

Matt held her by her waist while he nibbled on her lips, dotting kisses down her neck, following each shiver-inducing kiss with another one until her nipples tightened up, begging for his attention.

He smoothed his hands up her rib cage, his thumbs reaching her breasts first, and Allie's knees nearly buckled. She leaned into his chest, for support and to slow things down.

"Too much?"

"No," she said, although it was. She was feeling too much for someone she had barely met, despite her wild claims to the contrary about their dating history. Even worse, she had thought she could be happy with this brief moment, but all of a sudden she wanted more with him. Which was impossible.

How had this ever seemed like a good idea?

While her mind raced, she moved her fingertips across his chest, oddly soothed by the motion.

"God, that feels good."

She lifted her head at his words. His eyes were closed, but there was no mistaking the bliss on his face. She unfastened the top button of his shirt with shaking fingers. His eyes shot open. He watched her the entire time she unbuttoned his shirt, exciting her with the way his chest rose and fell as he waited for her to touch his bared skin.

She pulled the shirt open. He was beautiful. She almost sighed at the perfection on view. It was next to impossible to tear her eyes away from that lovely spot at the base of his throat.

"If you don't put your hands on me pretty soon—"

Allie pressed a kiss to his chest. He sucked in his breath. She followed that by placing her palms flat against the smoothest skin she'd ever touched.

She couldn't stop the sigh. He couldn't, either.

She had to touch every bit of him. Her fingertips slid across his skin, and she finally realized he was doing the same to her, only on the outside of her clothing.

She stopped, stepping back a few steps.

"No!"

"I'm leveling the playing field," she said, reaching for the hem of her shirt. She loved the way his eyes lit up at that—until he realized it was the first of several she wore. He helped her tug the rest of them over her head in one quick swoop and started to toss them behind her.

"Not on the floor!" Allie grabbed the T-shirts just in time. "I have to wear these again."

"That's a real shame." His thumbs caressed the lacy bra, pulling it aside so his mouth hovered over her bare nipples.

Her head dropped back, and she somehow tucked the shirts into the back of her waistband. Her lower body rubbed against him slowly. He growled and slid his hand down to her butt, pulling her tighter against him.

Thank God the room was so small. They had to stay close to each other, making it absolutely perfect. She didn't know how she was going to stop. In fact, her hands were at the top button of his jeans, and she was trying to figure out how to shimmy out of hers...

The door handle rattled. Someone pounded on the door behind Matt.

They both caught their breath at the same time. His widened eyes were filled with "You have got to be kidding me." Allie nearly laughed out loud. Instead, she buried her face in his chest. He sighed and dropped his head against the door in resignation. He also slid his hand up into her hair, stroking it while they both silently prayed for the intruder to leave—and quickly.

The door handle shook again. "Maybe it's stuck," they heard

the man say to someone.

Matt leaned down to whisper in her ear. "It sounds like he's going to knock down the door pretty soon."

"There's not enough room in here for anyone else," she answered with a giggle.

He kissed her, a short, hot, sweet blast that made her want to throttle whoever was outside.

Matt yelled, "It's out of order. We're, uh, doing some maintenance in here right now."

"Oh," the man answered, clearly befuddled. "That's what they said in the last car."

Allie snickered, especially when Matt gave her a wink. "Sorry for the inconvenience," he added.

Allie couldn't believe it. Talk about a major inconvenience. She was tempted to say something to the intruder, but Matt stopped her with another kiss.

Boy was she going to miss these after today.

Matt couldn't stop kissing her. He kept telling himself it didn't make sense to feel attracted to this crazy woman with the big blue eyes and the whopping huge lies. He couldn't listen to logic, though, not when his body was convincing him she was perfect for him. She fit into his arms as if she had been designed specifically for them. Her skin was warm wherever he touched it, and it soothed him at the same time it made him fantasize about having her completely bare.

He nearly lost his balance at that thought.

If it hadn't been for the guy outside putting the brakes on things, Matt knew they would have been headed toward nakedness.

He pulled away in an effort to get his head on straight, but that was nearly impossible when she mewed in protest, kissing him again. His heart pounded. Maybe he could track down the waiter to see if the guy knew of someplace private where Matt could be alone with Allie, exploring all kinds of passion for the next hour or two. He would have willingly given up the next few years of his contract just to be inside her, hearing her moan his name over and over.

But in the next instant he realized that wouldn't be enough for him. Allie deserved more than an impromptu hookup in an office or supply closet. Not that he would have regretted it—not for a minute. But he couldn't take the chance that it might end up in the tabloids, turning it into something sordid when it was anything but.

Allie would have a real Matt Kearns story to add to her fake ones, but it wouldn't be at all pleasant for her to be subjected to that kind of scrutiny.

He wasn't sure what to do next. He wanted to keep seeing her when the train trip came to an end. She tantalized him in so many ways, and not just with her kisses and her passionate responses. He couldn't wait to see what she would say, or do, next. There had never been a woman like her in his life.

There was only one thing he knew for sure. He wasn't about to let her go like that fool Matt Kearns had.

Chapter Six

"I've always wondered what it would be like to be kissed on the caboose," Allie said.

She would have stayed in their tiny hideaway forever, and it had definitely seemed like Matt had wanted to keep things moving along too. But to her surprise and disappointment, he had suggested they get some fresh air. They'd put their clothing to rights, taking as long as possible in the process, and then meandered through the train until they'd reached the end.

Her heart nearly sank at that thought. Fortunately, the fresh air of the open observation deck came with a lot of fresh kisses.

She squirmed closer to Matt, relishing his warmth while the breeze from the moving train did its best to cool them down. No chance of that happening while Matt's gentle laugh warmed her insides. And that wasn't counting the places where his talented hands were touching her.

"I love kissing you on the caboose." He leaned forward, ready to deliver another scorching one to add to the million other kisses they'd shared.

He could make a girl completely forget her own name. As well as his name—

"Dude! It's Matt Kearns."

Allie froze for a moment. She blinked, trying to figure out why someone was reminding her of Matt's name. In the next instant, she felt Matt's shoulders sag with undeniable defeat.

They'd been discovered.

There was no place left to escape. The only exit was blocked by several excited young men wearing baseball caps that matched Matt's. The logo on their T-shirts left no doubt of who their idol was, either. They'd finally tracked their quarry, and they weren't about to let him get away without talking to him.

Allie heard Matt sigh, and she wanted to cry out in protest that she and Matt couldn't have this moment to themselves. He gave her an apologetic look and straightened, turning on that megawatt smile, ready to confess who he was—and probably sign autographs for the last available hour of the excursion. He did his best to block Allie from their view, keeping their attention focused on him.

She admired him for being such a pro. She could only imagine what it took to constantly be in the spotlight. The poor man was hounded no matter what he tried to do. He hadn't even been safe locked in a bathroom.

In the back of her mind, she realized how much worse it would be if he was part of a publicity campaign based on him taking his shirt off, and she could understand why he'd refused. She was actually having second thoughts about sharing that magnificent bare chest with the rest of the world. Even if it was for charity.

But Matt was a first-class kind of guy. He knew they had no way out of the situation, so he made the best of it. His fans were beside themselves with glee, cackling and slapping hands as they congratulated themselves on cornering their favorite baseball player.

"Can you believe it?" one of them crowed. "It's Matt freakin' Kearns."

Matt's smile was forced, but it still counted as a smile. "Yeah, I get that all the time, actually."

He gave Allie a quick wink. If he was willing to try to brazen this out, she would do everything she could to make it work.

Allie stepped around Matt and gaped at the fans. "Ohmygod, you think *this* is Matt Kearns?" She started to laugh hard, holding her sides. She noticed the young men giving her a cocky look, so she knew she'd have to up her game. "Look at him. The *real* Matt Kearns is way hotter."

Matt gasped behind her.

"Seriously?" one of the young men said, clearly not believing her.

"Oh, yeah." She fanned her face. "Like, blazing hot. Scorch. Ing."

Matt said in a wry voice, "I thought you didn't kiss and tell."

She flushed. "I'm not. I don't. I'm merely telling them what should be obvious to anybody who knows Matt Kearns."

He cleared his throat, but it was possible he was covering up a laugh.

"Put the two of you side by side," she continued, "and it's going to be completely obvious who's hotter."

"It sure looks like him," another young man said, his voice filled with doubt. At least he'd dropped the camera phone to his side. She was making progress.

"That's because you've got your wine goggles on. Heck, you probably thought I was that girl from that TV show."

"I told you it wasn't her!" one of the men hissed. He received a punch in the arm from his buddy.

"I still think he looks like him," the most stubborn of them said. "Exactly like him."

"Well, of course he looks similar," Allie said with a snort. "If you looked like Matt Kearns, wouldn't you play that up?"

The young men stared at each other while they puzzled that out and then grinned in unison. "Yeah, we totally would."

To ensure they were convinced, Allie placed her hand on Matt's biceps, squeezing the world-famous pitching arm. She nearly quit breathing at the thought of how wonderful his arms had felt around her. All she had to do was wrap up this fiasco, and they could get back to those delicious kisses.

"Does this arm look like it could throw a baseball? Let alone a ninety-eight-mile-per-hour fastball straight across the plate?" She rolled her eyes. "There's no way anyone would put this man half-naked on a beefcake calendar, either."

The young men looked sheepish. "Hey, man, we're so sorry."

"I don't know how we could have made that mistake."

"Hope you don't mind."

"No worries." Matt gave her a funny look. She'd have to apologize to him afterward about disparaging his physique. She

236

truly had no complaints about it, but she might have gone a little overboard trying to get his fans to leave him alone. Hopefully he'd understand her reasons.

"We really thought—"

"I understand. I'm a fan of his too." He smiled. "In fact, it happens so much, one of these days I'm gonna say I *am* Matt Kearns."

Allie turned away to keep from laughing. He was such a good sport. He chatted with the guys for several minutes about baseball stuff and what they would have told Matt if he'd actually been Matt.

"Yeah, you're right," Matt said. "Once he gets done with rehab, he'll no doubt be ready for the new season. I'm sure he's gonna be great."

The whole encounter earned him a place in the young men's affections that had previously been taken up by their hero worship of Matt Kearns. There was a lot of hand-slapping and high-fiving, and then Allie and Matt were alone again.

At last.

Allie could finally exhale. She'd saved Matt from unwanted publicity—and saved herself from being plastered in the tabloids, which wouldn't do much to further her cause with him or the charity calendar.

They'd dodged a huge bullet with their quick thinking. Maybe they could track down some celebratory champagne. She stepped closer to Matt, ready to resume their interrupted kissing.

She was in for a big shock.

Matt's blue eyes were sparkling, only this time it wasn't from amusement or desire. She would definitely call his expression an accusing one.

"You knew who I was all along!"

Matt stared at her, his chest tight with anger and disappointment. "You lied to me!"

"And you lied to me!"

"I told the truth."

"But you told it like it was a lie," she answered defiantly, her fists on her hips.

She didn't back down from his anger, which he admired in a way, but he was frustrated and more than a little hurt. It was hard to accept that she had pretended not to know him in order to get closer—merely so she could get what she wanted from him.

He had been so sure she wasn't like everyone else. That what they had going between them was different.

Matt snorted. "You lied about knowing me."

"No, I just didn't let you know I knew who you were."

Her cheeks were flushed the same way they'd been when they'd kissed. She still tempted him. Had she also lied about her attraction to him? Was that part of her act? He shook his head, as much at his own weakness as her deception. Maybe he'd never learn. And that angered him even more.

"That's a lie of omission," he said.

"And that's an oxymoron. How can I lie if I'm not saying anything?"

"I'm not sure." He wanted to stomp around, but there wasn't any room on the small metal platform, which increased his aggravation. "You said you'd dated me. That was a lie."

"And you knew it was a lie. Because we've never dated."

He threw his hands up in the air. She was maddening. It was impossible to have a regular argument with her.

Allie inhaled deeply, and just like the first time she'd sat down next to him, it looked like she was gathering her courage. But he wasn't about to give her a chance to duck the question. Or utter another falsehood.

"You're the one who's been calling my manager about posing for that calendar. That's how you knew about it."

She nodded, biting her lip.

This time he felt like he'd been punched. He shrugged, acting as though it was no big deal. But it bothered him more than he expected. How had he been so wrong about her?

"I truly didn't know it was you when I came over to talk to you." Her eyes pleaded with him to have faith in her.

"That's hard to believe," he said. "In fact, almost everything you say is hard to believe."

Her cheeks reddened, and he felt a twinge at causing her distress.

"I know," she said. "And I apologize for that. But I thought you might feel more comfortable if you didn't have to be, well, *you*, for a few hours."

He stopped his pacing. She was right about that.

They'd had a chance to get to know each other without his celebrity getting in the way. In fact, the only time it had caused any problems was when he'd had to duck his fans. And that had led to some sizzling kisses. His body reacted to the thought of the passion they could be exploring—once they figured out what the truth was and who was telling lies.

"Why is this damn calendar so important to you?"

Her chin jutted out. "It will give my marketing company a huge boost. I've recently started my own business, and I work a million hours a day on it. This is actually the first time I took a break from work—"

"Only you were working me."

She flushed. "That's not fair. That's not what I was doing. I haven't enjoyed myself like that in years."

He desperately wanted to believe her, but he didn't know if he could. He had to sort out his thoughts. How had one woman scrambled his brain like this, in less time than it took for him to finish nine innings? He needed somebody to decipher all the signals he was getting, only there wasn't a coach on the sidelines telling him what to do.

"I've got to go," he finally said.

Chapter Seven

Matt found Troy sitting in the midst of several lovely females, and damn if the guy wasn't preening. Normally he'd tease his friend about it, but he had other things on his mind.

"Hey, buddy," Matt said. "Can I steal you for a minute?"

Troy's shoulders slumped until he saw the expression on Matt's face. "Sure. No problem." He jumped out of his chair and swung both index fingers toward the women. "Ladies, I'll be right back. Don't go anywhere."

They all giggled at his witticism and poured more wine for each other.

"What's up?" Troy asked as Matt walked them to some chairs a fair distance away. "Are you having a good time?"

"Yeah. I was. But—" He plopped down into the club chair.

Troy sat on the edge of his, impatient. "But what?"

"I met this woman. She's sexy and funny, and I can't remember when I've had such a great time."

"High five, man. So how's that a problem?" Troy's forehead wrinkled as he tried to figure that one out.

"She lied to me."

Troy shrugged. "About what? She's got fourteen kids? Two husbands? A prison record?"

Matt laughed. "No, she lied about dating...well, me."

"Now I'm totally confused. Did you date her?"

"No! That's just it. She came over to me and said she was going to tell me three things and one of them would be a lie." Matt chuckled as he remembered her approaching him. "Actually, she started out saying it would be three lies. She messed the whole thing up, and it was pretty cute—"

"So she told you right off the bat she was going to lie to you."

Troy nodded slowly, considering that. "I might have to steal that one for the future. Sounds like a good strategy."

"Would you listen for a minute?"

"I am listening. So she said she was going to lie, and then apparently she did. Wait. She lied and said she'd dated you."

"Well, not me exactly. Matt Kearns."

Troy shook his head. "You know you're Matt Kearns, right?"

Matt laughed again. The whole thing was absurd. And the more he tried to explain it, the more outlandish it got. It would probably make more sense if he had another glass of wine. Or a whole damn bottle.

"I told her I was Matt Kearns, and that's when she said she had dated me. Him. You know what I mean."

"Hell, she sounds like fun. Did you get her number? I'd love to give her a call."

Matt's blood pressure doubled. "Don't even think about it. I told you I like her. A lot. I'm trying to sort my thoughts out here."

"What's to sort out? She knew who you were—"

"Because she's the one who's been trying to get me to pose for that calendar!"

"Okay. Well, it shows she's smart too. She knows who you are, but she keeps it to herself, instead of busting your balls about refusing to do the calendar."

"True."

He hadn't considered that. The minute he'd mentioned his name, Allie could have started promoting her calendar, but she hadn't said a word about it.

"And she knows how to have fun," Troy continued with a boisterous laugh, "because damn, she must have gotten a kick out of telling you what it was like to date you."

"Actually, she wouldn't give details. She doesn't kiss and tell. I was starting to get jealous of myself."

"Which makes her perfect for you. You know she won't be running to the tabloids."

Matt's heart lurched. Troy was right. Allie had done everything possible to keep the fans away, convincing them he wasn't the baseball superstar they'd been following all day long.

When he'd confronted her about why she hadn't let on that she knew who he was, she hadn't tried to deny it. She'd explained why the calendar was so important to her. He knew what it was like to make work paramount. But instead of commiserating with her, he had blasted her for doing the exact same thing he did all the time.

Matt slumped down in his chair. "I'm such an ass."

Troy raised his fists in the air. "Finally! Somebody believes me."

"How do I make this right?" Matt frowned. "I haven't messed this up, have I?"

"You can't be serious. This is when you're at your best, when the pressure is on and nobody thinks you can pull out a win."

Matt gave him a look.

"Except for me," Troy rushed to add. "You know I always bet on you to win." He grinned. "Because you always do."

"I can't believe I messed this up."

Allie took another sip of wine, although she'd had way too much already. She'd never consumed so much wine in a three-hour period before. Of course, she'd never had reason to. Today, she'd had excellent reasons. First, she'd been hanging out with the sexy hunk Matt. Now she was recovering from the sexy hunk Matt.

After this fiasco, she might swear off wine forever.

"You didn't mess up anything," Sandra said. "You actually achieved what you set out to do."

"I was trying to get out of a dating slump. I didn't set out to derail my business and smash headlong into heartbreak."

Sandra rolled her eyes. "Stop being such a drama queen. Although you're doing a great job of it."

Allie laid her forehead on the table. "Great. I've tried to end my dating losing streak and in the process I acquired skills for my next career."

"Look at me."

Allie shook her head, although it felt funny with the tablecloth rubbing against her forehead. She finally lifted her head, and Sandra reached over to smooth down her bangs.

"Your goal was to end your dating slump, remember?"

"True. Although it feels like I ended it by starting another one." She sighed. "That wasn't exactly what I had in mind."

"Did you have fun?"

"Yes. I haven't laughed that much, or kissed that much, in so long. Only now I'm going to miss it. And—" She held up a hand to hold off a protest so she could finish the thought before it escaped her. "And now I'm going to hold everyone up to the Matt Kearns standard."

"The real one or the fake one?"

Allie frowned. "What do you mean?"

"I mean, is the Matt you spent the afternoon with the one you're going to compare everyone to? Or is it going to be the one you think did everything wrong?"

She had to think about that for a while. "He didn't really do anything wrong," Allie admitted. "Not that I did either. I started that lie thing before I realized who he was, and when I did realize, I didn't want things to get uncomfortable. I mean, I would have been tongue-tied if I'd thought he knew I knew who he was."

"So you liked the real Matt."

"I think that was the fake Matt."

"Now I'm confused. Who's the real Matt?"

"Both of them," she said. "I liked the one I made up, and the one I told about the fake one. I'm going to miss both Matts."

There was so much to miss. The sexy smile, the irresistible kisses, the way he playfully went along with all of her crazy comments about the man he supposedly was impersonating. Until he'd accused her of lying for the wrong reason.

"You don't have to," Sandra said.

Allie blinked. "I don't have to what?"

"You don't have to miss them. You could tell them—him—how you feel."

Her stomach clenched, remembering the look on Matt's face before he'd left. It had been a mixture of hurt and disillusionment, and she was sorry she'd put it there. "I know what you're saying, but I'm pretty sure he wouldn't listen. He thinks I only wanted to get him to pose for the calendar. And I did, at first, but then I was having so much fun, I completely forgot about the damn thing."

Sandra's shocked expression was priceless.

"I know! Me, not thinking about work. But he has no reason to believe me. Why would he, when I lied about everything else that involved him?" She felt like moaning or crying or leaping off the speeding train. Any of those would feel better than the ache in her chest.

"It's possible he won't believe you," Sandra agreed. "But you don't know for sure. Why did you keep calling his manager about the calendar when you kept hearing 'no'?"

"Because I'm stubborn?"

Sandra laughed. "Or because you're willing to pursue something you believe in."

Allie stopped, the wineglass halfway to her mouth. Her heart thudded painfully while she thought about explaining her feelings to Matt. But she couldn't do it. It had been tough enough when he'd stalked away the first time. She wasn't ready to experience rejection again, not this soon. The prospect made a dating slump seem downright comfortable.

But deep down, she knew Sandra was right. Even if she failed with Matt, she had to try at least once more. She had to let him know how she felt, how he'd helped her see she needed to realign her priorities in life. It might not matter to him, but she could go home knowing she'd done her best to make things right.

Most importantly, she had to let Matt know she wouldn't be bothering him anymore about the calendar. After spending one afternoon with him, she understood why he wouldn't want all the extra attention it would bring. She couldn't bear for him to deal with that on her account. And she was pretty sure the rescued greyhounds would understand too.

There were lots of other ways to get her fledgling business off the ground, but there was only one man her heart wanted. All she had to do was catch him before he left the train.

She stood and grinned at Sandra. "Cancel those stripper-pole lessons. We won't be needing them."

Matt strode toward the car where he'd last seen Allie. He was in a hurry, but unfortunately so was everyone else. The train was slowing down as it got closer to the station, and the passengers had started to mill around, standing in the aisle during the last minutes of the excursion.

Matt shifted impatiently, trying not to bump into anyone. He had to reach Allie before she left the train. He'd overreacted, too willing to believe she had spent their time together just to get him to do her calendar. It had been a knee-jerk response, one based on years of experience, and he hoped she'd understand when he explained why he'd reacted so harshly.

He also hoped she'd accept his apology—as well as his offer to take her to dinner that evening. The thought of seeing her again made him impatient, and he almost plowed into a crowd of people trying to get past him.

"Excuse me." He stepped aside, smiling, but the delay nearly killed him. He couldn't wait to get to know more about Allie. Hell, he couldn't wait to have her in his arms again, kissing her, listening to any sweet lie she wanted to tell him.

He was so wrapped up in his thoughts of her, he didn't hear the buzz of excited whispers until it was too late.

"Oh, hell," he muttered, tugging at the bill of his cap. He wished Allie was there to deflect the attention, like she had with the last bunch of fans.

"You're Matt Kearns, aren't you?" The young woman's eyes struggled to focus, but her attention was trained squarely on him.

"I get that a lot," he said automatically.

He almost laughed at how easily the lie came to his lips. And he had the audacity to give Allie a hard time for lying? He was a natural at it too.

"It's him," the woman's friend said, her voice rising with excitement. "I'm pretty sure it is."

He ducked his head and tried to slide past them, needing to get to Allie, but the train stopped abruptly. The first woman's arms flailed as she tried to catch her balance, which she finally did—by throwing herself against Matt. His arms wrapped around her instinctively to keep them both from falling and knocking the rest of the passengers down like dominoes.

The woman was busty, and attractive in an overly made-up way, but she wasn't Allie. And Allie was the only woman on his mind right then. The only woman he wanted wrapped around him like a second skin.

He grinned with genuine pleasure at that thought.

"Are you okay?" he asked the woman. She nodded but didn't take her arms away from him. Matt glanced up, looking for a way out of the tangle he was in. A sharp whistle blast announced their arrival at the station, and he knew he didn't have much time left before everyone left the train.

He had to find Allie.

He finally saw her—as well as her dismayed expression—right before she turned and fled.

Chapter Eight

Allie deleted another message from Matt's manager. She felt bad about ignoring his calls for the past month, but she wanted to tell Matt in person that she had changed direction on the calendar. First, though, she'd had to wait to hear from her client that they approved the change. Thankfully, they had, that very morning.

She picked up the tickets to the exhibition game—great seats, right behind home plate—and wondered if Matt wanted her to be there tonight when he showed the world that his arm was in perfect shape. Or maybe he'd meant for her to raffle them off to help out her business. Either way, sending them to her had been a thoughtful gesture. She would be sure to thank him when she finally talked to him.

Her heart skipped at that thought, but she reminded herself why it was important to keep things between them on a professional level.

For a few fleeting minutes at the end of the train ride, it had seemed like a good idea to tell Matt how she felt about him—until she saw the woman flinging herself at him, professing her adoration. Luckily, Allie had escaped the train before doing something similar, mortally embarrassing herself and Matt.

The way he had smiled with that woman in his arms—it had been exactly how he'd smiled at her. That's what it had taken to make Allie understand she'd read too much into their time together.

As much as she'd loved being with Matt, they'd been talking past each other the entire time on the train. It wasn't possible to build a relationship on a foundation of so many lies.

Still, the afternoon had served its intended purpose. It had been a fun diversion, as well as a much-needed reminder of why business shouldn't always be given top priority. In time, she would quit thinking about Matt and his kisses. Her feelings for him would eventually fade.

And one day she might even believe all the lies she had just told herself.

Allie picked up her phone, dialing Matt's manager to see if he could arrange a meeting with Matt. She hadn't gotten past the first three numbers when she heard a commotion outside her office door. There was a definite buzz of excited chatter, along with the sound of other office doors in the hallway opening. While her business was improving every day, it still wasn't well-known enough to have that kind of activity.

The knock at the door was determined. She walked calmly to open it, telling herself it was probably the UPS man, or the mailman, or any man except the one she really wanted to see.

She gripped the knob and swung the door open.

Matt stood there, smiling, looking sexier and more delicious than he should have. Allie wanted to throw her arms around him and kiss him, but she managed to refrain. He'd probably had to fend off several women on his short walk from the parking lot.

"Matt, it's so good to see you." She held out her hand, doing her best to stay professional, though it nearly killed her.

A flash of confusion crossed his features, but it was quickly replaced by something that looked like resolve. He took her hand. Instead of giving it a brisk shake, he held it, smoothing his thumb over her skin. The same way he'd done on the train. She kept from shivering only through sheer force of will.

"It's great to see you, Allie."

"I'm so glad you're back from Triple A. And better than ever, according to the papers."

His eyes widened. She shouldn't have let him know she'd been following the news reports about him. But how could she resist? Despite her best intentions—and her earlier self-deception—she couldn't think about anything but him. She'd tried to end her dating slump, and instead she was in a Matt slump. There was no simple recovery from that one. Not that he needed to know that.

"Yeah, I'm doing great," he said.

"I'm glad to hear it. Oh, and thanks for the tickets. That was so generous of you."

"I was hoping you would be at the game, but I decided it might be a good idea to ask you in person." He winked, a simple gesture that nearly melted Allie on the spot. "Your phone doesn't seem to be working."

"Oh, that. Well." She couldn't think of a suitable lie. In fact, she might never be able to tell a good whopper again, thanks to the wine-train debacle. "That's because—"

"I miss you, Allie. I think about you all the time."

Her heart lodged in her throat. Maybe she hadn't been wrong on the train—maybe they did have something real between them, something special. Before she could explore that, or hope for a future between them, she had to let him know a few truths, including what she'd been too afraid to admit on the train.

A cough in the hallway snapped her back to the present.

Each time she'd fantasized about this moment, she had been glib and eloquent, and it was only her and Matt standing there.

In reality, she was speechless, and every neighboring business owner was leaning forward to get a better look at them.

Allie wasn't about to let the public in on this private moment. She gave a breezy wave of her fingers to the onlookers and pulled Matt into her office, closing the door behind him. He leaned against it, smiling in the same sexy way he had in the train restroom. She shook that image off before it could derail her.

"Matt, I need to be perfectly honest with you." She inhaled, gathering her courage before it could skitter away. "I don't want you to do the calendar."

His eyebrows shot up. "I think I liked it better when you were lying."

She laughed, nervously. "I thought you'd be glad to know I won't be hounding you anymore."

To her surprise, he didn't seem all that happy with her announcement. "So how will this affect your business? Not doing the calendar, I mean. I want to help you make it a success, any way I can."

She gnawed on her lip, debating how to tell him of her new plans.

"Do you have somebody else?" He gave her a mock glare and pushed away from the door. "It's not that Matt Kearns guy, is it? I'll rip this shirt off right now and audition if I need to. I've been practicing all kinds of sexy poses."

Talk about a tempting offer. It made her remember those incredible moments with his bare chest, and his kisses, and—she had to get her thoughts back on track, and soon.

Matt took her hands in his. "Allie, I needed to see you. So I could tell you how much I missed you." He lifted her fingers to his lips. "And how crazy I am about you."

Allie's heart nearly stopped. So much for trying to think clearly after the curveball he'd just thrown her way.

"I hated how we left things," he added. "I'd just figured out what a complete ass I'd been, but I couldn't get back to tell you before you left."

"When I saw you with that woman—"

He sagged. "I was afraid you'd seen that, and I wanted to explain."

Allie shook her head. "You don't have to."

"Yes, I do. I want to. That happens to me all the time. I've kind of gotten used to it. But after spending that day with you, it made me realize how much you tried to keep all of it away from me. First, by pretending you didn't know me. And later, when you made sure the college boys thought I was an imposter. I accused you of using me for your own ends, but you weren't."

"But I was," she protested. "Maybe not in quite the same way, and it was for a charitable cause. But even after I saw what you go through, I still wanted to persuade you to do the calendar."

"You were actually shielding me. Giving me privacy so we could get to know each other, like regular people do."

"I dragged you into a bathroom so we could make out!"

"See what I mean? You're resourceful too. Only I was so used to being defensive, I didn't see it at first."

"Probably because I was lying about dating you. That couldn't have helped much."

He laughed and pulled her closer. Her breath hitched, though she tried to hide her attraction.

That was one lie she couldn't tell, though. Not anymore. Her body wouldn't let her.

"I didn't know what to do when you wouldn't return any calls." Matt's voice was definitely regretful. "I was stuck in Triple A until my arm was completely rehabbed. The trainer expected me to be there at least a couple of months, but he didn't know how motivated I was to get back here."

"Matt—"

He wrapped his arms around her waist. "I just want to say one thing."

"Fine." Allie put her fingers against his lips. "But not until I'm finished. I have three things to tell you." She inhaled, gathering her courage once more.

"I don't want this to be over," Matt blurted. "I want to see you again. Tonight. And tomorrow. And the next day after that."

"That's the third thing I was going to say."

"What's the second thing?"

She tilted her head back so she could see into his eyes, and Matt took the opportunity to kiss her, a succession of sweet, hot kisses the entire length of her throat. She couldn't hope to stop the shivers, or the lustful response of her body. "Stop," she whispered, "or I won't be able to finish what I have to say. It's important."

"Okay," he said, not even trying to halt the kisses. "I can do that."

"Liar."

She felt his grin against her throat. "Takes one to know one."

"I have another idea for raising money to rescue the greyhounds," she breathed in between his kisses. "Something that might appeal to you, I hope. What would you think about a celebrity auction?"

Matt lifted his head, incredulous. "You'd rather sell me in the flesh than have women ogling my picture?"

"No! Not that kind of auction. Which is actually the second

thing I want to tell you. I understand now how tricky it is to have a life separate from your baseball existence, and baring your pecs doesn't help with that."

"So if it's not a bachelor thing, what is it?"

"I was thinking of an event where your fans could bid to spend an afternoon with you. On the wine train."

"Hmm."

She wasn't sure if that was an "I'll consider it" or "I hate it" kind of sound. She had to erase any doubts he had about her motives. "It's okay if you don't like it. I understand. Honestly, I do. I have no intention of making things worse for you—"

"Us," he amended, giving her nose a kiss. "I really like that idea. It would give fans a chance to talk baseball, up close and personal. And I could enjoy it too. It could be a lot of fun."

Allie sighed her relief. "And we could have you pose for some pictures—with your shirt on, of course."

Matt winked. "Of course."

"I'd much rather you be the face—not the chest—of the charity's fund-raising efforts."

He laughed and gave her a squeeze. "Go ahead and say it. You want to keep me all to yourself."

"I cannot tell a lie." She sighed, wrapping her arms around his neck. "Which is the final, most important thing I want to say. I'm completely crazy about you."

Matt leaned down for another kiss. "That may be the best thing I've ever heard from you."

She tangled her fingers in his hair, glad he wasn't wearing a baseball cap. If she had her way, neither of them would be wearing much of anything soon. "I can't believe how this all worked out."

"I know. Everyone should start out with three lies."

Allie giggled. "I'm glad I messed up that part."

"Me, too."

He dotted some tender kisses along her temple. "Tell me another lie. And make it a really good one this time."

She didn't have to think about it.

"Did I tell you what a great kisser Matt Kearns is?"

He growled, right before giving her a kiss to drive that man from her mind forever.

About the Author

Donna Cummings has been an attorney, a tasting-room manager at a winery, and the owner of a retail business, but nothing beats the thrill of writing humorously-ever-after romances.

She resides in New England, although she fantasizes about spending the rest of her days in a tropical locale, wearing flip-flops year-round, or in Regency London, scandalizing the *ton*.

She can be found on Twitter (@BookEmDonna) talking incessantly about her true loves—coffee and writing.

You can also find her at her website (www.AllAboutTheWriting.com), blogging at Heroes and Heartbreakers (www.heroesandheartbreakers.com), or on Facebook (www.facebook.com/Donna.Cummings.Author).

Big Boy

Ruthie Knox

Dedication

To Twitter, without which the *Strangers on a Train* stories would not exist.

And to Meg, Serena, Donna and Sam, with thanks for all the laughs.

Chapter One

He always meets me at the gate. The chain link swings open, and I pull my car through at a crawl. I don't look to the left where he's standing. I don't want to know who he is yet.

Until I step onto the train, he's nobody special.

"Are my seams straight?" I ask, pausing in my walk so I can tip the arch of my foot toward the floor of the train car and point my toe. I glance over my shoulder, the epitome of coy.

I'm Marilyn Monroe from *Some Like It Hot* tonight. I coaxed Lisa into sewing the black satin dress for me, adding fringe from a flapper costume I found at Goodwill. Lisa says that in this dress, my ass looks like two puppies fighting under a blanket.

The banked fire in his eyes tells me that's a good thing.

He wears a leather jacket and a newsboy cap. He carries my luggage. When we get to my berth, I'll tip him, and he'll smirk at me the way he does.

Rocky is his name. I asked when I handed him my hatbox.

He's five or six inches taller than me, his body lean and sculpted by hard work. I bet he looks grand with his clothes off.

I toss him a smile, another form of gratuity. "Well? Are they?"

He shakes his head as if I'm doing something to him, and it's painful, and he'd like me to stop. But all he says is "They're straight, ma'am."

I'm ma'am tonight. I like that.

I think it means I'll get to be in charge, but I'm wrong.

As soon as we pass through the narrow doorway of the berth, he's on me, his hands spanning my waist, sliding over the curve of my hips. His skin catches the slick material of my dress. He puts his lips on the pulse at my throat and lingers there. I hear him draw in a deep breath, reverent.

I missed you too.

And then his mouth is moving down, down, until he reaches the tightly cosseted swell of my breasts.

"Stop me if you're gonna stop me, lady."

I want to lift my leg up and wrap it around his hip, but I can't lift anything. I'm wearing a garment designed for mincing around. I know, because I designed it.

"You're awfully fresh." I can feel the smile on his lips as they brush my nipple through the satin. The tease.

"You married, ma'am?" He addresses the question to my cleavage.

"You care?"

"I don't truck with married women." He lifts his head to tell me this, his hound-dog eyes all soulful and dark. He's lost the cap. I see it on the floor where our feet have tangled together, Glen-check wool next to beat-up cordovan oxfords and two-tone pumps with bows on the toes.

I spent days finding the right shoes.

"A cad with principles." I furrow my fingers through his hair. He's slicked it back, but I loosen it. I like it falling in his eyes. "That's rich."

"Who says I'm a cad?"

He squeezes my ass, his long fingers pressing close to where I want them but not close enough.

"Jeez, fella," I say on an exhale, dropping my head to the wall behind me and letting my eyes drift closed. "I sure as hell hope you're a cad."

I imagine the vibration of the train in the wall behind my back as he peels the satin off my shoulders and puts his mouth on me. As he drops to his knees and pushes the dress up my hips. The fringe ought to be an impediment, but he's the sort of man who can handle a little fringe.

He's not a cad, though. Not really.

The babysitter is sick, and I hate her.

This makes me a bad person, I know. She sounds so pathetic on the phone, frog-voiced and snotty, and I'm supposed to comfort her. It feels like emotional blackmail. Why do I have to be nice to her when she's ruining my day?

"I can still come if you want me to." She means *I want to stay in bed and watch reruns of bad television.* "I just don't want to get Josh sick." *Only a very bad mother would expose her child to this pestilence. A very bad, very selfish mother.*

I'm not a bad mother. Not usually. But there's no room in my life for sick babysitters. I have to teach in forty minutes, and I haven't done my class prep yet. I have office hours afterward, meetings with nine separate students to talk about papers they haven't started thinking about writing. I have a dissertation chapter to finish if I'm going to manage not to get fired when I come up for my contract renewal in the fall.

Sometimes Josh gets the short end of the stick, but I console myself with the thought that I get it a lot more often.

I'm not a bad person. On the other hand, I'm not such a good one that I'm going to tell my babysitter to stay home. This will be a life lesson for her: Don't say yes when you mean no.

Maybe if I'd learned that lesson sooner, I'd have told my sister no when she asked me if she could put me in her will as her children's guardian. Then, when Paige and her husband and my three-year-old niece, Ava, got killed by a drunk driver, I wouldn't have become the mother of a nine-day-old infant.

But if I'd done that, I wouldn't have Josh now, and not having Josh has become inconceivable.

Sweet as pie, I ask the babysitter, "Why don't you come on over? He has a strong immune system. If you feel really crappy, you can show him cartoons."

Of course, Josh gets sick the next day.

He sleeps badly, waking up every hour and calling for me. I set up a humidifier in his room, rub his back and soothe him to sleep, but by the third time he wakes, I've given up on the idea of getting any sleep myself. I rock him in my arms for hours, singing folk songs when he gets fussy.

He tucks his head against my neck, breathing warm against my skin, and I feel so guilty. So inadequate.

I should've canceled my office hours and stayed home with him. I should put him in daycare, but I can't afford it. My salary is pitiable, and I have loans to pay off. So I make do with a couple of babysitters, telling myself he's better off at home, spending as much time as possible with me.

But when I'm at home with him, I'm a distracted mother, always trying to get away with as much work or as much cleaning as I can. He wants nothing but me—my attention, my love—and I want to give it to him, only I want so many other things too.

When Paige and I were kids, we both thought we'd have big families one day. I imagined a husband and three children, every little girl's version of domestic bliss. Then I went to college, and I spent the summer after my sophomore year as a camp counselor in Colorado. The job was relentless. Cabins full of eight-year-olds for three weeks at a stretch. They never stopped needing me for one second. I felt like I was suffocating.

That's when I decided I wasn't cut out to be a mother. I was always the better student, anyway. I focused on school and let Paige focus on motherhood. She found her husband, her scrapbooking group, her happy domesticity. I went to grad school and fooled around in an unserious way with unserious boys.

I pet Josh's back, breathing against the solid weight of his sleeping body pressing into my neck, my breasts, my belly. I wouldn't trade him for the world.

I want him to have everything, but all he has is me.

Lisa's students call her Lisa. Mine call me Professor Sharp. I suspect this is no mere accident. I'm a nice person but a hard grader. I kick them out of my classroom for texting, and I tell them things about Indian nations and white-male privilege that disturb their comfortable worldviews.

My students walk into my classroom expecting odes to the American frontier and walk out disgusted with their ancestors, incapable of waving a flag or watching a Fourth of July parade without deconstructing it.

Some of them dislike me for this, but the best ones love having their eyes opened. They sit in my office and wax enthusiastic about prejudice and abuse, nattering on about how the readings I've assigned them have recast the way they look at everything.

I used to be like them. It's hard to remember now, but that sort of critical idealism is what got me into grad school in the first place. These days, I fill my grocery-store cart up with packaged baby foods and state-government-subsidized milk, and it's harder to get fired up about any of it. The condition of my bank account and Josh's diaper seem to be about all the worries I can handle.

I'm a professor of American Studies at the University of Wisconsin–Green Bay, the most recent hire in an abysmal job market. I got the job three months before I got Josh. I was packing up to move when Paige died and everything changed.

Now I'm in my second year in Green Bay, and I like it well enough. It's the sort of place people don't move away from, which means I'll be an outsider even if I live here until I die. Which I might. There are pitifully few jobs in my field, and I hadn't liked being on the market. So many sharks fighting over so little chum.

I'm Mandy to my friends, Amanda to my mother when she calls, which is not all that often. She lives in Oregon, and she's mourning Paige's death with long stretches of silence and solo camping trips that worry me. I've tried to talk her into relocating to Wisconsin so we can have each other for company and she can help me with Josh. She says she needs the quiet and the high desert to heal.

Josh calls me Mama, which is my favorite name. I love him with a ferocity that scares me. I once made myself retch thinking about what would happen if he died in a plane crash or got sick or abused.

But having a baby is like having a bad boyfriend. Josh will kiss me one minute and smack me in the face with a sharp-edged block the next. If he could talk, he'd say, *I need you, Mama. I need you so bad.*

It wears me out, being needed.

Lisa calls me a martyr and tells me to stop trying to save everybody and take care of myself.

I do, I tell her. *I do.*

But it's not exactly true. One night a month, I let somebody else take care of me.

Chapter Two

After Rocky has me thoroughly sullied, he helps me clamber up on top of the train car, and we look at the stars.

His idea. He has all the fun ideas.

Technically, there aren't any stars, of course. The Pullman car is housed indoors. But the train is real, unyielding beneath my back. He's real too, holding my hand and breathing beside me in the dark. It's easy enough to pretend.

When I'm with him, anything can be true.

"Do you ever think you were born into the wrong life?" I ask.

It's not an idle question. Our role-playing has brought all these other versions of me to the surface. Some of them come so easily and feel so real, I wonder if they're authentic echoes of the person I ought to be.

I like the women I am with him.

"Do I want to be rich, you mean?"

"Not rich, necessarily. Just somebody else."

Maybe it's an odd question. Maybe porters named Rocky don't think about such things. But he's not always Rocky. Last month, he was a vacuum-cleaner salesman from Spokane. The month before that, he was an investment broker.

Every fourth Tuesday night, we're both somebody else.

He rolls to his side and leans close to kiss my temple, which makes my eyelids flutter closed. "Every day."

"Who would you be?"

"A Rockefeller." I open my eyes to catch a glimpse of his confident smirk. "All the oysters I could eat."

"Oysters are vile."

"Nah." His expression turns mischievous, the way it does when he's about to say something he knows will wind me up. "They taste like a woman."

"*You're* vile," I accuse with a smile.

He tangles his fingers in my hair and kisses me. The hot sweep of his tongue into my mouth erases my disappointment in his answer. He hadn't said what I wanted him to say. I don't know what I wanted him to say.

"A complete cad," he agrees. "But that's what a woman like you needs."

"What kind of woman am I?"

"You're a racehorse. You need a man who will work you up to a good lather and rub you down right."

"Maybe you should give that a try."

"Up here? We're liable to fall off and break our necks."

I twist sideways so I can pull him closer, sneaking my hands inside his jacket to find the ridged plain of his rib cage with my palms. He smells like leather and thrift stores and the peppermint candy he offered me right before he hoisted me up.

"Tell me a secret," I say, reckless. "Tell me something nobody knows."

I know all about him. He hates the smell of lilies. His grandmother died in a factory fire. He wants to visit Fenway Park one day.

The trouble is, I don't know what's true, or if any of it is. He's better than I am at disguising his real self.

Tonight, I want a sliver of honesty to pierce the illusion. A splinter of reality to carry in my pocket all month, to cherish with my fingertips, thinking of him.

He presses me onto my back and stares down at my face, his irises seeming to stutter as he considers my lips, my forehead, my chin. One finger traces the shape of my cheekbone, and he says, "Nobody but me knows the way you look up here in the moonlight."

Pretty words. There's a tenderness in his expression that I don't think he's faking. I feel cherished and fragile—a rare experience, considering that I spend a lot of my time being smeared with food and climbed all over by a rambunctious toddler.

But on the other hand, there is no moonlight.

He kisses me so gently, I think I might break, and then he lies back down, tucking my head into the hollow of his shoulder. He strokes my arm, humming a tune in my ear I don't recognize. I can imagine it playing on a phonograph, the blanket of white noise overlaying both of us. The static pop of the recording.

All we ever do is lie to each other. Fool that I am, I'd hoped he would tell me the truth.

We met online. How else?

Lisa wants to find a life partner, and she'd talked me into thinking online dating made sense. I blame sleep deprivation. Josh was four months old then, and I hadn't had an uninterrupted night's rest since I took custody of him.

I moved through the days in a fog, mainlining coffee to keep from nodding off during any silence that lasted longer than twenty seconds. In my profile picture, I looked like a zombie, but the algorithm the dating service relied on kept matching me up with brainless men. After three hapless, awkward dates, I tried sifting through the profiles on my own.

That's when I found him. Viscount Curzon. In his profile picture, he wore a cravat and a monocle.

In another one, he was Benjamin Piatt Runkle, a Civil War soldier. Under *Accomplishments,* he'd typed, *Survived the Battle of Shiloh.* His picture was tinted sepia, like a daguerreotype.

The third one, for Frank Sinatra Jr., made me laugh out loud. *Dislikes: Living in father's shadow. Likes: Loose women.*

I found eight of them altogether, each with its own picture. He did a remarkable job of looking like eight different men. I mean, I could tell it was him—he had the same hazel eyes, the same sandy-brown hair in every photo. But he inhabited the disguises.

I showed Lisa, and she told me he was weird. I'd already figured that out. Still, I was surprised how much stock she put in it. His weirdness was what appealed to me. I felt so unfocused so much of the time in those days—like I wasn't myself anymore, but I wasn't a new person either. I was a blob with feet.

This guy knew something I didn't. He knew how to change

identities nimbly, with a gleam in his eyes that said *I'm having more fun than you are.*

I sent him an email. It had to go through the dating service, so he only knew me as Mandy, and I only knew him as Chet Baker. *Likes: Porkpie hats, West Coast jazz, heroin. Dislikes: Rigamarole.*

He told me he had rules. He didn't want to know my last name or what I did for a living, and he didn't want to tell me anything about himself, either. It was the very opposite of what the dating service encouraged us to do.

I accepted his boundaries and tried to engage him in chitchat about music, movies, books. He asked me out. Sort of.

He proposed to meet me at the gate of the National Railroad Museum at eight o'clock on a Tuesday night. I had to wear something appropriate to 1957.

Lisa said he was a crackpot and I should stay away. But I liked the idea of meeting him in costume. If he could pretend to be Chet Baker or whoever, I could pretend to be the version of myself who didn't have a four-month-old. I could be the superseded me, a competent grad student who never burst into tears at the drop of a hat.

I suppose I was betraying the new me, but I didn't like her much.

Lisa agreed to babysit. She helped me find a boiled-wool travel suit and locate a source for heavy silk stockings. We curled my hair with rags.

When I got out of my car in the parking lot, I noticed the angle of his hat first. He wore a dark checked jacket with a pocket square, held a cigarette in his mouth that he never lit, and had a louche way of leaning against the brick side of the museum that put me at ease.

"You can be whoever you want," he told me before he led me to the Aerotrain. "Just stay in character."

The National Railroad Museum—a considerably less grand operation than the name implies—houses a couple dozen trains. Some are scattered around the grassy grounds, but most, including the fin-tastical 1950s Aerotrain designed by General Motors, are lined up in a huge outdoor shed that's open on both ends to the elements.

Only the very best trains—the rarest, the well preserved—are indoors, in the Lenfestey Center. The main building also houses a few exhibits, staff offices and a gift shop. Four times a day, they offer a train ride around the tracks that circle the property.

It's a quaint museum, neither large nor small, funded entirely with donations, grants, admissions and membership fees. Sort of medium-impressive for a city of a hundred thousand people. Very Green Bay.

I'd never been there before that night.

The Aerotrain's engine was a sleek bullet, but inside, the cars smelled of mouse nests and spent oil, and I had trouble pretending at first. I focused on the wedge of his back moving through the car in front of me. The way his hat sat over his ears.

Lisa had cautioned me to be safe, to keep my hand on the pepper spray in my purse until I knew he was no psychopath. But as I watched him walk, he became just a guy on a train, and I wasn't afraid of him. I was Florence from Pottsville, Pennsylvania, taking the Saturday special to visit my sick sister in Harrisburg. If I had butterflies in my stomach, they were only because I wasn't accustomed to traveling, and because I didn't normally have opportunities to meet such nice-looking men.

His name was Philip. He took me up the steps in the dining car to sit where it was quieter, and he bought me coffee and pastry.

It was an unimaginable relief to talk to him. For one stolen hour, I was somebody else. We swapped stories. Told jokes. We laughed a lot.

When we finished drinking coffee that didn't really exist, he escorted me back to my seat, his hand settled at the base of my spine. I would've let him kiss me goodbye, but he didn't try.

He waited another two months to kiss me.

I think about him in the days between our dates. I figure out what I'm going to wear when I see him again, who I'll be. The anticipation is so sweet, sometimes I wonder if it'll make my teeth ache eventually, turn my stomach, and that will be that.

We've been on nine dates in nine months.

I didn't sleep with him until the fifth date, and I might not have done it then, except it was wartime, and my sweetheart had died in the Eastern Theater. I'd decided not to waste any more opportunities. When he kissed me in the stateroom of General Eisenhower's train, I pulled him down to the floor by the lapels and asked him to make me forget.

For an hour after I left that night, I drove around in circles, an endless loop on the interstate. I kept touching my lips with my fingers, unable to think about anything but the way he'd felt inside me.

I wonder if he has other women on other nights. Does his Thursday-night girl search for lipstick that's just the right shade of red? Does she comb through the Internet to find lingerie appropriate to 1944?

It's possible. Nine months since we met, and he's never taken down all those profiles on the dating site.

I think sometimes he must be the director of the train museum, but he's got a workman's hands. He's probably the janitor.

I refuse to figure it out. I'm a scholar, a researcher by training. I could do it easily.

I don't want to.

Instead, I commute the ten miles from my apartment to campus and look for him behind the wheel of every car I pass. He drives a Jetta, I think. He drives a pickup truck. An SUV. An ancient Oldsmobile.

He's told me nine different versions of his life story. One night, he was a feed salesman who loved the smell of the ocean. Another, he was a farm kid from Nebraska who'd worked his way through college. He's an only child, sings a passable tenor, loves heights. He has a good pension coming to him. He's Philip, Dexter, Rocky, Charlie, Slim.

I know the way his hair curls at the nape of his neck. I know his body, the way he moves, the way a suit jacket hangs on his shoulders.

When he moves inside me, I think I know what's in his heart. But after I leave the museum, I remember it's all a game. He's a stranger. He's nobody.

Chapter Three

"Have you met Tyler? He's here with Soo Yun."

It takes me a minute to catch up with the conversation. I'm at a back-to-school-again party for work, talking to my department chair, Jon, and it's too loud for me to concentrate. There are people everywhere, twinkling white lights wrapped around steel beams.

The restaurant brewery is known for excellent food and creative cocktails, but I don't like it here. The floor and walls are concrete, like a meat locker, and the air conditioning makes it feel like one. The ceilings are too tall. There are too many voices.

"Hmm? No, I don't think so."

"He works at the train museum. I think you'll like him. Let me introduce you."

Jon is gone before I can answer, loping toward a man who has his back to us. A stranger named Tyler who wears blue jeans and a red cowboy shirt with white piping, and whose sandy-brown hair curls at the nape of his neck.

I know him before he turns around, of course. I know him instantly.

Jon leads him over by the elbow, makes the introduction, and then abandons us for the bar. I'd suspect him of matchmaking, only Jon isn't that socially advanced. I think he threw the two of us together from a sense of occupational necessity.

Tyler is the photo archivist at the train museum. I'm the newest Americanist at the university, a specialist in the intersections of US history, literature and culture. In a city as small as Green Bay, we're supposed to know each other. He's my peer.

He's my lover.

He pretends not to recognize me.

"So how do you like Green Bay?" he asks.

"It's nice," I say. "I grew up in Oregon, so it's pretty different."

"Did you go to grad school out there?"

He's holding a glass of beer and offering me just the right amount of polite attention for the situation. Standing close enough that we can converse easily, but not so close as to be inappropriate. He's very adept at this. That, or he literally doesn't recognize me—a horrifying thought.

"No, in North Carolina, actually. NC State."

"Oh, yeah? I've never been to the South. Did you like it?"

"Yeah, it was great. They have a real spring down there. The trees bloom and everything. It's beautiful."

He smiles, and it's like I've never seen him smile before. I'm an ordinary woman meeting a handsome man at a party. I'm a creature of whooshing blood and inconvenient perspiration. My conversational skills are severely impaired by how white his teeth are and how nicely his jeans hug his thighs.

I want him to like me. I admire the pearl snaps on his shirt, which *has* to be vintage, and I want him to ask me out.

"What about you, are you from here?" I ask.

"Yeah, I grew up here."

"How'd you get into history?"

He shrugs. "I always liked it. Seemed like a good fit, and I did an internship at Heritage Hill one semester in college and couldn't resist the allure of the low pay and complete lack of respect that comes with museum work."

"I was the same way. As soon as I found out about the grad-school-debt to starting-salary ratio, I was like, *Where do I sign up?*"

I give him half a smile, pushing my hair behind my ear and hoping he thinks I'm pretty. I'm wearing tall brown boots and tight, dark jeans, a cream sweater, a scarf. I look like a college professor at a faculty party. He looks like a really hot photo archivist who moonlights as a cowhand.

I feel like we're wearing another set of disguises, alluring and new, until Soo Yun comes up behind him and takes his elbow. Soo Yun, who teaches physics and has perfect skin and no children.

Soo Yun, who rises to her tiptoes and whispers something in his ear.

He smirks, and it's not for me. It's for her.

He extends his hand. "We have to head out. It was nice meeting you."

The light scrape of his calluses over my palm makes me wet, a disgusting bit of Pavlovian biology.

I liked him better when I didn't know his name.

The first thing Lisa says when I open the door to her is "He's not cheating on you with Soo Yun." She's all lit up with the news, happy as an elf stuffing stockings.

"It would be impossible for him to cheat on me. I'm not his girlfriend."

She pushes past me into my apartment, unbuttoning her coat. After dropping it unceremoniously to the floor, she crouches down to say hello to Josh, who's stumbled his way into the entryway, listing like a drunk.

"How's my best guy?" she asks him.

"Eees!" It's the closest he can come to "Lisa". He lunges for her hoop earrings, but she blocks him.

"Stick with the necklace, Joshie," she says, guiding his hands to the leather lace around her neck. He finds the beads there and begins manipulating them with total absorption.

"You've been out with him a bunch of times." Lisa drops her voice to a whisper. "You're *sleeping* with him. That makes you his girlfriend."

I roll my eyes and walk into the living room, and Lisa scoops Josh up and follows. When she sits down on the beige carpet beside me, he flings himself into my lap and begins humping his butt up and down like an inchworm.

"What is he *doing*?" Lisa asks.

"I don't know, but he does it all the time lately."

He lifts his head and grins, then stands up and totters off, bent on destruction. I need to feed him lunch soon if I want to avoid a meltdown. After that, it'll be time for his nap, and Lisa and

I are going to work on my next date-night outfit.

On Tuesday, I'll meet Tyler in the engine compartment of the Big Boy. It's the largest, most powerful steam locomotive ever built—I looked it up. I'm hoping the engine room is filthy and hot. I have a lot of filthy, hot ideas.

"You understand that when I say 'He's not cheating on you,' I mean that I asked Soo Yun, and she told me they're not together?" Lisa asks.

"Nooo," I say slowly. "I didn't understand that. Why would you do that?"

"Because you like him."

I do. I like him. But it's such a bad idea.

"Don't do that again."

"Why are you so weird about this guy? You don't want me to ask around about him, you won't admit you like him, and you only go out on these bizarre role-playing dates where you don't tell him your last name or anything important about you."

"I don't know."

I *do* know. I don't want to explain it.

"I googled him," she says. "Want me to tell you what I found out?"

"No."

"He went to college at—"

"Shut up." I stick my fingers in my ears, because I know she won't.

She doesn't. I hear her say "Marquette" and then "Civil War", and I have to start going "la-la-la-la-la" to drown her out.

Josh finds this amusing, and he runs back over and spazz-tackles me, knocking me down on my back. He pulls up my shirt and puts his cheek on my belly. My stomach is his version of a security blanket, which can be embarrassing when we go out in public.

I stroke his silky black hair. He looks like Paige's husband, and I find that comforting. It would be harder if he looked like my sister.

When Lisa's mouth stops moving, I take my fingers out of my

ears.

"You should ask him out on a real date," she tells me.

"I can't."

"Why not?"

"Because that would be changing the rules."

"That's weak."

I know it is. But it's more complicated than that, because when I met him, what I wanted from him was his ephemerality. I needed him to be a stranger on a train, to snap into existence when I got out of my car and snap back out of it when I walked away.

For a while, he gave me exactly what I needed. Only, when I wasn't paying attention, I started needing something different.

I'm not sure what it is, exactly, but I don't think I can get it from Tyler. He doesn't know me. He doesn't *want* to know me. When he saw me at the party, his eyes didn't light up with recognition. His lips didn't widen into a smile that said, *There you are, at last. The real you.*

It was a game to him. It's always been a game.

And I knew that, of course. He put all those profiles on the dating site, his way of saying, *Anybody want to play?*

I signed up. I agreed to his rules. I can hardly change them now.

Josh gets up, trips, falls down. He lies still for a second, sprawled on the carpet, as if he's not quite sure how he got there. Then he pushes himself up and grins at me, and a long strand of drool falls to the floor.

Such a disgusting mess, babies.

I pick him up and pat his diapered butt with affectionate vigor. He wriggles violently, craving freedom, so I set him on his feet and wait for him to find his balance before I let go.

Tyler is deliciously filthy.

He's wearing colorless canvas pants, a half-unbuttoned work shirt with the sleeves rolled above his elbows. He's got a bandana tied around his neck, sweat-stained and greasy, as though he's been wearing it for endless days of backbreaking labor. He has some kind of cotton work cap on, striped blue and dingy gray.

I can't see his face, but there's coal dust on his neck and a spot of grime on one ear.

Part of me appreciates all the trouble he's gone to. Where did he find coal dust? I imagine him breaking into the coal yards by the Fox River and climbing over the piles just for me. I see him leaning in toward a bathroom mirror somewhere, carefully examining his reflection as he smears theatrical crud on his lovely face.

He's the fireman tonight. The Big Boy consumes tons of coal on every journey over the Wasatch Range, and it's his job to make sure the fuel gets to the engines and the fire stays stoked. An auger that's at least twelve inches in diameter feeds the coal from the tender into the furnace, but it gets stuck. When I reached the top step and passed into the dark cavern of the engine room, he was muttering something about "fucking clinkers", his face buried between the steel butterfly doors of the firebox.

He has such a big wrench in his hand.

He has such a great ass.

I'm the engineer, I've decided. It's historically improbable, but not unheard of. There were a few female engineers on the western railways. I'm dressed like I imagine Katharine Hepburn would be, or Meryl Streep in that one movie where she has the African coffee plantation: high-waisted flannel trousers with wide legs, a short-sleeved ivory blouse. I've swept my hair up and pinned it in place.

I want to order him around. I intend to tell him to call me "Boss". Maybe it will be payback for the way he made me feel at the party, I'm not sure. My plans are elaborate but incompatible. I've made so many over the past few weeks. I've had so many different kinds of feelings about him.

It turns out not to matter. He suddenly turns around and drops the wrench to the floor of the car with a deafening metallic clatter that wipes my head clean of thoughts, and he stalks toward me with a leer on his lips.

Angry, and not faking it.

The sight makes my toes curl inside my sensible black boots. He's normally so poised. I've never witnessed him lose control except during sex, when he's balancing on the knife's edge of an orgasm, his face lit with pleasurable agony.

This is different. He's just plain pissed off about something and incapable of hiding it. I'm seeing the real Tyler, undisguised. I'm embarrassed to say how instantaneously, shamefully wet that makes me. Just the way his mouth twists up with the force of his fury. The furrow between his eyebrows. God.

I've been waiting, hoping something like this would happen. That he'd open up and give me access to himself. I want to know him better. Even the ugly parts. I want to know everything.

He gets two fists full of silk at the collar of my blouse and rips it open with one effortless tug. I keep backing up, backing away, until I bump into the edge of the driver's seat, which faces ahead, ready for forward motion that will never come.

He's never been so rough before.

I'm not afraid of him, far from it. But menace is a presence in the car, joining all the rest of us—the real Tyler, the pretend one whose shirt identifies him as *Mack*, the real me, the lady engineer, and this ribbon of violence, twisting through the air between us.

So inexplicably, primally exciting.

He doesn't say a word, and that's not like him either. He's a talkative man, the kind of guy Mom would say has fallen in love with the sound of his own voice.

Tonight, it's just his grimy palm on the pale white of my bare breast. His hard cock grinding into the soft space between my thighs as he crushes me against the seat.

The edge of the upholstery hits the small of my back all wrong. My knees are bent, I'm on tiptoe, and when he presses into me I lose my purchase on the floor.

He brings his mouth close. That's when he hesitates. One breath, his lips hovering. Two.

"It's okay," I whisper. More than okay. I crave this dark, physical truth from him. His passion. His need. "I want you."

He crushes his lips to mine, ravenous. Rough hands fumble with his zipper, then with mine, but he can't find it. It's on the side. I help him, yanking it down, pushing my slacks to my ankles. He doesn't bother to remove my peach tap pants with the lacy blue trim. He just shoves them out of the way and takes me, hard.

I can't keep my balance, so I cling to him. He drives into me, his eyes squeezed tight shut, and he's shuddering, trembling with the motion of the train car. Thirty tons of coal. Six thousand horsepower. All that energy and mess.

I hold on tight and think, *This wasn't part of the deal.* He's a catastrophe tonight, a broken man.

I take him in. I want to put him back together.

When he comes, I arch my back into the palm of his hand. My lips make the shape of his name.

Not Mack. Tyler.

He staggers from the car afterward, tucking his shirt in as he moves away. He didn't use a condom. He always uses a condom.

I'm on the pill. I ought to be afraid of disease, of disaster—of him—but I'm not. I'm afraid *for* him. He was a cad.

He's suffering, and I don't know why.

I hear his footfalls on the iron catwalk, then down the steps that connect the engine compartment to the ground fifteen feet below. He stops before he gets to the bottom. I imagine he's sitting there, thinking, *What the fuck just happened?*

Me too.

I get myself in order as best I can. My blouse doesn't have enough buttons to make myself decent, and I feel swollen and bruised between my legs. *Rode hard and put away wet.*

I sit beside him on the steps and wait for him to say something.

He pulls a crumpled package of cigarettes out of his pocket and lights one up.

I think he could get fired for smoking inside the building. But I suppose he could get fired for fornicating on the trains too, and I've never let that stop me. When he offers me a cigarette, I take one. I let him light it, and I take a drag off it that goes directly to my brain and makes everything sharp and too bright. I don't like to smoke. I hold on to the cigarette, though, to keep him company.

He smokes half of his and then pinches it out and puts the butt in his pocket, the gesture practiced but almost certainly faked. He never smells like smoke.

"You ever think maybe you're living the wrong life?" he asks me.

"I did," I tell him. "I used to."

"Sometimes," he says slowly, "I think that if there's one more thing I have to do, I'll lose it."

Oh, honey, I think. *You just did.*

But maybe he means something different. Maybe he means he'll start screaming or crying. That he'll walk into a public cafeteria and start shooting people.

"They're using me up."

He's got his head down. The back of his neck is grimy. There's coal dust in his curls.

I can't seem to separate him in my head, Tyler from Mack. He sounds like he's talking about The Man, about oppression and hard work. He sounds like he means it, like he's sick to the depths of his soul about it.

I wonder what he's really talking about. It seems impossible that this could be a conversation about photo archiving. I'm not sure it's a conversation about anything.

"Don't let them."

I trail my fingers up and down his back, settling at the space between his shoulder blades. I want to take him home and clean him off, which is new. I want to take care of him.

A long exhale. He turns his head. "Did I hurt you?"

"No."

"I'm sorry I did that."

All the answers that come to mind are so grotesque, I keep them to myself. *You can do that whenever you want. I didn't mind. I want to make you feel better.*

I'm supposed to be a feminist.

"I said you could." I scoot a little closer and put my arm around his waist.

"I should've taken care of you. I wasn't thinking straight, I—"

"Next time."

He turns, urges me up by the hips, pulls me into his lap. "This is where I want you."

His blunt fingers toy with one of the two functioning buttons of my blouse. "I wrecked your shirt."

With his thumb, he finds the smooth wedge of fabric where the cups of my bra come together between my breasts, and he follows it beneath one cup, around toward the back. I'm wearing a peach bra with lace trim to match the panties. Stiff, reinforced. Practically a nuclear armament.

"I'll dock your pay," I tease.

"I don't ever want to hurt you."

You're going to break my heart.

I hadn't known, but I know now.

Chapter Four

We usually have a lot of fun. He tells hilarious stories, always in character. We crack period-appropriate jokes, and he tickles my rib cage until I'm helpless with laughter.

One night, he brought a flask, and we sat on top of the Atchison, Topeka, and Santa Fe engine and drank gin as we watched the sun come up. It was 1934. We were both dirt-poor, our dreams shattered, our families broken apart. But we made each other laugh until we had to climb down because he was afraid I would fall off the train.

That was the first time he kissed me. He leaned against the car and pulled me into his body, and I thought I was breathless afterward because of the laughing. Then he kissed me again, and I changed my mind.

I've told him all my secrets, only they've been in disguise. I told him what happened to my sister, but I made it the story of how she went through the ice when her husband was driving her across the bay in the winter. People used to do that—cross the bay on the thick sheet of ice. Mostly, they survived it.

They used to harvest the ice too. It was a big industry, back when families had iceboxes.

I told him about being afraid I might lose my job. I was a clerk-typist that night, so I talked about layoffs and how one of the other girls in the secretarial pool was sleeping with our boss.

I've described Lisa to him on three separate occasions, with three different names.

I even told him about Josh once. How his parents were gone, and nobody could find them. How I was looking out for him in the meantime.

Tyler is a good listener, a good friend. I think I'm a better person since I met him, and while that might not be all down to him, he's helped. Getting away from my life and talking about it has made a difference. Playing with him has reminded me that I can be Josh's mom and still be myself. I can be a new version of myself.

The first time we had sex, on the floor of the Eisenhower, I was a little embarrassed afterward, when the high of the orgasm finally wore off. I'd kind of attacked him.

But the next month, there was Big Band music playing over hidden loudspeakers. We danced on the wooden floor of the postal car. He'd put short, stubby candles in some of the mail sorting slots. He swung me around, twirled me and spun me, and then he took me to a narrow bed in one of the sleeper cars and made love to me for hours, so slow and thorough that I felt like he was branding me with his hands and his tongue, claiming me with every thick stroke into my body.

I was Veronica Lake that night, until he took off my dress. Then I was me. When he's inside me, I've never been anyone but myself.

I think I'm in love with him, and I don't know what to do.

I google him.

Tyler Janssen attended the University of Wisconsin–Green Bay. He got his master's in the Public History Program at Marquette University. He's a part-time photo archivist at the National Railroad Museum who at one point spent a lot of his weekends wearing homespun and carrying a rifle, traveling around the state as an amateur Civil War re-enactor, though he doesn't seem to do that anymore.

He's seven years younger than me.

He lives in a house in Astor Park. I drove by it. It's a pretty brick house in a solidly upper-middle-class neighborhood. His father might have owned a jewelry store once, though it could've been somebody else. There are a fair number of Janssens in Green Bay.

His mother is dead, but his dad is still alive. The house where he lives is the house where he grew up.

In high school, he was in the Key Club, the National Merit Society, the Drama Club.

He posts in forums for re-enactors, railroad buffs, photo-restoration specialists. He is friendly and helpful. He never engages in bad Internet behavior.

All eight of his original profiles are still up on the dating site, and there are a few others too, that I hadn't found before. Carl Froch, the boxer. Yortuk Festrunk, who I recognize as one of the brothers from the old "wild and crazy guys" *Saturday Night Live* skits when I read his "likes": *Swinging, foxes, big American breasts.*

I'm in love with a very hot photo archivist. An ordinary Green Bay geek. An extraordinarily strange man.

But I knew that already.

He's Mike Brady, but better looking, and with lighter hair. His shirt is white, open-necked, butterfly-collared. It's printed with the most hideous chevrons, brown and orange and gold.

He's grown sideburns. *Sideburns.* I saw a picture of him online from a few years back where he had muttonchops at a Civil War encampment near Prairie du Chien.

I'm officially cyber-stalking him now.

It's hot tonight for September, muggy in the empty car. We're in one of the outdoor trains that sits alone at the back end of the lot. We're pretending to be passengers, strangers on a train. Pretending it's daytime, pretending it's 1977. The air of the train car is thick with his cheap cologne. Brut, I think. It smells awful. He's reading *Octopussy* in the dim glow from the security arc light mounted outside.

I'm a girl in a minidress. Tall black boots, short black skirt, hair teased up at the crown of my head, smoothed over, curled up at the ends like Mary Tyler Moore's. I don't even know who I'm supposed to be tonight. Some kind of working girl. Some Rhoda who believes in women's lib and open relationships.

He's a used-car dealer in brown polyester pants, and I want him so bad I'm squirming.

"You got a problem?" he asks me. He sounds kind of New

York, kind of Jersey. Kind of arrogant and mean, like Travolta in *Saturday Night Fever.*

"I do. I need to get fucked."

Oh, yeesh. Now we're in a porno. He shoots me a player's grin, and I remember what he said that first night. *You can be whoever you want to be. Just stay in character.*

Apparently, tonight my character is Cheap Floozy in a Trashy Movie.

"I might be willing to help you out."

Shameless, I stare at his package, lovingly outlined in brown polyester. His fly has orange topstitching with tiny little arrows that point inward, as if to say *Here's my jock.* Seriously, where does he find these clothes? I think he must spend more time than I do, and I put an embarrassing amount of effort into it.

Geek, I think, with affection.

"You sayin' you got what I need in there?" I ask.

"I know I do, baby."

"Take it out." If I had gum, I'd be snapping it. If I had long, manicured fingernails, I'd be buffing them. "I wanna see if you're all talk before I make up my mind."

He takes it out. It looks pretty good, but he makes me inspect it closely. He suggests that I taste it, and I lick him like a lollipop and suck until he's panting. When we swap places, he pushes my minidress up and makes me lose my mind with his tongue, my boots perched on his shoulders. The whole time, we're teasing, talking in thick, terrible accents, saying, *Oh, yeah, baby. You like that, sugar? You're a dirty whore, aren't you? You're one foxy thing.*

There's a smile behind every line, a sparkle in his eyes. Nobody has ever played with me the way he does, and the freedom of it is intoxicating. To be able to put on another self, a body, a persona. To be wearing the clothes, saying the words of an imaginary person, but to know he's making love to me, to me, only to me. I think he must care about me, to be this way. He must.

We flip positions again so he's slouched on the seat beneath me. I sink down onto him, watching his face turn helpless and strained.

I trust him enough to have sex with him bare, but not enough to tell him I have a son. I'm a freak and a coward.

I don't know what that makes him.

Oh, mama, he says, smiling, and I laugh. I cup his face in my hand for a second, my forearm braced on top of the seat behind him. I look in his eyes as I ride him, letting his smile soak through my skin and lift me up, lighten me.

I'm anchored by his cock, by the grunting, sweating reality of us, the slapping sounds and the firm grip of his hands at my hips, moving me the way he wants me to move, tilting my hips so his pubic hair rubs against my clit. He's still wearing the pants. Those little arrows.

I'm so happy. Incandescent.

"Come on, foxy," he drawls when I get close, and he rises up, wrapping his arms around my back to bring me closer. "Come for daddy. Lemme hear you."

He lowers his mouth to my breast and sucks, flicking with his tongue, and I'm laughing when I start to come, until the bright pulse of pleasure gets too big and I have to throw back my head and squeeze my eyes shut. I make a porn star noise, the loudest orgasm in the history of womankind.

It sets him off. He lunges forward, and I'm suddenly on my back on the floor and he's pumping into me. "Jesus, Mandy," he says. "Jesus Christ."

His breath catches, holds. His hips pin me to the floor. I hear my own name, my real name, over and over again as he shudders and groans in my ear. In the silence afterward, the crickets chirping, the white shushing noises of the cars on the highway a few miles away.

When a light flickers in the train window and a man shouts, I can't make sense of it, but Tyler is much quicker on the uptake. "Fuck," he says. "Get those boots off. We're going to have to run."

"What's going on?"

"Security guard."

"What security guard?" I'd always thought there was no security guard. Tyler unlocks the gate every month. I'd understood that the gate was all the security a bunch of old trains required.

"Shh. He's just supposed to drive by. He must've seen something weird. Or heard you come. You were pretty fucking loud."

He's peeking out the windows as he says it, but he turns around and grins at me, and I choke, snorting my amusement into my fist like a girl.

There's a barefoot chase in the dark over damp grass. An escape from a uniformed rent-a-cop. My heart pounds. My thighs are wet.

Tyler holds my hand, pulls me along, and all I can hear is the sound of his voice, saying my name.

Chapter Five

I can't keep away from him. That's what it all comes down to.

Hitching Josh up higher on my hip, I pull open the glass door to the National Railroad Museum and pass through the entryway into the lobby. I'm headed for the gift shop, where they have a train table that Josh loves.

We've been coming here for months. We have a membership, which isn't as desperate as it sounds. It only cost twenty-five bucks, so it paid for itself after a few visits.

Josh toddles over to the table and begins moving the cars around the track, over the bridge, into the roundhouse. The trains have weird gray faces that I used to find eerie and disturbing. They've ceased to bother me. I no longer find it strange to personify trains. Everything for children is personified.

Josh has his own words for Thomas, Percy, Henry, Gordon. I tell him in the deep voice of Sir Topham Hatt, "You have caused confusion and delay," and he giggles every time. He's a sucker for Sir Topham Hatt.

We usually play with the train table for forty minutes or so and then wander through the big hall where the indoor trains are. Josh likes to climb the steep iron staircases, to toddle down the carpeted hallways on board and touch things he's not supposed to.

I like to think about Tyler.

I've never seen him here, but I always anticipate the possibility. Now that I know his job, I know which office is his. It's all by itself in the corridor that connects the exhibit area to the indoor trains.

His office door is closed when Josh and I pass by. It always is.

We walk through the Pullman car and poke at the multimedia consoles outside the train. There's a brass railing around the exhibit, and Josh ducks under it over and over again, squealing and running away when I try to stop him.

I know I shouldn't be letting him turn it into a game, since he's doing something I don't want him to do, but I'm too lazy today to care. If I stop him, he'll scream, and I'll have to parent him intensively. I'd rather drift, running my fingers over the cool brass and living in my memories of this place. Living in anticipation of my next date.

Josh slips under, and I make a pretend grab at him, just to hear him shriek with laughter. This time, instead of running back around and up onto the platform again, he runs away, looking back over his shoulder and inviting me to chase after him.

I oblige. I chase him down along the length of the Big Boy to the birthday train, which Josh always insists we climb on. He likes the streamers inside, and he makes me tell him all about how he can have his party here when he turns two. How we'll invite Lisa and both of his babysitters and all his little friends.

When we walk off the car, he wants to hang from the metal railing along the steps—another thing I let him do one time and shouldn't have. It was months ago, but he's never forgotten. I spot him so he doesn't fall and get hurt.

That's when I hear Tyler talking behind me.

"Little brats," he says. I hear the words distinctly, though I miss the sentence they're embedded in. I hear because he says "brats" with the sort of venom that attracts notice.

I keep my hands hovering over Josh's hips but turn my head. Tyler is bending over a table, cleaning up what looks like the remnants of a birthday party alongside a female colleague I recognize from the gift shop.

"They're not that bad," she says.

"They steal the toy trains and make a mess."

"That's true, but they pay for the privilege."

"Not enough," he says. "And the screaming gives me a headache."

He's throwing paper plates into a plastic garbage bag, but he stops to rub at the space between his eyes. I think of Josh, shrieking just moments ago. He spilled his Cheez-Its in the Pullman car, and I had to go down on my knees and pick them up. I'm sure I missed a few. I can never get anything all the way clean. I have frosting smeared on my jeans from the cupcake I let him eat at lunchtime.

Josh is a good sort of baby, but if he ever had a party here, he'd make a mess, and he'd definitely try to steal the trains. He'd shriek, he'd play, he'd have a wonderful time.

And Tyler would hate him for it.

"Come on, sweetie," I whisper, planting a kiss behind Josh's ear and holding him tighter than I ought to, tight to match my clenched teeth. "Let's go outside and play on the wooden engine."

I carry him away, unwilling to hear more.

I've made a mistake coming here. It's not the worst mistake I've made.

"But that's just stupid," Lisa tells me.

"Thanks."

She's leaning in the doorway of my office, having crashed my office hours for the purpose of lecturing me about my life. "No, seriously. You heard him make a couple of offhand remarks to a colleague. He was cleaning up a bunch of kid shit, and he said something callous about kids. That doesn't mean he's an asshole. I bet you said stuff like that all the time before you had Josh."

It's true. I'd only ever been able to handle babies in small doses. I have an innate distaste for bodily fluids. I never even got a cat, so grossed out was I by how they're always horking things up or licking parts of themselves I don't want to think about.

"I say stuff like that now," I tell her.

"Exactly. So why isn't he allowed to?"

"He is."

Lisa frowns. She doesn't understand why I'm agreeing with her. "Exactly. So why have you decided you have no future with the guy?"

"He's seven years younger than me. He only works part-time. He lives with his dad—hell, he probably sleeps in his childhood bedroom. He doesn't like kids—"

"So far as you know."

"—so far as I know, right. And when I met him in a public setting, he pretended not to recognize me. All of this suggests he doesn't have the emotional maturity I might reasonably be seeking in a mate."

"He's good in bed, though, right?"

I turn away and make a point of checking my email.

"Oh, come on. He's got to be hung like a horse, or you wouldn't get so excited about these dates."

"That's crude."

"Tell me he has a cocktail weenie, then."

I'm outraged on Tyler's behalf. "He doesn't have a cocktail weenie. He's...built to scale."

Lisa fans herself. She saw him at that faculty party, so she knows he's tall. She knows an awful lot about Tyler, having been my companion on this bizarre journey from the beginning. "If he's that good, he's worth going after."

"Except for all the reasons I just told you, which add up to him *not* being worth going after."

"God, you're such a coward."

She says it like she means it, not teasing at all, and it makes the hair on my arms stand up.

"What do you mean? I'm not a coward."

"You are. You know how many dates I've been on since we signed up? Twenty-three. I counted them up the other day. I've lowered the bar so many times, it's rolling around in the dirt, and I still haven't found one guy, not *one guy*, who made me feel even a tenth as happy as you look every single morning after a date with your weirdo."

I don't know what to say to that. It seems like *Also, I'm in love with him* would be the wrong direction to take the conversation.

"You're making up excuses not to go for it because you're scared," she says. "It's cowardly. Flat-out."

"Don't hold back. Say what you mean, please."

"Oh, screw you." She smiles when she says it. "Screw you and your built-to-scale, weirdo boyfriend. Even if he lives in his parents' basement and spends his days playing retro Atari games, you should tell him about Josh, and you should ask him out on a date somewhere other than the train museum. Even if he's an underwear sniffer, you should do it."

"An underwear sniffer?"

"Or some other obscure brand of pervert. You're not going to find out unless you try. And I'm sick of helping you find costumes."

I twirl back and forth in my office chair, looking at the books on my shelves and thinking about Tyler and me and Josh and this whole crazy mess I've gotten myself into.

"It's so complicated."

"It's really not. Girl meets boy. Girl likes boy. Girl asks boy out to dinner."

"What if he says no?"

"Then you keep pretending you don't know him when you see him in public, and meanwhile you carry on screwing him on trains until you get arrested for it. The real question is, What if he says yes?"

She has a point. If he said yes, it might mean I could have Tyler in my life. Every day. Or even every week. I could learn him. I could love him, maybe.

I have to try.

A few days later, I leave Josh with Lisa, promising to be back within an hour because she has to teach a class at three o'clock.

There are photographs all along the wall of the hallway leading to Tyler's office. I've never looked at them before, but now I know he might have picked them out. They might be an example of his curatorial genius. So I look.

They're train wrecks. Literally.

Giant engines beached on their sides like whales, or crumpled up in the snow. Wreckage and steaming metal, vivid pictures that conjure up burning creosote smells and sobbing and disaster.

I am not encouraged.

I pause outside his door, staring at his nameplate. His no-nameplate, actually. It just says PHOTO ARCHIVIST.

I wonder what he does when he's not here. If he smokes weed in a basement or helps old ladies across the street or bags groceries at some store I don't shop at.

I want to know. That's why I knock. Because I want to know.

"Come on in," he says.

His eyes widen when I open the door.

I took care to dress like my normal self, as a sort of ambassadorial gesture. *Here I am,* my outfit says. *The sort of woman who wears jeans and very dirty old running shoes and a dark blue lambswool sweater that's unraveling a little at the cuff. The sort of woman who hasn't showered today and probably won't, and who has to instruct the hair stylist not to cut her hair in a way that requires any particular attention, because she uses her blow dryer so rarely, it smells like burning dust whenever she turns it on.*

Here I am.

"Hey, Mandy."

I'm grateful—*so* grateful—that he doesn't act as though we've never met. Which, it occurs to me, is setting the bar a little low.

"Hi." I look at my hand on the doorknob. "Do you have a minute?"

He stands up. "Sure. Come on in." He moves a stack of manila folders off the chair by his desk and waves me into it. "Sorry, it's kind of a mess."

Tyler at work is Tyler in an untucked dress shirt and a V-neck knit vest with a gray-on-black herringbone pattern that ought to make him look like he's trying too hard but doesn't. He's got on jeans and Vans. Casual Friday at the train museum, I guess.

The fluorescent lights pick up the fine lines at the corners of his eyes and the shadows beneath them. He looks tired, older than twenty-seven. He's got photos spread out over the top of his desk, and the sort of magnifying thing jewelers use. A loupe, I think it's called.

"Train spotting?" I ask.

It's a terrible joke. Not even a joke, actually, just an inanity.

He half-smiles, but not in a way that puts me at ease.

"Sort of," he says. "I'm trying to identify which of these pictures are our Big Boy and which are the other ones."

"I didn't know there were other ones."

"Sure, there's a bunch. Couple dozen."

His shoulders are tight. I think I'm making him uncomfortable, and he'd like me to leave, but he won't ask. My heart does this really pathetic squeezing thing, and my throat gets thick and tight.

"Is it a problem, me being here?"

"No. I guess not." He shrugs. "Want to tell me what's up?"

I'm suddenly fascinated by my knees. I've never been good at this part of being human. The part where you have to tell other people embarrassing things. I let Paige's hamster out of its cage once, and it got away and disappeared. I didn't tell her it was my fault, not even when we found it dead in the back of her closet. Especially not then. God.

But I'm pretty sure this is what life requires of us. That we learn how to tell the truth if we're going to call ourselves adults. So I open my mouth, and when nothing else comes out, I swallow, give my knee a fierce squeeze, and try again.

"I have a kid."

Tyler doesn't say anything, and I don't look at him, so I can't possibly know what he's thinking.

"His name is Josh. He's a year old, and he was my sister's baby, but she got killed, and he's been mine since he was tiny."

Still nothing from Tyler. I glance up as far as his desktop, but that only tells me he hasn't fallen down dead. I can't see his hands. His torso isn't saying much.

"I was hoping I could...see you. Outside the train museum, as myself, and you as yourself. But I thought I'd better tell you first about my kid, because "

Uh-oh. This is a conversational pit. *Because I know you hate children* is one possible way of finishing the sentence, but not a good one. I decide to go with "...because it seemed like something you should know. About me."

When I do look at his face, finally, after seventeen stupid

heartbeats of cowardice, it's not so bad. It's not so good, either. It's disturbingly neutral.

"Do you want to see me?"

I don't know why I ask him. It feels like committing hari-kari right in front of him. *Sword, meet soft underbelly.*

He presses his lips together. His eyebrows draw in, his forehead wrinkles. It's a face of sad perplexity. A denial face. He holds it for a few beats as he shakes his head from side to side.

Oh, Christ.

In that moment, I revise the story of everything that's ever happened between us. I become his pursuer, the crazy woman who emailed him because she liked his joke profile. The woman who flung herself at him and screwed him on the floor of a train like a succubus. The woman who dressed like a hooker and had sex in public with a strange man who doesn't want to know her name, who doesn't like her, who didn't ever expect to have to talk to her in the real world.

It's ridiculous. I know this even in the moment. There's only so much revisionism the tale will bear, and I'm taking it way too far. But the denial on his face…the embarrassment. It's for me. He's ashamed for me. His expression is all sadness and empathy, which makes me feel like a victim, and that's the very worst thing. The thing I can stand the least from him.

I get a lot of pity. A lot of *Oh, you brave woman, how good of you to take on your sister's son. How ever are you managing?*

I pity myself too, though I try to keep it to a minimum.

He's never pitied me before. I thought he saw something in me, felt something.

I'm just a dope, I guess.

I go ahead and act dopier. My tongue is functioning on autopilot at this point, impelled by the inertia of my humiliation.

"Why not?"

He plows his fingers through his hair and blows a puff of air out on an exhale. "It was just for fun. It was only ever supposed to be, you know, kind of a lark."

"But it's more than that now, don't you think?" *A lot more.*

I'm not a big enough idiot to think he's going to agree, that he'll leap out of his chair and kiss me and this nightmare will turn into a great big scoop of Wonderful. I guess I just feel the need to crash the train more thoroughly.

"I don't...want it to be more."

"Because I've got a son."

His fingers drum against the arms of his desk chair. "Because I can't handle the responsibility."

This time when I look at his face, I revise everything I've ever thought about him. Again.

He's seven years younger than you, only marginally employed, and he lives in a fantasy world of his own making. He can't "handle" the "responsibility" of a real-life relationship. That's not your problem, and it's not your fault.

I'm not sure it's me who thinks this. It might actually be Lisa. She's fond of air quotes. But whoever it is, I'm grateful for her, because she gets me out of the office before I start to cry.

Chapter Six

Even so, I go on one more date with him.

I know.

But in my defense, I went into it with my eyes open. In the office, I hadn't really said goodbye to Tyler. I just ran.

Tonight, I want to take leave of him—to bid farewell to all the different men he's been for me, and to the warm, happy glow he lights in my body. I couldn't have done that in his office. I can only do it here, on the train.

I'm not playing along this time. His text said it would be 1911, and I should meet him on the snowplow train, but I came in jeans and a plaid flannel jacket, and I only peeked my head into the snowplow to look at him. He's all bundled up in a peacoat and watchman's cap, with a hand-knit striped scarf. Very working-class, though not dirty like he was that night on the Big Boy.

That night. It doesn't fit my new sense of him. Something was wrong with him then, he wasn't playing, but whatever opening it might have given us to follow our relationship somewhere deeper, somewhere new, he didn't take it.

I look at him like he's one more exhibit, and then I wander off. I run my hands along the giant wheels of the Big Boy, clicking my fingernails on the sign that labels all the dials and knobs and levers in the engine compartment. I climb up a ramp to let my peripheral vision skate over the blank windows of the Eisenhower. I walk through the indoor displays, the movie theater, the gift shop. I go outdoors, certain the entrance will lock behind me. I'm not sure I care whether he's following me until I hear his footsteps and I know he has, and that's what I wanted.

I walk all the way to the back end of the lot and climb the observation tower. Dozens of steps leading up into the night. At the top, a view of this small, ugly city I've adopted. The wide cut of the

river. A man beside me who I don't know, not really. A man who
doesn't want to know me.

We've been doing this for a year. I thought at the beginning he
knew a secret, and he'd teach it to me—that he could show me how
to put on a new role and inhabit it. I needed that twelve months
ago. I was lost, adrift somewhere between my old life and my new
one. The clothes, the makeup, the courtship, the sex—they all
helped me. The newness of him, every time, and the comfort of
attraction, flirtation, banter.

It's funny that he doesn't want to be involved with me in part
because I'm a mother. At least, that's how I interpret what he told
me. I can't be sure it's what he meant. He wasn't exactly effusive.
But it's funny because he was the one who showed me a path
through the maze of new motherhood. He was the one who helped
me see I was still in there, tangled up and turned around. He was
the one who led me back out.

He's standing at the railing next to me. "Take off your coat," I
tell him.

I take it off for him. He stands still, watching me, as I
unbutton it and push it over his shoulders and down his arms. I
unwind his scarf. Unbutton the shirt he has on underneath, too,
and keep going until he's standing in front of me bare to the waist
in the brisk October air, covered in goose bumps. Quizzical but
patient.

I'm not sure what I'm up to. I guess I just want to see him one
more time without the costume.

My hands slide over his shoulders, my thumbs balancing on
the ridge of his collarbones. His biceps, the inside of his elbows, his
golden forearms, his hands. I still don't know why he has a rough
man's hands, or so much lean muscle. Maybe he's a gardener. A
runner. Maybe he teaches Pilates.

I'm not ever going to know, and the thought is a sort of final
punctuation mark on our relationship.

I measure his waist with my hands, smooth my fingers over
his stomach and chest. I'm not trying to turn him on. I guess I'm
trying to memorize him.

He stands there and lets me. When I'm finished, I kiss him,

and I think at first he won't kiss me back, but he does, hard. He holds my head with his fingertips, as if I'm delicate, but he kisses me with a hunger I'd forgotten somehow.

Something in there. Something between us. But it's not enough.

I draw back, descend the steps and drive away.

I don't need him anymore.

I see him on the highway. He drives a Smart Car, a hybrid SUV, a semi with a load of logs. His name is Johnny, Ray, Clint. He's the Man with No Name. He's nobody.

He's every single man I walk past, every corner I walk around, every thought in my head.

It's disgusting, the way I mourn. Bottomless. Completely out of proportion.

My contract gets renewed, Josh starts talking in sentences, and still I'm preoccupied. Obsessed.

But it's all quiet, private, because Josh is with me a lot of the time, and he needs me to play with his blocks and change his diapers and feed him applesauce. I can't be Misery Barbie with Josh; he knows the difference between having my attention and not having it, and he wants it every moment he's awake.

Look, Mama! he says, pointing to a bird overhead.

Read it! he says, plopping into my lap with a board book.

Pick you up! he says, demanding that I lift him and carry him around the apartment.

I am his mother, and I don't resent it. But Marilyn-me, Rhoda-me, Hepburn-me keeps making sneaky escapes. She keeps running off to the train museum in my memories to look for Tyler. She plays maudlin records on her Victrola, drinks too much sherry, cries until her mascara streaks.

I don't know what to do with her. I leave her alone. She got her heart broken, I guess. She needs time to heal.

The fourth Tuesday of November comes and goes. She's not better yet.

We're not even close to better.

Chapter Seven

I'm feeding Josh a waffle for breakfast when the phone rings and I think, *Fuck.*

At seven fifty-five, the only person likely to call is the babysitter, and the only reason she'd call is to say she's not coming.

Briefly, I consider not answering, but then I remember that magical thinking is useless when it comes to babysitters.

It's not her, though.

"Hi, Mandy. It's Tyler." He clears his throat. "Is this a bad time?"

The sound of his voice is a spike of wobbly anxiety in my stomach.

I'm getting syrup on the phone. I'm wearing flannel pajama pants with skunks on them, and I have to figure out how to warp time so I can turn Josh over to the sitter, shower, dress, eat, and get to campus for my class at nine.

This is a terrible time.

"No, it's all right. What's up?"

I check that Josh is occupied with making a waffle mess and walk into the living room.

"I'd like to see you."

I don't say anything for a moment. I'm busy putting myself in a yoga pose on the floor, pressing my forehead into the nap of the carpet. It's an important pressure point, I heard once. It's supposed to be soothing to push your forehead into things. I guess that's why cows do it, and horses.

I'm too excited. I'm going to end up disappointed. He wants to see me for some work-related reason, and I'll die of it. Or he wants to see me so he can win me back, only that would be a disaster too, because he's not the guy for me. I proved it already.

Somebody needs to tell my heart.

"Why?"

"I— Can I just come by? I know where you live. I'm in the parking lot, actually. Maybe I could come up."

"I'm with my son." *There are skunks on my pants.*

"That's fine. I'm not—" He sighs, and in my head I see him in a car, raking his hand through his hair. "Please."

He's kind of...begging? Is that possible?

Begging isn't a tone I associate with him, but I decide I like it. If he wants to crawl through the apartment on his knees, just saying please to me for a while, I'll be okay with it.

He and the babysitter arrive at the same time, which piles one awkwardness on top of another. I let them both in, and Josh gets terrified toddler eyes, complete with wobbling chin, because he doesn't know Tyler, and he doesn't like this babysitter very much yet. Once he warms up to her, they're fine. It's just one of those separation-anxiety things. It sometimes takes me twenty-five minutes of concentrated wheedling and reassurance to get him to stop clinging to my leg like a screeching barnacle.

I don't have time for that this morning. Tyler's here, he's got his hands in his pockets, and he looks come-to-Jesus handsome. "Becky, this is Tyler. Tyler, Becky. Can you guys go in the living room?" I point. "I need to do something real quick."

Josh is already whining. He's seen Becky. He knows the score. I open the kitchen drawer that contains my secret arsenal and fish out three fun-size candy bars left over from Halloween. Back in the living room, I find an episode of a vapid cartoon that Josh likes and put it on the TV. I refuse to think about what my ass must look like in these pants from where Tyler is standing.

I return to the kitchen, grab Josh's high chair and roll him into viewing range of the screen. His face crumples at the sight of Becky and Tyler staring at him. I open a candy bar, hand it to him and turn up the TV.

"Come with me," I say to Tyler, and I lead him into my bedroom and shut the door.

I wonder briefly how this looks to Becky, but then I get distracted by my room, which is a mess. There's nowhere for Tyler to sit. I haven't made the bed. I don't even have a grown-up bed, just a mattress and box springs on the floor. I keep meaning to buy one, but it's not a high enough priority. Neither is the laundry. There are dirty clothes in a pile in the corner.

I turn around, and there he is. Tall. He smells like winter, crisp and cool. He looks like a male model, and I'm wearing skunk pants.

"I don't have much time. I have to get ready for work."

He swallows, and I stare at his throat. His coat is unbuttoned, and underneath he wears a soft-looking black sweater. I want to press my forehead against his chest. *It would be calming,* I tell myself, but this is a lie. It would be the opposite of calming.

"I made a mistake," he says. "I made a lot of mistakes."

I order myself to wait, breath caught in my throat. My cells stop dividing. My blood stops circulating. My heart keeps beating, though, and Josh squeals with happiness in the living room. That would be the candy doing its work.

"I shouldn't have said no to you. I want you to give me another chance."

"What kind of chance?"

"A date."

"What kind of date?"

"The kind where I'm Tyler, and you're Mandy, and I pick you up at seven and drive you to a restaurant and buy you dinner."

This sounds like my kind of date. But he's not done yet.

"And afterward, we talk about our childhoods over coffee, and you make me laugh, and then I kiss you good night and feel like skipping on my way back to my car because you're so fucking fantastic."

I think I go into some kind of a fugue state then. I must, because I don't consciously remember how his hands come to be wrapped around my upper arms, and I don't know why he looks so concerned all of a sudden, or why he's saying my name.

"Sorry," I say. "I'm having trouble processing, uh, you."

He kisses me, and it doesn't help one bit, but it feels dangerously good. His fingers dig into my arms, pulling me higher, closer, as his minty mouth moves over mine, and I fall into him. Plummet, really. His teeth on my bottom lip, his tongue in my mouth. He doesn't let go until I'm thrumming and wet, and then he does, but it's too late, because all I can think about is sex. The bed right behind me. What he feels like inside me, and how much I missed him, and how badly I want everything between us to be okay.

My brain has been hijacked by my libido.

"That was a mistake," I say.

"It felt great."

"No more of that." My thighs are still reflexively clenched. "It's totally unacceptable for us to have sex, ever again."

He closes his eyes with a little groan that makes me want to die. In a good way, though. *Le petit mort.*

"That was just kissing," he says, with his eyes still closed. "Now you've got me thinking about sex."

He reaches blindly for my waist, but I smack his hand away.

"Okay, look." I try to steer through the flotsam in my head. "You saw the toddler out there, right? That's Josh. That's my son. And this"—I lift my hand up and sweep it around, encompassing myself and everything in the room—"is my life. This is how I dress a lot of the time. I have to go to work in a few minutes. That's basically all I do—work and take care of Josh. It's not glamorous or interesting, and I can't keep going on dates with you because they're fun. I lost that luxury when I became a mom. I have to be responsible, okay?"

I lower my voice. The apartment is small, and I have no idea whether Becky can hear me through the door. I hope not. Christ, I'll never be able to look her in the eye again. "And you make me want to do crazy, irresponsible things, which is why I liked you so much, but I can't—"

He cuts me off. "I'm in love with you."

He's in love with me. I can't even...no. Just, no. "You don't *know* me."

"I want to." He takes my hand, flattening it between his palms and no doubt smearing syrup all over himself.

He has the prettiest eyes. Hazel. In the dim light at the museum, they'd always looked brown, but in my bedroom, with the clear light of a cold December morning streaming through the windows, they're whiskey shot through with blue, an eye color that doesn't particularly make sense unless you've seen it, and then it's your new favorite.

He looks so damn sincere. Six weeks of nothing, six weeks too late, but he really *means* it now, this confession of love at the wrong time, the wrong speed. I want to cry.

It's too much. I'm condensed under the weight of the way he's behaving. I wish I could reroute his words in some way so that my heart hadn't heard them, but it did, and it's so incongruously happy, while the rest of me is panicked and confused and disappointed.

"You can't handle it. You told me so yourself. We don't fit together right. I'm an adult, and you're— Well, you're just skating along, aren't you? You have sort of half a job, you live with your parents with no real responsibilities... Did you know I'm thirty-four? And having Josh makes me, like, forty-four. I'm too old for you. I think you might have gotten the wrong idea about me on all those dates. I'm not the sort of woman you're looking for."

"You're exactly the sort of woman I'm looking for."

"If that's true, why did it take you six weeks to come here?"

"I've got..." He pauses, staring over my shoulder for a second, and then shakes his head and starts over. "I was being an asshole. But you have the wrong idea about me. You need to give me time to explain myself."

"I don't have time. I have to get ready for work."

"So let me take you out. Tonight. Tomorrow. Anytime you want."

"I'll think about it."

He reaches for me again, my shoulders this time, and I let him catch me. "That's not good enough. Give me a chance. Please, Mandy."

I duck out of his arms before he can make me any weaker than I already am. "Don't push me. I'm not yours to boss around. I said I'll think about it. Now back off, huh? I have to get ready for work."

To his credit, he does. He's got the hound-dog eyes, the wounded expression, like a tragically misunderstood silver-screen hottie. "Okay," he says. "You'll call me."

I nod. "I'll call you."

When he goes, I have to sit on the bed and take deep breaths for several minutes before I'm ready to face the fact that I have to put on clothes and go out in the world and be a professional.

I teach a three-hour seminar class, The Myth of the American West, and I'm horrendous. Basically, it's two hours and fifteen minutes of group work and video clips and phoning it in, and then I send them on their way because I can't keep my mind off the subject of Tyler.

I can't decide if he deserves a second chance. I can't decide what to think about the real-world version of him, the man who so cruelly denied me twice and then showed up on my doorstep penitent, six weeks too late.

I still haven't decided when I step out of the classroom to find him in the hallway, waiting for me.

"Have you thought about it?" he asks.

He says it kind of quiet and humble, which strips me of the ability to hate him for being so pushy. "Yes."

"Have you made up your mind?"

"No."

He nods, as if this is what he expected. "I want to show you something. It might help you decide. But I'll have to drive you to my house. Is that okay? Or do you have to go home to Josh?"

I have office hours scheduled, but early December is the doldrums before exam panic sets in, and I don't get a lot of students showing up to see me. Plus, I think whatever this is between Tyler and I, we'd better figure it out soon, because I wasn't doing all that hot when I was walking around bleeding internally for six weeks, and I'm doing even worse now.

"Let me put a note on my door."

So we go to my office together, and I unlock it and write a note that I'll be missing my office hours, and I tape it to the door. All the while, Tyler examines the spines of my books. He's an exotic creature in my office. He doesn't look young or immature. He looks like a man who's comfortable perusing scholarly books—like a man who actually gives a damn about my chosen profession, which is exceptionally rare.

It occurs to me that if our relationship weren't doomed, we could be great together.

He drives a Nissan. Black on the outside, gray on the inside, totally immaculate. He doesn't look too young when he drives, either. With his hands on the wheel, navigating through the streets of Green Bay, he looks competent, adult, and extraordinarily hot.

For a long moment after he turns off the car, we sit in his driveway, immobile. Finally, he glances at me over the ticking sound of the cooling engine and says, "You told me your sister went through the ice. What actually happened?"

"She got killed by a drunk driver. Her, and her husband, and my niece."

"I'm sorry."

"Yeah. So am I."

He smoothes his hands over the wheel, from twelve o'clock to six o'clock in two hemispheres. "When we go in there, I just want you to watch, okay? And I want you to know, I told you all this, same as you told me about your sister."

I have only the sketchiest notion what he means, and no idea what I'm agreeing to. "Okay."

I follow him inside. The side door takes us into the kitchen, where there's a large, older man at the table being fed soup by a raw-boned woman in scrubs.

"Hey, Ty!" she says. "We didn't expect you back for a while."

The man is hunched over the bowl. He looks at Tyler sidelong with mean, squinty eyes. I think he must be over six feet tall, carrying the weight that all men seem to pack on in their latter years in the Upper Midwest. He has a few days' growth of beard, a wrinkled white T-shirt, sweatpants.

Tyler makes a gesture with his hands and says, "Hey, Nancy. I wanted to bring Mandy by to meet Dad."

"Oh, this is Mandy?" Nancy sizes me up in a friendly way, and then gestures at the older man. Tyler's father. "Look, Paul! Tyler brought Mandy to meet you. Doesn't she seem like a nice young girl?"

Tyler's dad makes an awful, choking, moaning sort of noise and glares at me. The hand that isn't holding the spoon rises from the table and carves out a rushed, jerky shape in the air.

"Nice girl," the nurse says. "That's right, Paul, she is a nice girl." She picks up the napkin and wipes his mouth.

I'm slow on the uptake, but I guess I've figured out enough. That he's deaf, and declining in one way or another. I remember that Tyler told me once, on our second date, that he grew up on an isolated farm in Appalachia, and his parents were both deaf, so he learned to sign before he could speak.

Not a story. The truth. More or less.

"Well, we've had a busy morning," the nurse tells Tyler, signing so Tyler's dad will understand. "I got him to drink some orange juice with the thickener, and I tried to get some toast in him for breakfast but we just didn't want to eat today, did we, Paul? And we refused to get dressed."

Tyler winces. "He didn't hit you again?"

She shakes her head and stops signing. "He took a swat at me, but I saw it coming. I thought it wouldn't hurt him to stay in his sweats until you got home. It might be getting on time to let him wear the sweatpants all day, anyway."

"He would've hated that."

"I know, honey, and I know you want him to have his dignity, but you're doing everything you can for him. Part of keeping sane with this illness is just accepting the changes as they come."

Tyler nods. "I'll think about it. But for now, I think I'll get him dressed." He starts signing again. "What do you say, Dad? Want to get your clothes on for the day?"

His father grunts and slashes at the air. Definitely a no.

I stand back against the wall and watch the rest of it play out. Tyler coaxes his father out of the chair and helps him shuffle slowly—painfully slowly—out of the room. Paul leans on Tyler's shoulder with one hand and uses a three-footed metal cane in the other. He looks heavy. So heavy.

The house falls silent as they move into what must be a bedroom out of sight, and then I hear nothing but a bump and the creak of weight on a mattress to the accompaniment of Tyler's muffled grunt. It takes them a while. Afterward, Tyler helps his father to the bathroom.

The nurse looks at me. "He wears himself out," she says quietly. "Day and night. His mother was just the same."

"You've known him a long time?"

"I started coming over a few hours a week when Paul first needed extra care and Mrs. Janssen wanted to run out for groceries. Tyler was in school then, commuting down to Milwaukee for classes and living at home to help his mother."

"But she died," I say in a whisper. "And he took over."

He'd told me that, too. A story about his sainted Aunt Beedie, and how she'd taken care of his uncle when he got dementia until it plumb used her up. How he'd had to arrange for his uncle's care, because it was what Beedie would've wanted.

"How much do you help him?" I ask.

"Not enough. Just when he's working at the museum, and a few hours here and there so he can do his errands. And I used to come by one night a month so he could see you." She looks down at the table, maybe thinking she's overstepped.

Tyler and his father come back into the room, a process that takes a good five minutes before Paul is completely resettled in his chair. The nurse feeds him some crackers. Tyler is unusually disheveled now, his hair falling in his face, but Paul's is neatly combed, and he's wearing navy slacks and a cardigan over a button-up shirt. Dignified.

My father was a natty dresser, Tyler had told me. He'd polished his nails on his sweater and blown on them, a teasing light in his eyes. *Runs in the family.*

You're vain, I'd said.

Gotta flaunt what you've got. Mama always said it was those peacock feathers of his that grabbed her attention in the first place. I reckon it takes a little something extra to win a girl who's worth it. How about you, sweetheart? You fancy a fella with nice feathers?

I do fancy him. I fancy him like crazy, and it dawns on me that if he's been a complete jackass, so have I. We were both groping for a connection without being willing to take any risks.

I'd thought we were poorly matched, but it's the opposite. We're too similar. Too many burdens in our ordinary lives, too much joy in the escape, and no fucking sense whatsoever about how to find each other, how to share ourselves, how to tell the truth.

But maybe we can get better at it with practice. I sure want to try.

Tyler's talking to Nancy, making plans for the rest of Paul's day. "You want to see the house?" he asks me when they're through.

I do. He shows me around, starting upstairs with his bedroom, which isn't a kid's bedroom at all. He has a nice headboard, actually, a sleigh bed in antique cherry. A neat stack of clean laundry on the chair. He shows me the bathroom, the office, the guest room, the dining room. I see the couch in the living room, close to his father's bedroom, with an afghan folded over the arm and a full-size pillow on the back. *That's where he sleeps,* I think. *To be nearby if his father needs him.*

In the basement, he shows me an eight-foot-tall climbing wall that he built himself, for bouldering. It wraps around three walls. I don't know what bouldering is, but when I test my grip against one of the holds, I understand why he has rough hands and corded forearms. I imagine him working off his stress down here at night, moving along the walls, elegant as a spider. Loosening up all the places that tightened from the heavy physical work of helping his father through his days.

I've always liked to climb things, he'd said as he helped me up the ladder to the top of the Atchison, Topeka, and Santa Fe train.

Ever since I was a boy, my ma called me a monkey.

I can imagine his whole life. He's told me most of it, just as I've told him mine.

He leads me outside, and we sit on the front steps in the cold, looking out over the quiet street. His yard is well groomed, tidied up for winter. He must have done that. He must be always doing things, always feeling hopelessly behind, feeling needed.

That night on the Big Boy, when he'd lost control with me, I'd tried to be what he needed, but I hadn't understood.

I understand now.

"You didn't think there was room for me."

He looks out at his yard, pushes his hands down his thighs and over the tops of his knees. "No, I didn't."

"I didn't think there was room for you, either."

Tyler turns toward me, meeting my eyes. He puts a hand on my shoulder. "I'm still not sure how to make it work."

"Neither am I. But I think we could start with a date."

"An ordinary date."

I nod. I think we've found the correct path forward, but I have to ask him one more thing. "Do you hate children?"

"No. I don't really know any. I was an only child."

"They grow on you," I tell him. "Or, mine does, anyway."

He brushes his hand over my cheek, catches a lock of hair and secures it behind my ear. "My father doesn't grow on you."

"I'm not worried about that. He's your dad. He belongs to you."

"I want you to belong to me."

I scoot closer until we're hip to hip, knee to knee, and then I tip sideways, resting my head on his shoulder. "Yeah. I want that too."

The train car is crowded, but the man in the fedora only has eyes for me. I smile at him over my shoulder and put a little extra sway in my step, just because I can.

When I slide into an empty seat, he sits beside me and leans in to whisper in my ear. "Lady, you're going to get yourself in trouble, walkin' like that out where people can see you."

His folksy drawl makes me smile. "What kind of trouble?"

"The best kind."

Josh sticks out his hands and launches himself from Tyler's arms into mine. "Goin', Mama?"

"We're going to ride the train."

"*Goin'?*" he insists, flattening his palms on the window and looking out at the grounds of the National Railroad Museum.

"Just twice around the museum in a loop, buddy," Tyler says. "But we can pretend we're going to Topeka if you like that better."

"What's in Topeka?" I ask.

"Nothing special, sweetheart. But it's a long way to Topeka. I figure a guy like me could use the time to his advantage."

I stiffen my spine, feigning offense. "What's that supposed to mean?"

He leans down and whispers something in my ear that makes me blush.

"What a scandalous man you are. I should have you thrown off the train."

He just smiles and puts his arm over my shoulders. "You should keep me around. Scandalous men are more fun."

I lean in, and he catches my face in his hand when I kiss him.

"How long would it take to get to Topeka?" I ask under my breath.

"Days." After a moment's pause, he adds, "Nights too."

The whistle blows. The train starts to move.

I think I will keep him around, all the way to Topeka and beyond. I think I will.

About the Author

Ruthie Knox graduated from Grinnell College as an English and history double major and went on to earn a Ph.D. in modern British history that she's put to remarkably little use. These days, she writes contemporary romance in which witty, down-to-earth characters find each other irresistible in their pajamas, though she freely admits this has yet to happen to her. Perhaps she needs more exciting pajamas. Ruthie moonlights as a mother, Tweets incessantly, and bakes a mean focaccia. Visit her website at www.ruthieknox.com to keep in the loop or just wave hello.

Some hearts only want what they can't have...

Headstrong
© 2011 Mey Maguire

Libby Prentiss is ready to simply be herself. After half a lifetime rebelling against her privileged family's expectations, she hopes her biological research trip to New Zealand will cut the cord for good.

It doesn't take long to spot the hopelessly amateurish spy her overprotective father has hired to keep an eye on her. Fortunately, Reece Nolan's desperation to save his family's pub makes it all too easy to convince him to turn double-agent. Yet there's something different about him. His icy reserve sets her on fire...and ignites a secret yearning to let him see the mass of insecurities she hides behind her provocative persona.

Where Reece is a glacier of cool self-control, his brother Colin is a hot-blooded, unpredictable volcano. Libby's instant friendship with Colin is more satisfying than anything she's ever known—and traps her in completely foreign territory. She's caught between one man determined to hold her at arm's length, and another who offers her the intense connection she's worked so hard to avoid.

Something's got to give or the fallout could tear them all apart...and put the Nolan family's future in serious jeopardy.

Warning: Contains an emotional love triangle guaranteed to launch your heart into your throat.

Available now in ebook and print from Samhain Publishing.

SAMHAIN
PUBLISHING

It's all about the story...

Romance

HORROR

www.samhainpublishing.com

CPSIA information can be obtained at www.ICGtesting.com
Printed in the USA
BVOW08s0004060214

344083BV00002B/38/P

9 781619 216822